AUDUMN'S
LOVE

12-23-20

To: Gennavonah

Be Blessed +

Calvin

ISBN 978-1-952320-73-6 (Paperback)
Audumn's Love
Copyright © 2020 Calvin Denson

Yorkshire Publishing
4613 E. 91st St,
Tulsa, OK 74137
www.YorkshirePublishing.com
918.394.2665

Printed in the USA

AUDUMN'S LOVE

A Novel By:
Calvin Denson

TULSA

I dedicate this book to Shanae Settles who's taught me what the word Love really means in Audumn's Love's title. Keep being an inspiration to those around you. Kisses and be blessed.

INTRODUCTION

"Come they told me, Pa rum pum pum pummm. A new born king to see, Pa rum pum pum pum….."

"Audumn I'm leaving!" Lawanda yells when she hears the store's overlapping Christmas song come to an end for the night.

Audumn is hanging up the last leather sports jacket when Lawanda's voice travels down the empty aisles of the once over-crowded store for Christmas shopping. "Lawanda did you finish everything I asked you to do?"

"Yes Ms. Humphrey! Everything you've asked me to do I've done!"

Audumn appears from the numerous racks of clothes as if she's just stepped out of the wilderness. "Thanks Lawanda for staying late, and yes, you're free to go home. By the way, don't forget Marcus will be coming in tomorrow at eight so be here earlier than usual this Saturday to open the store for him."

"Yes ma'am and I'll see you Monday." A silent whistle from the wind blows through the door as it is opened and shut from Lawanda's exit.

Staring through the 10' x 6' windowpane, Audumn looks at the luminescent sign for A Touch of Elegance across the parking lot flicker before going completely dark. *Finally, today's chaos is all over,* she thinks as she presses enter on the store's Brink's alarm system to activate the alarm. Stepping outside, her hair sways to the back of her shoulders as dead leaves skip endlessly through the vacant parking lot. Cherry, which is the nickname for her cherry colored Cadillac her ex-boyfriend, Tree, gave her is parked perfectly in between the white lines next to the empty spaces surrounding it. Audumn presses the keyless remote pad and the car alarm chirps as she quickly races over to the driver's door to get in. A sigh of relief leaves her lungs as she rubs her heel while turning the key in the ignition.

The streets are scarce tonight because of the strong winds and the tiny raindrops that are starting to fall on her windshield. Stopping at a traffic light, the rain from the thick dark clouds above her starts to come down a lot heavier and more rapidly than they were two minutes ago. Her driver's side windshield wiper blade isn't fit for the weather at hand, so she has to squint and peak around the two inch streak that is blocking her vision.

It's getting late when she notices that the bad weather has had her poking along the feeder road of I-45 for nearly thirty minutes. Audumn's day is free tomorrow so there's no need to rush, but her fatigue from her 14 hour work shift causes her to step on the gas a little harder. With her vision distorted and her restlessness tugging on her body, the debris that is all over the road up ahead can't be seen until it's too late. Swerving, she dodges an empty bucket from the back of someone's pickup truck. "Thank you Jesus," is all she can say while looking through her rearview mirror and then turning to focus back onto the road. She feels the coast is clear, but a six foot ladder is only a few feet in front of her. Her reaction time is not fast enough as the car's front left tire runs completely over it. "Damn it!" she screams as her car's digital dashboard tells her that her tire is flat.

Audumn slows down to nearly 5 mph and tries to make it to the Shell gas station a few exits up off of the interstate on Hollow Tree Lane. The speed she's going causes a five minute ride to turn into ten minutes as she pulls into the station next to a gas pump. Her day has been longer than usual, so she sits there to get a grasp on what she felt was a near death experience. After catching her breath, she dials her boyfriend Secorion's number three times only to keep getting his voicemail. She knows his phone is going straight to voicemail because he's working in a power plant and doesn't get off until 4:30 in the morning. The only thing she can do is leave a message and change her own tire like he taught her to do in case of an emergency.

Taking a deep breath to clear her mind, she steps out and runs to the trunk to get the spare and hardware needed to change her tire. Back to back lightning along with unbelievable thunder startles her and makes her hands slip off the 4-way while she's trying to break the nut loose off the tire that has become only a rim. Looking around for a savior, she sees no one is around to help her do the physical job that she's trying to do. "Where are all the men at when you need one?" she asks herself as she places the 4-way back onto the nut she was trying to break loose before.

Suddenly, a set of head lights are in her face, but then they shut off as soon as she looks to see who is blinding her. The rain pouring down on the awning that is covering her is all she can hear until a familiar voice comes from the driver's side window of the car that has just pulled up behind her. *It couldn't be, or could it?* she thought. *Gayriale did say a few months back that her brother got out and is doing good for himself.*

"Audumn are you okay?" Tree jumps out of his Mercedes Benz and runs over to the once love of his life's rescue.

"Torrance Wingate Jr., where are you coming from this time of the night?" Audumn asks, thinking he's back to his late night drug selling ways.

"A Christmas concert they had at my father's church. It was over around 10:00, but I'm in charge of locking the building after the janitors and ushers clean up."

His answer makes her feel a little ashamed because everyone from his neighborhood, Northborough, have been constantly telling her that Tree isn't the same guy anymore. "I'm sorry for prying, but I thought you were up to no good like you used to be back in the old days. I mean, you got to understand with you pulling up in a brand new Mercedes Benz and all."

"Oh that's just a little something I bought with the $116,000 you brought to my mom's house when I got locked up. As for that other lifestyle I used to live, that's over with completely because I lost too much that last time around in the penitentiary." Tree looks away in pain as Audumn begins to stares into his eyes that hold the love that he still has for her.

"I'm sorry Tree, but the love I had for you wasn't good enough for you to stop doing everything you had gotten yourself into back then."

"It's all good Audumn because I hear you're happy and as long as you're happy, then I'm happy, baby." Audumn cringes at the word baby coming out of his mouth and grabs her X's and O's necklace, which she never takes off, off her neck. "I see you're still wearing that necklace I bought you 8 years ago and from the looks of it, I see you taking good care of ol' Cherry that I gave you too."

"Please don't think I wear this necklace because of you because it's not. The reason why I wear it is because it's a very pretty necklace and it's mine. And as far as this Cadillac, I deserve it after all the bullshit you put me through."

"Okay, okay," Tree says, putting his hands up as if to say he surrenders. "I believe you and good job on taking care of the car."

"Thanks, now can you help me or not because it's getting late and my boyfriend is at work."

"Please don't insult me like that, Audumn, you know I'll always be there for you no matter what."

"Good, because the past is the past and I need to get home out of this bad weather asap," Audumn replies with a little anger in her voice.

Tree changes her tire without saying another word about their past relationship. Today is the first time he's seen Audumn and he doesn't want their encounter to end on a bad note like when he left her by herself the last time he went back to jail for the second time. He knows in his spirit that she still has a place for him in her heart, but the hurt he always placed upon her only turns that place into hate every time she thinks about what happened between them.

"All done Ms. Audumn Danyalle Humphrey, you're free to go." Tree closes the trunk after putting her busted tire inside of it.

"Thanks Tree, and I'm sorry for snapping at…"

Tree stops her before she can finish her sentence. "Audumn you don't have to apologize to me, I understand completely."

Audumn drives off leaving Tree standing next to the gas pumps. Her heart is in knots because no matter how hard she tried to hate him, she couldn't. Looking into her mirrors, she sees his tall muscular frame grow smaller and says, "Tree knows he looks good," while her phone begins to ring with her boyfriend Secorion's ring tone.

CHAPTER 1

T he clock is blinking 12:00 a.m. when Audumn yawns and stretches to start her day. Everything for a second is a blur as her hazel eyes adjust to the bright noon's sunlight. Peeking through the blinds, she notices that a few branches have fallen around the canal on the backside of her apartments, Columbians Greens. The storm had passed making its mark throughout the night and leaving some traces of its presence for today.

Her apartment is nice and cozy this afternoon because even though the sun is out. the December's temperature is still in the 60's. Audumn feels anew while looking through her closet for something to put on for this beautiful day. Half of her energy burst came from the long hours of sleep she had gotten during the night; the other half came from being wrapped in Secorion's arms during those long hours of rest after he came home from work. Thinking about him causes her to wonder where the man she's given her heart to could be.

Audumn becomes curious all of sudden when walking to her closed bedroom door that is usually opened. Reaching to turn the knob, she pauses and puts her nose to the door because on the opposite side something smells like sweet perfume and bacon. Quietly, she opens it and sticks her head over the ledge looking for the source of all her bemusement. The answer to her curiosity is quickly visible in a small mist of smoke that is traveling from the kitchen. Audumn decides to tip toe across the living room and secretly hides behind the refrigerator. Before she can fix her lips to speak, her heart and eyes quickly mute her because Secorion is fixing two breakfast plates with a big smile on his face. Rose petals are on the floor of the kitchen along with a single rose and perfumed incense in the center of the dining table.

"Good morning my love." Audumn's voice is soft and sexy as the words fall from her lips.

"I'm sorry baby, but it's not morning anymore." Secorion chuckles as he grabs her small hand and escorts her to her seat.

"What's all of this for baby? Did you get the raise you were talking about?"

"I'll answer your questions later because as of right now, all I need for you to do is enjoy your breakfast and look pretty." Audumn blushes and does what her man wants her to do.

Breakfast felt like the 4th of July because of all the sparks that were flying each time the two of them took a bite and stared into each other's eyes. They're both happy this afternoon and their happiness causes their words not to come forth. Secorion's meal isn't the best of meals that has been prepared for her, but it was very sentimental and from the abundance of his heart. Also, the rose petals all over the floor made Audumn feel as if she's the apple of his eyes.

"Secorion Woodson!" Audumn blurts out with a blank expression. "I can't take it anymore. Why all of this today, baby? Please tell me before I go crazy."

"Shh," he romantically whispers with his index finger over his lips.

Secorion slides his seat back, stands, and goes to open the kitchen drawer. An envelope appears in his hands out of nowhere as he's turning and he hands it to Audumn over the kitchen table. "What's this?" she asks, wondering again why is today so special.

Audumn opens the envelope and a beautiful heart shaped card is inside of it. Her hands are hesitant as she opens it to read the words, "Will you marry me!" which are written across the paper full of imprinted wedding rings. Standing to her feet, she presses the card against her chest. Secorion face is shining like the sun as he falls to one knee and looks up with a small velvety texture box in his hands.

"Baby I don't know what to say." Audumn places her hands over her mouth.

"Say yes, my love! Say yes."

"Yes, yes, yes, yes, and yes!" she exclaims rapidly. "Yes I'll marry you Secorion Woodson!"

Secorion jumps to his feet in glee and removes the ring from the box. Audumn holds out her left hand and hangs it there waiting for her fairytale dreams to finally come true.

"It fits." Secorion said as Audumn looks down at the diamond ring she has awaited all of her life. "Do you like it baby because if not, I can take it back and get you another one?" Secorion asks in a bashful way.

"I love it and it's the most beautiful ring I have ever seen in my entire life."

"Really baby?"

"Yes honey, it really is a pretty ring and I'm honored to be wearing it."

Audumn face is as red as the rose petals on the floors when she leans over and gives her new fiancé a kiss he will never forget. The kiss is long, wet, and has a little tongue fighting in it. Secorion's penis is rock hard and Audumn knows it as she slides her ring finger hand down through the slit of his boxers. His hormones are bubbling through his skin and he decides to take his bride to be on the kitchen table where he proposed to her. Audumn is all in and slides her panties off as Secori, which is Secorion's nickname, pushes everything on the table to the floor like he's in a movie about to have the dirtiest sex he's ever had.

Kissing her neck and caressing her perky breast, Secori decides to let his tongue travel between her cleavage, down her stomach, and into her fragranced garden that is now his for the rest of his life. Audumn moans and presses the back of his head hard into her vagina as waterfalls flow from between her legs and begin to moisten the front of his face.

"You like that baby? I love you."

"Yes my love, I like it a lot." Audumn sits up on the kitchen table. Kissing Secorion she says, "Make love to me, Secorion Woodson. Make love to me right now."

Secorion pushes himself inside of Audumn unhurriedly because today he plans on taking his time with the precious gift God has given to him to be his happily ever after. Audumn's garden wraps around his stiff tree as he tills her ground up, down, left, and right in her rich soil until planting himself near her boundary. Squeezing into her high yellow skin, he releases his seed inside of her for the first time since they've been together. Before, they would use a condom or he would pull out in time, but today, they are both on one accord because of the covenant they both agreed on in getting married.

Kissing the side of his neck, she says, "I love you, baby and I promise to be yours for the rest of my life," as she begins to grind her hips until every last drop of his sperm is wherever it needs to be to make a baby.

Secorion lifts Audumn in the air, carries her to their room, and lays her in the bed. After tucking her in, he kisses her forehead and goes into the kitchen to clean up the best mess he's ever made in his life. While cleaning, he's all smiles as he picks his boxers up off the floor and puts them on. "Wow!" he says aloud. "I'm about to get married."

Audumn is in the bed half asleep when her future hubby lays next to her. Feeling his masculine presence, she snuggles her body into his as he wraps his strong arms around her. Secorion gave his all in consummating their engagement and he's tired as well. "I love you Audumn," he mumbles before he passes out next to her from exerting to much energy earlier. Audumn hears nothing because she's been out for the count ever since he begin to cuddle with her.

The alarm clock on Secorion's nightstand blared loudly through the stillness of their one bedroom apartment. He thought he would get up an hour ago to take care of unfinished business and run an errand, but afternoon sex changed his schedule. Sitting up on his side of the bed, he turns off his alarm clock and looks back at his fiancée.

"What's wrong baby?" Audumn asks, groggy from waking up a second time.

"I'm sorry love, but I have to go to work."

"Work!" Audumn sits up. "Aww baby, why do you have to go to work today of all days?"

"Honestly baby, I was going to wait until Sunday to ask you to marry me because that's my only off day. But, seeing you lying next to me looking like an angel this morning I couldn't help myself, so I decided to just go for it. I can call in if you like, babe."

The glow on Audumn's face becomes dim because it's Saturday, she's engaged, and she wants to spend the rest of this unforgettable day with the man who made it unforgettable.

"What do you want me to do, babe?" Secori breaks the brief silence in the air. "But, if we can wait till tomorrow to celebrate, it will be better for me because Saturdays are the only days I can get a permit to finish up this switchgear I'm building on the live side of the power plant I work at."

Secorion is an electrician who works for Bechtel Construction in Baytown, Texas. He's a lead man and he and his foreman are the only two people out of their crew that can get a permit and today his foreman is at his classmate's funeral.

"Okay, okay my love. I hate that you work nightshift, but you know I'll never come between you and your career. And as the future Mrs. Woodson, we're going to need every dime to pay for this wedding."

Secorion walks around the bed and kisses her on the lips. "I love you, Audumn Humphrey," he says, gazing into her hazel eyes. "And thanks for saying, yes."

"Yes, yes, yes," Audumn repeats over and over until he closes the door to the bathroom to take a quick shower.

Lying in bed, she stares out the window at what's left of today's sunlight. Night time is only about an hour away and from the looks of the daylight, Secorion is running behind his usual schedule. Baytown is thirty minutes away and it takes him an extra thirty minutes minimum to get inside the plant if everything goes accordingly.

"Baby!" Audumn yells.

Secorion bursts from the bathroom door naked, while brushing his teeth. "I know, I know baby. I'm going to be late," he says digging through his socks and underwear drawer.

"Slow down baby before you hurt yourself." Audumn laughs, seeing him stumble as he's putting his right foot inside his boxers.

"Baby, you don't understand. My foreman isn't in today. He went to a funeral and said he wasn't going to be able to get the proper rest he needed in time for work tonight. Had he been, I would have just called in and chilled with you regardless if I had to work or not."

"Oh."

"Yes, oh. Oh and I've got to get the hell up out of here so that I can get my guys lined out for tonight's task on that switchgear we have to put in."

Secorion is fully dressed when he rinses his mouth out twice and spits. Seventeen minutes have passed since his alarm clock went off and he wishes he could have gotten dressed in ten. Before racing out the front door, he blows Audumn a kiss and takes the steps down to the ground by twos until he jumps inside his Charger and leaves. Audumn gets up to check to see if he locked the door and sure enough he didn't.

"Hey baby, could you check and see if I locked the front door. Love you! Thanks…" she reads in a text message when she gets back to her bedroom. *I already did, my love,* she thinks, taking off her t-shirt so that she can take a bath.

In the tub, Audumn's mind is in a happy place as she sits in the perfumed oils that keep her skin soft as a baby's bottom. Twirling her left hand through the air, she looks at the water drip from her hand as the lights above send an array of colors through her diamond ring before her eyes. Her ring is beautiful, but looking at the gold band evokes memories of her first and the only love she had for a guy before she met Secorion. What's ironic is that the past love she's thinking about was the Superman who saved her last night from the night's treacherous weather. "No, no, no, Tree. I will not let you spoil my precious day today by thinking about what we could have had together," she says aloud, while reaching for a towel.

Kizzy and Diana are the first two she calls after she's dressed. Kizzy is from New Orleans and her and her three kids came to Houston after Hurricane Katrina. Audumn met her shortly after that at a Little Wayne concert and the two of them have been friends ever since. Diana, on the other hand, is another story. She has known Audumn a little longer then Kizzy and, to her, she has seniority in certain events and situation in the best friend Chica trio they've got going on. And being that she's a 6'1" black, country Texas girl, Audumn and Kizzy just go along with it to keep her mouth shut. Kizzy can be a handful as well. She's the shortest of the bunch, but when she's mad and she gets New Orleans ratchet, Audumn and Diana just stay out of her way because there's nothing that can stop that Category 5 storm.

"Hello." Kizzy answers the phone on the first ring when seeing it's Audumn.

"Guess what, girl?"

"Oh Audumn, just spill it already. You know how I get when it comes to the guessing game."

"I'm getting married!" Audumn exclaims. "Secorion asked me this morning during breakfast!"

"Audumn stop playing games, yeah." Kizzy accent is distinct now that her bff has gotten her attention. "Wait, are you serious?"

"Yes, I'm serious! I said yes!" Audumn shouts with joy.

"You're getting married Audumn!"

"Yes, yes, yes. I said yes!"

"Girl, I'm so happy for you and Secori!" Kizzy pauses to think. "Hold up Audumn. I better be your maid of honor, yeah."

"Kizzy not now. I just got engaged like 6 hours ago. You are the first person I told and besides, I have to call Diana and my mom next."

"And what's that supposed to mean? I thought I was your girl."

"You are Kizzy, but we haven't set a date yet and here you are planning the wedding for me already."

"Might as well start now. I'm ready to see you come down that aisle to kiss the man I always told you had googly eyes for you."

"Yes, I can honestly say you did best friend."

"Well, act like it then when you choose your maid of honor."

"Okay Kizzy, I'll remember that when I cross that bridge."

"Whatever. Bye girl and congratulations again. You deserve it Audumn."

Audumn called Diana next and she is pissed because Audumn didn't tell her first. Not wanting to break Audumn's day of happiness, she subsides and allows her best friend to tell her everything that happened from the beginning detail by detail. She tried to leave out the hot kitchen sex, but Diana wasn't trying to hear all that because if Secorion is going to marry Audumn, he had definitely better have come correct on his proposal.

9

"That's what's up, Beaumont." Diana is the only person in Houston who calls Audumn by her hometown, Beaumont, Texas. "I'm happy for you for real, for real. Now get dressed because the night is still young and we're going to toast to the future Mr. & Mrs. Secorion Woodson. Plus, drinks are on me tonight."

"But...."

"And I'm not taking no buts or nos for an answer!"

Audumn thinks about it and agrees to go. "Okay, Diana. I guess I don't have a choice," she says excitedly, wanting to get out of the house. "Call Kizzy and see if she wants to come. Give me about an hour and I'll meet you at your place. I still have to call my momma and tell her that I's a getting married now."

Laughter comes from both ends of the phone at Audumn's shenanigans as they both press end to finish what they were doing. *Time to celebrate with the Chicas*, Audumn thought as she listened to her mother's phone ring through the receiver.

CHAPTER 2

I t's Saturday night and Pappasito's on FM 1960 is packed. Audumn and Diana are next to be seated as they both look through the vast windows to see if Kizzy is walking up. She said she was coming after she fixed her kids some nachos, but Diana said that was shortly after she got off the phone with Audumn.

"Right this way, Ms. Ross. Your table for three is ready." A male waiter with a fuzzy red Christmas hat on said after he walks up and greets them.

"Come on, Audumn. I guess it's just me and you till she gets here." Diana tugs Audumn's sweater when seeing the waiter has already left to show them to their table.

"But I really wanted her to be here tonight to celebrate with us."

"Girl come on! Just text her when we're seated."

"Okay."

"Okay, is right. Okay we're about to get drunk up in the place for my bff's engagement with or without our girl, Kizzy. And besides, that's just more alcohol in our system for us two. Remember, drinks are on me tonight and once my cash gets low, I'm done. Unless you want to get a round or two when that time comes." Diana gives Audumn a slight elbow.

Kizzy walks through the entrance and waves. Audumn waves back as she is sitting down at their table. *I knew my girl wasn't going to let me down on a special night like this,* she thinks, smiling to see that this awesome day of endearment will end celebrating with two of the people she loves with all of her heart.

"Girl, this Christmas shopping traffic is terrible tonight." Kizzy sets her wallet on the table and takes a seat.

"I know right." Diana replies. "Especially with us being in the Willowbrook area and all."

"All that's in the past ladies. As long as we're all here, I'm happy."

"You're right, Beaumont. Enough with all that, let's get this party started. Who wants to take shots?"

The waiter beckons to interrupt their conversation. "Hello, my name is Julio Perez and I will be your waiter for tonight." Julio hands each one of them the menu and they all begin to thumb through it. "Can I get you anything to drink while you see what it is you desire to eat or shall I come back later?"

"Shots por favor!" Diana blurts out. "We want shots!"

Kizzy laughs at her friend's outspokenness and wannabe Spanish. "Diana you're as crazy as a New Orleans girl on Bourbon St, baby."

Diana waves her off to the waiter as if to say, *don't mind her.* "We would like two shots of Patron for all of us with salt and lime."

"Two a piece, Diana?" Audumn asks.

"Yeah Diana, two a piece is a lot to start off with. What, you got a Christmas bonus on your check yesterday?"

"Ha ha, Kizzy, but today my bff got engaged so it's only right we turn all the way up for her."

"I guess." Kizzy replies, pondering on what she's going to do about the drive home later.

Liquor is in their system when Julio brings a skillet of sizzling fajitas out of the kitchen. As soon as the food touched the table, jokes began to be told about their wild Chica adventures. Loud laughter rises from their section when Audumn tells her friends how Secorion ate twice for breakfast and how one of his dining's was not food, but her. Audumn is fixing herself a taco when Diana decides it's time to give a toast on behalf of her engagement. Kizzy is all giggles because she knows this is about to be funny because Diana is tipsy already.

"Can I have your attention please?" Diana clangs the side of her glass of Long Island Iced Tea with her fork. "Today I would like to congratulate my friend Audumn Danyalle Humphrey on getting engaged to one of the best guy's I know, Secorion Woodson."

Audumn shrinks in her seat after seeing that the whole restaurant is being attentive to Diana's drunk toast when, suddenly in the blink of an eye, Kizzy is standing holding her glass of Long Island Ice Tea as well. *Oh no, not you too Kizzy?* Audumn is shaking her head no to the both of them, but that doesn't stop either of them from continuing on with the charade.

"And I would like to give a toast to the first girl I befriended after Hurricane Katrina placed me and my kids in Houston seven years ago. I'm usually not the one to do things like this, but tonight my girl got engaged to a guy who's handsome, a hard worker, and most of all, loves her for her." Kizzy pauses when her eyes begin to water from all she knows about what Audumn's been through and where she's at today. "Audumn, we love you and me and Diana wish you and that hunk of a sexy man, Secorion, all that God has in store for the both of you when you become one." Kizzy walks around the table and hugs Audumn. "Congratulations my friend and this is only the beginning."

Pappasito's customers weren't rude at all during their toast to Audumn. As a matter of fact, they were the exact opposite because they begin to chant congratulations from every corner of the restaurant as soon as Kizzy finished. Not feeling embarrassed anymore, Audumn stands and embraces Kizzy tighter and Diana joins in. It's been a long time since they had a group hug and tonight is a hugging night because the tears flowing from all of their eyes says that it is.

"Thank you, Kizzy and Diana. Tonight, I thought wasn't going to go well for me because I wanted to spend it with Secori, but he had to work." They all sit down at the table after their small huddle is separated. "All the sadness I was feeling when he left today changed when Diana insisted on celebrating tonight and I want to say thank you to the both of you for making this lovely day special for me again."

"Audumn you know, Kizzy and I will do anything to make sure that smile stays on your face."

"I know you will, Diana. I know the both of you will and that's what makes this night everlasting all the more."

The girls are stuffing their faces when the table begins to tremor and a small buzz sounds from somewhere on it. All three of them search their personal belongings only to find that Audumn's phone is the only phone that's amiss. "I got it. I got it," she says, inebriated, tossing the silverware cloth from on top of it. Diana and Kizzy laugh at her slurred speech as she squints to see that Secorion is the one calling her. *How did my ringer get off,* her my mind wonders trying to recall when the last time she heard it ring was.

"Hey babe!"

"Audumn?"

"Yes, my love it's…it's me." Audumn stammers. "And guess what?"

"Ummm, that you're drunk." Secorion replies, putting two and two together after hearing how she said babe and asked her garbled question.

"No silly. I mean yes, kinda. I mean, maybe just a little." Audumn looks at her friends and winks as they all cover their mouths to snigger. Remembering the question she asked him, she blurts out, "But that ain't what I asked you Secori!"

"Yes, you did bae. You asked me to guess what."

"All right bae. I believe you. You're confusing me with all these big words."

"Huh?" Silence takes over their phone call for a brief second. "Hello?"

"Secorion, I'm out with my friends celebrating for us and I should be with you. You're not here and I understand, but all I asked was for you to guess what."

Secorion gives in when hearing Audumn put on her whiney voice, that to this day he can never resist. "Okay sweetheart. What is it that you want me to guess?"

Audumn titters. "That I love you, miss you, and can't wait to be Audumn Woodson."

Secorion shakes his head at his fiancées answer. "Is that it, bae?"

"Yep, that's it! Well, that and I can't wait till you get home from work so we can have hot butt naked sex on the kitchen table again."

"Now that's what I'm talking about, Beaumont! Go for what you want, Audumn! That's your husband and if you want to have sex at the clothing store while trying on a summer dress in the middle of October, then god damn it, do it! By all means."

"What?" Audumn, Secorion, and Kizzy said at the same time to Diana's comments.

"You heard me! That's yo man Audumn and you can do it whenever and wherever you want."

Audumn and Kizzy are laughing their tails off when she remembers the phone in her hand still has Secorion on the line. "Baby, I got to go. I'm drunk and I'm out with my Chicas. I love you and wake me up in the morning for round 2. Byeee."

"I love you too…" Secorion tries to tell her he loves her back, but his response was only heard by the speaker of his phone.

Kizzy gives Diana a high five and tells her she's a fool for telling it like it is to Audumn. Audumn wants in on the fun and high five's the both of them just because she's in the high fiving mood. The drinks have truly settled in their blood, but that doesn't stop Diana from standing, raising her shot glass, gulping it down, licking salt on the back of her hand, and then sucking a lime.

"I think you've done that backwards, yeah. I think the lime comes before the salt."

"Oops, my bad, Ms. Goody Two Shoes from Louisiana. Last time I checked, we were in Texas. And if I'm not mistaking, us Texan gals always save sucking for last. Ain't that right Audumn?" Diana slams her empty shot glass down and gives Audumn another high five.

Audumn turns to Kizzy and says, "Yeah! What she said," while drunkenly nodding at Diana.

"I guess, girl."

"What you really mean is that I guess I need to get with the program."

"No. That is not what I meant, Diana."

"Well it needs to be." Audumn interjects to instigate.

"Oh Audumn, don't you start too." Kizzy decides to change the subject because she notices people are starting to listen in on their Texas girls sucking conversation. "But on the real Audumn, 2013 is really looking up for you. You're going into the 2013 new year engaged and you only have one semester of school left until you graduate from U of H with your bachelor's in science."

"And I'm going to be like, hell yeah, when she do!" Diana blurts out, gazing into the air thinking about when Audumn walks across the stage. "I'm sorry Kizzy, but you might not want to sit by me because I'm gon' be turnt all the way up in that gymnasium."

"You're not the only one who's gon' be happy for her when she graduates, Diana. You best believe I'm going to be screaming at the top of my lungs too."

"Yeah, I know Kizzy, but screaming at the top of your lungs is one thing and squeezing the crap out of an air horn while shouting through a bullhorn is another, N.O."

Audumn and Kizzy picture Diana in the stands with both an air horn and bullhorn. "I don't know, girl. Diana's got a point."

"You're right, Audumn." Kizzy chuckles. "I may have to reconsider my seating arrangement on that day if Miss I Can't Hold My Liquor is going to be doing all that."

"Whatever you say, Kizzy. I'm just trying to give you a heads up because I already know what I'm going to be doing in June when my bff walks across that stage to get her Veterinarian degree."

"And she ain't lying either. As a matter of fact, when I hear Diana's big mouth come through that bullhorn, I'm going to break the crowd off with the Cabbage Patch dance and the Roger Rabbit as I cross the stage."

"Dang Audumn, if you do that, you gon' take it back to the 80's for real when you get your diploma."

"Girl do what you do. It is going to be your day, Audumn." A thought crosses Diana's mind. "You know what?"

"What now Diana?" Kizzy retorts. "What? You gon' do the Michael Jackson moonwalk too with your little airhorn and bullhorn in your hands?"

"Nope!" Diana shakes her head from left to right then points her finger at Kizzy. "But you're close, though."

"Oh Lord, I don't want to think about what these shots of Patron and Long Island Iced Tea has made run across your brain."

Audumn is sitting there quiet, but the look on Kizzy's face when she said, 'Oh Lord!,' has brought forth her giggles again because she knows Diana is about to say something stupid. Suddenly, the scraping sound of chair legs scuffing the wooden floor sends slight vibrations under their feet. And before you know it, Diana is up on her feet and decides to grab everyone's attention around their sitting area. Looking down at Kizzy and Audumn, Diana claps her hands and shouts, "Cotton candy sweet as gold, let me see that Tootsee Roll!" before executing the early 90's dance where she's standing.

It's something about being out with her Chicas that brings out the spontaneous butterfly in Audumn and before you know it, she jumps up and gets beside her best friend and is doing the dance, 'The Tootsee Roll,' right on side of her. "To the left! To the left! To the right! To the right!" she continues on with the lyrics Diana has already vocalized while moving her hands, hips, and feet to the imaginary beat they both seem to hear.

Diana reaches down and grabs Kizzy's arm. "Girl get up here!"

Kizzy may be the prudent one of the bunch, but she is by no means a party pooper and gets up on the other side of Diana. "On three, on the beat," Kizzy exclaims while snapping her fingers and moving her feet in sequence with Diana and Audumn. "One, two, three!"

"Now dip baby, dip! Now dip, baby dip!" the three say in unison as they break The Tootsee Roll dance down to the floor and burst out laughing when Diana goes too low and falls on her backside.

Diana is sitting on the floor when she looks up at Kizzy and says, "And bam! Just like that, Kizzy, is how I'm going to be when my Chica get her degree in front of errybody. Now help a bitch up so I can rethink how I'm going to do the dip part of the song at the graduation without falling on my ass!"

"That's easy." Kizzy reaches down to help her up. "Don't get drunk."

"I guess, Kizzy, but I can't promise you nothing because I might have a shot or two of Jack Daniels in my purse to loosen me up a bit in the bleachers."

Diana stood tall in her heels as she is pulled to her feet. The waiters and the Pappasito's customers loved every bit of the three amigos show so much that they begin to clap for an encore. Audumn waves them off with laughter and smiles as she took her seat, saying thank you. Diana, being Diana, was still holding Kizzy's hand and forced her into taking a bow with her to the restaurant's cheering. "Girl let my hand go." Kizzy mumbles between her teeth when seeing that Diana was going to try and make her bow again.

The food is gone and the drinks are gone as well as Audumn's December 6, 2012 wedding engagement extravaganza comes to an end. Not only has their night come to an end, but the restaurant is closing and the customers are down to Audumn's group and another table of two. Diana paid the tab for the drinks without stressing the price while Kizzy paid for the food. Audumn pulled out a twenty to tip Julio when he began cleaning off the table, but he insisted on giving it back because he made good on tips tonight and he believes it's because of the show they put on earlier.

"You see, Audumn how good God is. Tonight is truly your night."

"You can say that again, Kizzy." Audumn replies and then holds up the twenty dollar bill she just saved. "Won't he do it!"

"You stupid for real, lil Beaumont. I'm talking for real for real."

They joined arms while walking to their cars because for one, they were drunk, tipsy, or whatever they wanted to call it. And two, they were in heels. If you add the two together, most women will agree that it's not a pretty site if tragedy decides to happen. Kizzy made it to her car first and she departed by telling them to be safe and to call or text her when they make it home. They all agreed to call each other, but when walking arm in arm with Audumn, Diana wondered, *How did Kizzy get a better parking spot then us and she got to the restaurant last?*

"Audumn I don't know how she did it, but she did."

"Huh? What are you talking about now, girl?"

"Kizzy."

"What's up with Kizzy?" Audumn looks to see if Kizzy is still in her car, but the parking space she occupied is empty.

"Nothing, but I want to know how in the hell she got a better parking spot then us and she came last?"

"Girl it's late and I'm not fixing to play with you tonight. Goodnight Diana." Audumn closes her car door and rolls down the window. "Be safe and thanks for the drinks tonight. I really had fun, Chica. Now, could you please get in your car so I can get my butt home?"

Parked under a tree, Audumn grabs the steering wheel at the 10 & 2 position. Staring at the Christmas lights that are reflecting off her hood from the tree she's under, she notices that the holiday colors are also dancing through her diamond ring on the steering wheel. Placing her wedding band over her heart, she thinks about how special this Christmas is going to be when she shows off her engagement ring with her soon to be husband to her family.

Speaking of family, she thinks about her second mom, Ms. Boswell, who taught her about God as a child and who is there for her whenever she needs motherly advice. Ms. Boswell loves church and today is Saturday, so Audumn tells her intoxicated self that she will go to Fallbrook church with her in the morning. Feeling her stomach bubble brings her back to the empty parking lot she's the only one sitting in. Backing out, her phone vibrates in the cup holder and startles her. Two texts are on the glimmering screen. One is from Secorion saying that he loves her and to drive home safe. And the other is from Kizzy saying, "About to be home." Audumn only texts Kizzy back, "Ok", and then drove off saying aloud, "I love you too, Secorion Woodson. I love you too."

CHAPTER 3

T oday is Sunday, but it's not the Sunday she wanted to go to church with her play mom, but the Sunday after. Last Sunday didn't go as planned because she didn't wake up until after 1:00 pm. When she did wake up, she woke up to Secorion fondling her and before she knew it Round 2 and 3 was in effect. At the end of their bout, their sex match was declared a double knock-out because they both were out for the count until Secori woke up and took his soon to be wife to dinner.

But that was last Sunday and not today's Sunday. This Sunday, Audumn made time purposely for the Lord because 2012 has been a good year for her and now it's going to end a great year with her getting engaged to Secorion Woodson. Also, she doesn't want to miss too many Sundays of church with Ms. Boswell whom she loves unconditionally. She hoped Secorion could come with her more to church, but his job is having him working all kinds of crazy hours.

She's on her way out the door when she remembers she didn't put on mascara. Audumn likes her eye lashes full and fluffy, so she uses a thick, densely bristled brush for the lashes she's looking for. "There, all done," she said, batting her eyes and blowing a kiss to herself in the mirror. "Muah!"

The drive to Ms. Boswell's house is peaceful. 97.9 the box is playing gospel hymns and Kirk Franklin's, "The Holy Lamb God," lyrics are coming through the speakers. The soothing beat and the choir harmonizing on one chord makes Audumn feel good inside. Her life in Houston has had its ups and downs, but through it all God has kept her afloat for the present day she's living in now. She never in a million years thought that she would have a relationship with God, but it was Ms. Boswell who taught her about Jesus as a child and the sacrifice he made on the cross for the forgiveness of sins for the world.

Listening to the music brings faint tears to her eyes because visions of her selling weed in Northborough and going to jail for her ex-boyfriend, Tree, pierces her soul for how foolish she was living. The handcuffs on her wrists, standing before a judge, probation, and going on a high-speed chase from the police with him causes her to swallow hard because it could have been worse. *But God,* she thought. "But God," is what Ms. Boswell would tell Audumn and her three sons when something miraculously happened in her life or in someone else's. *But God,* she thought again when she looks down at her ring and then into the rearview mirror at the woman she has become.

Christmas lights adorn the front yard, trees, fence, and the roof of Ms. Boswell's house. With her left boot on the pavement, Audumn steps out of her car and Christmas tunes began to sound through the air with each step she took. The caroling stopped when she stopped walking, and that's when she realized that motion detectors had to be

23

along the passageway to the door. Audumn's finger is about to press the doorbell, but the metal cross on the outside of the house brings back memories of her childhood. The cross is rusty, but it's the same one she helped Ms. Boswell's sons hang on her house when she was a child in Beaumont, Texas.

"Audumn wake up. You're home."

"Already, Ms. Boswell? It seems like we just left the church."

"Come on baby, it's late and thanks for coming to this summer's Vacation Bible School with us."

Audumn lifts Ms. Boswell's son, James, head off her lap and looks out the church van window. *"Thanks Ms. Boswell and I really had fun making this clay cross. I can't wait to put it on my dresser when I get in my room."*

"Anytime Audumn, and even though Vacation Bible School is over, tell your mom and dad I am still picking you up for church Sunday mornings."

"Yes ma'am and thanks again Ms. Boswell. I love you and goodnight."

The door hastily opens and snaps her off of memory lane. "Come in. Come in," Shanay said after unlocking the burglar bars that secured the front door. Shanay is Ms. Boswell's oldest granddaughter and it was through her and her cousin Kendra that Ms. Boswell and Audumn reconciled in Houston after not seeing each other for over ten years. Kendra stayed in Northborough during Audumn's hustling days and Shanay used to visit Kendra when she would come to visit her grandmother from college. Christmas is around the corner, so she must be in town for the holidays.

Audumn steps inside and immediately takes off her shoes because Ms. Boswell doesn't allow anyone to wear shoes in her house. All Shanay can do is smile because her grandmother, who she calls Nana, has been having her company take off their shoes since she was born. Ms. Boswell reasons for the Chinese customs came from her raising three boys in a house with white carpet. Even though all her sons are grown and no one hardly ever visits her, she still does it because she hates having to shampoo it as much as she would have to if she didn't.

"Hey Nana, look who's here." Shanay said, escorting Audumn to the kitchen table where her cousin Kendra is sitting.

Ms. Boswell is turning the oven dial to low so that her Sunday dinner roast will slow cook while they're at Sunday morning service. "Hey my sweet and beautiful Audumn. Thanks for coming with us to church this morning." Ms. Boswell gives her a hug and looks her over because Audumn's red blouse and skirt she picked out for church fits her well. "I love that outfit Audumn. It looks so good on you that the mannequins in the stores would be jealous if you walked by their window while wearing it."

Kendra chuckles at her aunt's compliment. "Yeah girl! It is cute though."

"Thanks, I got this blouse and skirt on a 50% off sale at my store, 'A Touch of Elegance.'"

Shanay takes a seat at the kitchen table and Audumn asks, "So, how's Prairie View been treating you?"

"It's been good, I guess, besides the fact that I still haven't decided on a major."

"Trust me Nay Nay, you'll figure it out and before you know it, you'll be graduating in no time." Audumn replies, referring to Shanay by her nickname.

"Speaking of graduation Audumn, are you ready for your last semester of college so you can start Veterinarian Institute of Technology (VIT) school?"

"Yes Ms. Boswell, and I also can't wait to go to VIT so that I can be one step closer to helping animals who are severely hurt like my dog, Lady, who died when I was a child."

"Is that why you got Lady tattooed across the back of your shoulders?" Kendra asks.

"Yes, and it was a birthday gift from my girl, Pepper, who used to work with me at the strip club, Magic City."

"Girl, I always thought that you had that on your back for who you are and how you carry yourself."

"I know right. Everybody does. Lol!"

"So Audumn?"

"Yes ma'am?"

"First, how is your mother doing since she's been in remission the past five years? And two, where is this engagement ring you raved to me about so much last Sunday?"

"My mom is doing great and still serving the Lord through the bond we've had since battling her cancer together five years ago. It's amazing how God changed her life being that she didn't go to church much when I was growing up. But, it's better late than never because I just love the woman and mom she is today."

"Amen and thank you Jesus for your mother's glorious healing and worship to the most high God the Father," Ms. Boswell replied.

"Engagement ring?" Shanay looks at Kendra with the, *I don't know* anything *about any engagement ring,* look as soon as her Nana finished her sentence.

Audumn sees her play sisters haven't seen her ring yet and hangs her hand in the air for display.

"Wow!" Shanay exclaims, wondering how much the ring cost.

"Wow is right, Shanay!" Kendra said taken aback that her friend who is like a big sister to her and her cousin is getting married.

Ms. Boswell grabs Audumn's hand and is bedazzled at how Secorion, who she hears so much about but only met 3 to 4 times, has stepped up to the plate and asked her adopted daughter to be wed in holy matrimony. "It's beautiful Audumn and everything you told me about your ring on the phone last week is just how you described it to me. Simply beautiful, Audumn," She says again, but this time turning away to wipe tears forming in the corner of her eyes. "You deserve it."

"Nana we have to go, like now. Church starts at eleven and it's already twenty minutes till."

Ms. Boswell looks at the clock on the stove. "Shanay get my purse hanging on the side of my headboard and the shoes I'm wearing should be on the floor right under my purse."

"Yes ma'am." Shanay goes and retrieves what her Nana has asked her for.

"Great. Now let me hurry up and put on my stockings and then I'll be all set to hear the word of God with my three favorite girls in the world."

Fallbrook is a megachurch on the northwest side of Houston, Texas. The members are friendly, the deacons go out of their way to help members in whatever ways possible, and the Pastor's heart and love travels throughout the congregation endlessly. Visitors come and immediately feel at home as soon as they come through any of the numerous doors and are greeted by the smiling greeters. Everything positive they say about Fallbrook is true and the neighborhoods on the northwest side love all the church does for the homeless and the youth in the community.

Christmas pictures are being taken today during and between both services for anyone looking to take a picture in front of their 20' tall bedizen Christmas tree. Kendra and Shanay knew their Aunt and Nana wanted to take a picture with her niece and granddaughter this morning. That's why they made it their business to attend church service with Ms. Boswell today because she had asked them to shortly after Thanksgiving dinner at her house three weeks ago.

This morning the line is short to take a picture. This is because church has already started and the members and visitors are getting to their seats. Waiting in line, the four of them watch the TV monitors along the walls of the foyer so that they can keep up with the service even though they are not inside the sanctuary. The mass choir and congregation are singing the old hymn, "Amazing Grace," when Kendra gesticulates that it's their turn to go. Audumn steps to the side as the three of them step in front of the empty Christmas wrapped boxes perfectly placed around the bottom of the tree.

"What are you doing, Audumn?" Ms. Boswell asks with a blank expression.

"I thought this was a family picture and you wanted to take it with your family."

Ms. Boswell steps off the red velvet Christmas tree skirt and goes and stands beside of Audumn. "Audumn you are my family sweetheart. You are the daughter I never had and whether you like it or not, I played a part in raising you into the woman you are today."

"But Ms. Boswell, I really don't won't to impose."

"Excuse me Miss, but the line is waiting for your family to take your picture," the photographer's assistant said, hoping she didn't have to skip them.

"Yeah Audumn! Come on." Kendra and Shanay both try to pump her up to take a picture with them.

"I'm sorry ma'am, but it looks like I will not be taking a picture either if my Audumn doesn't take one with us."

Audumn sees that the assistant is about to escort her friends from in front of the Christmas tree so that the next family can take their picture. "Oh, okay. Hold up. I'll take a picture with them."

"That's my girl. And thanks for regarding my wishes." Ms. Boswell holds Audumn's hand as they both step onto the Christmas skirt next to her niece and granddaughter.

The picture is immaculate. Ms. Boswell had on her favorite white dress and Kendra and Shanay were dressed alike in all red. With Audumn wearing red and gray, the four colors they had on meshed together really well. Audumn stood in the middle next to Ms. Boswell while the girls stood on the side of each of them. The snap from the photographers came as soon as they all looked into the camera because they were already smiling just from being in each other presence. Huddled around the digital printer, the four of them watched as their picture printed out before them. Immaculate is right, in view of the fact, that the matriarch of their small family had on all white putting her on somewhat of a pedestal in the picture where she belongs.

"Oh, it's beautiful girls and thank you from the depths of my heart for my first Christmas picture with all of you. I can't wait to have it blown up and hung over my fireplace." Ms. Boswell looks at the monitor and notices that a guest preacher is trekking across the immense stage to the podium and concludes that the pastor is not preaching today. "Come on girls. Let's find our seats fast because the word of God is about to be preached."

Pastor Terrance Grant Malone of the St. John Missionary Baptist Church where Martin Luther King once preached in Houston Texas is the guest speaker today. Just as Ms. Boswell and the girls are about to sit, he asks everyone to stand for the Lord's prayer. "Our Father who art in Heaven," he begins and the congregation repeats after him the preeminent prayer until he says, "Amen and you may be seated." The Lord's prayer is something he does before preaching the messages God has given him so that he won't go overboard with a long drawn out prayer that makes his audience lose interest in what he's about to say.

"Foundation," he says into the microphone to the thousands of members and guests who are attending this morning's 11:00 a.m. service. "Today Fallbrook we are going to be talking about the word foundation and what's the significance of this word is in the Bible and in you and in your kids. Amen."

"Amen!" replied the multitude of people from the top row all the way down to the pulpit in which Pastor Grant is standing.

Pastor Grant continues, "Church, before we go to scripture, we must first know and understand what the word foundation means." Pastor Grant sips some water that is placed on the dais as he turns the page of his notes. "According to the numerous dictionaries I've looked the word up in, the definition of foundation is: A.) A basis upon which something stands or is supported, B.) An underlying base or support, C.) A body of ground in which something is built up or overlaid. Now, keep in mind that there are other definitions of the word foundation, but today I would like to focus on these three because it is these three definitions that today's text derives from."

Pastor Grant holds up his Bible and ask those listening to turn to Matthew chapter 7, verses 24 & 25. As he waits for the house of worship's pages to stop turning, he makes it perfectly clear that the scriptures they are about to read are from Jesus himself.

"The scriptures read: 'Therefore everyone who hears these word of mine and puts them into practice is like a wise man who built his house on the rock. The rain came down, the streams rose, and winds blew and beat against that house; yet it did not fall, because it had its foundation on the rock.' Foundation," he repeats again before proceeding. "The Bible says throughout the Old and New Testament that Jesus was a carpenter, right?"

"Yes!" comes from different corners of the prodigious church while others nod their heads in agreement.

"As a man of God, I tend to ask myself and God, 'Why?' on some things that perplex me in my studies of the Holy Bible. Such as, out of all the positions in the world God the Father could've placed his only begotten son in, he chose a carpenter to be the stepdaddy to assist in grooming Jesus into the Christ we know and love today. Why?" he exclaims through the microphone with great emphasis. "To my understanding, a carpenter is a person who makes and repairs wooden structures. I know, I know, some of you are wondering where I'm going with this, but let me explain. Take this building for instance or better yet, the very chair you're sitting on. As a carpenter, Jesus had to know that if he made the chair you are sitting in, the four legs under the seat must be supportive enough for a certain amount of weight to be supported for anyone who decides to sit in it. With that said, what would the legs of your chair be considered as, church?"

"Foundation," they all said in unison.

"Yes Fallbrook. You are exactly right. The legs of your chair are the foundation of
the chair."

"Preach pastor," a lady on the front row shouts, understanding where the Pastor is going with his message.

"Fallbrook, this is a big church, but did you know that before it was built someone had to first stabilize the ground and lay cement so that someone else could come and build on it? Once again, what did the workers have to put in place before someone built this gracious building?"

"Foundation!" the church bellowed in concurrence.

"Amen Fallbrook. Amen. Moving on to answering my initial question on why.

God the Father revealed to me that Jesus being a carpenter would give him the knowledge as a child to an adult on what he was going to become for the world. Which is what Fallbrook?"

"Foundation!" The entire congregation shouted visualizing how Fallbrook was constructed and collating it to how Jesus is the foundation that the church is built upon.

Pastor Grant sees that he has their undivided attention and is overwhelmed at how much they've been participating thus far in his sermon. "In Psalms (102:25) the Bible says that in the beginning

God laid the foundation of the earth. In Jerimiah (10:12) the Bible says that God made the earth by his power and founded the world by his wisdom. In other words, His wisdom is the foundation of the earth we live on. In Timothy (3:15) the apostle Paul tells his pupil that God is the pillar and foundation of truth. And last, but far from the least, in 1 Corinthians, chapter 3, verse 11, the apostle Paul bluntly tells the church of Corinth 'for no one can lay any foundation other than the one already laid, which is Jesus Christ.' What does all of this mean, Fallbrook?" he asks rhetorically. "What it means is that God the Father made it his business to make sure his son had a solid foundation in his life. In doing that, His son Jesus would be prepared to lay down his life on Calvary for the future foundation of the church in which we are built on today." Pastor Grant pauses for a brief moment and allows the Holy Spirit to flow throughout the believers. "I said all that to say this. What foundation are you as Christians laying in your life to build on? Or better yet, what foundation are you laying in your kids' life so that they can have something to build on when they become adults? Earlier I asked for those willing to turn their Bibles to Matthew chapter 7 versus 24 & 25 and now I ask that you read versus 26 & 27."

A flutter of pages turning sounds lightly through the assembly.

"And Jesus said: 'But everyone who hears these words of mine and does not put them into practice is like a foolish man who built his house on sand. The rain came down, the streams rose, and the winds blew and beat against that house, and it fell with a crash.' Amen and I pray that something was said here today that gives you the understanding of what the word foundation means in the word of God and how it applies to your life and your kids' life. My time here is up, but before I walk off this pulpit, I would like the church to shout as loud as they can the word foundation one more time for our Father and his son Jesus Christ, our personal savior."

Roars of the word foundation ripple through the rows of chairs as members and guests begin to stand one by one for such a profound message on finding stability in your life. Pastor Terrence Grant Malone waves to the crowd one last time before he exits out of the side entrance to the stage. Pastor Nance, the youth pastor, follows Pastor Grant's message by asking all visitors desiring to join church or looking for prayer to please get with any of the ushers and that they will escort them to the prayer and dedication room in the back. After closing with a prayer, Pastor Nance says, "Amen and Sunday morning service is over."

"Wow what a wonderful message," Ms. Boswell says, exiting into the foyer thankful that the young ladies God has placed in her life heard it as well.

"I know, Nana. It's like everything he talked about made me think about how you raised me."

"And how you raised me too, Auntie."

"What about you, Audumn?" Ms. Boswell asks. "What did you get out of today's message from that outstanding young preacher?"

"What I got out of that message is that without a foundation nothing can exist and if it does exist without a foundation, it won't last long because it doesn't have one." Audumn replays the words she just said in her mind. "Hold up. Did I say that right?"

"Yes, you did Audumn. Yes, you did. That's exactly what Pastor Grant-Malone was talking about." Ms. Boswell stops in the foyer and looks at the three of them. "I'm proud of all three of you ladies and I'm thankful for being in each of your lives."

"Awww, we are happy to have you in our lives too, Nana."

"Yes Auntie, I don't know where I would be without you."

"Me neither." Audumn added in understanding that while she was growing up her mom wasn't big on church like she is now and that it was Ms. Boswell who laid the spiritual foundation in her life she has today with God.

"Great! I hope you guys are hungry because I have a big juicy roast in the oven waiting on the four of us." Ms. Boswell looks at her Christmas picture and then back at the girls. "Let's go home."

CHAPTER 4

A ll set and ready to go, Secorion has his bags packed for the week they have planned staying at Audumn's parents' house in Beaumont until the new year. Audumn was packed too, but due to the limited space for her and the Christmas gifts, she had to revise her excessive packing situation. Secorion tried to tell her that she didn't need to bring two of everything for each day of the week, but that was like talking to a brick wall because she would always retort with the question, "What if?"

As usual, he was right when it came to packing the limited space they had in his Charger or her Cadillac and he refused to entertain that they should take both cars. In other words, Audumn is going to have to put something back and if it was up to him, he would start with her bag of shoes. As much as she hated to, that is exactly where she is going to start because, *'What if'*, she spilled something on her outfit she was wearing for the day or worst, *'What if,'* she slipped and fell in the mud.

"Come on, come on already. It's like almost 1:00 and we still ain't left Houston." Secorion taps his head on their opened bedroom door in frustration.

"Oh, be quiet Secori. It's not like you're trying to help me out. And besides, you whining ain't gon' help me move any faster." Audumn zips her last bag she has to lighten up for their trip.

"Now are you done?"

"Yes Secorion, I'm all done. But just fyi, we would have been gone already if we had taken both cars."

"Whatever." Secorion exclaims and then mumbles, "Women. Can't live with them and you damn sure can't live without them."

"What's that you just said under your breath?"

"Huh?"

"You heard me."

"I didn't say nothing, baby. I just want to go already."

Christmas traffic in Houston seems to be at its all-time high this year. If it wasn't for the gigantic red and green bows along the lights of I-10, one would think Hurricane Rita or Ike was doubling back for revenge on how quickly the city rebuilt after all the water rescinded a few years back. Bumper to bumper, they poked along in Secori's Charger hoping and praying that they can get their speed up to at least 50 to 60 mph. Their prayers seemed to be working, but that's until they came to a complete stop for about twelve minutes.

The car is silent because Secorion has his radio off and is angry because they didn't leave earlier like they planned on doing the night before. Audumn is mad because he's not talking to her and she knows it's her fault that they probably won't make it out of the city until about three o'clock.

"So, that's how you're going to do me on our first Christmas Eve together as a soon to be married couple?" Audumn places her left hand on top of his on the centered gearshift. "I'm sorry, baby. I'm sorry for not listening to you from the beginning and now look at us sitting here not even moving an inch."

"Baby you know how Houston traffic gets during the holidays and yet we still left our apartment like we're some rookies to this city's chaos."

"Baby I said I'm sorry."

Secori looks over at her and sees Audumn is just as irritated as him. "I'm sorry too, baby. I should have helped more back there and complained less. Had I done that, who knows, we probably would be ahead of all this traffic by now."

"I love you so much my love, but this one is on me. I'll take the blame for our delay and I promise you it won't happen again."

Loud horns from the cars behind them jolts them out of their bumper to bumper apologies because the cars in front of them proceeded about thirty seconds ago. Secorion presses the gas to catch back up to the 20-mph flow, but inwardly fights himself from giving everyone in his lane behind him the middle finger.

"Finally," Audumn says, letting out a deep sigh when crossing over the ship channel. "Beaumont Texas here we come!"

"Well it's about damn time." Secori replies when seeing that their destination is only 50 minutes away.

"Aww baby it's Christmas Eve and I'm on my way to see my family with the man I am going to spend the rest of my life with."

"Okay. So what is that supposed to mean?"

"It means that we're out of the city and we're out of that terrible traffic so let's enjoy this beautiful holiday." Audumn caresses the side of his face and a smile cracks his lips. "That's it, baby. Only happy thoughts and making treasured memories from this day on."

"Starting now?"

Audumn sits back and faces forward. "Yes Secorion Woodson. Starting now."

I-10's traffic begins to dissipate when they get into Anahuac and the highway opened up to press the pedal to the metal if he wanted too. Enjoying the beauty of nature's landscape, Audumn asks Secori to roll the windows down for some fresh air. Secorion complies, but ends up only cracking them when a December cool breeze comes swooshing through the car sending chill bumps along both of their arms. The breeze is cool, but the fresh air circulating through the car gives Audumn the fresh start she's looking for to a day that started out bad for her and her future hubby.

"Oh, that feels good, doesn't it my love?" Audumn lays her seat back, takes her shoes off, and puts her feet on the dash.

"Yes babe. I've got to admit, the fresh air does feels good. Especially after I put some drawls on the windows and turned the heat up."

Audumn chuckles to Secori laughing at his last statement. "Yes baby. Thanks for putting them drawls on the windows. Don't know what I'll do without you or your drawls."

"I know right," he jokes.

Secorion laughing was the fresh start he needed to a day that started out bad for him and his future wifey. Everything that happened earlier went out the window when he rolled them all the way down before rolling them back up again. With the weight of grief, unhappiness, and anger off his shoulders, he turns the radio on, but

Audumn quickly puts the station on 102.5, which is her hometown's radio station.

"Looks like we're almost home," Audumn says as the three-lane highway changes into two lanes in Winnie Texas. "Beaumont is only twenty minutes away."

"Now that's what's up. I can't wait to see what your brothers have been up to lately." Secorion smiles inwardly, thinking about how her younger brothers had him wilding out in Temptations strip club in Vinton Louisiana last Christmas when he visited.

"Yeah I bet you do want to see what they've been up to." Audumn puts her index finger to his temple. "As long as your black ass don't end up in some strip club throwing all my money."

"Your money?" Secori asks, wondering how long has she known they went to the strip club that night when she went out with her classmate and friend, Khamil.

"Yes! Like I said, my money!"

Secorion sees where this conversation is going and changes the subject quickly. "So, how's your mom and dad been doing?"

"They're fine and don't think I didn't recognize how you just changed the subject."

"I'm sorry baby. I thought we put the past in the past when we left H-town earlier."

"Yeah I bet you did." Audumn gives him a beady eye and sits back in her seat quietly.

Secorion pulls into her parents' driveway at approximately 5:00 on the dot. With a toot of the horn, Aubrie, who the family calls Brie, comes running down the tall steps of his parents' house to greet his favorite sister, which is also his only sister. Hugs, kisses, Merry Christmas, and how are you comes all at once from her baby brother who loves her ever so dearly. Recognizing the bond her and his future brother in law has, Secorion realizes that he has to watch what he says and does in front of Brie because her baby brother must be Audumn eyes and ears when she's not around.

"What's up Secori! What's been going down in the H?" Aubrie goes to the driver's side of the car to give him a fist bump.

"Shit, just chilling, doing me, and staying out the way trying to get all the paper I can get on the job I'm on. Other than that, really nothing special besides your sister saying yes to marrying me."

"What marriage?"

"What do you mean what marriage? What; you don't know?"

"Know what?"

Audumn runs around the car and places her hands over her brother's eyes.

"What are you doing sis?"

"Keep your eyes closed when I take my hands off your eyes and I'll tell you when to open them."

"Anything you say sis. I'll play along." Aubrie wonders what the surprise is.

"Okay lil bro. You can open them."

Aubrie opens his eyes to his sister standing next to Secorion with her wedding ring hand on Secorion's chest. "So, what's the surprise?"

"The surprise is that I said, yes!"

"Yes to what?"

"She said yes to marrying me, brother in law."

"Brother in law." Brie's mind slowly wraps around the good news his sister and her fiancé are telling him. With wide eyes he shouts, "You're getting married sis! Wow, I am so happy for you and that ring is bling blinging for real though, bro." Aubrie playfully punches Secorion in the arm.

"It better be because your sister is my everything and that's exactly what I'm going to give her for the rest of my life. Everything."

Aubrie is too excited. "Can I be in the wedding sis? Pleeaassee!"

"Of course you're going to be in the wedding silly. The wedding won't be a wedding if my baby brother, Aubrie Jean Humphrey, isn't in it."

"Yeah brother in law, I wouldn't have it any other way."

"Brother in law, huh?" Aubrie likes the way it sounds coming from his boy Secori. "I got to admit, it does have a nice ring to it."

"Whelp Secori, you've done did it now!"

"Did what?" Secorion asks.

"Got my little brother's head in the clouds with all that brother in law talk."

"Sis it ain't even like that. Now get your butt up them steps and go tell the fam hi while me and my brother in law get these bags and Christmas gifts inside the house."

Audumn looks at Secorion and shakes her head. "See, I told you." Before walking up the steps she turns and tells Brie, "And you better not say nothing until I say something because it was supposed to be a surprise!"

Yeah, a surprise I didn't know nothing about. Secorion thinks before loading up as much of their belongings as possible and following Brie into the house.

Audumn opens the Christmas wreathed doors and pokes her head inside. Dex and Nick, which is short for Dexter and Nickolas, have their backs to her playing Call of Duty on the PS3 and doesn't notice that their big and little sister just came through door. Big because she's Nickolas' big sister and little because she's Dexter's little sister. Setting down the bag she carried in, she walks in front of the tv and shouts, "Merry Christmas brothers, I'm home!" All at once, both controllers smacked the floor as Dex and Nick jumped to give her a bear hug.

Her dad and mother, Geary and Yolanda Humphrey, are in their room when they hear all the commotion coming from the living room. Investigating the noise that livened the quiet house so suddenly, they both came out of their room with ear to ear smiles upon seeing their only daughter standing next to her three brothers. Robby, her oldest brother, is the only one not there, but his flight comes in at ten tonight and he should be home after midnight if his rental car is ready when he gets to Jack Brooks Airport in Taylor Landing, Texas. But that doesn't stop Mrs. Humphrey from savoring this precious moment of having four of her five kids under the same roof since last year's holiday festivities.

"Well hello there Secorion. Nice to see you again and Merry Christmas."

"Merry Christmas to you too, Mrs. Humphrey." Secorion extends his hand for a handshake. "And your Christmas tree is beautiful."

Mrs. Humphrey pushes his hands down and gives him a warming hug. "Son, go on with all that handshaking mess. In my eyes, you're family and my daughter loves you and you take good care of her. What else can a loving mother, like me, ask for in a man for her only daughter?"

"Yeah son." Mr. Humphrey puts his arm around his shoulders and looks over at his daughter having a jovial time with her brothers.

"Audumn is my baby girl and will always be my baby girl. And honestly son, my wife was right in everything she just said about you."

Audumn leaves her brothers when noticing that Secori is being besieged by her parents. "Excuse me mommy and daddy, but can I have my boyfriend for a moment?" Audumn pulls Secorion by the arm and brings him over to the decorated fireplace. "Mom, Dad, Dex, and Nick, me and Secori have an announcement to make."

"An announcement?"

"Yes daddy, an announcement." Audumn clasps Secorion's left hand.

"Hold up. Why you didn't you say Aubrie?"

"Oh shut up Nick and let her finish." Aubrie nudges and shushes his big brother because it looks like he's about to say something anyway.

"First, I want to say Merry Christmas mom and dad and I love you."

"We love you too baby and Merry Christmas to you too. Now, what's this announcement?"

"Well Mr. Humphrey, it's like this."

"Come on son, spit it out. Remember, my wife said you're family."

"On December 6th I asked your daughter to marry me and she said..."

"Yes!" Audumn screams. "Mommy I said yes, yes, yes!" Audumn runs over to show her parents her ring and her brothers run over to welcome their new brother in law into the family.

"Oh Audumn," her mom exclaims, looking down at Audumn's pretty ring on her finger. "I am so happy for you." Mrs. Humphrey looks over at Secori and back at Audumn. "I'm happy for the both

44

of you, sweetheart. Audumn he's perfect and your ring is beautiful. I knew from the day I first met Secorion he was a good man and would make a fine husband and father someday. I knew from how he spoke with such great respect for his elders and that told me he was raised right. And not to forget, he's very handsome."

After the exciting news, hugs, and Mr. Humphrey and Secorion's one on one talk at the kitchen table, the boys helped them put their presents under the tree and bags in Audumn and Brie's room. Her mom went into the hall closet and found an old Christmas stocking and wrote Secori on it to hang over the fireplace next to the other five she's hung on the mantle for her kids. The spirit of Christmas is in the air when she pushes the thumbtack into the wood to put Secorion's stocking next to Audumn's. Brie grabs the remote and puts the tv on a Christmas caroling channel while Nick grabs some playing cards.

"Who wants to play spades?"

"You shouldn't be allowed to say the word spade, Nick. You don't remember how me and Audumn tore you and Brie a new butthole last time during the holidays?" Secori replies, being respectful of his language because Mrs. Humphrey is in the room.

"I don't know what you're talking about." Brie comes over in defense of his big brother.

"Yeah I bet. Audumn, you feel like taking your little brothers to school again just to show them they ain't working with nothing when it comes to playing us in spades?"

"I don't mind, baby. Like you said, they are my 'Little' brothers." Audumn laughs because she knows Brie hates to be teased about anything.

"Well it's settled then. I'll go get the paper and take score for the four of you and the best out of three wins." Dex goes to his room to get some paper.

"It's on then! Best out of three wins and they get bragging rights."

"I don't know about all that bragging rights talk you're talking about Nick, but I'm ready whenever you're ready." Secorion loves the excitement and thinks about how him and his brother Cori used to play cards growing up in Chicago. "Audumn, remember if I go high, you go low and I promise we got these suckas." That's what he used to tell his little brother and they would always win. *Next year we are definitely going to the Chi to see my fam for the holidays,* he thought sitting Indian style across from Audumn.

"I got next after y'all three." Dexter said, sitting in his dad's chair ready to take score. "First hand bids itself!"

CHAPTER 5

Robert slightly taps his fingernail on the door to Audumn and Brie's old bedroom. Trying not to creak the door too loudly, he peeks inside to see his baby sister lying in her bed. Secorion is across from her in his baby brother's bed because Audumn's full-size bed isn't big enough for the both of them. Being careful not to make a sound, he reaches over the wooden bedframe and pulls her hair. Audumn moans and swipes at her face as if something is on her forehead, but then rolls over and begins to snore. "Audumn," he whispers. Robby tugs on her hair again, but this time Audumn knows she's not dreaming and that nothing is on her and sits up.

"Audumn it's me, Robby, wake up," he repeats twice in his quiet voice.

"Robby, is that you?" Audumn squints.

"Come here. Come here. I'm not trying to wake Secori up."

Audumn gets up and silently takes two wide steps to the door. "Robby! Robby!" she loudly whispers, jumping into her big brother's arms. "I missed you so much this past year. Especially with you not coming home for Thanksgiving."

"I know, right? I missed you too, lil sis. It's just that I used all of my vacation time at the beginning of the year staying an extra two weeks with momma. And what I had left, I wanted to use to be at home for Christmas and the new year." Robby pauses and recalls that his brothers told him that Audumn is getting married last night when he got in and she was asleep. "So, what's this I hear about my baby sister getting married?"

"Baby sister?" Audumn steps back. "Robby, I'm your only sister. And from the looks of this ring on my finger, I'm not a baby anymore."

"You can go on with all that sis. I don't care what you say, do, or how many rings you get on your fingers; you will always be my baby sister."

"And I should be because I was just playing, Robby." Audumn kisses her brother on the cheek. "Merry Christmas Robby and next time I don't see you in a whole year, I'm coming to Florida and I'm gon' kick your behind all over that orange state."

"Whatever you say sis, and Merry Christmas to you too." Robert knows his sister loves him unconditionally and brushes off her boxing threat. "But that doesn't answer my question about how you're supposed to be getting married soon."

Audumn snaps out of her morning stupor and remembers Robert wasn't there yesterday when she told the family about her engagement. "Oh, I'm sorry Robby. I guess getting up this early in the morning made me forget that you weren't here yesterday when I announced us becoming one next year." Audumn shows her brother her ring. "I said yes, big bro. If God says the same, this time next year I will no longer be Audumn Danyalle Humphrey, but Audumn Danyalle Woodson."

Robby embraces her head into his chest and kisses the top of her head. "Congratulations baby sis. And yes, God will say the same, Mrs. Woodson."

Robert and Audumn shared the morning making breakfast for the entire family. Audumn made the eggs and grits while Robby made the bacon, sausage, and toast. They would've made biscuits, but they decided to make a sheet of Christmas cookies and a pan of brownies instead. Secorion loves brownies, but Nick and Brie smoke weed and always have the munchies afterwards. That's where the sheet of cookies come in at because between the two of them, they can eat a pan of brownies like it's nothing.

"Whala! All done." Robby looks at the clock on the wall. "Do you want me to make you a plate? It's almost ten o'clock. I know the boys stayed up late playing spades, but they should be getting up any minute now to check and see if Santa came or not."

"Sure. Don't mind if you do." Audumn replies in an English accent. "Cheerio."

Robert burst out laughing. "Sis, you are silly as hell! Cheerio means goodbye, crazy."

"Not as crazy as you saying the boys are going to be waking up any minute now to check to see if good old St. Nick done come down the chimney or not." Audumn puts the cookies and brownies in the oven and presses start on the timer.

"Here you go, sis." Robby sets her breakfast plate on the table and pulls out a chair for his sister to sit in. "It looks good too, Audumn. I got to admit, we always did put it down in the kitchen when it came to making breakfast ever since we were little, huh?"

"And you know this, mannn!" Audumn replied in her Chris Tucker voice from the movie Friday.

Robert takes a seat at the table and grabs her hand. "Thank you Jesus for us being home with our family during the holidays and for the breakfast you blessed our family with from me and my sister's hands. Amen."

"Amen."

"So, when's the big wedding date so that I can tell my boss I want off on that day?"

"I don't know. We haven't decided yet."

"Well when you do, let me know asap. Preferably before February or March.

That way I can put in my request before anyone else on my floor at my job does for the month you choose."

"I got you, big bro. I'll let you know in February whatever date we came up with." Audumn holds up two fingers. "Scout's honor."

"So now you're a girl scout." Robby chuckles and holds up two fingers. "Scout's honor it is, sis. And for what it's worth, I'm happy for you and Secorion will be a great husband to you."

"Jingle bell, jingle bell, jingle bell rock. Jingle bells swing and jingle bells ring. Snowing and blowing up bushels of fun, now that the jingle bell hop begun..." Bobby Helms 1957 "Jingle Bell Rock" interrupts their sister and brother time and brings their Christmas breakfast to an end. Just as Audumn is scraping up the last bite of her grits, Dex, Nick, Brie, and Secori come through door and begin demolishing the breakfast she and Robby made for all of them.

"Come on sis. Let's bring mom and dad some breakfast so our bros can sit down." Robby says, getting up and throwing both of their paper plates away.

Mrs. Humphrey is already up when Audumn left the kitchen to bring her some breakfast. Humming to the Christmas tune, she joyously separates everyone's gift by name under the tree. "There, all done," she said to herself and then sees Audumn approaching from the corner of her eye. Audumn hands her the plate she made for her and sits on the couch to allow the love of her family around her to soak into her spirit. Her mom was on her way back to her bedroom to eat, but decides to sit next to her daughter instead.

"Thank you for the breakfast, Audumn. It looks good."

"It should be. I learned from the best." Audumn lays her head on her mothers' shoulder. "Merry Christmas, momma."

"Awww, would you look at that?"

"Oh, shut up Dex. Don't be hating because mommy loves me more than you."

"You know what, sis?" Dexter takes a seat on the couch on the other side of their mother and gives his mom a big kiss. "It's Christmas and I love you too much to even go there with you today. And please lil sis, don't tell me to shut up when you need to be telling momma to shut Pop Pop's old Christmas records up that she plays every year."

"Oh, shut up Dex. Ever since I was a little girl, my poppa used to play his records during the holidays to keep us in the spirit so that we won't lose hope at the lack of presents we got each year." Mrs. Humphrey looks at the stockings thumbtacked to the fireplace and remembers how her dad would dress up as Santa. "I guess I've made it a family tradition and I pray someday you can pass Pop Pop's record collection down to your kids."

"Momma, Pop Pop's records are cool, but for one, they're old, and two, the entire collection is white people music."

"Um sir." Audumn looks across her mother at Dexter. "I don't know if your brain has processed this, but momma is white so that makes you white as well."

"Half white. And all that sounds peachy coming from you, but you need to tell that to the cop that keeps pulling me over because I fit the description of a light skinned black man all the time."

"Boy you're crazy, and stop lying all the time, son. You know darn well that there isn't any cop on BPD that's pulling you over for your skin color." Mrs. Humphrey hands her son her empty plate. "Boy, go throw that in the trash and tell my boys to come open these Christmas presents. Audumn, you go and get your dad while I make sure I haven't misplaced any of the gifts."

"Yes ma'am," they both said at the same time as they got up to fulfill their mother's request.

"By the way, Dex, can you take those cookies and brownies out of the oven since you are going to the kitchen? Tell Nick and Brie I made them especially for them." Audumn winks her eye at her brother and goes to her mother's room to get her father.

Everyone came to the living room at their mother's entreaty. When all of her family is seated, Mrs. Humphrey hands each one of her family members the gift she and her husband bought for them. "Here Secorion, this is for you." Secorion looks up in shock at how big his present is over everyone else's. Brie frowned because his gift is small, but quickly changes his attitude when looking over at all the unopened boxes in his section under the tree. Tearing the wrapper off, Secorion pulls out a Klein tool bag and inside is a $50 gift card to Home Depot. "God bless you and Merry Christmas my future son in law and I pray that this gift Geary and I got for you will help you in some kind of way with your electrical trade."

Opening the first gift led to all the gifts getting opened and before you knew it, boxes and wrapping paper are all over the floor, couch, and the fireplace. Audumn got the Ugg boots she wanted and Brie got the expensive Beats headphones by Dr. Dre he begged his momma for. As soon as their mom saw that all of the gifts were opened, she asked everyone to help clean up. But that's all she did was ask because when she asked them, all of a sudden everybody had something to do.

The boys went outside to fly the drone Nick had gotten from his parents for Christmas. Secorion followed the three of them, but Robby stayed back to help with the cleaning. Audumn gives her fiancé a look he knows isn't good and tells Secori not to forget about the conversation they had in the car on the way to Beaumont. Her look makes him remember that he can't say or do too much in front of her brothers because somehow their little strip trip to Vinton, Louisiana got back to her and he didn't know when or how.

Her dad left next after noticing his sons had disappeared before he could make his exit. His excuse was that he had to visit some friends just in case his job called him into work later. Mrs. Humphrey thought that sounded strange because for one, he's the head cus-todian for French Elementary, and two, what school do you know that's open during the Christmas holidays? Let alone on Christmas day. This entire year he's been pulling stunts like this, but she didn't want to pry on behalf of the fact that her husband is known for pick-ing up odd jobs to make extra money. As he went out the door, Mrs. Humphrey wanted to say something, but with Audumn and Robby helping her clean-up she decided to speak her mind on this confound matter later.

"Momma." Robby calls. "Momma, where do you want me to put this box of ornaments and Christmas stockings?

"Huh?" Mrs. Humphrey is staring into space at the closed front door her husband just walked out of and doesn't hear her son calling her name.

"Momma, what's wrong with you?" Audumn asks. "It's like you've just seen a ghost or something."

"Yeah mom, I've been asking you for the past minute where to put these decorations and you haven't said a word."

"Sorry kids, my mind must've wondered off."

"I know, it's like you saw a ghost or something after dad left."

"I did. As a matter of fact, he is that ghost. One minute he was here and the next minute he is gone. I mean, really, who does that on Christmas day?"

"Mom, what are you talking about? Daddy said he was gon' go by some friend's house just in case he got called into work." Robby defends his dad.

"I guess you're right, son." Their mother pushes back her suspicion for now and gets back to the task at hand. "Robby, all the boxes go inside the attic above my closet and anything else you can put inside the garage. And Audumn, get the broom and dust pan so that you can sweep this floor after you pick up all this wrapping paper. As for me, I'll clean the kitchen. You can leave all the decorations on the walls, but as for the rest of this house, I want it back to normal before Nick, Brie, and Dex get back inside and decide to tear it up again." Mrs. Humphrey clapped her hands and all three of them went their separate ways.

Christmas day ended with Audumn and Secorion hoisting up one of Dexter's baseball trophy's to represent being today's spade champions and their dad coming in around eleven o'clock. His kids didn't think too much of him coming in so late because who are they to question their father's whereabouts? But their mother, behind closed doors, studied her Bible and prayed herself to sleep, waiting for her husband to come home. She tried to stay up for an explanation, but tomorrow is Friday and she has it all planned out to spend with her daughter. Before closing her eyes, she thanked God for her family being in good health and asked for Him to give her a discerning spirit so that when she does decide to question her significant other it will be the right time and the right thing to do.

Friday morning isn't as busy as yesterday morning. Also, it isn't as noisy either. Last night, Brie and Nick went back to their apartments to give their guests some space and to get out of any yardwork or chores their mother would've had them do around the house today. Secorion was asleep when Audumn heard her mom in the front room fumbling around. He's asleep because last night he decided to have sex with his fiancée. Why, you might ask? It's because, for some reason, he thought it would be funny to do it in the same bed and room she grew up in. Audumn felt some type of way at first, you know, with her mom and dad being in the other room and all. But that changed when her drunk friend, Diana, popped up in her mind at Pappasito's screaming, "Secori is yo man and you can do it whenever and wherever you want!"

"Audumn, you ready to start our mother daughter day?" her mother asked, hearing Audumn walk up from behind.

"Yes ma'am. Do you mind if Khamil comes with us? I invited her last night when she said she didn't have nothing to do because little Cody is at his granny's house for Christmas."

Mrs. Humphrey turns around with a big smile. "Audumn, you know I don't mind and your friend Khamil is practically like a daughter to me as much as she spent the night over here when you two were little girls."

"Thanks mom. She just texted saying she's on her way."

"Great. And today is going to be perfect. I can't wait to show the both of you what I've got planned for us."

Today's temperature is moderate. The high is 76 degrees and the low is 65. Being that it's December, the windchill is present, hence, long sleeves and a pair of jeans is appropriate. Dressed for this morning's weather, Audumn drives them in her mother's jeep to eat brunch at Bettie Jean's Homestyle Cooking on Dowlen road. It's her mother who instructed her where to go. She chose Bettie Jean's because the owner is her sister in Christ, the food always touches the right spot, and it's in the same parking lot as the Korean Spot Spa & Massage.

Mrs. Humphrey enjoyed every word said and every bite of their threesome brunch. Seeing Audumn and Khamil sitting across from her in the booth made her admire how much they've grown to be beautiful successful women. Khamil drives school buses for B.I.S.D. and Audumn is the manager of a successful clothing store and a soon to be college graduate from the University of Houston. The neighborhood used to call them Black and Yellow when they used to be together in the streets of South Park. Khamil's dark chocolate skin and Audumn light-complected skin is where the phrase Black and Yellow was derived from. Sometimes the kids would go too far and make them cry, but today they sit before Mrs. Humphrey with their heads high and confident in the skin God has blessed them with.

"So, what's next Mrs. Yolanda? The chicken and waffles I ate was awesome. It's not even twelve o'clock and I'm full and having too much fun with you two."

"What's next is that I'm about to take my momma shopping and get me something to wear for the week." Audumn turns towards Khamil. "Secorion made me put a lot of my stuff back before we left, but what he didn't count on is me going shopping with my mom like we always do when I come to Beaumont."

"What are you talking about, Audumn?" Khamil looks at Mrs. Humphrey and then back to Audumn.

"Long story, but just know that I'm standing up for all women and I won't let us down."

Mrs. Humphrey sits back and laughs. "You two are still the same little girls that used to run around my house."

"I know, right? Every time my girl leaves back to H-Town, I be missing her like crazy."

"You and me both, Khamil. I know Houston is only an hour and half away, but she's busy and I'm always busy trying to catch back up from when I was sick with cancer." Mrs. Humphrey looks at her wristwatch. "Come on, ladies. It's time to be pampered like the women we are. Our appointment at the Korean Spot is at noon."

The Korean Spot Spa & Massage is three doors down from Bettie Jean's. Once again, Audumn or Khamil have never heard or been to the place, so entering through the tinted doors they were kind of leery of what goes on in there. They're greeted in the foyer by a man and a woman wearing black scrubs with the Korean blue and red symbol on their sleeves.

"Welcome to the Korean Spot. Merry Christmas and I'm Jang-mi and this is my husband My-Sung and we are the owners of the Korean Spot Spa & Massage."

"Good morning or shall I say good afternoon, Mrs. Jang-mi. My name is Yolanda Humphrey and I have an appointment for two today."

"But momma, what about Khamil?"

Mrs. Humphrey slaps her daughter on the back of her hand and tells her to be quiet. "Like I was saying before I was rudely interrupted, I have an appointment at noon for two. but I was wondering if it will be any problem to add one more?"

My-Sung goes to the countertop and checks the spa's schedule for the day. "Honey, it looks like adding a third party to their appointment wouldn't be any problem at all."

"Great." Jang-mi exclaimed. "Well, there you have it. Looks like you're good to go. Right this way, Yolanda and…"

"Khamil, and this is my friend Audumn, which is Mrs. Yolanda's daughter."

Leaving the foyer, My-Sung stays at the front desk while Jang-mi brings them on a short tour of what her business has to offer their customers and clients. The place is huge and there is a section for everything. At the Korean Spot you can get a manicure, pedicure, facial, waxing, and a massage. There's also a hot tub, pool, and various saunas with different temperatures from super-hot to super-cold. Mrs. Humphrey paid for the deluxe package with gift cards she's been saving all year for this special occasion. With the deluxe package, every sauna room is accessible, therefore, they decided to start their pampering with the shower room to get their pores opened up for today's Korean experience.

Each girl was given a robe and a locker to put their belongings in. Stepping into the shower room, the three of them dropped their robes and stepped under one of the shower heads along the walls. The showers are motion sensored, so the warm water rains down on them unexpectedly. When the water came on, Khamil reached for a bar of soap, but then realized that this isn't that kind of shower.

"I saw that." Audumn giggled when seeing Khamil's hand searching for a soap dish.

Khamil laughed with her. "I got something you can look at," she said smacking her black bare bottom.

"Dang Khamil, you really filled out after you had little Cody."

"Yes ma'am. I sure did, and I'm all woman now."

"Is that because of your big butt or your big head?"

"So there you go with the jokes," Khamil replied standing akimbo. "Don't be mad at me because your momma didn't bless you with none of this."

"I'm standing right here, Khamil."

"Yeah Khamil, my mom is standing right here."

"I didn't mean it in a bad way. At least, I don't think so."

"I was just playing Khamil and even though I'm not black, I think I work what I got real good for a 51-year-old white woman."

"Yes you do momma and I think I work what I got real well too for a mixed black and white girl."

"Yes you do sweetheart." Mrs. Humphrey marvels at how Audumn's naked body reminds her of herself when she was that age.

Suddenly, out of nowhere, they both smirk at each other and look over at Khamil and smack their wet backsides like she did when she was bragging about her African American curves. All Khamil could do is shake her head because both of them are as nutty as a fruitcake and she didn't know where she would be if she didn't have them in her life when she was a child.

"What's this?" Audumn notices a small trough of light green water at the exit of the shower room they're leaving out of.

"The sign says, 'Mugwort Tea Bath Benefits.'" Khamil points to the sign and pot above the trough. "It's for boosting your blood circulation and leads to healthy hair and scalp."

"And look momma, it also relaxes the nerves in time of shock."

"Yes, I see that. It also says it's good to strengthen your uterus. Something good for you too, Audumn so that you can give me my first grandchild."

Khamil picks up the pot and dumps tea over her head. "Well, I don't know about all that uterus talk because I ain't trying to have no more kids no time soon. But what I can use is some healthy hair and a healthy scalp."

Audumn runs her fingers through her hair. "Ha, ha! Good thing I took after my momma and not my daddy in that department."

"Ha, ha! There you go with the jokes again." Khamil fills the pot up with tea and dumps it on Audumn's private area. "I'm sorry best friend, but my play mom wants a grandchild and I plan on helping her get one."

"I guess." Audumn replies, taking the pot from her and dumping a pot of tea onto her mother. Before you know it, they were splashing in tea like little girls playing around a fire hydrant.

After experiencing all the sauna rooms that they can bear, they decided to do the massage therapy next, and everything else they wanted to do they did before they left. Such as the facial, manicure, and pedicure. Audumn and Khamil ask for a masseur and Mrs. Humphrey ask for a masseuse. She really wasn't supposed to be doing too much of anything that involves heat because of her being in remission, but going to a spa with her daughter is something she always wanted to do on her bucket list. She also knows that her body isn't the same since the surgery and chemo years ago, that's why she decided to have a woman massage her instead of a rough man.

Overall, the Korean Spot Spa & Massage was well worth their gift card experience. The laughter, the massage, and the time spent with each other is just what all three of them needed going into the new year. Audumn and her mom had never done anything like this together and today's optimistic fun is something that they'll be duplicating in the future. Khamil also had the time of her life. Her body felt light has a feather and she couldn't stop looking at her bright yellow fingernails and toes. They spent 2 hours at the Korean Spot and being that they were on Dowlen road already, Audumn proclaimed that it's time to do what girls do best during this time of the year, which is shop, shop, and more shopping.

"Parkdale Mall here we come!" she shouted, jumping into the driver's seat of her mother's jeep.

"Yeah, that way!" Khamil pointed down Dowlen road towards the mall.

CHAPTER 6

I t's crunch time and the 4th quarter of getting her bachelor's degree in science started one week ago on the 22nd. New years came and the fun with her family popping firecrackers made her remember the good ole days when she used to watch the fireworks show on the banks of the Neches River in downtown Beaumont. God, Secorion, her family, and friends is what drives her to completing what she started four and half years ago and the finished product will be making everyone proud, including herself.

Three classes are left in fulfilling her prerequisite for the Veterinarian Institute of Technology in Houston, otherwise known as VIT. Physics, which is the hardest course of the three she takes, is on Mondays and Wednesdays so that she can have more time to do her homework. She takes Chemistry and Animal & Veterinarian Science on Tuesdays and Thursdays. That way, she can have Fridays off to manage the store, A Touch of Elegance.

"Class, it is now a quarter till ten and I know some of you are going to be very sad to hear this, but Thursday I will not be here. Therefore, your homework will be to read Mole Concepts in its entirety in your text-books and answer Exercise 1 on Oxygen and Nitrogen of particular gaseous mixtures. This assignment and today's assignment will be due next Tuesday and I expect all of your homework to be on my desk prior to you sitting at your desk. Now," Professor Baron Banks looks over his Chemistry class to see if anyone has something to say or needs to ask a question. "Class dismissed and enjoy your six-day weekend."

Audumn exited Professor Banks class at ten o'clock sharp. Her next class starts at 10:15 and is in one of the outside buildings not joined to the main building in which she's in. January and February are a lot cooler in Houston than it is in December, so her attire is a bit warmer than what she had to wear during the end of the 2012 year. Knee high boots, jeans, a turtle neck sweater, and a U of H scarf is what blocks the wind and the coolness of the 57 degree weather. Usually, she would grab a bacon, egg, and cheese croissant with a caramel mocha iced latte out of The Nook Cafe, but being that everyone runs late the first two weeks of school, the lines are too long, so she settles for a Coke instead.

Animal & Veterinary Science is up next and even though the class just started, Audumn anticipates the fun she will have in this class because of all the different animals she will learn so much about and get hands on experience with. Last week, Professor Armstead took the class on a tour of U of H's barn, aviary, and pigsty to give her students a look at all the different animals they would be working with throughout the semester. Professor Armstead also took them on this tour to weed out anyone who's allergic to certain animals or had a disdain for certain animals. By applying this method early in the year, her students can have an ample amount of time to get out of her class before it's too late.

Audumn strolled through the door of her classroom, not knowing the classroom setting was going to be a lab. Finding a vacant stool at one of the lab tables in the middle, she sits next to a slender black guy and introduces herself. "Hi, I'm Audumn," she said, taking a seat, only to get a nod and a slight smile for a reply.

"Good morning class and I'm glad to see that everyone who signed up for my class has somewhat of a soft spot for animals. Before I go any further, I want to say that the person who you're now sitting next to is your lab partner for the remainder of the year, so get to know each other because your grade in the lab projects will be the same for the both of you. Last week, we dealt with all of the animals we're going to be tending to in this class as we move forward throughout the year. However, in order to properly move forward in caring for what U of H has bestowed to us, we must learn how to collect blood from the cephalic vein and the jugular vein. We collect blood for many different reasons when treating animals, but we also collect blood for what our profession calls Routine Preventive Care. Routine Preventive Care and Pre-Anesthetic Blood Tests will be our subjects for next week's Tuesday and Thursday class when we are dealing with the different colors of rubber stoppers for vacutainer tubes that tells the person collecting blood if any additives have been added to the tubes or not. We also will be learning the meaning of EDTA, what are red and white blood cells, serum, and how to use our blood separating machine, a Centrafuse."

"My dad told me that when using the Centrafuse that you should always put water or blood in the empty slots to balance the spin and to keep the machine running smoothly while separating the clotted blood cells from the serum."

"Yes, that is exactly what a Centrafuse is used for and I must say that I'm quite impressed Mr.....""

"Tigner. Jerick Tigner is my full name and my dad has his own practice as a veterinarian out in Sugar Land, Texas."

Amazed that her non responsive lab partner knows a little something, Audumn disregards that he brushed her off earlier when she was trying to be polite. *Hmmm, I think Mr. Tigner here will be of some help when it comes to sticking these animals with needles,* she thought, thinking about her dislike for syringes.

Professor Armstead walks to the back of the lab and brings back a muzzled Labrador from one of the twelve cages. With the palm of her hand, she taps the top of the lab table in front of the class, making the canine jump on top of it, obeying her command. "Class this is Matt and he's two years old, and today, I will be demonstrating how to collect blood from the cephalic vein. There are two types of veins we use to collect blood in dogs. One is the cephalic vein, which we use for collecting small amounts. And the other, is called the jugular vein, in which we use for collecting large amounts." Ms. Armstead pauses to see if anyone is taking notes. "Um, this will be a good time to get out your pen and paper to take notes because that may be a test question."

"Yes ma'am," a few students muttered as notepads begin to open and pens begin to write.

Professor Armstead went on to teach. "In this class, we will collect blood the correct way and the safe way, always using the proper safety precautions our school and practice requires when drawing a blood specimen. As you can see, I have on scrubs and in the shirt pocket of my scrubs I have a Sharpie and a fine point Sharpie." Ms. Armstead holds the Sharpies up for her class to see. "These two sharpies are a requirement in this classroom and you will need them for labeling files or vacutainer tubes after collecting blood samples. I suggest that you have these Sharpies by class on Thursday because you're not using mine. Also required for this class is a stethoscope. Keep in mind, we do have stethoscopes in the sterilizing cabinet to my left, which is your right. And as your professor, this is something that I must make available to you, but me personally, I would never put anything in my ears that I'm not the only one using on a daily basis." The class quickly writes, *"Get a stethoscope,"* in their notes after pondering on how dirty the earbuds on the school issued ones would be after a day in and day out use. "Now, the scrubs are not a requirement and if you don't have the means or desire to buy any, then along the walls of this laboratory there are lab coats of all different sizes to choose from when being in this class. With that said, I would like everyone to find a lab coat off the wall that fits you and gather around Matt so that I can demonstrate how to collect blood from the cephalic vein." All the students get up to follow the professor's instructions. "Please make a mental note that when you enter this class, you are required to have on scrubs or a lab jacket the entire time class is in session. This is for your safety and something that will roll over into whatever field you may be going into. After today, I will not say this again concerning the lab jackets or Sharpies and will be deducting a half a point from your final grade each time you don't meet my class requirements. As far as the stethoscope goes, I'll give you two weeks to purchase one before it will become a requirement for you to wear the class issued ones the University of Houston provides or a half a point will be deducted for that also." Standing around Matt, Ms. Armstead emphasized that when drawing blood from any animal that you must have the proper restraints or an assistant to hold the animal still while collecting a sample. "Jerick, will you be my assistant since you have some knowledge of what we're about to do today in class?"

Jerick walked around the backs of his lab mates and then sifted his way through a few girls to get to the lab table where Matt is propped up for display. The professor wraps her arms around the dog to show Jerick and the class the proper way to restrain a canine during this procedure. The class nods their heads one by one to show they understand as Jerick follows the teacher's example so that Matt is ready when their instructor is ready to stick him. Step by step, Ms. Armstead breaks down the do's and don'ts of using syringes and strongly suggested that if you have a fear of needles then her class is not your class and that the student should rethink the profession they have chosen to be in. "All done," she said as she took out one of her Sharpies to write Matt on the vacutainer tube in the stand next to him.

Behind in her normal class schedule, the professor decided to divide the class up into two groups so that in Thursday's class she wouldn't have to go back and teach a lesson from today. One partner from each lab section must stay with Matt to learn how to collect blood samples, while the other partner had to take notes for the both of them on dog anatomy from the charts on the wall.

Jerick kept his head down when Professor Armstead gave the ultimatum of allowing the partners to decide who stays with her or who goes and take notes for them and their partner. Audumn took this as a, 'Get out of jail free card,' and crawfished her way back to the opposite side of the room and begin drawing her best version of a German Shepard from the chart in front of her. Her artwork is not bad because she always did enjoy drawing ever since she was a child.

Just as it is in the chart, she drew lines along her drawing's body while labeling each body part such as the Neck, Muzzle, Sternum, Skull, Loin, Stifle, Hock, and Withers. She did the same thing for the dog skeletal system chart but her dog's skeletal pictures weren't as good as the first so she decided to take a picture instead with her phone and work on her drawing back at her lab table. It's not like she had too because the picture is good enough for studying; but, she wanted too because she learns things better when she writes it down or says it out loud.

Audumn's phone rings in class and causes a disturbance.

"Class, I don't know if I mentioned it in my introduction to this class, but one of my pet peeves is that I can't stand phones ringing or any kind of alerts in my classroom. So please, for your prerequisite's sake, put them on silent because trust me, you will not need any outside disturbances in what this semester has up ahead for you guys. Thanks, and as you were."

Embarrassed, Audumn digs inside her book satchel and pulls out her phone to put it on silent. As she's pressing the sound key, it begins to ring again, but this time she silences it as soon as the first musical tone aired through the silence of the lab room. Though she caught it in time before the professor could respond, that didn't stop the student's necks from turning towards her at the same time as if they were all on some kind of mechanical mechanism. Ignoring them all, she discretely sticks out her tongue and grins as she notices that her mom has called her twice. *Sorry mom, but Professor Armstead doesn't like phones and I already got one strike against me.*

11:10 came and all of the students fell into the hallway heading for the exits to eat lunch or hang out in the cafeteria. Some students just hit up the vending machines or drive off campus to the nearest fast food restaurants whilst others found a corner to cram for a test they didn't study for the night before. On Tuesdays, Audumn goes to work at 12:30 p.m., therefore, she can't do anything. Her hangout days in The Nook Cafe with her college cronies are on Mondays and Wednesdays because on those two days she goes in from 2 to Close. Pressed for time because she's hungry, she heads straight to Lot 9 where she's parked.

The sound of her blaring alarm and blinking lights catches her eye from the curb at the edge of the parking lot. Quickly, she presses the panic button to shut it off after identifying where she's parked throughout the scores of cars. The sun is out, but that doesn't stop the wind from swishing the naked trees back and forth with a sudden cool breeze. Not wanting her hair to become disarrayed, she quickly scurries to her car and jumps into the driver's seat. Cherry senses the keyless remote in her sweater's pocket and cranks right up when she pushes the start button.

Heat spewed through the vents to warm her chilled body. Sitting there, she lets her body warm up and takes her cellphone out of her book bag lying on the passenger seat. The screen displayed four missed calls from her mother and the envelope for text messages had the number six next to it. *What can be so important?* she thought, when seeing that she had three text messages from her mom, one from Nick, Brie, and her dad. Suddenly, her mind quickly turns for the worst and her memories of her mother's dreadful battle with ovarian cancer pushes its ugly face to the front of her eyes. *Oh no! Please*

Lord don't let anything be wrong with my mother! She's been through so much and I can't handle another scare like last time.

Her thoughts and the four missed phone calls made her call her mother first. "Momma, it's me, Audumn. Is everything okay?" Audumn speaks as soon as her mother picks up, but the person on the other end doesn't say anything in return. "Hello, momma are you there?"

A loud wail barrels through the receiver of Audumn's phone. Her mother is on the other end and her heart is in shambles because the head of her household has more than one household. At least, that's what the evidence says. Money always coming up short for the bills, he's always gone, he's always at work, not showing any interest in her, and talking to the homewrecker on the phone kind of put the icing on the cake as well. And to make matters worse, the woman worked at St. Elizabeth, the hospital where she got her chemo treatments at back when she had Stage III cancer at the end of 2007.

It just so happened that Geary and Jennifer grew up together in the north end of Beaumont and had a fling in middle school with each other. Jennifer is single with two sons and is willing to be Geary's mistress because he promised her that it's been too much secrecy for too long and that he will separate from his wife the day before this upcoming Valentine's Day. How Mrs. Humphrey found out was when her husband was in the shower before work this morning, his phone began to light up on the nightstand from a caller named Boo Thang.

"Momma no! Please don't be telling me what I think you're telling me about daddy. Please momma, don't say that about daddy. Daddy loves you. You've got to be mistaken. Daddy would never do that to you or us. Daddy loves us, mommy."

A loud sob cries from the opposite end of the line when Audumn mentioned that her dad loves his family.

"Love!" her mother squelches. "Yeah, he has love all right. Love for that Boo Thang he's been sleeping with for the past five years. I can't believe I was that blind to the bullshit lies he's been telling me about how he's working late tonight or how B.I.S.D. needs him to wax the floors on his off days."

Audumn is dismayed to the fact that her mother is cursing and is telling her about the man who raised her. She loves her dad and thinks very highly of him, but her mother doesn't have any reason to lie to her about something this grave. *Dang daddy, I remember sacrificing everything when mom had cancer and there was nobody there to help me but Robby until he left and went back home to Florida. Is that what you were doing when mom needed you most? When mom was fighting the fight of her life to be with us, including you? I remember how you were always gone to work and coming in late. I remember.....* Audumn remembers something her mother said to her on Christmas day about her father.

"Audumn, are you still there?" Mrs. Humphrey stops crying after realizing what her daughter may be feeling. Especially since, in her eyes, he's always been a Super Dad to her and her brothers. "Sweetheart, I'm sorry if I hurt you by telling you this, but I needed you to know that your dad will no longer be staying here."

"Huh? What do you mean, momma?"

"What I mean is that when he got out of the shower and saw me on the phone with his Boo Thang, he told me it's over and it's been over for the last three and a half years."

"So, he just left?"

"Yep! He took his clothes and just left. Oh, but not before telling me he will be back for the rest of his shit later." Her mom begins to cry again over the phone because that was her husband's exact words before he stormed out their bedroom door.

"Momma, I'm so sorry that you have to go through this drama after overcoming so much for us and that man."

"Audumn, he's still your father."

"Momma, I'm furious and you're a great woman and your walk with God has brought us closer together and has transformed me into a better person because life is short and anything can happen. He's wrong, wrong, wrong, momma. No matter how you look at it, it's not right and nobody deserves to be spoken to or to be treated that way after thirty-three years of marriage and thirty-six years of being together. Frankly momma, this is inexcusable and the man I thought was my father is not my father after all."

"But Audumn."

"I love you momma, but this cut me deep and I simply don't want nothing to do with him right now. I don't want to talk, text, or see his ugly face right now!" Tears start pouring out of Audumn's eyes and into her palm she's covering her face with. "Momma, you're a great mother and you don't deserve this."

"Audumn, please don't cry sweetheart. I'm sorry for stirring you up this early in the afternoon. I didn't mean to hurt you."

"Momma, forget him!" Audumn screams to the enclosure of her car. "I'm not a kid anymore and he's wrong and I don't want nothing to do with him because there's nothing he can say to me to justify these inexcusable actions he's been doing against this family over the years by not being able to keep his dick in his pants."

Yolanda doesn't question her daughter's judgement or choice of words, because the fact of the matter is, that her daughter is grown and is about to be thirty-one years old this year. Audumn is her best friend and she needed to know that the house she came to on Christmas will no longer be that house when she comes to visit again.

After letting her daughter vent and allowing the steam to die down, Mrs. Humphrey broke the silence and said, "Audumn, thank you, my love, for calling me back and always being a shoulder for me to cry on. I love you and I'm sorry if I ruined your day with this god awful news. Be blessed and call me later to check on me and also so that I can know that you're okay."

"Yes ma'am and I love you too, momma."

"I know you do sweetheart. Goodbye."

The conversation lasted almost thirty minutes. Noon is around the corner and her job she has to be at by 12:30 is about thirty minutes away. The windows are misty from the hot air coming from her breath and the heat still blasting from the vents that she forgot to turn off during all the madness. Still angry at her father, she notices that he texted her two times while she was on the phone with her mother. Her love for him is what made her middle finger press the envelope message button on her phone. The first text message said, *I love you*. The second text message said, *I can explain*. And the last message said, *Call me!* Audumn doesn't want to hear from him now or ever again because as she put her car in drive, she thought about how she and Robby defended their dad to their mother when he left on Christmas day. *I'm sorry momma for not hearing you sooner,* she thought, pounding the steering wheel before calling her job to let her employees know that she's going to be late.

CHAPTER 7

P eople are everywhere. Mostly men and children, but there are also women in the Gateway Shopping Plaza looking for last minute love gifts. The sky is clear today and the wind cone on top of the Chase bank across the street is pointing south. The cool air is still, but the sun above them gives Cupid the window he needs to come out and shoot his arrows in his usual attire, which is nothing.

Fondness is in the hearts of all people during this time of the month that the United States has purposely ordained to show affection for your parents, friends, and your significant other. Well, that is for most people, because truthfully, a lot of Audumn's love was ripped from her heart when her mother told her that her dad has been cheating on her for years and has left her for another woman. Distraught from the news that broke her into pieces, Audumn has been walking around apathetic to the Valentine's Day spirit that the atmosphere brings.

"Excuse me Ms. Humphrey, but there's a delivery guy out here with a big box from Gardenia's Floral Arrangements."

Audumn is in her office doing paperwork when Lawanda knocks on the door before entering. Usually on Friday's Audumn's out mingling with the customers or helping Marcus restock the store, but the daddy piece to her puzzle is missing right now, therefore being all lovey-dovey just isn't happening this year. No matter how she tries to look at the situation from both sides, she still can't fathom that the man she looks up to did this to the woman she adores and would give her life for.

"Tell him to go away; it must be a mistake. Valentine's Day is tomorrow and I know it's not for me because Secori and I are both off tomorrow."

"I don't know, Miss Humphrey. Royalty gave me this to give to you and from the way they spelled your name with a D and not a T, tells me that, "Somebody Loves You Baby." Lawanda did her best version of Patti Labelle when saying her hit single's title at the end of her sentence.

Audumn cracks a smile. "Girl, you are crazy and this better not be no gift from a secret admirer because then me and my new employee, Royalty, is about to have a talk."

Lawanda shakes her head and then hotfoots it behind Audumn because she forgot to mention that the box is from a secret admirer and doesn't want Royalty to get into trouble on her second week of work. "Miss Humphrey, wait! I forgot to tell you...." she exclaims, but Audumn has already made it to the delivery guy about to give him a piece of her mind if this box is a bunch of nonsense like she thinks it is.

"Good afternoon Mr. flower delivery guy, but I don't except gifts, let alone flowers from people I don't know."

"How do you know if you know them or not if you don't open up the gift, Ms...?

"Humphrey."

"Your first name might not be Audumn by any chance?"

"It is."

"Well this is for you from your secret admirer." The delivery guy bowed as he waved his hand towards the enormous red box and stepped back.

"Come on Miss Humphrey, just open it." Lawanda said when seeing her boss turn red to the delivery guy's corny presentation of the gift she doesn't want.

"Yeah Boss Lady, it's not every day you get a gift like this from someone. This guy must really like you."

"What makes you think he's a guy, Marcus?"

Marcus clears his throat and chuckles. "Trust me Boss Lady, it's a guy."

"Yeah, Miss Humphrey. Ain't no women giving no other woman no gift like this unless you know something I don't know."

"Oh, shut up, Lawanda. You sound ridiculous and don't you have some customers to tend to?" Audumn points to the line that's building up on line 2.

"Sorry Miss Humphrey." Lawanda sprints over to her register to help Royalty who has been working the lines by herself for the past fifteen minutes.

"So, what you want to do with this here box, Boss Lady?"

Audumn turns to the delivery guy and shoos him out the door before he can say something to make her regret keeping the intriguing big red box on the floor of her store. "Get out, get out," she said, handing him a five dollar bill out of her back pocket. "Marcus, can you help me open this box so Lawanda and Royalty can get back to work and stop watching me so close?"

"Anything you say, Boss Lady."

Marcus and Audumn both walk around the box looking for the best way to unwrap the gift that was brought in on a dolly. The heart shaped bow on the front is only a gigantic sticky pad and when Marcus pulled it off, nothing happened. The only other thing that protruded from the box is the tag hanging from a long string that said, 'To: Audumn.' Carefully inspecting the tag, Audumn notices that the back of the tag has the words, 'Pull Me,' in bold letters stamped in the center of it. "Hey Marcus, look at this."

Audumn pulls the tag just as she is telling Marcus to come see what she has found. Suddenly, like at a magic show, the sides of the box started to fall one by one until Secorion is standing in the middle of it holding a box of chocolates and a dozen brown and yellow roses. "Happy Valentine's Day my love, my fiancée, and my future Mrs. Audumn Woodson!"

A Touch of Elegance erupts with claps, Happy Valentine's Days, and congratulations to Audumn and Secorion's soon to be holy matrimony in becoming one. Customers in lines are all smiles as they look on to the love offering of the young man holding the flowers displayed for the store to see. With the atmosphere being surreal, Audumn jumps into Secorion's arms and begins kissing him all over his face while hugging his neck with the utmost of joy because no one has ever done anything like this for her before, not even her ex, Tree.

"And to think, I almost sent you back out the door with that delivery guy." Tears begin to gloss her eyes when pondering on how she almost rejected such a well thought out gift from the man she gave her hand to.

"Aww baby." Secorion consoles her. "Trust me my love, I wasn't going to let you put me out and if you did, I would have been proud anyway for respecting me and not accepting gifts from strangers on Valentine's Day."

"But baby…"

"But baby, everything went according to my plans and I'm right here my love." Secorion finishes her sentence so that her negative thoughts can be diminished before they are planted and watered in her mind.

Audumn looks him in his eyes as he's wiping the tears from hers. "I love you so much Secorion and you really surprised me with this one."

"Trust me baby, this is only the beginning of all the gifts I am going to give to you for the rest of our lives." Secorion passionately kisses her on the lips and hands her the flowers and chocolate. "Baby, I know you don't get off until eight, but I rented a cabin on Lake Conroe at The Timber Reserve for two days and if possible, could you leave at five so that we can start our Valentine's Day weekend a little early since it's our first and only one we're going to have being engaged?"

The woman of the hour complied with her fiancé ever so graciously and Lawanda didn't mind running the store for the remainder of the day. Frankly, her boss needed the early time off from all the grief she's been through trying to figure out how, why, and what in the hell her dad was thinking when he decided step out on her mother.

Secorion felt the same way as Lawanda did; that's why he showed up a day before Valentine's Day with his gift because Audumn's heart being broken by her father has leaked into their relationship at home.

Secorion's stuff is packed when they got to their apartment to get Audumn's belongings for the small vacay. Trying to make her mind and soul at ease as much as possible, he already had her traveling bag opened on the bed with her toothbrush and deodorant tucked away inside it. Audumn recognizes the gesture and effort. And kid you not, for the first time since the phone call from her mother, it felt like a weight is being lifted off her shoulders each time she tossed something into the bag for her getaway with her bae. "I'm ready, Secorion. Please, let's just get out of here."

I-45 North traffic leaving out of the city is not heavy, but it's not light either. Secorion didn't mind what the traffic looked like anyway because Audumn has already dozed off in the passenger seat. Her beauty is fetching as he tucks her in with his Chicago Bears blanket he always keeps in his car for his lunch breaks at work. Lately, Audumn has been mentally distant from him as well and he needs her mind to be back in the game for what he's about to tell her on their first enchanting evening together in their log cabin.

Willis Texas is where The Timber Reserve is located on the shores of Lake Conroe. After driving down the long road Thousand Trails, the GPS finally said their destination is .09 miles away. Secorion is relieved when he gets to the arrowed sign that reads, 'RV Park to the left and Log Cabins to the right.' Theirs is Cabin #4, so all he had to do is follow the graveled road about a hundred feet around the bend and he would be there.

The fourth porch light on the cabin not being on is what made him know he had found the cabin they will be abiding in. And with the music being off and the windows being cracked, the sound of the crunching rocks underneath the tires is what wakes Audumn up from her daytime nap that's slowly turning into night. Wide awake, she raises her seat up to see the wooden structure she hopes to regain some of her happiness back in. That, and the sparkly dim horizon reflecting off the lake not too far from their doorsteps.

"Baby it's beautiful. And you are sooo getting some of this cookie when we get inside there." Audumn leans over and kisses Secorion while groping what's hers between his legs.

"Now hold on baby." Secorion opens his door and jumps out quickly because he felt his package move towards the upward position.

"Yeah, right. Is that you talking because it felt like to me that your other head wants to come out and play?" Audumn flashes her boobs and blows him a kiss when he reaches in the back seat to get their bags.

"Okay, okay. If you want to do it that bad, I guess I can squeeze having hot, butt naked sex as soon as we get here into our schedule I had planned for us tonight."

"I guess, you guess." Audumn gets out and grabs whatever he didn't take out of the backseat. "I don't know if you realize this yet, but your ass belongs to me now and if I want to do it then that's what we're going to do."

"Yes Miss Humphrey, but please remember that same declaration when I start to have my urges."

"Ouuu, look at him using them big words." Audumn drops her bag and closes the door. Taking Secorion by the hands, she leads him to bed and pushes him down. "Since you want to get me all hot with them big words, let's see what else has gotten big as I find out how many licks it takes to get to the center of your lollipop." Audumn grips his manhood hard with two hands. "And don't think I didn't hear how you called me Miss Humphrey either. From now on, you have to address me as Mrs. Woodson or my singing career on your microphone will cease to exist if you keep playing with me. Got it?" Audumn went down on him as far as she can go.

"Got it, Mrs. Woodson." Secorion palms the back of her head and pushes her head down further. "Oh yes baby, I got it."

Sex wasn't long, but it was the beginning of the relief she needed to transition back into her normal self. After showering the past turmoil off the both of them, they both changed into a warmer outfit for the dropping temperatures. Secorion started a log fire with the wood the last couple left by the fireplace. Despite the fact that a light switch brings them light, everything else about the cabin is real as cabin life can get and Secorion couldn't be any happier about it. For one, he's never been a Boy Scout, and two, he forgot to bring his nonexistent oil lantern he kept on the nightstand by his bed.

"I'm ready, my love, to take a tour of The Timber Reserve."

"Great, and I'm ready to see what all two lovebirds can get into around here for Valentine's Day." Secorion finds some marshmallows and graham crackers in the cupboard. "And look bae, I found two of the ingredients to make some gooey smores for when we find an outside firepit to snuggle up to."

"Secori, that sounds romantic."

"I know, right? Come on bae. Let's go find a snack machine and buy two or three bars of Hershey's up out of it. I can't wait to be sitting next to you with a marshmallow on my stick over the fire."

"Sounds like a plan to me. I'm down."

Before looking for the firepit, Secorion wanted to range over the landscape with the brochure he found on the clip outside the cabin's door. He already knew what The Timber Reserve had to offer from the pictures he viewed on his phone but now he has a map of the property in his hands and he's ready to quicken his love's heart again with having a good time away from the drama that life brings. Hand in hand following the map, they walked through the hard-wintered grass and all you can hear for a brief moment is the wind slightly wailing in the open terrain. Besides the lake that sits twenty feet from their log cabin, the nearest attraction is the eighteen hole putt putt mini golf course that's up ahead under the prodigious canopy and lights.

A handful of children are the ones putting at the time. As the kids race between holes to see who can put their golf balls in first, they pushed and shoved each other in laughter until the girl sinks a ball in the cup and screams because she won the battle between her brothers. Secorion doesn't know it, but the girl winning their friendly sibling match took the last weight off of Audumn's shoulders that was holding her down from being her everyday self. It is also that winning feeling that has uplifted the sadness that has engulfed her soul and has put a dark cloud over her life. It is also that winning feeling that has made her realize that in life you win some and lose some. And it is that same winning feeling that she needed to say to herself, *it's my dad who has lost out on a good family that will go on without him.*

"Secori, why do men cheat?"

Secorion feels like he's having Deja vu because the first time Audumn came to his apartment back in the day it was because Tree was cheating on her. "Baby, all men don't cheat because I would

82

never cheat on you." Secorion lifts her chin up with his hand and stares deep into her hazel eyes. "I love you, Audumn Woodson."

"I know you love me Secori, but I thought my dad loved my momma and it turned out he was in love with some heifer he had a thing for in middle school."

Secorion continues to follow the map to one of the three outdoor firepits displayed on the threefold paper. "Baby, your mom is a beautiful, proud, white woman and any man who leaves such a sweet strong woman like that is a fool and it's sad to say, but there's no good going to come to him for it."

Audumn rests her head onto his shoulder as they talk and walk towards the flicker of fire on the meander they are strolling on. "Thank you, my love. I really needed this."

"I know you do, my love. That's why I brought you here."

Six wooden Adirondack chairs sat in a semicircle around the chiminea that was thought to be a firepit. Two of them were occupied with a mixed couple warming themselves up under the stars above them. Audumn said her greeting before taking a seat next to the woman while Secori went to the vending machine and bought as many Hershey bars ten dollars can buy.

On his way back to the marble rock floor and chiminea setting, Secorion couldn't help but to overhear that Audumn had already made her a new acquaintance. Taking his seat next to her, he says, "Happy early Valentine's Day, by the way, my name is Secorion or Secori for short."

The woman said "thank you" and "my name is Jaqkie," in response to his politeness, but her husband got up to introduce himself properly and to give Secorion a firm hand shake.

Enjoying the night by the fire, Audumn and Jaqkie hit it off by sparking up a conversation on how her mother is white and her dad is black. It's kind of the same, but not the same because in their relationship, Jaqkie is black and her husband, Mark, is white. Though the circumstances are switched, her new friend can definitely relate because Audumn is probably how their child will someday look when he or she is grown.

"So, how long have you two been married, Mark?"

"Going on seven months. How about you two, Secori?"

"Oh, we're not married yet."

"So when's the lucky or shall I say the big day?" Mark replied, looking at the ring on Audumn's finger.

"Honestly Mark, we haven't decided on it yet or started planning the wedding. But what I do know is that we're getting hitched sometime this year."

All four of them spent the night by the fire making smores and relishing in each other's company. Jaqkie gave Audumn ideas on wedding planning and Mark and Secorion talked about how the Baltimore Ravens beat the New England Patriots in the Super Bowl ten days ago on the third. Both of them said they'd lost money on the game, but they also both agreed that Ray Lewis deserved to get another ring before he retired. With the night getting darker by the minute, Mark and Jaqkie decide to turn in early to relax by their cabin fire and listen to the oldies station until they fell asleep in each other's arms. When they faded into the night on the meander in which they came, Secorion decided to break the news to Audumn about the project his job is trying to send him to on March 2nd.

"Baby." Secorion looks as the reflection of the fire lights up the different colors of brown in Audumn eyes. "I have something to tell you."

Audumn sits up when seeing Secorion really has something on his mind. "What is it, bae? You know I'm team Secorion in whatever you are thinking about telling me."

"It's funny that you say that because…."

"Because what, bae?"

"Because my job wants to send me overseas to Dubai to help get a project that's behind schedule back to where it needs to be for annually payouts from the contractor."

"But baby, we just got engaged and we haven't even set a date or started planning the wedding."

"I know baby, but this is a great opportunity for us. I'll be making $64.00 an hour and $175.00 a day per diem. On top of that, it's non taxed up to the first $80,000 and they say when I get back, I'll be foreman on the job we've got coming up in Corpus Christi, Texas."

Secorion has Audumn's full attention now. "But baby, what am I supposed to do while you are gone and what about our wedding?"

"Well for starters, I will leave on the second of March and I will return for your graduation at the end of May for one week and then I'll leave again and won't return until the fifteenth of August."

Audumn stands up and goes to stand in front of the fire. With her back turned towards Secori, she says, "It sounds like you've already made your decision without me."

"No baby, I didn't. I told my job I have to talk it over with my fiancée first and they said they can meet any of my requirements I need if I decided to go." Secorion places his hands on her shoulders.

"Baby, nothing is set in stone until Monday when I give them my answer on whether I'm going to go or not."

"So, are you going?"

Secorion turns her around. "How can I go if I don't bring it to the attention of my better half first and see what she says?"

"I don't know, baby. Four months is a long time to be without you."

"I know it is Audumn, but just think of how much money we are going to have so that you can have the fairytale wedding you've always dreamed of."

"Well, it would be great if we didn't have to ask anyone for help on our special day together when we get married. And Kizzy and Diana will love the fact that we can go all out for my wedding like I know they want too."

Yes! Secorion thought. "You see baby, everything's going to work out perfectly and I will get the promotion I always wanted in this electrical trade since I moved to Texas."

After carefully going over the facts about the project he has to leave four months for, they both agreed that it would be best for their future family if he goes and do what his employer asked of him.

"I love you, Audumn. And thanks for supporting me on this. I promise you that me being gone will be over with before you know it."

Audumn rests her head on his chest. "It better be," she mumbles. "Or the rest of Team Secorion will be in Dubai dragging your ass back home."

Secorion pictures her in Dubai, but quickly shakes the thoughts away before he starts laughing. "I'll keep that in mind bae the entire time I'm out there." Secorion pauses and thinks about their discussion on the walk to the chiminea. "Audumn."

"Yes, my love?"

"There's one more thing I need you to do for me."

"What?" Audumn pushes back off of him.

"I'm sorry about what your dad did to your mother, but Mr. Geary is a good man and has always made me feel welcome in his home. Please my love, when the time is right for you, could you please return your dad's call because until you truly confront your demons you will always be in bondage in here." Secori touches her heart with his index finger.

"But…" Audumn stops speaking and remembers that she is on Team Secorion now. "As you wish my love, and I can't wait to kick your butt in putt putting tomorrow."

And I can't wait to let you win. He thought, thanking the Father in Heaven for the woman he fashioned for him since the beginning of time.

CHAPTER 8

T his month is the month of the beginning of every girl's dreams. It only seems right that this is also the month of the beginning of spring where the bright colors that bring life to this world covers the deadness from what the winter has left behind.

March 3rd is when the phone calls on behalf of the wedding begin to get the wheels turning for today. Secorion left for Dubai the day before, but Audumn made sure he left the phone numbers of all those who needed to be contacted for their holy matrimony before he left. For two weeks, she and her two Chicas have been calling numbers and getting addresses for the invitations they will soon be sending out and today is their first official meeting at their official meeting spot.

Kizzy is the one out of the three Chicas who has a house and Audumn couldn't be more obliged that it's Kizzy and not Diana's place where headquarters is going to be to plan her illustrious day. Diana is her girl, but punctuality and seriousness is not always a part of her repertoire when it matters most because Diana's time table for life is different from the time table the world has put in place for us to follow.

Just like I thought. I knew she wasn't going to be here on time. Audumn drives up and sees Diana's car is nowhere to be found. *I guess I'll have to let her make it this time because I'm late myself.* Audumn toots her horn and closes her car door. *But we definitely have to address this issue today because we're on to short of notice to mess up my wedding day over being late all the time.*

Audumn walks to the door, but Kizzy heard the horn and opened it before she could ring the doorbell. Rounding the corner to the living room, Diana comes from behind her and yells, "Boo!" Audumn gasps and drops her purse while Kizzy and Diana laugh it up on how they knew she wasn't going to be expecting Diana to be on time for the meeting.

"Diana, your big behind scared the crap out of me!" Audumn pushes Diana on the shoulder. "Don't you ever, ever, ever do that again. I almost wet my pants playing around with you."

"Uh huh, I knew you thought I wasn't going to be here on time because I'm always late to anything that doesn't involve me at the center of the attention. But, you're my Chica Audumn and I'm here to let you know that you can count on me and I'm at your disposal."

"Whatever." Audumn is still a little shook from being spooked as she bends down to put her belongings back in her handbag.

"Oh my God, we really scared her, Diana! I am so sorry, Audumn. I thought we would have a little fun with you since we knew you weren't expecting her on time."

Audumn's nerves calm down and the joke that her bff's played on her brings her sense of humor back. "You two got me, but trust me, this isn't over with by far, Ms. Diana Ross."

"And what else?" Diana replied with a big smirk on her face.

"And you girls are right, I didn't think you were here on time and I apologize."

"Why thank you, Audumn. Apology accepted." Diana gives Audumn a hug and apologizes for scaring her like that.

"Are you girls finished yet because my son and daughter are going to be home at 4:00, yeah. And we have already wasted twenty minutes of our two-hour meeting on some stuff that ain't got nothing to do with this wedding."

"All right N.O. There's no need for you to get all New Orleans up in this place."

"Diana, not right now and both of you need to have a seat so we can get started." Kizzy replied.

Kizzy rolls a magnetic dry erase board onto the carpeted living room floor. On it, at the top in bold and underlined letters is, **Audumn's Wedding Planning.** Underneath is the to do list, which consist of photographer, flowers, music, reception hall, rehearsal, bakery, and other things she could think of off the top of her head for today's wedding planning meeting. She also hands Audumn and Diana a mini wedding planner notebook and explains to them that they are for taking notes in the meetings and for jotting down ideas for whatever you want to bring to the dry erase board in the meetings.

Kizzy holds up her book. "As you can see, my notebook is a lot bigger than yours because I'm personally taking charge of the wedding planning unless any of you two want to do it and therefore, we would switch notebooks and I would step down." Audumn and Diana look at each other and don't say anything. "Moving on," Kizzy responds to her friend's silent response of them saying they're cool with her being in charge of the wedding planning. "First thing's first.

Audumn, we need a date so that we can know what our time frame for making your day as beautiful as you want it to be is."

"After a long discussion, Secorion and I decided on September 13th."

"September 13th I think we can do. I mean, with today being the 23rd of March and all. What do you think about it, Diana?"

"I think whatever Audumn wants her date to marry that fine ass man named Secorion Woodson to be on, I'm down with it." Diana sits up. "But why September 13th, Beaumont?"

"Yeah, why September 13th, Audumn?"

"Because for one, it is my fiancé's grandmother on his mom's side's birthday, who died after giving birth to his mother. Secorion never met her, but loves her just as much as if he says he did. Her name was Serina Swain and he wants his wedding date to me to commemorate his grandmother who is one of the main reasons he was brought into this world to me."

"Aww...that's so sweet that your date means something so heartwarming." Diana takes a piece of tissue off the coffee table and wipes her eyes. "I can't believe I let you get me all teary eyed up in here."

"Yeah girl, that's really touching that you two are deciding on that date to honor her when you get married."

Audumn stands to her feet to announce something else her and Secori had decided. "And two, I'm deciding on that date because my name is Audumn and September is in Autumn. And......"

"And what?" Diana blurts out.

"And I want the wedding to have autumn colors and an autumn theme."

"I like that, yeah. I think that'll be a beautiful wedding best friend and guess what?"

"What Kizzy? You and Audumn need to stop it with all these damn guessing games all the time and learn how to get right to the purnt!"

"Purnt? All right now, Madea."

"Yeah, purnt, Audumn. You know what I meant though, I betcha that!"

"You two stop it and you both are crazy." Kizzy shakes her head to the comedy show that the three of them always put on. "If you two are done, I can get back to the purnt at hand."

"You stupid, Kizzy for real, for real." Audumn leans back and giggles.

"I guess, but like Diana said Audumn, you know what I meant though. I betcha that."

"Bam! Thanks for having my back, Kizzy. Now please, let's get to the purnt."

Kizzy laughs and then spews out what she's been excitedly trying to say. "We now have a date and a color and the theme we're going to go with for the wedding." Kizzy pulls the black marker off the magnetic board and writes everything down they have discussed thus far. "Come on Audumn and Diana, it would be nice if you two could write this down in them $6.00 mini wedding planners I bought you. Also, you both need to write down that we have almost six months to get all that we need done." Kizzy writes a big six on the board and circles it. "Now, Audumn we need two more things before today's meeting on wedding planning is over and we move to our next topic on physical fitness."

"I don't even want to think about what that topic is about because it sounds like my fat behind is about to work out."

"Audumn, what's our budget and who's going to be the reverend that's going to be doing your wedding ceremony?"

"Well, as far as who's going to be the preacher, I've chosen Pastor Colbert, my childhood pastor from Paradise Baptist church who was the first person that I heard that Jesus died for my sins from. I haven't asked him yet, but Ms. Boswell assured me that he will do it after he realizes who I am from long time ago. And as far as the budget goes, we've agreed that money isn't an issue and that we would like the cheapest and most beautiful wedding money can buy. But, if we must put a dollar amount on our max price, it would be $25,000 from us not including what our parents and family will pitch in and not including our honeymoon that we haven't decided on yet."

"$25,000! Girl, we about to be on some Princess Diana stuff up in here come September."

"Child, you just said that because her name, Diana, just like yours."

"Face it Kizzy, like I said time and time before, you are a natural born hater and until you admit that you will never appreciate my greatness."

"Girl, stop it with all the foolery." Kizzy raises her shirt and her face becomes stern. "What are we going to do about this?" she asks, grabbing a chunk of her belly fat. "I refuse to be your maid of honor when I'm looking like a fat pig."

"Yeah Beaumont, and I refuse to be your second maid of honor looking like a tall cow. And that reminds me, who's going to be Secorion's best men because I refuse to walk down the aisle by myself when it's all over where you just got hitched from."

My bad, I forgot to tell you that he's going to have two best men to match my two maids of honor. His brother, Cori, and cousin,

Brian Woodson from Chicago, are going to be his best men and we already talked to them and they said yes. And my four brothers Aubrie, Nick, Robby, and Dexter are going to be his groomsmen."

Kizzy clears her throat after writing the best men and groomsmen on the erasable board. "That's good to know Audumn, but like I was saying before I was rudely interrupted by no other than the rudest person I know, Diana Ross."

"Go on with all that N.O., you know damn well we needed to know that. That's why you wrote it down on that wack ass board of yours."

"Please Diana, can I finish our first meeting before my kids get home? I ain't trying to be here all day messing around with you two." Kizzy's angry and Diana knows it, so she sits back in her seat and allows her friend to continue on with what they were discussing. "Um, oh yeah, what I think is that all of your bridesmaids whose schedules permits or who wants to participate should work out twice a week together every other week until at least the end of August."

"It sounds good to me because my big ass gotta be fine as hell when Audumn walks down that aisle!" Diana jumps up and runs her hands down her jumbo breasts, waist, and hips to outline her BBW curves.

"Me too. I'm sorry Audumn, but everybody's not skin and bones like you."

"I don't care. I'm down and I think it will be something fun to do with the girls up until the wedding day. The only thing is that I don't want to hear no hating when I turn these skin and bones into a gourmet dinner."

"More like a chicken dinner, Audumn," Diana replied.

"Okay well, it's all set then. This meeting is adjourned until Wednesday after next and when we leave here, we are going to call the bridesmaids and tell them to meet us at WOW's Fitness Gym on highway 290 and Tidwell next Wednesday at 8 pm. And on Sunday at 5:00 pm every other week until August 15th."

"Sounds good to me. I'll call Shanay, Kendra, Khamil, and Gayriale tonight and let them know. But I doubt Khamil can make it on Wednesday's living in Beaumont and working a 9-5 with a child."

"Hold on, hold on!" Kizzy butts in. "What do you mean Gayriale is going to be in your wedding? What happened to Tamera, your other childhood friend you said you were going to ask?"

"Yeah Audumn, what kind of shit is that? Does Secorion know you invited your ex-boyfriend's sister to the wedding, let alone made her one of your bridesmaids?"

"Yes, and he's perfectly fine with it too, so mind your business. I have nothing to hide from my man and besides, I want her there because my life changed the day she invited me to Fallbrook Church when I was doing community service at the airport. I am a new person in Christ Jesus, even though I know that I've slid back a lot since the 2013 year began. Also, I did get in touch with Tamera, but she is on a project in California for her job. She said she's sorry she couldn't be one of my bridesmaids, but she will definitely be at the wedding."

"If you say so. But please remember that the reason your yellow behind was on probation and had to do community service was because of the gun charge you took for that sorry ass brother of hers." Diana stated, making sure she got the last word in.

Diana and Kizzy made it to WOW's Fitness Gym early and got the seven of them set up with some special passes that they put together with the owner. The owner's name is Jann Pink and she strongly professes the importance of women knowing their worth and omnipotence. So out of love for all women's health and wanting them to feel and look their greatest, she has a package deal for five months for the bride and bridal party. Ms. Pink/WOW's Fitness Gym caters to the women more than men because the gym's sole purpose is to make their clients and customers wow you when they leave her gym from working out. But men are strongly invited as well and because of all the women always present at the gym, they're there on the regular to show their support so they say.

Church let out at one and Kendra and Shanay decided to jump into the car with Audumn and her friend Khamil, who has come down for today's Sunday workout with the girls. Khamil has never visited Fallbrook Church and the immenseness of the congregation and building truly left an impressionable expression on her face. She loves her church, St. Peters in Beaumont, Texas, but since she's made it a commitment to work out every other Sunday with the bridesmaids. She will come early to Houston to attend service with her childhood best friend.

Gayriale is checking in with one of the employees when Audumn and her bridesmaids walk through the electric doors with Academy duffle bags in their hands. "Hey girl, how's everything been going with you. I'm sorry I couldn't make it Wednesday, but my daughter's basketball games are on Wednesdays."

"It's all good, Gay. I know we all have our lives to tend too, therefore, I totally understand. And for what it's worth, you're not the only one who can't make it on Wednesdays so don't feel bad at all."

"Yeah, Gay." Khamil pauses. "That is your name, right?"

"Yes, and Gay is short for Gayriale."

"Nice to meet you Gay, I'm Khamil, Audumn's friend from Beaumont." Khamil extends her hand and Gayriale shakes it. "Being from out of town, I can't make it on Wednesday too."

"Me neither because I'm in school and it's not possible for me to make it here from Prairie View on Wednesday with my work and school schedule." Shanay chimed in to let them know they are not the only ones who missed the first workout session.

Khamil and Gay hit it off really good after they put on their workout tights and Nike sport bras. Both of them have a dark chocolate skin tone and curves that made all the men they walk by put their weights down and stare at them for a minute. Khamil is an inch or two taller than Gayriale and has a country swagger that most people are attracted to. Gayriale, however, thinks she's America's black Barbie and if anyone says something different, she would call them a liar to their face. It's amazing how they're the exact opposite in character, but their black beauty has brought them together.

Shanay and Kendra got their whistles and stares from the guys too and Audumn couldn't help but admire how her bridesmaids and maid of honors are so beautiful. Approaching the treadmill where Kizzy and Diana are running, she bends over and does a few toe touches before finding her spot on one of the rows of exercise machines behind them. The rest of the gang followed suit and did their stretches just as Audumn did and then joined the bride to be on the nearest machine to get fit with the rest of the group.

"When you girls get done working out, me and my homies over here got y'all on the protein shakes in the lobby if any of you fine tenderonies want one!" One of the guys shouts from the pull-up bar section before going back to talking with his gym buddies on the low.

"Men." Diana shakes her head and turns her machine off. "What's up, ladies? I'm Diana Ross for those who don't know me and I'm the maid of honor. Me, Audumn, and Kizzy decided to put this together so that we can be the finest bitches in the world when my homegirl jumps that broom in September. You feel me?"

"I feel you, Diana. You know, I'm ready to get my work out on with the three Chicas. Especially for my big sis from the hood, Audumn. If we can go out together, we can work out together!" Kendra replied, speaking about the past when her and her cousin Shanay would go to the club with them.

"That's how I feel too, cousin. Audumn is my big sis and my Nana's Goddaughter. Whatever Audumn wants me to do for her wedding, I'm down with it." Shanay nods her head to her cousin Kendra as if to say, *let's do this.*

"And I'm Kizzy!" Kizzy pulled the red stop button string and turned to the girls starting their treadmills. "I am Audumn's second maid of honor and what we are looking for during my bff's last days as an unmarried woman is something spectacular and an unforgettable experience. Our desire is for everyone to have fun, so that the girl we all fell in love with since the day we met her will know that we have her back and that we give her our full blessing in becoming the future Mrs. Woodson. At the end of our work out, we will be giving out the next few months schedule for what we've got coming up for the bridal party while on this awesome journey with Audumn. Such as, the rehearsal at the Holiday Inn on Walden road in Beaumont,

Texas where we've recently decided to have the wedding ceremony and our trip to my hometown, New Orleans, as a little getaway and stress reliever for her big day."

"New Orleans!" Gayriale exclaims, walking on a treadmill a few rows back.

"Yes Gay, New Orleans. We are now at the end of March and our trip will be on the 11th & 12th of September. We will be leaving for New Orleans on that Friday the 11th at 6:00 in the morning from Houston and we will stop in Beaumont to pick up Khamil and Audumn's brothers around 7:30 on our way to the Big Easy. We will be traveling by SUV's we've already reserved with Enterprise and we will be staying at the Marriot, which we also have already reserved."

"Sounds good to me. Especially since September is still crawfish season and I can get some real Cajun food in my life."

"Cajun food?" Please Gay don't be getting me all hungry right now thinking about crawfish in New Orleans with that corn and sausage and that garlic butter." Khamil licks her lips and turns the dial up for more speed.

"Enough of all that talking and let's get to walking! I'm on my fourth mile and I'm feeling that burn like crazy! September 13th is only five months away and we gon' shut the Holiday Inn down when we walk in there with our toned-up bodies strutting what God blessed us with for all men to see!"

"That's right, Diana. Enough of all that talking and let's get to walking!" Audumn starts a light jog on her machine. "You heard my maid of honors, ladies. Turn them machines up and let's get it!"

All the girls hush their mouths, put their earbuds in, and get focused on the task at hand, which is making sure Audumn is beyond happy on her wedding day because she undoubtedly deserves it.

CHAPTER 9

I t's early in the morning and Secorion is lying down in his four-star hotel in Dubai. The room is not the best money can buy, but it is decent enough to enjoy the peep show on Facebook's facetime app on messenger. His roommate, Manny, knows that his friend and leadman needed some privacy because of the big bottle of baby lotion Secori has on the nightstand next to his bed. That's why, when Manny got up this morning, he made it his business to get lost and that's just what he has done.

Lying there, Secorion is all smiles as he waits for his fiancée to pick up and give him a peep show at her moist lips below her waist that only opens up for him. His birthday suit is his attire and with his laptop between his legs, he wants Audumn to see every inch of him. Including his pole that has no flag waving in the wind. It's been almost two months since he's been gone and even though the natives love to party with the Americans, he has remained faithful to the woman he's going to marry in September. His love is the foundation of his constancy. However, the sessions they've been having at the spur of the moment has helped keep the spark in their flame when the distance between them tries to smother it out.

"Hey my love, are you…" Audumn stammers at the sight of Secorion already on homeplate with his bat in his hands. "Oh wow! I was going to ask if you were ready, but your two baseballs look like they are about to throw me a pitch." Audumn laughs at her own analogy. "Get it!" she laughs again. "Two baseballs."

"Yes, I get it baby, but I'm really horny and I'm trying to see what that gift between your legs that keeps on giving do." Secori laughs to his own analogy. "Get it?"

"Yes, my love, I get it, but are you ready to see that gift that keeps on giving is the real question? Now close your eyes because I bought something just for your eyes to seethe over."

"I'll close my eyes, but I'll be the judge of how seething it is when I'm through painting this monitor white with the sperm that's not gonna make it to the eggs inside you."

"You're stupid, my love. Now close your eyes or I'm not going to show you my surprise."

As requested, he closed his eyes, but then opened them to who should be Victoria Secret's next top model for their lingerie selection. His eyes widen and his mouth is open as he drooled over the woman who is his online porn star for today. Audumn is in the squat position when she gives him the okay to look at the blessing God has given him. Slowly rising to her feet, she does a slow turn in the red pumps she bought last week for this special occasion.

Secorion's penis is throbbing at the sight that's being displayed on the computer and he's trying his hardest not to stroke it. Lying there astonished at how Audumn has turned their peep show sessions up a notch, he decides to go for two orgasm today instead of one.

Especially since in the background of their apartment he hears that she is playing the song "12 Play," by the freaky Pied Piper himself. And everyone knows what happens at the end of that song.

Her outfit is a raunchy 2-piece neon pink strappy lace and mesh teddy with a garter lace on each leg. Her cheeks are out because the string from her mesh panties is being overcome by her apple bottom that Secorion wishes he can take a bite out of at the present time. One hand is in her panties and the other is holding the phone as she explores the inside of her lake that is slowly seeping down her inner thighs each time she played with her clit. Next, she fell to their bed and began to moan when she showed him how wet her fingers are. "You like that, baby?" Audumn says, squeezing her erect nipples and licking one of them.

Secorion has seen enough and can no longer fight the urge to do a little target practicing. Squeezing his pistol, he lets off a round, knowing that the sexy woman on his screen will give him the opportunity to shoot another round off at her again real soon. Relieved from all of the pressure he just released, he lies back smiling at the fact that technology has made the 8,165 miles distant between them null and void when it comes to getting their freak on. Well, at least for one day so to say. As the song comes to end, Audumn looks into the camera and licks her juices off her fingers. "I love you, Secorion Woodson. Hurry home." *Goodbye...*

Secorion reads her lips saying goodbye. "Hold up, baby! I'm not finished yet." He replied to a blank screen before a message popped up in his inbox that read, *I hope you liked my surprise. I have to go pick out a wedding dress today with my mom and Ms. Boswell. I'll facetime you later and be careful out there. Muah!*

Audumn hung up the phone with a devious smile on her face because she knows that she's left her fiancé hanging. And that's not just figuratively speaking either. Secori thrills came from her doing her best performance as an exotic dancer and her thrills came from seeing the expression on his face before she pulled the wool over his eyes and said goodbye. No matter what, she is content in knowing that her fiancé's magic wand still lights up when he sees her and that her strip teases keeps his mind solely on her until he makes his way back to the states.

Ms. Boswell and her mom knocked on the door shortly after she got out of the shower. Glad that she kept her online performance minutes down to a minimum, Audumn rushes to get dressed because her mom reminded her that they have an appointment today for 9:30. The appointment slipped her mind because this week she had testing at school and also the store had to be flipped around to this year's spring addition. "Almost done!" she yells while putting on a dab of makeup to put some color in her cheeks that seem a little pale today.

Audumn walked into her living room to two of the three people who have laid the foundation in her life. It took her some time to fully understand the message Pastor Grant preached back in December, but since then she understands who the pillars that have upheld her from the time she was born are. Her dad, who taught her the highs and lows of life while growing up. Her mom, who taught her to never give up on yourself and to always stand up for what you believe in. And Ms. Boswell, who taught her who Jesus was as a little girl and what he did for her on Calvary when he died on the cross for the sins of the world. All three of them played a part in her foundation and even though her mom didn't teach her about Jesus as a child, she's doing it now in her everyday walk with Christ.

"All done." Audumn gives Ms. Boswell a hug and kisses her mother on the forehead before she can get up. "Come on, come on, ladies. We have an appointment for 9:30 to keep."

"Oh, might you be a little peachy this morning?" Mrs. Yolanda says with endearment.

"Probably because today I'm going to pick out my wedding dress with the two people who have always loved me unconditionally." Audumn's words make her cry because for a long while her and her mother didn't talk when she first moved to Houston. Seven years to be exact and it was all because of pride and not being able to talk to one another to explain one's self.

"Audumn, this is supposed to be a happy day for you so let's see that beautiful smile of yours." Ms. Boswell picks Audumn's chin up and looks her in the eyes. "We love you Audumn and we are beyond happy for you and we want to be a part of making your wedding day special like the woman you grew up to be. That's why me and your mother have decided to split the cost for your dress, so don't hold back if you see something you like and it's a little pricey."

"Any dress?" Audumn replies with a twinkle in her eyes, pondering on whether she should she get a wedding dress like Princess Snow White's or one like Princess Cinderella's.

"Yes, my Audumn. Any dress that's reasonable and worth the price on the tag."

"OMG, momma this is so amazing! Thank you both so much! I love you two from the bottom of my heart and today it will be my pleasure to have you two with me when I pick out the dress I will be getting married in."

"And it is my pleasure that you chose your mother and I to share this day with you."

"Audumn it's 9:10, let's go because me and Janice paid for you to have this appointment and it's nonrefundable."

Audumn thought, w*ho pays for an appointment to pick out a wedding dress? What kind of appointment is this?*

Ms. Boswell made it to their appointment three minutes late, but those three minutes would have been like ten if it were her mother behind the wheel instead. Mrs. Humphrey lives in slow motion Beaumont, Texas and hates driving to Houston, let alone driving in Houston. But today, she's with a longtime friend and her daughter so she's ready to spend some quality time with the both of them. It's been a while. Audumn didn't have to drive if she didn't want to, so she hopped in the backseat and enjoyed the ride. Not to mention the company she's around are her mothers, therefore what more can a woman ask for on a day as significant as this?

The bell hanging over the door jingled when the three of them stepped foot inside the elegant bridal store. No one is in sight, but the music coming from above is exuberant and yet enchanting at the same time. Audumn looks around at all the pretty dresses until her eyes fall onto a whiteboard on an easel that reads, **Welcome to One on One with Joann, the future Mrs. Woodson.**

One on one? What does that mean, momma?"

"I don't know. Why don't you press the bell and see?" Mrs. Humphrey points at the red bell on the counter next to the easel.

"What do you two got going on?" Audumn walks over to the bell and curiously looks over at her mother. "This bell!" she exclaims as she taps it rapidly five times.

Suddenly, the black curtain divided behind the counter and just like that, Joan herself appeared. "Welcome to Joann's Bridal Fashions! These are my assistants, Javier Garcia and Veronica Perez, who run the store for me when I'm off doing shows and bridal events." Joann stepped to the side to allow her assistants to come onto the floor.

"Let me guess, you must be Audumn, the bride to be, and welcome to our store." Javier shakes Audumns' hand and walks around her while squeezing her shoulders and taking a measurement of the small of her back. "What an awesome shape you have, and I already have something in mind for you."

"Why thank you, I guess." Audumn looks at her mother with animation eyes because she has never had professional tailors and designers at her service before.

"I'm Veronica, and Javier's right, you do have the perfect shape for a wedding dress. Not too much butt, but just enough. Slim waste, straight shoulders, and the right weight to take risk with if you decide to show some skin." Veronica does her walk around the bride while giving her professional opinion. "To my understanding, you're having an autumn wedding in autumn. If that's true, I want to say I'm very impressed and I have the perfect color in mind for your dress already, Audumn." Ms. Perez emphasized her last name to let Audumn know that she understands the concept of what she wants her wedding to be remembered as.

After politely allowing her assistants to introduce themselves, Joann ushers them to a plush white sofa with a glass coffee table in front of it. On the table are two bottles of wine and three Baccarat Crystal glasses. One white and one red for those who have a preference of which wine they drink. Horderves, crackers, and fruit sit decoratively on a crystal tray next to a pitcher of ice water. There's also souvenirs with different bridal sayings on them, just in case they don't want to forget this looking for a wedding dress experience.

"This is where you two beautiful ladies will be sitting while Audumn and I try on dresses from the selections we have on display. I am the designer of every dress in this store and your mother and Ms. Boswell thought it would be a wonderful experience for all of you, including me, to have your wedding dress custom made by the designer himself. In my case, herself." Joann does a curtsy bow between her sentences. "Please, feel free to change up anything you want changed to suit your taste. That way, we know without a shadow of a doubt that you feel confident and amazing when you walk down that aisle to the man you are giving your life to. Now, to find a good dress for our bride to be, we need to know how it feels when you walk in it. Are you good with the material, and most of all, do you feel pretty wearing it? Please keep in mind that any dress you pick we can make in any color you choose to go with from our cloth selection. But first thing's first." Joann claps her hands. "I want all six of us to pick out a dress and hang it in the dressing room with the purple curtain. As for you two ladies, please feel free to partake in any of our refreshments after you pick out the dress you wish this beautiful bride to be in."

Small butterflies quickly enter Audumn's stomach from out of nowhere, but she quickly drowns them with a big gulp of red wine she poured herself when she first felt them flutter. "I'm ready now, Joann. For a minute there it felt like my palms were trying to start sweating." Audumn feels the wine meshing with her bloodstream. "But trust me, I'm good now." Her eyes look past Joann at Javier who's eyeballing a modish wedding gown draped sexily over a mannequin. "Wow!" she exclaimed, slightly pushing Joann to the side to get a better look at how the train falls graciously from the dress waistline. "That dress is sooo beautiful."

The dress is everything a bride can ask for if she is looking for the sexy, classy, all eyes on me look. Since it's official that this is the wedding gown Audumn is picking, Javier winks at Joan because the night before they both put it on display from off of the measurements her mother gave them over the phone. Veronica picked out what she thought would look good on Audumn and hung it on the clothes rack in the dressing room next to Javier's choice. Ms. Boswell and Mrs. Humphrey, however, have always looked at Audumn as a princess and decided to go with a more enchanting wedding gown and therefore, chose a dress that a queen would be getting married in on her wedding day.

"Great." Ms. Joann waits for the elder ladies to sit down from hanging their preferred wedding gown in the dressing room. "First, I would like to say that all three of you have great taste and I also want to thank my assistants for having a great eye and knowing what looks good on our bride to be. As for I, I will not be picking out a dress for the bride today because every wedding gown on the floor was put here purposely due to Audumn's proportions and from the personality outlook you two gave me on behalf of our beautiful bride. Therefore, all three dresses that were chosen today are my choices because I chose them specifically for Audumn after going over all the information I have for her." Joann waits for Ms. Boswell and Mrs. Humphrey to fix themselves a snack and some water so that she can regain their full attention. "Now, if there's not any questions, please be prepared to be amazed at what you're about to see."

Javier is waiting with his tape measure when the curtain opens for Audumn to come out. The only thing is is that Audumn is staring at her hour glass figure in the mirror that is wrapped in the most beautiful white material her eyes have ever seen. Her viewers can only see the back of her dress and you can hear Ms. Boswell gasp and her mother yelp, "Oh my God, look at her butt!" Joann couldn't help but to laugh at their response as she helps Audumn to a pedestal so that everyone in the room can get a good look at how the gown fits her.

The gown is sexy. Everything about the dress says Audumn as she models for her mother and play mother to get their opinion. Her face is red with glee and Javier can't help but to admire his eye because the dress fits her almost perfectly. It's the back of the dress that Audumn fell in love with the most. Not only her, but her mother as well as she begins to rave about how the white pearls that fell from her neck down her spine are very eye catching. And how the decorative lace brought out the shape of her back. Looking down on the dress that stood out the most to her, Audumn points out to Ms. Boswell how the skirt sits immaculately behind her on the floor and how the train overlaps the skirt leaving a silhouette to die for.

"And oh, by the way, the train unsnaps at the waist for when the bride is being social with all of her guests at the wedding reception." Javier unfastens the train from the waistline to show how the dress looks without it.

"Aww…" Ms. Boswell says speechless to Audumn's figure and on how much her little Audumn is not so little anymore.

The bodice has its perks as well and let's anyone looking at the bride know that the top is no less prominent than the bottom. Unseen designs embellish the material that can be seen as you get closer to the bride. Audumn doesn't have the breasts of her Chica, Diana, but what she does have the bodice has pushed up and makes her mother want to ask, is *there any way that her daughter can show less cleavage?* But, it's Audumns' day and the dress is not too inappropriate if that's the dress she feels she is the prettiest in.

"I love everything about it, Audumn!" Her mother exclaims hesitantly. "And no matter what dress you decide to go with today, you are going to make a beautiful bride."

"Yeah Audumn, you are definitely going to make some heads turns in that wedding gown." Ms. Boswell says with excitement, looking at the bust of the wedding dress.

"I know I will." Audumn steps down off the pedestal and does a successful walk test until she finds herself back in the dressing room wall mirror gawking at herself. "It's like I don't want to take it off."

Joann claps her hands to move on to the next selection. "I think we can all say that this is a dress we all agree that fits her well and that she feels confident and pretty in." Ms. Boswell and Mrs. Humphrey nod their heads in agreement. "Great!" Joann goes into the dressing room with Audumn and closes the curtain. "Next, we will be right out with the dress Veronica placed on the rack for our bride to be."

Veronica's pick is not as glamorous as the dress Audumn just took off, but it is different and different is what picking a wedding dress is all about. The decorative lace in her gown is stitched more heavily in this one and everything about the bodice of the dress is to Audumn's fancy. Especially how the lace forms a see-through shell around her breast and then runs up and down her shoulders until it reaches the small of her back in a V like shape. However, the slit up the skirt's middle is a little too high and makes her mother say that if she had to vote between the two, her vote would most definitely be on the first one.

"But mom, I do like the veil and how it makes me look more like the traditional brides that I always see in the movies or on television. Come to think of it, that's one thing I didn't like about the last dress I took off."

"That sounds all fine and dandy Audumn, but I refuse to have my baby girl walking around on her wedding day with all her stuff hanging out. Shoot, I already got to deal with your chichi's being in everybody's face when you go around to greet your guest." Mrs. Humphrey said that to also show her contemptuousness for the shell-like see-through lace that covered Audumn's breast on the dress she has on.

"I agree, Audumn. I like this dress and everything that it has to offer, but for some reason it's not screaming, 'Pick me!' like the last one you had on." Ms. Boswell added her thoughts to help sway Audumn into setting this gown to the side for now because she too thinks the dress isn't doing too much when it comes to covering up a woman's most precious jewels.

Audumn took her parent's advice and went back into the dressing room to try on the last dress hanging on the rack that her mom and play mom picked out for her. She wanted to speak up on her views of the dress, but being that it's their dime paying for it and she's outnumbered, she shuts her mouth and respects her elders' decision.

"Are you ladies ready to see what your eyes have picked for your beloved?" Ms. Joann shouts, stepping from behind the dressing room curtain with Audumn.

"Yes and we can't wait to see our princess in the dress we picked out for her." Ms. Boswell replies, scooting to the edge of her seat.

Joann swiftly pulls the immense curtain down the curtain rod. "Ladies and gentlemen, I introduce to you, the future Mrs. Audumn Woodson!"

Javier is the first to point out that the dress becomes Audumn and that the dress he picked out was classy and sexy, but the one she has on is sending a statement. Joann agrees and compliments the two ladies on picking one of her prized features in store. She also goes on to tell her customers what inspired her to make the ballroom wedding gown that would make any woman feel like a queen. She said, "Not everyone can be married inside a castle, but with the right dress on, a woman can feel like she is getting married in one."

Mrs. Humphrey and Ms. Boswell are speechless when seeing their beloved standing there gleaming from ear to ear with her hands on her hips.

"Holey moley!" her mother exclaims with tears of joy sparkling in her eyes. "Look at how my daughter has blossomed into the woman before our eyes."

"You're right, Yolanda and I must say that you did a fine job in raising her. Our God is an awesome and mighty God that we serve."

"You can say that again, Janice."

"So Audumn, how do you feel?" Veronica asks from behind Audumn who's now on the pedestal.

Audumn lifts the outside layer of her dress and shouts, "Unbelievable!"

"I must say you have the perfect shape for any of our selections in the store, but to me, this one is calling your name."

"I think you may be right, Javier." Veronica adds her thoughts. "I'm thinking a burnt orange reddish dress with shades of brown and gold or yellow."

Audumn pictures the color of the dress Veronica is describing with the puffy laced flowery skirt and all its layers and really starts feeling the look. Not only her, but her mother and Ms. Boswell are thinking how glamorous and enchanting the dress they'd picked out will look when she takes the wedding pictures with the groom, groomsmen, and the bridesmaids. Joann, however, has been sitting back waiting for the twinkle to be in all three of her client's eyes at the same time. And now that she's captured it, she hands Audumn a bouquet of assorted autumn colors.

"Oh my gosh, I feel like a Disney autumn princess and I love how the lace has a lot of hidden detail in it."

"And I love that you don't have your chichi's hanging out like on them last two dresses you tried on."

"Momma, but I really like the first dress that I put on! It made me feel sexy and up to date with the times versus how this one makes me feel like the girl in my dreams who would always marry Prince Charming before I woke up."

"So how does it feel when you walk?"

"Actually, being that the skirt is so poofed out, I can walk a lot better in this dress than the first one I tried on if that's what you're asking. Hell, I'm so free underneath all this lace that if you cut the right music on, I can drop it like it's hot right here in the store to prove it to you."

"Oh my! Ms. Boswell exclaimed. "Please keep in mind we're only here to find you a dress so you can save all that 'dropping it like it's hot' mess for Secorion when you go on your honeymoon."

"Yes ma'am, I sure am gon' save my dropping it like it's hot mess for the seven-day cruise me and my husband are going to be going on to the Bahamas after our wedding."

"You're a mess, Audumn." Ms. Boswell laughs.

"Yes, she is. But I love her more than she can imagine," her mother replied, thinking about how Audumn put everything to the side to help her overcome cancer.

Veronica emerges from the dressing room and pins a white shah in Audumn's hair so that they can get the full image of the bride to be in all her wedding apparel. "I really like how you look in this dress." Veronica poofs the laced skirt up a bit. "How do you think Secorion would like this dress?"

"I think he would like me more in the other dress because of how it grabs my shape and shows off the little curves that I have. But, and yes there is a but. But, I also think that he would be more surprised to see me in this dress and that's what seeing the bride for the first time should be like for every groom."

"I know Janice and I have given our comments on our pick, but Audumn, September 13th is your day so whatever dress you deem fit to your satisfactions, I'm giving you my full consent."

"And you have mine as well, Audumn." Ms. Boswell walks over and looks Audumn straight in the eyes. "Like your mother said, September 13th is your day and we're here to show you how much we love you and support your decision to marry Secorion Woodson."

Joann chimes in. "Personally Audumn, I feel that you have made some valid points concerning the groom and therefore, you can't go wrong with any of the two wedding gowns you choose to pick today. The first dress was made for you, Audumn. This dress was made for the Audumn in your dreams. I love how you feel beautiful in both of them and if my designs have achieved that today then I have done my job as an artist."

"But the other one didn't have a veil or a shah."

"Trust me, if you choose the first selection, I will make you one that your husband will remember for a lifetime when he throws it back to kiss the bride."

Audumn laughs underneath her breath. "So, which one momma?"

"Whichever one you pick Audumn is my choice."

"Ms. Joann, tonight I want to sleep on it and I promise you I'll give you my answer tomorrow."

"Sounds like wedding bells to me already and we can't wait to see which one you choose to go with." Joann claps her hands. "Javier, can you get our guest a book with the different colors of dresses we have to offer while Veronica and I help Audumn get out of the wedding gown?"

When the dressing room curtain closed behind Audumn, Ms. Boswell and Mrs. Humphrey gave each other a high five because of the impact the selection they chose had on her. Being old school, the gown Audumn picked showed too much and they hoped and prayed she will pick their dress because that's the dress that a princess would get married in. And in their eyes, that is exactly what Audumn is to them.

"All done!" Joann exclaims, opening the curtain. "And this concludes our one on one session with Joann's Bridal Fashions. Be blessed and I look forward to hearing from you Audumn tomorrow or the next day."

"Thanks Joann for undoubtedly a wonderful day." Audumn gives Joann a hug and then shakes her assistant's hands. "And thank you, Javier and Veronica, for making me feel special throughout this whole trying on wedding dresses experience."

"You are welcome, Audumn. And you will make a beautiful bride." Javier replied as he closed the door behind the three of them when they exited the store.

CHAPTER 10

Running late. Omw..., Diana texted with a picture of her U of H Cougar invitation dated June 3, 2013 attached over her message.

K. Hurry up, we're about to walk in. Audumn texted back.

About to pull up in 5. Don't graduate without me. Lol...

Everyone Audumn loves is present except for one, and Tree doesn't count because his love turned out to be no good for her. Secorion came in on the 26th and will be leaving out on the 5th. When he gets back to Dubai, the job will have less than two and half month left on the project and then he will be back in the United States permanently. Her mom and Ms. Boswell convinced her to start making amends with her dad because he does deserve to be a part of Audumn's commencement, let alone her wedding. It took a while to convince Audumn, but she conceded because they're right in so many ways. But, the only stipulation is that her dad can't bring his mistress around Audumn until she is ready to meet her.

I'm here! Jack Daniels on deck if u need a shot.

I'm good. Just hurry 2yo seat. I'm about 2 walk in. & P.s. U stupid Diana fr fr....

Bet that! & be listening for the airhorn.

Lol...smdh...

Pomp and Circumstances traditionally comes sounding from the band through every speaker in the TDECU Football Stadium. The music is loud, but that doesn't stop the uproar of proud parents and guests to pushing their voices through the tuba's bass down on the field. Audumn's last name is Humphrey, so that puts her somewhat in the front of the line among the graduates graduating today. Upon cue, she straightens her tassel and hand irons the outside of her black and red graduating toga. *Thank you, Jesus, for bringing me this far. I couldn't have done it without you,* she thought as daylight from the football stadium becomes closer each step she takes in the tunnel the football players run onto the field from.

Her mom and dad are the first two people she sees hanging over the side railing when the sun is through blinding her eyes and she's able to regain focus. Behind her parents is Secorion, then Robby, then Kizzy, looking down waiving endlessly with smiling faces. Audumn smiled back with cherry red cheeks and held up the broken toe cougar hand sign, which is holding the right hand ring finger down with the thumb towards the palm of your hand. The hand gesture dates back to 1953 when the Shasta mascot lost a toe in a cage door and the University of Texas fans began to mock the cougar's injury by making the gesture a laughing matter. Who would've thought, that on that day, something that started out as a joke will be cemented in time to represent the University of Houston until to the end of time?

The cameraman down on the field captures the excitement from all of the graduates. Some of the students do synchronized stomps with their feet in front of the camera while waving the broken toe hand gesture in the air from left to right. Others just wave cheerfully into the camera and then you have the students who have a stern face to portray the seriousness of them achieving a degree that will soon change their future. Audumn is not like any of these students because behind her smile is shyness from being on the biggest platform of her life. She tries to shake it, but this is the first time she's ever had so many eyes on her at once.

Two by two, the long line of summer graduates enter the stadium and walk along the walls of the bleachers. Scattered lines of officers and cameraman set an ushering barrier along the sidelines so that everyone can see the undeniable achievements that U of H is sending out into the world to help make a change for themselves and their country. The waiving ceremony is almost over when the tail end of the hundreds of graduates exit the tunnel with the rest of their class that is already on the field.

Audumn walks over the white tarp and red carpet where the honor students will be sitting in front of the stage and goes into the bleachers where she's assigned to sit until she's told what to do next. Her gown doesn't have all of the honor tassels or honor cords like those down below, but what she does have is the required credits to graduate and move forward with her prerequisites for the school Veterinarian Institute of Technology (VIT).

A loud horn finds itself to Audumn's ears and a muffled, "Go Audumn!" follows right behind it. Audumn turns her head to follow the sound and after narrowing down the section that it could've came from, her eyes find Diana jumping up and down like she's doing jumping jacks. She also sees all of her brothers, her Aunt Glynda, and her daughter Monica from South Carolina. Ms. Boswell is there too, along with Kendra, Shanay, Khamil, and her childhood friend Tamera who decided to pop up and surprise her. All of them are waiving and whistling to make sure Audumn knows that they're there. It is then, that everything about being shy vanishes from within her bosom and causes her to stand and wave back in glee at her profound support system.

Pomp and Circumstance's song drags to an end and a thunder of claps and stomps in the bleachers shakes the stadium before complete silence fills the air and you hear a woman say, "Please rise and remove your hats for the singing of our Star Spangled Banner." All of the graduates, staff, and guests complied and faced the Marine soldiers holding our nations red, white, and blue flags. Proudly, the U.S. anthem is sung with shoulders back and hands over hearts to show appreciation for the constitution our soldiers honorably fight for on a daily basis. When it's over, the soldiers do an about face and exit the stage in which they came.

"Graduates and guests, commencement is assembled." The woman's voice from earlier said. "Please welcome our leader and our President of the University of Houston, Dr. Nura Kahtor."

The claps of praise from the woman's introduction stop when the Doctor stepped to the microphone to speak. "Please be seated. Good morning and welcome to the University of Houston's annual commencement exercise." Dr. Kahtor pauses and allows a few chants for their school to be voiced from the honor graduates down below and then proceeds with the program. "Today, we the faculty, friends, and staff alumni administration are assembled to celebrate you, our graduates, as you complete your academic journey. I would like to thank everyone who has taken the time to share this special moment with you. In all academic institutions, the most important role is played by the faculty. Many of whom who are here with us this morning to celebrate with you. Please rise U of H to welcome our faculty members behind me in honor of their role that assisted in getting our graduates to this platform today." Everyone rises and claps when told. "Thank you. You may be seated." Dr. Kahtor waits for the assembly to be seated. "As I look around, I see a lot of familiar faces. You've all come such a long way. This is, without a doubt, my favorite part of my job and I know that the faculty members, Deans, and adminisstrators in attendance feel the same way. There's a special energy in the air at graduation that only happens on this day. That energy and electricity comes from a strong sense of accomplishment and achievement of long hours and hard work. It is also a road that you and your loved ones have traveled and now that it has come to end, the excitement of getting ready to travel a new one is already present after our graduates cross this stage."

Mrs. Humphrey starts to cry because she understands the hard work and love for animals that has brought her daughter to this glorious day. Her family couldn't afford to send her to college and even if she was to get a grant, she wouldn't have been able to go to school because she had to do her part in making sure their home ran successfully. Same thing goes for Mr. Humphrey, except he grew up black in a society at the time where black boys going off to college was scarce. When he completed school, he had to go straight to work at the rice mill because his dad died when he was sixteen and his mother needed all the help she could get around the house. Robby is the only one out of their boys who has taken college courses to get raises at his job, but he has never achieved a degree. Hence, making Audumn the first in their family to graduate from college.

"Today, I must say, that the sun is literally shining on you for this special occasion because for the first time in a long time. It seems to always rain or be a cloudy day at our outside commencements." Small laughter comes from the audience at the president's joke. "Today, you are graduating from a very special university. A university that is Tier 1. A university that has produced astronauts, scientists, actors, politicians, and Olympic gold medalists. But most of all, it is a university that you can call home and a university that you will always have bragging rights."

Audumn lifts her head up to the blue sky when hearing that her degree will be added with the success of the patriarchs and matriarchs of her school. She thought, *it is also the university that Audumn D. Humphrey graduated from and went on to start her own veterinary practice.*

"Before we move forward with today's commencement, I, the president of the University of Houston, would like to ask the parents, siblings, husbands, wives, aunts, nieces, nephews, uncles, cousins, friends, significant others, and guests to stand so that our administration can recognize you for the support you gave to help your loved one make it to the finish line."

The stadium went into a frenzy when the student's families stood to be recognized. All of the graduates shouted toward where their support system is seated because they knew that without them, this day wouldn't have happened. Audumn teared up and blew kisses to her family as they blew kisses back to show her that they caught them. "We love you, Audumn!" Her baby brother, Brie, shouted at the top of his lungs, but his sister didn't hear anything because all of the graduate's families are shouting at the top of their lungs as well.

"On behalf of all our graduates, we want to thank you and show our appreciation of you for all that you have done for the success of our 2013 class. And to our students, I want to say, that you're our cougars and if you can keep that same drive that has brought you this far, all of your dreams or conquests will be fulfilled. Congratulations class of 2013 for completing an awesome achievement. And now, I turn the mic over to Dean Hoit."

Keeping up with the time, Dean Hoit starts the ceremony of passing out the degrees without delay. "It is my honor to bring you greetings and to see all of you who have made it to this platform today. Graduates, you have survived your last finals week, your last anxious moments of waiting on your final grade, and your last battle for a good parking space among the numerous number of students looking for one. Now, without further ado, let's move on with our commencement celebration." Dean Hoit raises his hand to get the audience's attention. "In a display of respect to our graduates and families, please refrain from using artificial noise makers when the recipient's names, section, or study of degree is called. This will assure that the names of each our graduates or the degree of study in which they've earned is distinctly heard by both parties, including our graduate's family and guests."

Dean Hoit started by asking all the degree candidates for Architecture and Design to rise and remain standing so that they can certify the completion of them fulfilling all the requirements to receive their respective degrees. All the students asked to stand stood in their section with their heads high and sat when Dr. Kahtor stepped up to the mic and said, "By the authority invested in me by the board of regions by the Texas state university system, I confer upon you the appropriate respective degrees. Congratulations students. Please be seated."

Dean Hoit and Dr. Kahtor repeated this processed throughout the latter day of the university's commencement. It was like looking at a video on repeat. Dean Hoit asked a section to stand; crowd roars. Dean Hoit gives his speech; crowd roars again. And Dr. Kahtor closes by conferring their respective degrees. This went on because of the immense number of graduates that are graduating from such a great Tier 1 university. You would think that this process would take all day, but in actuality each section called upon only had no more than five minutes in today's spotlight. Therefore, Audumn's section came up quite quickly and when they were asked to stand, she stood proudly, knowing that she completed an overwhelming journey that she set out to do over four years ago.

"Degree candidates in the colleges of Science and Biology, please rise and remain standing," Dr Hoit spoke into the microphone with approbation because that was and still is his field of study. "Ladies and gentlemen, these class candidates have engaged in multiple disciplines in area studies in the humanities, biology, and sciences. They also have put theoretical and clinical training in practice throughout the city of Houston and the nation abroad. Today, they stand ready, having reached their goals and are equipped to take their place in the world. I also want to congratulate our future veterinarians who will be moving on to their next adventure with the degree obtained today and credits in Pre-Veterinarian Medicine. President Kahtor, on behalf of the general faculty and the faculty of the college of Science and Biology, I certify that the candidates standing before you have completed all of their academic requirements and are entitled to their respected degrees. Congratulations students, and I look forward to your bright futures."

Please Diana don't embarrass me, Audumn thought, waiting for something outlandish to happen after Dr. Hoit's speech.

"By the authority invested in me by the board of regions by the Texas state university system, I confer upon you the appropriate respective degrees in Science and Biology. Congratulations students. Please be seated."

"Thank you, Lord," she mumbled when recognizing that Diana didn't clown in the bleachers like she said was going to do.

Dr. Hoit went on to finish calling out the degrees until every section stood and received the honor in which they worked so hard for. When done, President Dr. Kahtor came to the podium to give her final remarks.

"Will all the Doctorate, Professional, Master, and Bachelor degree candidates please stand?" Dr. Kahtor waits for all of the students to stand and all of the guests to stop clapping. "Also, will the faculty members of our administration please stand?" All of the faculty stood up on the stage behind her. "By virtue of the authority invested in me, by the people of the state of Texas and the faculty of the University of Houston, you may now turn your class ring and move your tassels from the right to the left." Loud claps and chants came from every person in the vast arena when the president's last words came through the audio system. "Congratulations to all of our graduates and the best of luck to all of you. Go cougars and you are dismissed. Be blessed!"

After being dismissed, all of the graduates poured onto to the football field to find their invited guests. Audumn texted her fiancé and told him she is standing centerfield on the white U H stamped in the middle of the field. Secorion told her family and friends and they all sifted their way through the photographing people until they all reached Audumn and gave her uplifting praise. To Audumn, it was ironic because she felt like a football player with the football and everyone from her family was trying to tackle her. Only difference is that, unlike a football player, she was looking for the contact and not trying to dodge it.

Secorion found her first among the where's Waldo search of every graduate wearing a black toga, red and white stole, and black square cap. "Wow baby, you did it!

Audumn french kissed Secorion and looked up into his brown eyes. "No baby, we did it." She said pointing to her engagement ring. "There's no more I when it comes to us. Only we." Secorion nodded and Audumn french kisses him again. "I love you so much and this wouldn't have been possible without you by my side supporting me from the beginning."

Mr. Humphrey clears his throat to get his daughter's attention. "Okay son, we all know that you love her. If you don't mind, can I have my baby girl back for a second? I promise I'll give her back to you after I give her my love."

Secorion steps to the side and Audumn runs into her dad's arms. Embracing each other for the first time since him and her mother separated, she holds on to him, welcoming her father's touch, which she has missed during these past few months. "Look daddy, I did it." Audumn said with her head laid on his chest. "Daddy, I love you and I need you right now to be my father. What you got going on with mom, leave me out of it. All I ask is that you respect my wishes and don't bring your friend around me until I'm ready."

"Anything for you, my sweet and precious Audumn." Mr. Humphrey steps back and wipes his tears away. "Today is your day Audumn, smile and enjoy what you've accomplished as the first person in our family to get a college degree." Mr. Humphrey kisses her on the forehead and Audumn turns to meet and greet the rest of her entourage.

"Hey 1st cousin!" Audumn hugs her cousin, Monica, who came down from South Carolina with her mom, Glynda.

"Congratulations, cousin! Who would've thought that dog, Lady, we used to play with was going to lead to you pursuing to be a veterinarian in the future?" Monica exclaims. "Me and mom are so proud of you and we wouldn't have missed this day for the world."

"That's right, niece." Audumn's Aunt Glynda comes over and joins in on the hugging. "We wouldn't have missed this graduation for the world."

Audumn's mom and brothers were next to get their congratulation hugs and kisses in and Audumn couldn't wait to receive them. Right now, besides her fiancé and her Chicas, her parents and brothers are her everything. It is their faces that have pushed her this far in becoming the best Audumn she can be. Her mom and dad deserve to have a college graduate in the family and her brothers need to see that getting a degree can be achieved if you are willing to persevere to the end. They don't know it, but their genuine love has always sustained her and given her the fuel she needed to keep pushing no matter what the circumstances in life may try to throw at her. Friends come and go. Men are suspect, but the love from a mother, father, or a sibling is eternal.

Audumn goes to Ms. Boswell before she goes to her girlfriends who are patiently waiting to turn up with today's college graduate.

Audumn sees the joyous expressions on their faces and holds up one finger to let them know to give her a minute. Ms. Boswell is a major factor in her question and answer that makes her world turn in the right direction along her axis. Because of that, she deserves the proper respect and time for the part she played in making this day possible. And that is teaching her from a child that she can do all things through Christ who strengthens her (Philippians 4:13). When finished speaking amongst themselves, Ms. Boswell gave Audumn a sterling silver necklace and a cross pendant. In a low tone, she said, "Remember that in life all things are possible through Jesus Christ. If you don't believe me, look towards the cross." Audumn looked down at the cross pendant in her hand. "You see," Ms. Boswell points at the pendant. "Jesus is not on it anymore. Why, is because he rose from the dead. Now go, your friends are waiting."

Tam is standing next to Khamil, her childhood friend, introducing her to Shanay, Kendra, Diana, and Kizzy when Audumn strolls over walking with a limp like she's a pimp. Her cool breeze walk makes everyone laugh because as of right now, Audumn feels like she's on top of the world. Like honey, they all swarmed her like bees giving their acclaims on how her commencement was a great success and milestone she passed along this adventure called life. As the numbers of graduates on the field begin to dwindle, Audumn wanted to do what she sees all graduates do when they graduate from college.

"Stand back Chicas!" she shouted as her friends looked at her with unknowing expectations. "I'm about to toss my...." Audumn takes her cap off and tosses it as high as she can in the air. When she does, the students left on the field see it go flying and do the same from where they're standing.

127

Diana can't hold back the urge any longer and pulls out her air-horn from her purse and squeezes the trigger. The loud honk catches everybody's ears and draws their eyes to the big black woman with her arm in the air holding the horn. Diana sees she has most of the people surrounding her full attention and squeezes it again to make sure no one's head turns from her who is now on centerstage.

Diana shouts. "Cotton candy sweet as gold, let me see that tootsie roll!"

Kizzy and Audumn looked at each other and at the same time they screamed, "To the left, to the left! To the right, to the right! Now dip, baby, dip! Come on, come on. Now dip baby, dip!" as they begin to move their feet to the classic dance steps the 69 boys made to go with the hook.

Light laughter covered the field as once again the three Chicas take today's spotlight. When all the fun is over, Tamera wished Audumn the best and told her she had other family members to visit back in Beaumont so she must be going. "Great job best friend, I'm so proud of you. My flight leaves for Cali tomorrow at nine in the morning, so if I don't get to do anymore catching up with you, please know that I will be back in September and we can refurbish old times then. I love you and happy early 31st birthday since I'm not gon' be here Juneteenth to celebrate it with you."

Tam left and everyone else from Audumn's crew left a few minutes after her. Growing up, she loved eating at Golden Coral, so her father suggested that they go there to eat in celebration of his daughter graduating college. Not everyone is a big fan of the restaurant's enormous food chain, but that all changed when he said, "Dinner is on me." With hungry faces from today's two and half hour commencement, Mr. Humphrey found a Golden Coral on his phone that is only fourteen miles away. "I got it y'all! Everyone who's driving set your GPS for 3033 South Loop, West Houston, Texas." Audumn's group complied and set their GPS as told. When they reached the parking lot, Mr. Humphrey waved goodbye and jumped in his car so that he can get a head start on getting in line at the restaurant and a section big enough for twelve.

"I love you, daddy!" Audumn yelled with a big smile on her face when he was getting into his car, but she doesn't think he heard her.

CHAPTER 11

"Wake up Audumn, you're home."

"Huh?" Audumn raises the seat up and sees she's in a Mercedes Benz. "What happened and what time is it?"

"You were too drunk to drive, so I took you home and the time is a quarter after 2 a.m."

"Thanks for the ride home, I guess." Audumn slurred from the alcohol that has subdued her bloodstream. "I'll call someone in the morning to take me to go get my car."

"If you want, I could take you."

"You've done enough already and I don't know how I got here with you, but I shouldn't have gotten in this car because I hate you." Audumn pushes the side of Tree's head with her hand.

Tree hangs his head in sorrow. "I know you do, baby. I mean, Aud..."

"Don't call me that!" Audumn screams and grabs her forehead that started ringing at the sound of her voice. "I'm not your baby anymore. As a matter of fact, I never was."

"I'm sorry. I don't know how that slipped out. I meant to say Audumn."

"It slipped out because you know you lost a good woman and you still love me." Audumn stammers in her speech and opens the door for some fresh air. "Do you have the heat on because it sure is hot in here?"

"No Audumn, you're just drunk." Tree gets out the car and walks around the rear to help Audumn get out of the car. "Come on bae. Put your arm around my shoulders so I can help you up the stairs to your apartment."

"How do you know my apartment is upstairs?"

"Because you told me where you stayed right after you threw up in the parking lot at the club."

"I did?" Audumn tries to recall, but can't. "And how did I end up with you again?"

"The bartender, Sha, asked me to bring you home because she knew we used to be together back in the day."

"Oh I bet you liked her thinking that, huh?"

"I ain't gon' lie, I did and still wish things were different because I'm different."

"Oh well. That's your loss and my gain because I'm awesome."

"Yes you are Audumn, and that's why I will always love you. It hurts knowing you prayed for me to change my life and now that I have changed, you're not there anymore. Sometimes I question God about us, but then I realized that you made the right decision in leaving me because at the time I was no good for anyone, not even myself." Tree holds her steady by the waist so that she can get her unsteady hand under control to put the key in the keyhole.

The door opens and Audumn turns around towards Tree. "How do you know you still love me?"

"Because I think about you more than I think about anything else. And when I pray, I pray that you're happy and that you can forgive me for all the hurt I put on your heart when we were together."

"Tree, that was two years ago."

"I know and I'm sorry for feeling this way, but that doesn't stop the fact that I still love…"

Audumn spontaneously kisses Tree before he can finish what he was trying to say. She didn't know why she kissed him, but she did know it was wet, long, and felt like that's where her tongue and lips had always wanted to be. It was like she was having an out of body experience because she knows what she's doing is wrong, but her body is telling her that she's right. Tree's mind tried to make him back away, but his feet are planted and his branches have already embraced the season of Audumn. Standing there intertwined, Audumn uproots him and slams the door. What happened next is something that they both thought wouldn't have happened again in a million years.

It's Audumn's home, so she comes out of her clothes first to assure him that it's okay. Tree hesitates and tries to fathom if this is fact or fiction because he's been walking with the Lord two years now and has been saving himself for marriage. He knows that this is a test from God on his salvation, but he never was good at passing tests because he always cheated in the past. Knowing that, he thanks whomever for this opportunity and will ask God to forgive him later for what he is about to do.

"I so missed your touch, my love." Tree kisses her neck then her chest and then her breast. "I missed your hair, your hazel eyes, your hands and your feet, and most of all the treasure in between your legs."

"I missed you too baby, now take off those close and get to digging because X marks the spot." Audumn takes his hand and gently rubs her vagina. "You see bae, it misses you to too."

Tree pushes her to the sofa and falls to his knees to get a facial. As he's tongue kissing her second set of lips, Audumn's mind travels back in time to all the good sex they had when they were on good terms. She pulls the back of his head deep inside of her opening and moans when pondering on how good his tongue game has always been when it came to making her climax. "You're almost there Tree, don't stop. Please don't stop!" she exclaims, shivering from what is about to burst from inside her.

All wet from Audumn's showers, he stands and drops his drawers while Audumn lays with her legs as far as the east is from the west. Before going on to place his key in her ignition, he puts on a Magnum he's been keeping on his person just in case he fell short of a woman's temptation. The condom is six months old, but it will have to do because there's no way in hell he is about to go to the store to get another one. It takes him no time to slide it on and before you know it, Audumn and Tree are together again like they haven't been apart in years and like she isn't getting married in a few months.

Both of them have blocked out their better judgement. And both of them wants what's happening right now to continue. It's like their bodies are controlling them and their minds are locked away in a vault. Audumn loves Secorion and Tree respects the love she has for her fiancé out of the love he has for her and for his Lord and savior,

Jesus Christ. But just like that, all of their best thinking went up in smoke the moment he tried to measure her depths with his 9' ruler. In and out he went until his penis erupted inside of the condom and, suddenly, it felt like Audumn turned the waterworks on. Tree feels the atmosphere change from within, but keeps on going until every last drop of his sperm is released from his scrotum sack. Lying inside of her on the couch, they both fall asleep like dogs waiting to be unstuck from one another.

"I love you Audumn." he whispered in her ear.

I love you too, Tree, she replied in her mind as she fell into an intoxicated sleep and began to dream.

—m—

"Hey Sha." Audumn takes a seat at the bar. "I'll take my usual friend and don't forget it's my birthday weekend."

"Crown and Sprite coming right up. And by the way, when is your b-day, Beaumont?"

Audumn laughed because it's ironic that Sha called her Beaumont when she's waiting on Diana to have drinks with her tonight. "You should've said was and not is. My birthday was Tuesday, June 19th. I'm off Sunday, so I decided to do a little celebrating tonight with my friend Diana."

"You talking about your Chica Diana Ross who's loud and doesn't give a damn what nobody thinks of her?" Sha smiled and set Audumn's preferred drink on a coaster.

"Girl yes, so you already know how we about to turn up tonight in Claytons. As a matter of fact, you might want to tell DJ Chris to play that shaking ass music because I know I'm damn sho going to try to shake something later when he plays that song, 'It's your birthday bitch!'" Audumn gets up off her barstool and to do a little twerking before sitting back down.

"Well, this one is on the house because it's your birthday and the next one is on me. By the way, your ring is pretty."

"Why thank you, Pennsylvania."

"Please don't, Audumn." Sha shakes her head no and smirks. "Pennsylvania doesn't sound cool to be saying when calling someone by their city or state."

"I think you're right, Sha." Audumn downs her first drink in record time. "Pennsylvania is too long and I promise you I won't call you that again."

"So, who's the lucky guy?"

"Secorion Woodson. I don't think I've ever brought him here because this was Tree's hang out spot back in the day."

"Wow, so you and Tree are not together anymore?"

"No, but there's no hard feelings between us." Audumn turns her ring so that the diamonds can be facing upward. "I wish him the best though, and pray he finds his way like I did."

"That's what's up, Beaumont, but I honestly thought you two were going to be together forever."

"Me too, but forever ended two years ago."

The night is still young when Audumn finished her two drinks on the house, but that doesn't stop her from ordering another one. Kizzy is in New Orleans celebrating with her family and enjoying the emancipation from slavery parades throughout the party city. She asked Audumn to come with her, but Audumn had to work all week because her # 2 girl at the store, Lawanda, had an emergency to tend to out of town. Also, she will be in New Orleans for her bride and groom getaway before the wedding, so she didn't go because when she does go to N.O. she wants to do it with all her bridesmaids present.

Audumn is on her fourth drink within an hour that she didn't buy because the guys around the bar and club have found out its her birthday from Sha. Every time her glass gets low, someone new would signal to the bartender to get her another one and put it on their tab. This went on from the time she got there around 9:50 fresh off work until now when the club is starting to grow to its capacity. The music is jamming and the money pinned on her an hour ago is at about $96.00, so she stands with her hands above her head and does her white girl dance to celebrate. Men are gawking at her mixed beauty while some throw one dollar bills while shouting, "Go Audumn! It's your birthday and we gon' party like it's your birthday!"

DJ Chris takes a break around twelve and announces that he will be back in fifteen minutes. When he leaves, he puts on a slow jam mix he put together the night before for tonight when he decides to stretch his legs and mingle with the crowd. "Hey Audumn, I haven't seen you here in like forever."

Audumn looks up as she carefully collects the money off the floor. "Hey, DJ Chris. Thanks for playing my song because I really cleaned up tonight and the club still has got about an hour and a half left." Audumn stumbles, but braces herself on DJ Chris's chest and then the counter of the bar." Oops, my bad, I guess I'm a little drunk."

"Yeah, I guess so." DJ Chris replied, handing her a twenty to add with the rest of the money she's about to pin on her shirt. "Here, let me help you with that before you stick yourself with that safety pin." DJ Chris chuckles when seeing Audumn fumble with trying to thread the money with the needle. "There you go, big baller. I wish I could get money thrown at me like that on my birthday."

"Grow some tits and you will." Audumn winks and tries to tap his nose with her index finger, but ends up nearly poking him in the eye. "Oops, sorry."

DJ Chris shrugs off her mishap and sees she's by herself. "Where are Kizzy and Diana? Or shall I say the Chicas?"

"Hell, I don't know. I mean, who needs them on my birthday anyway? But I think Diana's coming." Audumn raises her hand for another drink, but then digs in her handbag for her phone. "Hmm, that reminds me…"

Sha brings Audumn another Crown and Sprite and DJ Chris tells Sha to put it on his tab. "Here you go, Audumn, this one is on me. Looks like my fifteen minutes is up, so let me get back to the turntables. Enjoy your birthday and let me know if Diana doesn't come so that I can make sure you get home safe."

Audumn sadly mumbles okay because she just read a text message from Diana that she sent an hour ago stating that she just got off and her feet hurt, so she's not coming out tonight. Sitting there, she says to herself that nobody loves her and that this is the worst birthday ever. Her man is in Dubai. Kizzy is in New Orleans and Diana is too tired. When you add up those three things, you get her being alone on her birthday weekend. *What else can go wrong?* she thought, looking at the melting ice cubes as she sipped another sip of her drink.

It was around 1:00 when Tree walked into the door and paid the door keeper $5 to get in. "What's up, Rudy? How's the club life been treating you?"

"So, so I guess, but this has got to be one atypical night because two used to be regulars I ain't seen in a long time came in here on the same night."

"Oh yeah. Who's the other one then if I'm one of them?"

"Your ex, Audumn. She's over there at the bar having a great time and all the fellas are showing her some love because it's her birthday."

Dang, it is her birthday. Well, it was four days ago on the 19th if I'm not mistaken. Tree gives the doorkeeper a fist bump. "Thanks Rudy for the info. I think I'm about to go over there and say hi."

"Anytime Tree. And oh, by the way, she's drunk as all out doors, so you might get lucky for old times' sake." Rudy gives Tree the wink and the gun and gets back to business as usual.

Tree walked off wondering how Rudy knew that they weren't together anymore. But then he seen a shimmer of glisten coming from Audumn's left hand on the bar and already knew she had told him.

"Hi Audumn." Tree sits his 6' 4" frame on the barstool next to her when a guy gets up to ask a lady for a dance. "Happy belated 31st birthday, beautiful."

"Oh, don't give me that crap. We both know you don't care about me. All you care about is your money." Audumn tries to focus on Tree's face, but it's hard because she sees two of him.

"I told you baby, I'm not like that anymore. As of matter of fact, I would sleep under a bridge before I try to make some money off selling drugs that will harm our people."

"Oh, just stop it. I'm not trying to hear how you changed your life for the better after I left your ass because you damn sure wouldn't do it for me." Audumn sassily retorts. "And don't call me baby!"

"I apologize and I won't say it again. It's just a habit, I guess. Especially with you being the last woman I was with when I got locked up back in the gap."

"Whatever, Tree. Why are you here? Last time we talked or I heard anything about you they said you were holy as Jesus himself?"

"Actually, no one can be holy as Jesus because he never sinned. And why I'm here is because I've been cooped up in the house for over six months and I thought it was time to get out and see some familiar faces."

"Let me guess, Chikora is the familiar face that you're trying to see here tonight?" Audumn said with disgust because she's the girl that broke them up once before. "You just can't seem to keep your dick out of her huh, Tree?"

"Well to put it in layman's terms, I don't talk to her anymore and as far as my dick goes, you are the last one I put it in." Tree said with some anger behind his voice because Audumn won't give him the benefit of the doubt that he changed his life for the better.

"It doesn't matter. You can have whoever or whatever you want." Audumn gets up and finds her balance. "I'm leaving."

Sha walks over and slides Tree a note when Audumn wobbly walks off towards the exit. The note said, *I know y'all are not together anymore, but Audumn is really drunk. Please take her home. I would do it, but the club doesn't close for another thirty minutes and then I have to clean up.*

Tree hastily got up after reading what the bartender gave him. Catching up with Audumn, he walks a few steps behind her to see if she can at least make it to her car. Audumn is just edging the corner to the parking lot when she stumbles over a tree root and hits the ground palms and knees first. Tree tries to help her up, but as she's trying to find her legs the acid in her stomach swooshes from left to right. It was like a brand new soda pop being shaken to a great extent because the pressure within her insides had built up and burst through her mouth.

"Audumn!" Tree throws her arm over his shoulders and helps her to his car. "I'm sorry sweetheart, but I can't let you drive home like this." After latching her seatbelt, he runs around the car and jumps in the driver's seat. "Audumn, where do you stay so I can bring you home?" Audumn answers by snoring to the sound of his voice. "Audumn wake up! What's your address?"

"Columbian Greens apt #327," she mumbled between snores, thinking it's her friend DJ Chris who's taking her home.

—ⱳ—

"Oh my god, what the fuck have I done?" Audumn awakes to the sunlight and Tree flushing the condom and wrapper down the toilet. The door to the bathroom is closed, but the sound of the swish echoed off the bathroom walls and caused her to wake up because she's usually home by herself. Tree has the door locked, so when Audumn tries to turned the knob, it was to no avail. His anguish is the reason why he turned the twist lock into the upright position and wonders what the outcome of this whole ordeal will be. Today is supposed to be one of the best days of his life because his entire time on lock he prayed and asked God to give him one more chance with the love of his life. But what happened in the wee wee hours of this morning is not what he was praying for. Therefore, it was the Devil presenting himself to him again and once again, like before when he went to jail, he failed tremendously.

Audumn pounds on the door with her fist. "Tree you have to leave now! This was a mistake and I'm sorry, but this will never happen again because I love Secorion." Saying his name makes her fall to the wall and slide down to the floor, crying. "Damn Audumn, what have you done?" she repeats over and over into the cup of her hands that are covering her face.

Tree opens the door and sees Audumn balling her eyes out on the floor and bends down to console her. "I'm sorry, Audumn. I don't know what came over me. I promise you when I offered to drop you off at home last night that having sex with you was not my intention." Tree squats down and tries to further explain himself. "When I was locked up, all I thought about was making it right with you for leaving you high and dry the way I did. But when you kissed me, it was like my body pushed the good Lord out of my mind and all I could see was the woman of my dreams throwing herself at me. Yes, you were drunk and vulnerable and I should've refrained myself because I'm a strong believer in marriage and..."

"And I think it's time for you to leave, Tree." Audumn stands to her feet and points towards the door. "The only thing you can tell me right now is, 'And you are leaving because this was a big mistake.'"

"But Audumn, I'm not finished yet. Something happened last night and as a man I must tell you."

Tree's tries to get out what he is about to say, but Audumn isn't hearing it. "Get out! Get out! Get out!" Audumn shoves him to door with her head down, not once looking him in the eyes. "Just go, Tree! Please just go."

Standing in the open door, Tree tries to explain what happened last night one more time, but Audumn pushes him over the threshold and slams the door in his face. *Audumn, the condom bust,* he thought, but for some reason his thoughts couldn't find his lips. When he got to his car, he looked up at her apartment, and asked God to forgive him for falling to the wiles of the flesh. He then vowed that from this day on, he will never be in the same room or place as Audumn because he's not ready to be the cause of breaking up a happy home.

Audumn, on the other hand, has a headache of revulsion pounding the back and the front of her forehead. And to makes matters worse, she got a text from Secorion right after she woke up that read, he will be home next week because he asked for a layoff to be back home with her.

"Dear Lord, what am I going to do?" she asked the ceiling as she threw three ibuprofens to the back of her throat. "And what kind of woman would I be if I keep this from my future husband?"

CHAPTER 12

Secorion made it back to Houston a little over three weeks ago and he couldn't be happier that he's back in the states with, Audumn. It was in mid-June that he had made the decision to come home because his fiancée was very disappointed that he wouldn't be with her on her birthday and that practically tore him apart. His job wanted him to stay the full extent of the contract, which ended in mid-August, but out of respect for his upcoming wedding, his general foreman went ahead and signed his release forms to return home earlier than expected.

Everything is good in his book, but lately his fiancée's attitude has changed and he doesn't know why. He hasn't said anything yet, but since he has her alone in the car today, he's definitely going to ask her why the attitude of despair seems to be a part of her demeanor and visage all of sudden. At first, he thought her stance was going to pass after they made love a few times, but even that didn't take the stricken look off her face. If anything, he feels that she's pushed him further away after each time they've had sex, rather than pulling him closer where he feels he belongs since coming home to be with her.

Today is Audumn's second, but Secorion's first, wedding rehearsal, so their destination is Beaumont, Texas. Being that Secori is from Chicago and she is from Beaumont, it made no sense to have their wedding in Houston so they both agreed to have their day in the sun in her hometown instead. That way, those who truly desired to come from her small city can make it no matter what their excuse may be. And besides, she felt deep down inside that's where her mother wanted the wedding to be anyway because she doesn't like to drive or ride on the highway too much.

Secorion passes Goodyear on I-10 and grasps the fact that he has about a ten minute window until they reach the Holiday Inn on Walden road for the rehearsal. "What's wrong, baby? Are you okay? Or did I do something?"

"No baby, you haven't done anything." Audumn looks out the window and watches the buildings come and go as they get ready to enter Beaumont city limits. "As a matter of fact, you are the best thing that has ever happened to me."

"Then why the sad face? And why can't you look at me when I'm talking to you? Or look at me when you're talking to me?" Secorion reaches over and grabs her hand, but lets go when she didn't clasp his back.

"I'm sorry, Secorion is all I can say."

"Sorry for what? Ever since I got back home, you haven't been the same."

Audumn turns her head towards him, but still can't look him in the eyes. "I'm just sorry and I don't deserve to be with a man like you."

"Wow, so just like that you don't want to be with me no more. I mean, for real? Like, what have I done?"

"It's not you, it's me." Audumn finally looks him in the face, but quickly turns and looks back out the window. "Secori, I love you and you love me, but sometimes love is not enough and people can make bad decisions to hurt those that they love."

"But baby, I promise you that I didn't do anything with the women out there. My heart and eyes are only for you, so please don't think of me that way when I know what I want because I got what I want."

Audumn starts crying when he pulls into a parking spot in front of the entrance of the Holiday Inn. "Baby, please don't say that because it only hurts me more when you tell me how much you love me."

"Please baby, look at me when I'm talking to you." Secorion tries to turn her face towards him, but she doesn't let him. "Please baby, you got to believe me when I say that I would never cheat on you."

"I know you would never cheat on me." Audumn opens the door to get out. "I knew that since the first day I met you, so please stop saying that too baby because it only hurts me more when you do."

"Then what is it then if I haven't done nothing?" Secori exclaims to her backside as Audumn gets out of the car. "What, you don't think I can make you happy or something?"

Audumn walks to the front of the car and waits on him to get out, but feels a little woozy. "I don't feel so good," she said, resting her hand on the hood to keep her balance.

Secori sees her stumble and runs to her side. "Baby, what's wrong? Do you want to call rehearsal off and go back home?"

"No, I'm okay. I don't know what came over me, but whatever it is it's gone now."

"Okay my love, whatever you say." Secori does a small observation of her facial features and notes that her eyelids and nostrils are a little red and her cheeks are a little puffy. "Come on baby, let's get you inside so that you can get a drink of water and sit down somewhere." Secori locks arms with Audumn's and walks her to the electric doors. "I'm sorry baby for grilling you like that on the way here. Now I know that you're just under the weather and probably starting to catch a summer cold."

Audumn didn't respond because yes, she's not feeling too good, but now is not the time to tell Secorion her last month's birthday secret. She didn't know when will be the right time, but out of the love she has for him, she would have to woman up and spill the tea someday soon and before the wedding.

"Let me get some water bae and freshen up before we go in there and meet everybody." Audumn takes a sip of water from the water fountain. "Go ahead and let everyone know that we're here and we'll be starting on time. Give me a sec, and I'll be right behind you. I know I probably look horrible so I'm going to go to the lady's room to powder my nose."

"Okay baby. Whatever you want." Secori kisses her on the lips. "I love you Audumn and always remember that no matter what you're going through, you will never look horrible to me."

Audumn thought, *Yeah, you say that now, but wait until you see how I look after you find out how I desecrated our engagement and wedding.*

146

Kizzy is in charge and she lets the wedding party know it as soon as the monologue clock over the entrance's big hand landed on the twelve and the little hand landed on the six. Time is of the essence because the Holiday Inn gave them their reserved room for the wedding or one similar to it for four one hour rehearsals as part of their wedding package. Their last rehearsal was in June and the groom and his best men weren't there. Today, the groom is here and since his best men won't be able to make it until the last rehearsal, Kizzy came up with doing the rehearsal on facetime because both of them have iPhones and that's one of the phone's new features.

Diana is like Kizzy's hands. What Kizzy says, she does without any backtalk because with only two rehearsals left after this one, she is doing everything possible to make sure nothing goes wrong with her bff's wedding. Being that she's a big girl, she's also taking on the responsibility of being the enforcer and getting everyone in order if she feels they are being lackadaisical when Kizzy is speaking. No one has time to argue with Diana because they can tell from her stature that she always gets her way. Therefore, when Kizzy speaks, they listen without questioning her leadership just to keep the peace that Diana brings when she's not opening her mouth trying to boss everyone around.

"First things first, yeah. I want everyone to come to the front of the aisle and find the piece of tape on the floor with your name on it." Kizzy points down the imaginary aisle with five spaced out chairs along each side to give an idea of how the congregation will be sitting.

"If you don't know what side your tape is on, the groomsmen will be on the right and the bridesmaids will be on the left."

"Diana is correct, and when you get there, I want you to picture the arbor, otherwise known as the wedding arch, in the empty space between you where our beautiful bride and her handsome man will be standing." Kizzy waits for everyone to find their names on the floor and stand on it. "I started tonight's rehearsal like this because I need all of you to remember these spots because they're your assigned spots on the wedding day. Also, I want you to know that when you're in this spot, you will always face the bride. What does that mean, you say?" Kizzy asks a rhetorical question. "Great, I'm glad you asked that." Diana and Audumn giggle under their breath because Kizzy is taking her job too seriously. "What that means is that when Audumn is in the back or coming through the door with her dad, you will always be facing whatever direction the bride is in. When she reaches the pastor, that's when I want everyone to turn and face her while she gets the shackle on her foot that will join her to her husband forever."

Everyone in the room started laughing to the joke Kizzy slid in to see if she has everyone's attention. "Great! I'm glad everyone is listening." Kizzy hands the wedding party a duplicate of the wedding program. "This is not the program, but the order on it is how we are going to perform our bride and groom's wedding. And just like the spots you're standing in, I want you to remember this program like your life depended on it. That way, we won't have any misunder-standings on what's going on or where we are at in the ceremony." Kizzy pauses to catch a breath. "Do you have any questions?"

"No." A few people replied while the rest remained silent.

"Are you ready to begin with the walk-in part of the ceremony?"

"Yes!" they all said at once because they're tired of standing in their assigned spots.

"Great! My name is Kizzy for those who don't know me." Kizzy speaks to the screen of her iPhone that's on a tripod facing her to Brian and Cori because they are the only two that haven't met or know her yet. "And I am one of the maids of honor who's in charge of putting this wedding ceremony together." Kizzy beckons for Diana to come see. "And this is my assistant and also the other maid of honor that you, Brian, will be walking with when the music starts and you two have to make your entrance." Diana waves at the camera and Brian waves back. "And if you haven't figured it out yet, Cori, I'll be walking with you." Cori waves in the camera and Kizzy smiles in return.

"Hey Diana and Kizzy, me and my cousin Brian are happy to be on board on my big brother Secorion's and my future sister in law Audumn's wedding day. Sorry my twins are not here tonight to view the rehearsal with us, but I don't think that Phil and Lil would've stopped playing to watch anyway. I promise you that they'll be there with bells on for their Uncle Secori's wedding day, though." Cori gives Kizzy a thumbs up. "I guarantee it."

Kizzy waits for him to finish talking and turns back towards the bride and groom's assigned spots and says, "Okay then, let's get started. Everybody go to the back and when you get in the hall, I want you to find who you are walking with and smile, laugh, cry, or do whatever you need to do to get to know each other because I don't want to see no cardboard people coming down that aisle when my girl is about to get married."

"Come on you Humphrey men with yo fine and cute asses! Chop, chop." Diana catches Audumn's brothers out the corner of her eye dragging their feet.

Everyone present is in the hall and awaiting further instruction from the director. Using Bluetooth, Kizzy plays the first of three songs on Audumn's playlist for the wedding ceremony off her iPad. When the music starts, she tells the bridesmaids and groomsmen that the first song played is for the parents and grandparents of the bride and groom, followed by the pastor, then Secorion. She also gives them instructions that Courtney Thibodeaux with Taking Images will be to the right when they get to the last row of chairs, so they must stop and smile big for the camera.

Kizzy walks over to Audumn and asks why are her mother and father aren't here for tonight's rehearsal. "Umm best friend, where are your parents because its already going on 6:30 and we only got the room till 7:00?"

Caught up with Tree on her mind and her not feeling too good, Audumn didn't even notice that her parents aren't there. "I'm sorry Kizzy, but I don't know how I even missed that. Give me a sec and let me call and check on my mom. As far as my dad goes, I will leave it up to him if he wants to be a part of this. He knows that tonight is rehearsal through the text messages I forwarded to everybody yesterday and this morning." Audumn goes to a corner of the room to use her phone.

"Alright guys and girls, are you ready? Because when this song comes to an end and the next one begins, that's your cue Kendra for you and Aubrie to start walking towards the front. And remember that when you get to the end of the aisle to...."

"We know, we know, Kizzy." Kendra butts in with a smirk on her face. "To stop and smile big for the camera."

"Well, all right then. I won't know it until I see everyone do it like it's supposed to be done. Because what I saw last month was half of y'all forgot to stop and take the picture before separating to your assigned spots." Kizzy puts her hands on her hips and speaks with a little sass in her voice. "Kendra, you two are up; the song is about to begin. Shanay, you and Nickolas are next."

Kendra walked in with Aubrie on her arm, smiling and waving at the guests who are not there. Shanay and Nick are next. Then Khamil and Dexter. Then Gayriale and Robert would come last, but since he stays in Florida, Gayriale walked down the aisle by herself. Kizzy would've facetimed him too, but he's an android user so the app didn't come with his phone. It didn't matter because he promised his little sister he would be there for the last two rehearsals like his life depended on it.

Gayriale made it down the aisle with her imaginary groomsman and stopped and did a small photoshoot for the imaginary photographer and the Taking Images portfolio. After taking four headshots and two full body shots, she blew a kiss to where Courtney would be standing and then proceeded to her assigned spot on the bride's side next to Khamil.

"Gayriale, I hope you were playing, right?"

"Yes and no, but you do have to excuse me because it's just something about the camera that seems to scream my name when I step in front of it."

"But it's a fake camera and it's not even there." Kizzy points towards the empty space Taking Images would be standing in.

"Yes, but you never know who might see your picture in Audumn's wedding book or who might be in the crowd."

Khamil is the same way about her black beauty and speaks out in Gayriale's defense. "She does have a point, Kizzy. I mean, sometimes you only get one shot to make a good impression."

"Listen here, baby." Kizzy feels that her New Orlean's patience is about to run out as each tick of the second hand ticks closer to their one hour rehearsal being over. "Khamil, you were doing a great job until you cosigned on Miss America taking pictures for her resume at my Chica's wedding rehearsal with a camera and photographer who's not here." Kizzy holds her hand up with her palm facing Khamil. "Therefore, you can miss me with that there, yeah, and talk to the hand. And as for you Gayriale, I'm sorry, but you need some help baby and I'll be wasting my time trying to make some sense out of anything you just said."

"Yeah Audumn, where did you get these boujee bitches from?" Diana yells to the entrance where Audumn is awaiting her turn to walk down the aisle.

"Oh my God, can we just get on with the rehearsal? It's Sunday and some of us have to go to work in the morning."

"My cousin Kendra is right. Fun time is over and we need to wrap this up asap because I want to be back in Houston at my Nana's house by nine." Shanay is getting frustrated and tired of all the she-nanigans. "Gayriale, you're cute, cute. Khamil, you're cute, cute too. I'm glad both of you are in my play sister's wedding and if there's not anything else, Kizzy can you cut the music on so Audumn can walk out and we can all go home already. Geesh."

Dexter sees where this is going and speaks out in Secorion and his sister's defense. "Listen up everybody! We have approximately eighteen minutes left, so let's stop all the bickering and get this over with for our soon to be bride and groom. I love my baby sister and I am so proud of the woman she has become and the man she's going to marry. September 13th is her day and if you love her like I do, then you will take all this seriously because that's what she deserves and she would do the same for you."

"Come on ladies. All six of you are beautiful and I can't wait to be seen on Shanay's arm when I say cheese for the picture." Nickolas looks across from him and winks at Shanay to let her know he's digging her style.

"And I can't wait to be seen with her cousin, Kendra, either." Aubrie elbows his brother on the side. "They say they want us to get to know each other better, I say, you and your cousin go on a double date with me and my big bro next weekend. So, what do you say pretty ladies?"

"Kizzy, I think that's your cue to turn on the music." Secorion laughs at how this was one minute away from being a catfight to now being a 2013 new season of, 'Love Connection.'

"Come on, you heard the groom!" Kizzy claps her hands twice to get the room's attention. "Diana, you're up next and I'm after you, so hustle your way to the entrance because I'm going to press play as soon as you get your big behind back there. And as for you Humphrey boys, get their phone numbers and call them later." Kizzy shakes her head and giggles because ever since Nick made his proposal to Shanay, him and his brother Brie have been giving Kendra and her the googly eyes.

Diana comes out holding Kizzy's iPhone to show Brian first-hand how he will be walking with her down the aisle. When she reaches the end of the folding chair which represents the seating arrangements, she looks into the camera and explains to him that this is where they will turn and take a picture. She then tells Brian that this is also where they would separate and he will go stand next to the groom and she will go stand in her assigned spot where the bride will be coming out shortly after them.

Kizzy is next, so Diana sprints back to the entrance and walks along side of Kizzy, but this time speaking to Cori who is on the phone and who will be walking with her until they reach their assigned spots. Between the four of them working together with today's technology, Kizzy feels that Brian and Cori get somewhat of an understanding of their role in the wedding.

"Audumn, you're next since the twins are not here. Had they'd been here, you would wait for Phillip to go first with the ring, followed by Lillian throwing the rose petals. Lil would start walking when her brother Phil gets halfway down the aisle and you will begin walking when she gets halfway down the aisle. Got it?" Kizzy's voice travels easily through the empty room.

"Got it!" Audumn holds her thumb up to let Kizzy know she heard all of what she had said.

"Great. We have a little under ten minutes left, so let's get this right the first time." Kizzy presses play on the third song on Audumn's playlist for the bride.

Audumn's phone dings with a text message right before the music turns on for her to walk out. "Pause it, Kizzy! My mom just texted me back from me calling to check on her earlier."

Mrs. Humphrey's text read: *Sorry I couldn't make it, dear. This morning when I woke up, I had an unwanted pain in my abdomen so I scheduled an appointment with my doctor. Enjoy your rehearsal love and I'll tell you about it later. About to get some rest. Not feeling too good.*

Audumn texted back that she would be by there later, but then texted back again saying that she will call her in the morning and that she should get some rest. "I'm ready, Kizzy! Turn the music on."

Kizzy runs up the aisle and hands Audumn a bouquet of flowers she made out of newspaper for the rehearsal. "Here girl. And don't forget to smile big for the camera," she exclaimed before pressing play on her iPad.

Audumn made it down the aisle without any mishaps or mis-understandings. The rehearsal was a little chaotic before the music came on, but when it did, everyone grew silent and looked on in amazement at the smile and beauty upon Audumns' face as she took steady steps to her husband to be. Secorion mouth is wide open when Audumn stood in front of him holding the fake flowers. He was like a deer caught in the headlights, but he snapped out of it when Audumn closed his mouth with her fingers. When he came to, he kissed her like he had never kissed her before and it was five seconds until he let her lips go. Both parties clapped and chanted them on because true love is hard to find.

Audumn feels woozy again after the kiss. "What was that for?"

"I don't know. I guess I couldn't help myself." Secori sees that Audumn face is becoming pale. "Baby, are you okay? You don't look too good."

"I don't feel too good either." Audumn regurgitates, but cuffs her mouth with her hand so her throw up can't escape onto the floor.

"Here sis." Aubrie hands her a small trashcan from off the floor and Audumn lets loose in it. "Let it out, sis." Brie pats her on the back. "Let it out."

Diana comes over to play nurse and check on her. "What's up, best friend? You good?"

"I was, but now I'm feeling nauseated and my stomach feels like a pot of boiling water that's about to spill over."

"Oh yeah. I've heard and had those symptoms before a time or two." Diana asks Aubrie and Secorion to let her have a word with Audumn for a second. As soon as they walk off, she pulls Audumn to the side and says, "Bitch, are you pregnant because that's what it sounds like to me?"

"Pregnant?" *Could this be why I'm feeling the way that I am?*

"Yes bitch, pregnant. Don't be acting all brand-new, like you and that fine ass man of yours don't be doing it raw." Diana remembers that she's always ready for anything that the birds and the bees may try to throw at her. "Meet me in the lady's room. I got something I want to show you." Diana goes to the corner and grabs her handbag from off the floor and exits.

"Audumn, are you okay and where's Diana hurrying off too?" Kizzy attempts to come over to see if her little weather bug has passed, but Audumn waves her off.

"Yeah bae, how are you feeling? Is that sickness trying to come back on you again?"

"I'm fine, honey. Go on and help Kizzy close out tonight. Diana says she has something to give me that may help me feel a little better. When you're done, I'll meet you in the lobby where we entered the hotel at. Tell everyone I said thanks for coming and that I'll call them tomorrow."

"Whatever you say, sweetheart." Secori hears the weakness in her voice and escorts her to the hall so that she can go meet Diana. "I love you baby and I'll give Kizzy the heads up on what's going on."

"Thanks love for always being my strength." Audumn kisses him on the cheek to make sure he doesn't catch what she's got. "Goodbye! See y'all next time and thanks for coming!" Audumn waves to her wedding party and exits before anyone can respond.

Diana is in the bathroom waiting for Audumn to come through the door. *I wish this girl would come on. I ain't got all night to be playing with her or Secorion.* On the counter she has a pair of latex gloves, two pregnancy tests, and a Plan B. And in her hands, she has a washcloth and a bar of Dove soap she confiscated from a hotel room. Not to mention, she also has on a pair of latex gloves and has changed her shirt just in case she gets some pee on her.

Audumn finally comes through the door. "What you got to show me, girl? Whatever it is, I know you're crazy."

"Audumn look, this is serious."

"First of all, what do you have on your hands and why did you change clothes?" Audumn looks down at the bathroom sink and then back towards Diana holding the washcloth and soap. "Diana, please tell me that you didn't have all that in your purse?"

"I'm sorry Chica, but a bitch gotta be ready if these dudes out here try to catch me slipping. Shit, I always keep two PT's on me and a Plan B because I'm not trying to have no kids until I find Mr. right ding-a-ling." Diana puts down the soap and hands Audumn a pregnancy test. "Now, go on in one of them bathroom stalls and piss on one of these sticks so that we can know what's up with all this nausea and throwing up and stuff."

"Really, Diana?"

"Yes really. But just know that if you're pregnant, then a Plan B is not going to work because you should've done that a long time ago if you're already at the throwing up stage."

"Girl shut up." Audumn goes into an empty stall and latches the door. "If I am, then I'm keeping my baby. Lord knows me and my Secorion need a new beginning after the sins I've committed behind closed doors."

Audumn steps out the stall and places the pregnancy test on a paper towel Diana has laid out for it. A minute passes by and a faint line begins to barely makes itself known on the display that tells you if you're pregnant or not. Diana begins to smile big and Audumn does too because one line means not pregnant and two means that you are. Just as the boldness in the color of the single line began to define itself, another faint line to the right of the first one shows up out of nowhere.

"I'm pregnant?" Audumn's back falls against this wall.

"Yes bitch, you're pregnant. At least, that's what this pee test says." Diana picks up the pregnancy test to get a closer look. "And your two lines are really pink too. It's not like some of the others I've used in the past. Sometimes you be like, is you or is you ain't, but this one is like, bitch you're pregnant."

"Oh my God Diana, I'm pregnant!" Audumn takes the test from Diana and begins to dance while looking at it. "Can you believe it, Diana?"

"Um yes. That's what you get when you don't use a condom."

"I know, right?" Audumn thinks about how Tree strapped up when they had sex. "Gotta use those if you don't won't no children. Good thing I don't need them because me and my love are getting married."

"Girl, don't you look much happier all of a sudden? Shoot, for the last hour you've been having a scowl on your face hidden behind a fake smile." Diana looks Audumn in her eyes whose countenance has changed tremendously since she found out the good news. "And why is that, Audumn? You know I know you like a book. Why earlier were you stand offish, but now all of a sudden, you're like woopty doo?"

Audumn remembers how her birthday extravaganza with Tree has been tearing her up mentally since she woke up on her sofa with a hangover. "I don't know what you're talking about Diana because from now on, it's only going to be me, Secorion, and this baby."

"Okay Chica, but whatever it is you had on your mind today, I pray that you'll someday confide in me or Kizzy about it and that it never comes back to bite you in the butt." Diana takes off the gloves and opens her arms. "Now come here and give me a hug best friend and I'm happy for you, Secori, and the little guy or gal you have in the oven."

CHAPTER 13

A udumn's mind is back in the game and her reason for being so high in spirits is because her prenatal appointment confirmed what she already knew. Last week, Dr. Belisima did a blood test and an ultrasound and they found out that they were having fraternal twins just like Secori's brother. The news took Secorion to another level of happiness because not only does he have one baby to raise and love for a lifetime, but now he has two. Audumn loved the idea of having twins to love on, but what mattered most to her today is that she could feel life in the lower part of her tummy starting to get firmer by the day.

Each day after she wakes up, she goes to the mirror to see if her baby bump has started showing, but as of yet, it has not. Some days when she's all alone, she would stand sideways and poke out her stomach or put a small pillow underneath her shirt to see if she's still pretty when she's as big as a house. To make a long story short, all the baby talk sounds great and Secorion is utterly beatific. But as far as Audumn goes, the stork that will soon be landing in their loving abode has put up a firewall in her conscience.

It is that same firewall that has prevented the fire of truth from spewing out of her mouth on how she stepped out on her birthday and got laid while being betrothed. Her secret is safe with her and even though she wanted to come out at first to tell Secori the truth, all of that has passed due to what will be here in a little under seven months. Practically, her drunken stupidity is dead and as long as she doesn't water it, then the seed of mischief will not sprout up into a tree. Unless Tree comes out and says something, which she knows he won't because he loves her. That makes the coast clear and Audumn will be saying, "I do," in three days.

Last night, the last wedding rehearsal was a success and since no one needed a room of that size over the weekend, the Holiday Inn went ahead and let the wedding decorator begin setting up the décor for the ceremony Sunday. All of the decorations weren't there, but the many rows of seats and the wedding arbor was put in its place. Hence, that gave the participants in the wedding a visual idea of how things will look in a few days. Ironically, Secorion's niece and nephew, Phil and Lil, took the cake when they entered in on the traditional, 'Cannon in D,' bride song. It was like everyone stopped and realized that this wedding is for real and they had to be on point and precise to make it the enchanting environment that their loved one is looking for. When it was all said and done, the bride and groom saw the first glimpse of what is to come when they put most of the pieces to their wedding puzzle together.

But that's enough about last night because today is Friday, or in Audumn terms, "Friyay," and it's time to turn up in New Orleans for the bachelor and bachelorette party. The Crescent City, which got its name from the state's odd shape, is about four hours away from Beaumont, Texas, so Audumn and her crew decided to head out at six because check-in time at the Marriot is at eleven. Secorion and the guys decided to follow behind them to make sure everyone got there safe and then they would part their separate ways when they checked into the hotel next to theirs at the Crowne Plaza.

Daylight is not being denied this morning as it pushes its rays through the night clouds that blanketed the city overnight. It's ironic how morning and night will always fight an endless battle, but the outcome is always the same because God's clock will never change and will always be right. Two Suburbans sat outside the Holiday Inn waiting for its occupants to jump inside and take the trip that Kizzy and Diana rented them for. Secorion's overseas job payed off well and all that Audumn desired for her wedding day to be has come true because of that. Such as paying extra for the four wedding rehearsals, the rental cars, and for two extra days in the three hotel suits assigned to the bridesmaids, groomsmen, and the husband and wife to be for their honeymoon.

On the elevator, Audumn looks down on the lobby through the glass walls that travel up and down the elevator shaft daily. Secorion is with her and is holding her hand when the doors divided onto level one. All the guys and girls are waiting for them when they step off the elevator, but the two of them already knew that from seeing everybody down below as they were being transported to the ground floor. Her bridesmaids brought duffle bags with a change of clothes, deodorant, and a toothbrush. While the groomsmen brought nothing because they didn't plan on going to sleep until the ride home tomorrow anyway. Audumn's oldest brother was the only one who bought a bag with his belongings in it so his little brothers threw their drawls, deodorant, socks, and toothbrushes in the bag with his.

Brian and Cori have never been to Texas, let alone New Orleans, so ever since they stepped foot off the plane, they've been on a mission to do everything possible in H-Town, Beaumont, and The Big Easy. Chi-Town is fun, but it's nothing like being on vacation when it's on someone else's dime. Cori is with his big bro and Brian is with his first cousin and that's all that matters to them in their book. Well, that and the fact that they have only come out of their pockets only twice for food since they've been in town for the past five days.

Not only them, but everyone in Audumn's wedding is being catered too. No one at any time has been asked to pay for or put money on anything but their dresses and tuxedos since the day they were inquired to be in the wedding. When the New Orleans trip was announced, Audumn had already let her maids of honor know that the trip was also an appreciation gift to the wedding party. The trip, the rooms, and not to mention the makeover glow up for the ladies and the haircuts and manicures for the men, was included in the appreciation gift to the wedding party as well.

Audumn waits for the two groups to make it to their rides for today and tomorrow. "Good morning. I know it's early, but we are now two days away from one of the biggest days of me and my future husband's life."

"All ready, big sis! And me and Kendra are ready to come strutting down that aisle like we own the place."

"That's right, Brie. We've been practicing and getting to know each other a lot better like Kizzy wanted us too." Kendra winks at Aubrie who's standing by his brothers.

"That's good to know, Kendra." Audumn looks at her Chicas with wide eyes. "Um, oh yeah, like I was saying before we found out that Kendra and my baby brother have been doing the nasty on their spare time," Aubrie shrinks when hearing his sister call him out. "I appreciate all of you for being here with me today, tomorrow, and Sunday when I give my hand to this wonderful man standing next to me."

"No problem, friend." Gayriale replies.

"Yeah Audumn, you've known ever since we were kids that I will always have your back and I will always be there for you when you need me."

"I know you will and that's why I couldn't do this without you. Not just you, Khamil, but all of you." Audumn tries to hold back the tears, but a few leak out. "When I'm old and grey and I look back on this day, I will thank God that I shared it with special people such as you."

"Aww thank you best friend, but can you turn off the faucet because I'm ready to get drunk as hell in New Orleans?"

"I hate to say it Audumn, but for once Diana is making some sense," Kizzy said.

"Okay Chicas, let's ride and remember that we have to be back here by five p.m. tomorrow to get our makeovers for the wedding. That goes for you too, guys." Audumn turns to Secorion and says, "You got that, Secori?"

"Yes, little sis, we got that." Robby interjects while putting his arm around Secori's shoulders. "Is there anything else Audumn because my plane leaves Monday and I'm ready to get this party started?"

"As a matter of fact, there is." Secori says to the groomsmen and bridesmaids with a smile. "Me and Audumn have an announcement to make." Secori turns to Audumn and nods his head. "Go on love, tell'em."

"Now?" Audumn replies a little bashful from being put on the spot.

"Now looks like a better time than any. Who knows how chaotic tomorrow may be with us during crunch time before the wedding? Also, we may not have everyone who took time out for us during this whole ordeal all together in a quiet place again."

"Yeah Audumn, tell us!" Shanay exclaims.

"Well, besides for my Chicas, my mom, my dad. and Ms. Boswell, Secorion and I haven't shared our bundles of joy with any-one because we're waiting on the right time to do it."

Secorion raises one finger to speak. "Bae, I forgot to tell you that I told my Uncle Andre too."

"What do you mean you told your uncle? You know he's going to tell his only sister the first chance he gets."

"My uncle can keep a secret. I told him not to tell momma until I do and he assured me that my mother would prefer if I would tell her myself, rather than him. And besides, what did you expect when he's my only family member living in Houston with me?"

"Hold up! Hold up! Bundles of joy? Shoot, last time I heard those three words in that order I was pregnant with little Cody." Khamil hears herself speak and realizes what Audumn is trying to tell them. "Pregnant, Audumn?! What you're trying to tell us is that you're pregnant?"

"Yes everybody, I'm pregnant with twins and I'm due in March." Audumn puts her hands over her stomach and smiles to her friends and family. "Also, this trip is all that we're doing for our wedding because me and my fiancé decided to cancel our honeymoon cruise until February so that we can save money for the new additions to our family. So, let's make this trip to New Orleans special guys and have some fun."

Audumn's brothers quickly rushed her when she confirmed the news. Smiles were everywhere as they took turns congratulating their sister and rubbing her stomach to see if they could feel the babies. Robby pushed his brothers to the side and gave his sister a gigantic hug and picked her up and spun her around like he used to when she was a kid. When he put her down, Aubrie fell to one knee and tried to see if he could hear something inside of his sister.

The girls waited for Brie to stop listening to whatever he is listening too and bogarted their way through her brothers and did practically the same thing. Except for the picking up or listening to a baby that's not fully developed, they too treated her like a pincushion trying to see if they can feel a baby bump. Diana and Kizzy just stood to the side with joy in their hearts because they've been raving about what is to come since Audumn revealed the news to Kizzy after last month's rehearsal.

"Congratulations, big bro. I'm finally about to be an uncle and Phillip and Lilian are finally about to have some cousins."

"You mean 1st cousins, Cori, like us." Brian gives Secorion a handshake and pulls him closer for a bro hug. "Congratulations, big cuz and I know without a shadow of doubt that you're going to be a great father like Uncle Secori was to you and to me since my father died in the 90's."

"Thanks cuz for being here all the way from the windy city to show your support." Secori opens his arms wide. "Come here you guys, it's time for a group hug."

"So, when are you going to tell mom and dad?" Cori mumbled underneath the huddle.

"During our wedding reception when we have everyone who means something to the both of us in the same room."

Brian hops behind the wheel of the Suburban meant for the men to drive because he has a 2004 model and he's not going to miss the opportunity to drive the 2013 edition. Robert said he would help drive, but that quickly is dismissed by his brother in law, Secorion. "Trust me Robby; my lil cuz got this all the way there and all the way back." Robert was only asking to help out, but Secori's words made him sit back and enjoy the ride because he's on vacation and he needs all the relaxation that he can get. As for the rest of the bunch, they laid their seats back when Brian got onto I-10 and put their Beats by Dre earbuds in their ears when Cori put on Bump-J, a Chi-Town artist in the cd player.

Diana isn't playing behind the wheel of the girl's Suburban. As of the moment, they've only been on the road twenty minutes and she's already approaching Orange Texas and after they pass that city, they will be crossing the Louisiana border. Her foot is heavy, but Kizzy hurried up and told her to take her foot off the gas when she read, 'Welcome to Louisiana,' when they crossed the channel of water that separated the two states. "Diana, you can't be driving like that, no! This is the boot, not Texas, and the po-po outchea don't play that driving fast, yeah." Being that this is Kizzy's hometown state, Diana decided to comply, but quickly is glad she did because a

167

Parish County police officer was hiding in the brush in the median that she just passed.

Their first stop is in a small town by the name of Rayne, Louisiana. Brian wanted to keep driving, but since he's following Diana he exited when she exited and parked beside of her at a mom and pop store. The girls had to pee and stretch their legs, so they got out in a little rush because they've all been drinking Pink Moscatos since they left the Holiday Inn parking lot. Some of Secori's crew was thirsty, so they jumped out of the truck to get something to drink and to stretch their legs as well, being that this is a better time than any to do it. Cori is a drinker and while he's walking inside the store, he sees Gayriale disposing the empty 6 oz. bottles into the trashcan outside the restroom that all the girls are in line for.

"Oh yeah, that's how y'all doing it on the way to New Orleans?" He asked, holding the door open for Gayriale like a gentleman.

"Why thank you Cori, but I thought men in Chicago were not into our down south customs when it comes to chivalry."

"I guess you can say that, but it looks to me that I'm in Texas, and last time I checked, my big bro told me that down here they treat the ladies with respect. Especially the pretty ones." Cori gives Gayriale a smile and she blushes when she passes by him holding the door.

Robert and his brother go inside the store shortly after Cori let the door close. Usually Robby never smokes weed, but the trip is long so he stepped to the side of the building with Brie and Nick and took a hit or two off one of the pre-blunts they have rolled up. That hit gave him the munchies along with his brothers, hence, now it's time to get some snacks for the remainder of the three hours they have left on the road.

What's crazy is that, in the past, it was Dexter who got wasted and lived his life on the edge, but he took his last drink or drug when he got saved six years ago on his sister's birthday. He doesn't knock his brothers for what they do because he knows they tolerated way more from him when he was coming home drunk every night. Or when they had to come get him out of jail for talking shit to the officers on the numerous number of times Jefferson County picked him up for being passed out on the side of the road.

Cori came running back to the truck with two brown bags in his hands. "Look cuz, they're selling real liquor in the store like they do in the Chi."

"Word." Brian replied, looking in the back at the two fifths of Hennessy and cups of ice Cori pulled out of the bag. "And I see you got the Hen dog too!"

"Our pops' favorite." Secori reached back from the front seat and took the cup his brother poured for him. "Where the cut at?" he asked after taking a sip.

"Oops, my bad bro. You know me and Brian likes ours on the rocks like pops do. I forgot you's a Texas boy now."

"Whatever, lil bro. You know it's Chicago all day with me! But I ain't gon' lie, I got much love for the H." Secori jumps out and runs inside the store to buy a 7UP.

"So, what's up with you Dex? You dranking or what?"

"Naw, I'm good, Cori. I've been sober now for six years, but I'm pretty sure my little brothers will take a shot or two with you."

"My bad bro, I didn't mean to try and knock you off the wagon or anything. It's just that in Chicago, this is all we do." Cori takes a shot from the bottle and says, "Aaahh," to the smooth burning sensation traveling down the back of his throat. "Not to mention, me and my cuz like to smoke that good green too."

Dexter chuckles at his comments because he knows his brothers are on a smoke break now. "Well, if that's what you like." Nickolas, Aubrie, and Robert open the doors with their eyes red and low. "Then you just missed it."

"Damn, y'all got this joint loud up in here! I didn't know y'all smoke green." Cori sees his brother running to the car because Diana is about to pull off. "Next stop, y'all definitely got to keep it one-hundred and let me and my cuz get in rotation."

"Most definitely." Nick replied. "You family now, so what's mine is yours."

"And what's yours is mine." Cori finished the famous quote while handing Nickolas the bottle of Hennessy.

It was in Baton Rouge that Kizzy remembered that they were supposed to be wearing the t-shirts the Chicas made for their trip to New Orleans. What made her remember is that she spilled wine on her shirt when Diana swerved to avoid a sack of sand in the middle of the highway. The three of them passed them out at a Speedy Stop they exited for, so that everybody can change shirts. The bridal party's shirts were burnt orange with brown and black letters that said, 'Last Night Single,' in a cursive font and underneath said, 'New Orleans Bachelorette Weekend,' and on the bottom to the left were their names. On the back is whatever part they play in the wedding and a picture of a diamond ring underneath the last letter of their status.

Secorion and his groomsmen threw their orange tuxedo t-shirts on after they saw how fly the girls were when they came out of the store prancing in theirs. The front of theirs is basically a picture of a suit with a brown tie and each of the guy's names was stitched on the handkerchief pocket imprint on their chest. On the back is whatever part they play in the wedding and that's it. When all of them put them on, they stood side by side admiring how fresh they look in orange in the reflection on the side of the black SUV. "We about to shut New Orleans down when we step foot onto Bourbon Street." Secorion said, turning his back to his groomsmen to show them his groom status for Sunday.

New Orleans is their next stop and the only thing in their path to get there after leaving Baton Rouge is the Causeway bridge that crosses twenty-four miles of water over Lake Pontchartrain. According to the Guinness Book of World Records, the Causeway bridge over Lake Pontchartrain is the longest continuous bridge passing over water since it opened its four lanes in 1955. It's design and structure is a site to see, and for eight of the twenty-four miles, you can't see land in any direction. In 2011, China built a twenty-six mile bridge by the name of the Jiaozhou Bay bridge, but our American Causeway bridge refuses to relinquish the world's longest bridge title to them.

But all that is irrelevant right now, because Diana knows that the Causeway bridge's four lanes of cement and steel structure is the only thing between her and her Chicas turning up for Audumn's bachelorette party. Her foot became like a block of cement when the SUV's front two tires touched the pavement of the bridge. It's a straight shot and the day is clear, so you can see the police up ahead if they're out with their radar guns trying to catch tourist coming to their city. The highway is only two lanes in both directions and the shoulder to the right of those lanes looks smaller, therefore, a cop would be a damn fool for trying to post up there to give somebody a ticket. Taking that into consideration, Diana raised the speed to 90 mph and the light posts alongside of the bridge began to zoom by until she saw the New Orleans skyline and started to slow down to the speed limit.

Brian is accustomed to speed and breaking the law, so when he saw Diana pick up the speed to 90, he did the same because he's never been left behind when it came to following somebody. Especially not by no girl, and especially not by the bridesmaid he's walking with in two days for his cousin's wedding. To him, that will give Diana bragging rights if she so chooses to use them and worse, his cousin Cori will tell his hometown that a girl showed him up on their way to New Orleans. *I'll be damned if she leaves me in the dust on this road trip,* he thought. *Hell, she's lucky I wasn't leading because I would've gotten us there before check-in time and not at 11:35 like the GPS says.*

They all pulled up to the front of their hotels, which are adjacent to each other and got the bags out of the back to go inside. A valet came to take the vehicles to the Marriot and Crowne Plaza parking garage, while the girls went inside the Marriot to check-in. The guys saw that Audumn and Secorion wanted some privacy, so they went inside the Crowne Plaza to get the rooms assigned to them so that they can be ready to party when it's time to go party.

The day is beautiful and the noise from the New Orlean's everyday life lit up Canal Street as the two of them stood hand in hand savoring the fact that they're almost over the threshold. People are everywhere along the sidewalks trying to sell things, doing magic tricks, and performing certain acts for money. The smell of Cajun food is what catches Audumn's nose and she can't wait to eat some crawfish and oysters with her friends. But for Secorion, his mind is on what his grooms have got planned for him and the famous Hand

Grenade alcohol beverage that will soon be in his system when they leave the hotel.

"Well, this is it, my love." Audumn gives Secorion a kiss and taps his lips with her finger. "And you better not do nothing I wouldn't do." Her statement made her think about her secret, but she quickly shook the negative thoughts from her mind.

"Come on now my love, you and I both know that my heart beats only for you."

Audumn raises her shirt up over her stomach. "And the babies."

"Yes, my love. And the babies." Secorion smiles at the love he has inside of him for her. "I love you Audumn and your bridal party shirts are cool," he said as she put her shirt down over her stomach. "Last Night Single, huh?"

"Don't do me. You know where my heart lies, but you got to admit our shirts do rock and when we turn that corner onto Bourbon Street it's gon' be on like Donkey Kong until we check out tomorrow."

Secorion thought, *shit, it's gon' be on like Donkey Kong when I get up to my room with all of the guys. Because if anyone knows how to act an ass and turn up to the fullest, it's my 1st cousin Brian Garland, a.ka. B.G.* "Have fun babe, and see you back here tomorrow."

CHAPTER 14

Night time has fallen in NOLA and everybody who knows Bourbon Street knows that daytime is good, but night time is where it's at. To some, the lights seem a little brighter at night and the music seems to have a little more New Orleans flavor. And then there's the food that seems to taste different and for some reason, the people are more sociable and friendly. In the daytime, you enjoy the scenery of the city's French Quarters and take pictures of all the high-spirited people getting into character for the tourists to enjoy and see. At night time, the daytime's alcoholic beverages have fully kicked in, so that's when the partying begins.

Audumn and her crew are on their level and it's no climbing down until they fall asleep and wake up. Tonight is Audumn's last night as a free woman, so she decided to have a drink or two, or three, or whatever count she's on with her Chicas and bridesmaids. She's on her last drink for the night and after gulping down the last of her vodka, she holds her cup up to admire the different colors of autumn rhinestones in her wineglass she had made for her and all of the girls. *Oh, how pretty,* she thought as she stared at the words, 'Bride to Be,' reflecting off the stones into her eyes, but then thinks about her babies. *Sorry little ones.* Audumn places her hands over her lower stomach. *I promise you that this will never happen again.*

Kizzy and Diana designed each wineglass to fit the bridal party's characters with Audumn giving them the description on how she viewed each one of them. All of the customized wineglasses are adorned in autumn rhinestones to match their shirts and the preferred colors for their friend's wedding, but the wording and the trimming is different. Such as, Kendra's glass has 'Country Swagger,' on one side and on the other side is her name with the number 4 underneath that, which represents the neighborhood South Park where her, Shanay, and Audumn grew up in.

Kendra's cousin, Shanay's glass has 'College Girl,' on one side and on the other side is her name and underneath reads, 'Where's the Party @?' Shanay wanted to drink a lot like all the other girls are doing, but her Nana, Ms. Boswell, taught her that if she's in a group of people and everybody is drinking, that she shouldn't drink as much because she might be called upon to be a designated driver. And besides, from the looks of Kendra's roaming eyes, she doesn't have to have another drink because her second cousin has had enough for the both of them. Hell, probably all of them.

Gayriale and Khamil's wineglasses are nearly the same because they are nearly the same. Well, in personality that is. Gayriale's glass says, 'Black is Beautiful' and Khamil's says, 'Beautiful is Black,' because they both love their Africa's first woman skin color. On the opposite side of both of their cups are their names and a mirror with a princess frame around it, so that they can always look upon their undeniable beauty.

Kizzy and Diana designed their glasses according to why tonight's Bourbon Street is so lit. Yes, Bourbon Street is always turned up on the weekends, but tonight it's really turned up because the Saints are playing the Texans on Sunday. Kizzy's glass has the New Orlean's Saints symbol, the fleur-di-lis, on one side and on the other side is her name and the state of Louisiana. Diana's glass has the Houston Texan's red and blue bull on one side and on the other side are the words, "I Am That Bitch!" And tonight, that's just how's she's feeling with all the numerous drinks flowing freely through her bloodstream. But that's only the half of it, her waist trainer has her BBW curves popping and her Red Bottom tennis shoes are letting all the women know that she has come to slay.

Houston is definitely in the house tonight and the Texan jerseys walking along the French streets of N.O. are just as plenty as the Saint's fans who are out supporting their hometown and the game in two days. Down below, sitting on crates, little boys play the bottom of buckets at a fast pace as if they were stepping onto the field to join a drumline. One even has a pair of Cymbals with a light up shoe tambourine on his foot jingling and clinging on beat at the precise time he knows to come in. Shanay is intrigued at their young talent and drops $2 into an old ballcap they had out in front of them.

The jazz music drowned the drummers out after taking only a few steps pass them. The tuba and the trumpet played in sequence, sending musical notes along with the accordion to the ears, bones, souls, and feet to everyone listening. Couples are swinging out to the music as Audumn and the girls stopped to look at a group of girls do some kind of New Orleans step none of them have seen before. Not even Kizzy, because she's been in Houston for the last 8 years. When the music came to an end, Kizzy went over and asked one of the girls to show them how to do the step that they were just doing, so that they can bring it back to Houston when they go out to the club.

"Come on, come on, ladies! The music is about to start again, yeah. And those girls over there from the Zetas are about to show us a new step to take back home to, Texas." Kizzy drunkenly chuckles because she just called Texas her home. "Hurry, hurry! Fall into place and let's show these people how Audumn's bridal party is turning up in the boot tonight." Kizzy urges all of the girls to get out there onto the imaginary dance floor, but stops Audumn when she's passing her. "I know I'm drunk and Kizzy's drunk too, but you can't drink no more because you're drunk and your babies might be drunk." Kizzy pokes Audumn's stomach with her finger.

"Huh? I don't know what you just said, but I'm drunk and Audumn's drunk too and I'm not drinking no more because my babies might be drunk."

Kizzy holds up the OK hand gesture and nudges Audumn towards the other girls. *I ain't understand nothing that girl just said,* she thought, walking behind Audumn. *Poor child can't even see that she's drunk.*

The jazz music really turned up when the large group of ladies stepped onto their platform. The Chicas love to step and to learn knew steps, so it took the three of them no time to catch their left and right foot up with the Zetas, who are calling out the steps so that all of the people watching can learn them. After the Chicas caught on, the rest of the bridesmaids followed their lead and after they got it down pat, they started adding the Texas version to it. Like dropping it down to the floor and bouncing your butt when your left foot goes back or shaking your hips and shimmying when the right foot goes forward. The crowd loved it and the men stepped back and let the onlooking ladies join in with the rest of the women on the street to have some fun. Laughter and chants traveled throughout the audience as the music extended and the cheers for the girls began to get louder. When the music came to an end, the band's bucket for donations is halfway full with change and dollar bills to show their appreciation for such a great jazz performance.

Everybody is sweating and are all smiles when they walk off down the street with the Zeta women from where they were performing. Earlier that day at Southern University, a few of the Zeta guys gave them a couple of $15 off coupons for a group of four or more for the Saints and Sinners restaurant and they gave one to Diana because they already used the other one earlier. Jade Mintz is the woman's name who gave it to Diana and she said that they must use the coupon today because it expires at midnight. She also said that later they're having a party in the dorms and that all of them are invited if they want to come.

"Here's my number. If you're serious about coming to a New Orleans Zeta party, then hit me up and I'll send you my location. If not, enjoy the crawfish because Saints and Sinners has some of the best food in town." Jade said, waving goodbye to her new friends. "By the way, the party starts at two. Toodles!"

Saints and Sinners is strictly about displaying their French heritage. There's high lights around the long bar, large bottles of booze along the wall behind the bartender, and Cajun music from the early 1900's playing from the speakers. Not to mention the smell of crawfish seasoning and crab boil that is tickling every sense in their noses as they part their way through the people drinking and having a good time on the floor.

"We up in this thang and I'm hungry like crazy." Diana said, letting a family pass by after eating their meal. "Come on Chicas, let's get those two tables that family just got up from before the waiter cleans them and gives them to somebody else." Diana hastens over and sits down. "What are you guys waiting for? She exclaimed. "I'm hungry and I'm drunk and I feel like sucking on something, so I guess it's gon' have to be some crawfish tonight." Diana catches Kizzy before she sits down with the rest of the girls. "Kizzy, go tell your people to come clean this table and that we're ready to order."

"Uh, uh, baby, I know you didn't. I'm not your maid, no!"

"Damn it, Kizzy, you hear the music they got playing up in this place?! I was just asking you that because these are your people and you may know the right words to say to get a big bitch like me something eat, like now." Diana turned towards the group to address the girls. "I'm sorry, but you got to excuse me because unlike you little bitches, I's get a little hungry from time to time."

"Ouu, you're lucky I don't feel like playing with you tonight, Diana because you crazy enough already." Kizzy looks over the tables and the girls look back at her with starving faces. "Okay girls, what are we getting?"

"I want crawfish." Khamil answered first raising her hand.

"Crawfish is fine for me too."

"I don't know why, but I should've guessed that, Gayriale." Kizzy looks down at Audumn and shakes her head.

"If we eating crawfish, we got to get the corn, sausage, and potatoes too."

"Shanay's right. You can't eat no crawfish without eating the corn, sausage, and potatoes with it." Kendra added her thoughts to the conversation. "Count me in. I'm cool with eating some crawfish if we gon' go all the way with it like my cousin say do with all the extra trimmings."

"Audumn, what do you think?" Shanay asks.

"Who me? I really ain't tripping because I'm drunk, hungry, and this is my last party night as a Humphry girl, so I feel like sucking on something." Everyone giggled at the table at Audumn's silliness.

"Well, all righty then." Diana exclaimed, leaning back to let the busboy slide the dirty dishes and trash onto a tray. "Excuse me, Mr. handsome New Orleans guy on Bourbon Street, could you please tell the waiter we're ready to order. I think it's safe to say that we've all come to an agreement that Audumn's bridal party is ready to suck on something while we're down here in the French Quarters."

"Will do, ma'am." The busboy's eyes got big after hearing Diana's request. "By the way, I love the shirts and enjoy the whole Saints and Sinners experience."

Everyone loved to eat the mudbug at the table, so when the 25 lbs. came with the extra additives, all the girls dug in with their plastic white gloves on. The gloves lasted only but a minute because Texas girls like to suck the spices off their fingers after they pull the tail off, peel it, eat it, and then suck the head like a Wendy's Frosty that refuses to come up the straw. This is the part of eating crawfish where men sit in the background and wait for the women around to suck the crawfish head like a pro, so that they can judge who's the best at what men love to get from women the most.

Diana looks to her left right after her and the crew were sucking a crawfish head at the same time. "Go on with y'all perverted assess!" Diana stands and shoos a group of white guys away and they start looking at it each other like, *Who me?* "It never fails when it comes to men. White, black, yellow, or green they all act like they ain't seen a woman suck a head before!"

"Oh my," Gayriale replied. "I'm a Christian."

"A bougie Christian is more like it, baby. And don't act like you ain't got no freak in you, yeah." Kizzy breaks the claw and sucks the meat and juice out of the shell. "Because I know you."

Audumn is pigging out and the juices from the crawfish is bringing her alcohol level down a bit. "Yeah Gay. We ain't about to have church up in here on my New Orleans night out on the town because I'm here to party!"

"Audumn's right! It's almost eleven o'clock and this crawfish got my drink coming down." Kendra pours beer into her glass out of the pitcher they got for free with the meal. "I'm from Beaumont, Texas and we don't turn down in a city that never sleeps!"

"What do we do, cousin?" Shanay asked, knowing that New Orleans is about to let out a monster.

"We turn up cousin because turning down isn't an option!" Kendra stands up and shouts, "Us Texas girls are in the house tonight, so watch out Louisiana because we about to get yo city lit from all our country swagger!"

"I'm down, Kendra." Khamil looks to see if her face is still on in the wineglass mirror Audumn gifted her. "I think it's about time to turn New Orleans inside out like we do in Texas."

Diana whispers something in Audumn's ear and Audumn whispers the message in Kizzy's ear. When they're finished talking amongst themselves and shaking their heads yes, they all extend their hand over the top of what's left of the crawfish platter in the center of the table.

Audumn is the first to speak. "Ladies, tonight we, the founding members of the Chicas, have come to the conclusion to do something that we thought we would never do between the three of us."

Kizzy followed behind Audumn after she finished her sentence. "But after spending these last four months with all of you and seeing the hard work you've put in for a woman we all love."

"And drinking with us, riding with us, partying with us, and taking our shit throughout this whole getting ready for the wedding process." Diana becomes a little teary eyed when she speaks because she sees that Audumn has people in her corner who are going to be there for her like her and Kizzy are.

Audumn sees her friend is tearing up and speaks up on her behalf. "What Diana, Kizzy, and I are trying to say is that we now extend our first invitation to you to be a part of our group, the Chicas. If you accept, please place your hand on ours in the center of the table."

All the girls placed their hands, one by one, on top of each other. Each of them have their own lives to live, but at the end of the day, good friends are hard to find. Gayriale and Khamil have more boy friends than girl friends back home and they've got to admit that being around the Chicas they've found someone who understands them. Kendra and Shanay have been hanging out with the Chicas a while now and were going to end up letting them know that they wanted to be a Chica soon anyway. Therefore, tonight's invitation and initiation just saved their breath from when they were going to ask later.

"On three, Chicas for life," Audumn exclaimed. "One, two, three!"

"Chicas for life!" they all shouted, catching the eyes and ears of every race in the Cajun bar and restaurant.

Back onto the pavement, the bridesmaids are officially Chicas and the party that they thought started earlier, they now realize has just begun. Walking past a man posing as a Saint's clown jester with two middle fingers up, the music from the statue man on a pedestal started playing up ahead and the man behind the silver costume began dancing. He's really getting his boogie on and has got more dance moves than you can count as he glides across the street like he's done this a time or two before. Also, being a professional statue artist, every time the music stopped, he would stop and stand as a statue.

The Swamp bar's neon green and black sign catches the eye of Kizzy first and immediately gives her an idea. "Hey, how about we ride the bull at The Swamp bar like they do in all the books and the movies about girls going on a girl's trip to New Orleans?"

"So now we're going from sucking to riding?" Kendra asked, ready to see if the fake bull can handle a sexy cowgirl like herself. "Ayeeee!!!" She shouts waving her hand in the air and shaking her butt to the beat of, 'Set It Off,' by little Boosie coming from the balcony as they approached. "I don't know about y'all, but I'm ready to set it off like Boosie and get my Country Swagger glass filled to the top with that swamp juice errybody be talkin bout when they come to the boot."

Entering inside The Swamp bar, all seven of them hear the first lyrics and bars of, 'Set It Off,' are about to be rapped and all at once they look at each other and screamed, "They call me Badass and I'll punish you! You ain't my equal, we ain't people, and I ain't one of you!" Not just them, but the whole bar went into an uproar rapping the whole song because Boosie is a Louisiana native and the song has been tested over time. The mechanical bull is out back and after everybody besides Audumn got their glasses refilled with the very intoxicating swamp juice, Audumn is the first into the square aired arena to ride. She didn't last but only a second, but quickly jumped back on only to be thrown off again in two seconds.

"Hold up, hold up! I got this." Audumn stops Gayriale from stepping onto the matt after she sees her bust her tailbone a second time. "Let me try one more time Gay and it's all yours. Promise."

Diana shouted, "Turn the speed up and let's see how much she really got this!" to the woman operating the on and off switch and the speed dial.

Meanwhile, not too far from the French Quarters, on the corner of where two streets form a V underneath a murky overpass and under a 150W outdoor LED street light is a strip club by the name of, She She's. Inside, you will find some of New Orleans finest, thickest, prettiest, and openly hospitable women the city has to offer at one in the morning for a groom and his groomsmen looking for a very special good time. It is here where Secorion's first cousin Brian allowed Google maps to take them in their SUV after drinking the famous Hand Grenades with the rest of the party on Bourbon Street. And with it being hurricane season, it is also here where they've been making it rain like Hurricane Katrina since they entered the building at midnight.

"Cuzo, this got to be some of the baddest bitches in town." Brian thumbs one dollar bills over the head of a redbone stripper giving him a lap dance. "I mean, look at the breasts on this fine specimen on top of me. It's like her areolas are telling me to kiss them." Brian puts one in his mouth and massages the other one.

"You stupid, B.G., for real." Secori laughs at his cousin Brian motorboating the stripper's bosom while putting ones in her G-string along her hips. "I see Cherry Pie fixing to break you real fast and real soon because you ain't let her go since we got up in this VIP section."

"More like she ain't let me go, big cuz." Brian laughs his famous laugh that sounds a lot like Tommy's laugh on Martin. "And don't be trying to stunt on me because I'm having a most awesome, exuberant, fantastic, great time."

"That's right B.G. tell'em to stop watching you and watch 5 Star who got her cat all up in his face!" Cori comes over and hand's Secorion a stack of ones. "Here, big bro, gon' on and tip her on me."

"I see you found you one, brother in law!" Brie shouts over the music at Secori tucking some ones in the crotch of 5 Star's G-string who has pulled back the gusset for him to see why she will never be broke. "I would ask for her next, brother in law, but I think she's taking a liking to you and you only."

The section is jumping and big enough for all seven of them to have a girl on each of them and one on the pole that they've purchased at top dollar for the groom. Even though they all can have a girl, doesn't mean that they all had a girl. Robby, Brie, and Nick are drunk and high and being that they have white blood in them, they were going to party like a rock star regardless if that's what they came to do. And by George, that's exactly what they came to do. The stripper Fantasy was fulfilling Robert's every fantasy, Erotic is arousing Nickolas sexual desires, and Brown Sugar is giving Aubrie a taste of just how sweet she can be for the ole mighty dollar. Everyone is having a good time, even Dexter, who is sitting in the back corner watching his brothers and brother in law go all out for their bachelor party. He's no party pooper, so he came along to spend time with his family, even though he's only drank water all day and has waved off each dancer until they got the picture that he's not interested.

Twerk music comes on and the beat really gets the strippers to bouncing and shaking their asses like they were in a contest. The DJ looks across the stage and sees She She's baddest chicks doing their best performance as Brian and Cori throw stacks of ones down upon them like they do in the Chi when they go to the strip club. Robby has plenty of money too and doesn't want Secori's kinfolks to show him up and therefore, opens the levies and when he does, his younger brothers followed suit behind him.

Money is everywhere and after the girls stuffed their Crown Royal bags, 5 Star pulled Secorion through a hidden door outside of the VIP section. No one noticed that he disappeared and honestly, no one really cared because of the waving titties and implanted assess in their faces. At first, Secorion's drunkenness didn't allow him to process that he was in another room in a matter of seconds. When he finally realized where he is, the red light came on and he's being pushed onto a leather sofa.

"So, I hear you're getting married in a few days?"

"Yep, you said it correctly." Secorion looks up at 5 Star as she straddles her leg over his lap to enjoy the ride. "Secorion Woodson will be getting married on Sunday to the beautiful Audumn Humphrey."

"Sounds like you really love her," she whispers in his ear and then nibbled on his earlobe.

"I do."

"I do, huh?" 5 Star brings her lips and eyes to his.

"I do! I do! I do! And when the preacher asks me Sunday it's going to be the same thing." Secorion replied, standing his ground, knowing that this red light special is only going to go as far as he lets it. "But that doesn't mean I can't enjoy a good dance from a vivacious woman such as yourself."

"Can I touch?"

"You can touch, but when I say that's enough then that's enough."

"Okay, big daddy." 5 Star runs her cold hands up Secorion's shirt and ruffles the small chest hairs he has in the center of his chest. "And just so you know, out of all my years in these strip clubs, there hasn't been one man who's turned down 5 Star and I let him get away with it. But, out respect for you, your marriage, and Audumn I'm going to let you make it, sugar."

Secorion sits back, knowing he can have her, but his love for Audumn made him think twice. "I got one request."

"Anything for you, big daddy." 5 Star is really aroused by Secorion and hopes he will give her the green light so that she can show the groom how she got her name.

"Tomorrow or shall I say today, I have a long day ahead of me getting prepared for my wedding Sunday. This is my last night as a bachelor and I want to have some fun, but not at the expense of violating my vows tomorrow."

"Aww, you're so sweet and handsome." 5 Star slides her thong off and her attitude changed from innocent to the aggressor. "Now shut up and let me show you what this pussy can do when you request 2 Star instead of getting the whole 5!"

Secorion is surprised by the sudden change of persuasion. "Yes, ma'am and please be gentle," he whispers jokingly as he relaxes and allows his eyes and hands to enjoy the show.

CHAPTER 15

I gotta tell her. For one, I should've told her when it happened. And two, it's been eating me up inside since my sister told me Audumn is pregnant in an early morning text before she went to New Orleans, Tree thought, driving 100 mph down I-10 to Beaumont, Texas. *The wedding started at five, but I didn't leave Houston until about a quarter til, so I should be getting to the Holiday Inn around six.* "Damn!" He shouts to the windshield while pressing harder on the gas pedal. *What have I done, Lord? I love Audumn. Everybody knows I still do, but if she's moved on and evidently, she has, then I need to keep it real and tell her the truth about my condom malfunction when we had sex on her couch.*

Tree opens the sunroof of his Mercedes Benz to allow some fresh air inside the car because his palms and armpits won't stop sweating. *Out of all the days I've had to do this, this is day I choose to do it on.* Tree shakes his head in disbelief that he's really on a mission to disrupt the love of his life's wedding day. *Please Jesus, forgive me for always ruining Audumn's life. First jail and now this.* Tree hangs his head in disgust, but quickly lifts it when construction workers along the highway make him merge from three lanes to two in Hankamer, Texas. *It just ain't right, Lord. No one deserves what I'm about to do on their wedding day. I just wish my sister would've told me earlier, so that it wouldn't have had to come to this.* Tree's thoughts bring tears to his eyes because this is the last thing Audumn deserves on top of everything else he's put her through over the years. *I'm sorry Father for my years of disobedience that never fails in letting you down as I strive to be a Christian. But, whether I'm wrong or right, Audumn deserves to know the truth before she says I do. Amen.*

It's 5:40 p.m. when Tree parked in between the white lines in front of the Holiday Inn. He doesn't know how he's actually going to play this, but what he does know is that he has to let Audumn know the secret that he's kept for the past two and half months from everybody, including her. Fast walking through the electric doors he goes to the front desk and taps the bell twice for service. Two employees quickly appear from a side door behind the counter, hoping that it's not a manager who rang the bell.

"Welcome to the Holiday Inn on Walden Road. and how may we help you today?" One of them asked while the other went back to the back to finish what he was doing.

"Yes, I'm looking for Audumn Humphrey's wedding. She's getting married here today to a Secorion Woodson." Tree pauses to let the clerk type Audumn and Secorion's names into the computer. "If I'm not mistaken, I think their wedding started at five."

"Here we go." The clerk replies, looking at the directory on the monitor. "Secorion and Audumn Woodson's wedding is in room #409, which is at the end of that hall to your left."

"Thanks, and sorry if I disturbed you by ringing the bell more than once."

"It's okay, sir. And if there's not anything else I can help you with today, enjoy the wedding ceremony."

Tree frowned when she said the word enjoy because there's nothing enjoyable about telling a woman that the babies she's carrying may be for him and not the man she's going to marry. Leaving the counter, he slowly walks to the edge of the hall the wedding is on and peeks around the corner to see if someone he may know is lingering in the hallway. Who he sees is the person he's in love with dressed in the most beautiful dress his eyes have ever seen, standing next to her father while two ushers hold open a set of double doors. Reacting quickly, he pulls his head back out of the hall and places his back against the wall to help brace himself. *There's no need to get cold feet now, Tree. Audumn is right there. It's either now or never.*

"Audumn!" Tree blurted out, pushing himself off the wall and into the hallway. The only thing is, is that she didn't hear him because the wedding music drowned him out as her and her dad start walking through the doors. "Audumn wait, it's me, Tree!" he shouts again as he jogs a light jog down the hall to room #409. But as he got closer, his chances of him telling her grew slimmer at the sight of the train of her wedding gown dragging through the doors and closing behind her.

Standing there, Tree wonders what to do next as he looks through the windows of the doors at Audumn's dad stopping and taking a picture with his daughter before giving her away to Secorion. His thoughts are in a sham because the smile on Audumn's face is priceless and to remove that smile with his terrifying news will not only hurt her, but him tremendously. Staring through the glass that separates him from her, his mind puts him in the burnt orange tuxedo Secorion is wearing and a smile graces his lips. The smile came from the thought of him marrying her, touching his heart in a way that he's hasn't felt since he had Audumn in his arms a few months ago. Star struck, he doesn't notice that Audumn has scanned over her guests in the audience and her eyes have stopped down the center of the aisle that divides the seating arrangement.

"Holy shit!" Tree says to himself after ducking beneath the windows. *Do you think she saw me?* "This is not right. I don't know what I was thinking driving way down here to stop the one person who has made me happy happiness. Yes, the condom bust, but so what?" Tree paces in the hall outside of the ceremony. "Me and Audumn were together for almost 7 years having unprotected sex and not once did she come up pregnant or have a miscarriage. So now all of a sudden I'm supposed to believe that my sperm knows how to swim instead of sink like they've always done in the past?" Tree sarcastically chuckles to his baby making dilemmas, but becomes serious again. "I love you, Audumn and I pray you and Secorion live your happily ever after. I'm out and be blessed from this day forward."

However, on the opposite side of the glass window, the same opposite side of the glass window Tree is standing on, lies an Autumn Princess waiting to be betrothed to her Prince. Her dress is an autumn red lace with a satin burnt orange background to match her sparkled heels and veil. The bodice grabs her figure, pushing up her breasts while flirting a hint of cleavage to add to her strapless shoulders, which in turns brings out her perfect neckline. Her waist is the size of the small part of an hourglass and her skirt poofs out like Cinderella's did when she took the prince's hand to dance on the ballroom's floor. Everything about her gown is breathtaking and as one continues to gaze upon the dress' beauty, the optical illusion of flowers with pearl centers begins to pop out more than once to the onlookers relishing in the garment's indisputable characteristics. Audumn is all that and more in the wedding gown her mom and Ms. Boswell picked out for her time in the sun. And yet, adorned in all her splendor, she's standing in front of Secorion, stupefied and as pale as a ghost. *Torrance?* she thought.

Audumn's dad found his seat next to her mother's and when he did, Pastor Colbert raised his hand and said, "Let us pray." Pastor Colbert bowed his head and begin to pray a prayer of love, forgiveness, contentment, and asked that the covering of the Father and his son Jesus continue to keep them under their wings as God would be the head of their household. During the prayer, you can hear people throughout the guests say, "Amen," in agreement to all the petitions the pastor has presented before the Lord in Heaven on behalf of the future Mr. & Mrs. Woodson. Secorion's head is bowed during the prayer, but he opened his eyes briefly to admire his queen only to see her eyes fixated on the entrance she just walked from.

"Say babe, are you alright?" Secori whispered to the shell of a woman in front of him whose mind is clearly not at the wedding that he's attending. Audumn turns toward Secorion, but her head slowly retracts back down the aisle. "Audumn, what's wrong? It's our wedding and you're clearly not standing up here with me."

"But I thought I saw…"

"What, a ghost?" Secorion lividly replied, so that only she can hear him. "Because that's exactly what you're acting like right now."

Pastor Colbert said, "Amen," and asked if everything is okay because he overheard Secori murmuring to Audumn throughout his prayer for them. Secorion nods his head to the pastor's question and Pastor Colbert, then proceeds with the ceremony.

"Today is a glorious day for Audumn and Secorion Woodson, but I would like the congregation to also know that it's a glorious day for me as well. My reasons for stating that is on behalf of the fact that I had the pleasure in watching Audumn grow up in my church from the time she was five years old up until the time she graduated high school. I remember her always attending Sunday school, Vacation Bible School, church services, carnivals, plays, and saying a speech or two in a few of our Easter and Christmas programs. But," Pastor Colbert pauses to gather his thoughts and his words that he has for the bride. "My fondest remembrance of her is when she was about eight years old and she came to me with her beaver teeth and asked me if she could be baptized." The congregation laughs at the picture the pastor painted in words for them to see. "I thought it was so cute to see a girl who never joined my church, but came faithfully with our member Sister Janice Boswell, to get up at the end of church service and say that she accepts Jesus Christ as her personal savior and that she wanted to be baptized as soon as possible. My heart went out to Audumn that day and she taught me that you don't have to be a member of Paradise Baptist Church to get saved because as long as one gets saved, they will find the church home God has called them to be a part of. Amen."

"Amen," came from everyone attending all at once.

Pastor Colbert continued. "I said that to make everyone aware that there's no other day as glorious as one getting saved, but what we are gathered here today for is right up there with it in the eyes of the most high God. This is why I am so honored to be the overseer of these two becoming one in the eyes of man and God. I watched this beautiful young lady grow in Christ before and after I baptized her and when these two's vows are complete, I will then watch her grow in Christ as the wife and helpmate of the man she chose to give her hand in marriage to. With that said, I ask, who gives this woman, Audumn Danyalle Humphrey, away today to be wed in Holy matrimony to, Secorion Woodson?"

"I do!" Her dad, Geary Humphrey, proudly stood and sat back down after the pastor told him to be seated.

I do, Audumn snaps out of her thoughts of what she thought she saw after she took her place with the groom. "I do!" she bellows out of her oblivion as she travels back down to earth to room #409 inside the Holiday Inn.

"Yes, my love, I do too, but we're not at that part yet." Secorion replied to her outspokenness.

Khamil has known Audumn since they were in pre-k and she knows something isn't sitting right with Audumn. *I hope my girl is okay because this isn't like her. Yes, she can be shy sometimes, but she has always been ready to live for the moment. Come on Audumn, snap out of it. Today is your wedding day, girl.*

"Oh." Audumn, shamefaced, covers her mouth with her hand and pushes Tree or whoever looked like Tree in the window out of her mind. "Sorry love, I don't know what came over me."

Secorion notices Audumn's skin color has returned and smiles because he feels his bride has regained her full consciousness. "Okay my love, I forgive you. I'm just glad your head is back in the game." Secori lifts her hand and kisses Audumn's knuckles. "I love you, Audumn. Now please, can we get on with our wedding?"

Pastor Colbert clears his throat to get their attention and they both straighten their posture to let him know they understand what he's trying to tell them nonverbally. "Dearly beloved, we gather here today in the sight of God, to join together this man, Secorion Woodson, and this woman, Audumn Humphrey, on this holiest day of matrimony commended to be honorable of all; and therefore, is not to be entered into lightly, but reverently, passionately, lovingly, and solemnly. Into this matrimony, I now present these two persons to be joined from this day and forever more. If any person can show just cause why they may not be joined together, let them speak now or forever hold their peace."

Please, please, please don't let Tree come busting up in here talking about how he loves me in front of all me and Secorion's family. Audumn thought, looking straight ahead while praying that the person she thought she saw doesn't make an entrance at this time.

Pastor Colbert allowed the silence to speak in the room before proceeding since no one stood or spoke up to object the vows that the participants of today's holy matrimony will soon be taking. "True marriage begins well before the wedding day, and the efforts of marriage will continue well beyond the ceremony's end. A brief moment in time and the stroke of the pen are all that is required to create the legal bond of marriage, but it takes a lifetime of love, commitment, and compromise to make a marriage durable and everlasting." Pastor Colbert pauses to allow Brian to hand Secorion some tissues because his eyes won't stop dripping tears upon his cheeks. "Today, you declare your commitment to each other before family and friends. Your yesterdays were the path to this moment, and your journey to a future of togetherness becomes a little clearer with each new day."

The room is silent as everyone listened to the pastor speak life and abundance over the soon to be Woodsons. Audumn's mom and Ms. Boswell are enjoying their moment in time because love is in the air and no matter how one feels at the present time, you can't help but feel what is no doubt in the atmosphere. Side by side, they sit in their matching autumn red dresses and big hats to show their support for the girl they raised for this specific day when Audumn found a man that will take care of her. Not only them, but also her bridesmaids are proud of the man she chose to take home to momma because they know from times past that Secorion has and will always be there for her by any means necessary.

Pastor Colbert opens his Bible and the rings the ring barrier, Phil, gave him are sitting between the pages, waiting to be placed on their new owners. "There's symbolism involved in the giving and exchanging of rings. Usually, if you look at rings with your eyes, you cannot tell where the rings begin, nor can we tell where they end. So, it is my prayer for you, Secorion and Audumn, that your love will be like this for one another and that there will be no end to your love for one another. But there's another thing that these precious rings also symbolize, and that's that we are fortunate that we're able to obtain these rings in their final state. But rings that are made of precious metals have to go through an intense purification process. Meaning that they are subjected to intense heat before they're given to us in the state that we see them in. It just may be, Secorion and Audumn, that your marriage may be tried intensely in the fire just as these rings and that the enemy may try to come against you with distractions to discourage you in what you already know our God in Heaven has put together for you. I want you two to remember that during this exchange of rings, know that, just as these rings survived the heat, it is my prayer that you two can also survive." Pastor Colbert hands Secorion the ring he's to put on Audumns' finger after he says his vows. "Secorion, I would like to ask if you will be kind enough to take Audumn's ring and while putting it on her left ring finger, please answer accordingly to what I am about to ask you under the eyes of God."

"Yes pastor, I will accept this ring to put on my love's ring finger, and answer truthfully to the questions you're about to ask me."

"Amen, brother Woodson." Secorion holds the ring in his fingers, ready to put it on the woman who stole his heart from the first day he laid eyes on her. "Do you, Secorion Woodson, take Audumn Humphrey to be your wife, to have and to hold from this day forward, for better or for worse, for richer, for poorer, in sickness and in health, to love and to cherish; from this day forward until death do you part?"

"I do."

"And Audumn, if you will take his ring and do likewise in putting it on his shaking ring finger," The crowd laughs at the pastor's humor and to Secori's nervousness that seems to have appeared from out of nowhere. "Do you, Audumn Humphrey, take Secorion Woodson to be your husband, to have and to hold from this day forward, for better or for worse, for richer, for poorer, in sickness and in health, to love and to cherish; from this day forward until death do you part?"

Audumn starts to cry as she's pushing Secori's ring on his finger. "I do."

"We will now have the pouring of the unity sand."

Secorion took his bride's hand and walked over to a table to his right that's decorated according to their wedding. On top are three glass jars. The jar to the left of the three is the shape of the letter B, which stands for bride and the color of the sand inside is autumn red to match the bride's dress. The jar to the right of the three is shaped in the letter G, which stands for groom and the color of the sand inside is burnt orange to match the color of the groom's tuxedo. The third glass jar that sits between the jars in which Audumn and Secori will be pouring from is empty and is in the shape of a heart to symbolize their love that was displayed on this day, September 13, 2013.

Each of them took their lettered jar that represents them and poured the sand into the center jar until the heart is filled to the brim with a beautiful mixture of their colored sand. When they're finished, Courtney snapped the perfect photo of the completion of the pouring of the unity sand to add with the others she took of them while they were pouring. "God bless you both, Mr. & Mrs. Woodson, and you two make a beautiful couple." The photographer stated before snapping more pictures of the newlyweds walking back to the pastor awaiting them under the wedding arch.

Pastor Colbert asks everyone to please stand. "Now for the moment we've all be waiting for. Could everyone please stand for these two beautiful God-fearing people who our Lord in Heaven has joined together in his son Jesus with the Father up above as the head of their household?" The crowd stood as requested. "Today, we have experienced on this evening the giving and the receiving of rings, the exchanging of vows, commitments made one to another, and the pouring of the unity sand. With that said, so it be that on this day, it's my pleasure that by the powers that have been invested in me, I now pronounce you, Audumn and Secorion, husband and wife. You may kiss the bride."

Secorion takes Audumn's veil in his hands and slowly rolls it up over the glossy eyes of his bride. "I love you so much Audumn and I always knew since I was a child that when this day came, I'd be right here kissing you."

"Aww…I love you too, Secorion Woodson." Audumn managed to say before their lips locked in a way that they've never locked before.

The kiss was long and it wasn't because of Secorion, but because Audumn wouldn't let his lips go. As she kissed him, she released her past completely. And she made a conscience decision that all her wrong doing and guilt that she's held up until this time for Tree will no longer hinder her in becoming the best wife and mother that she can be for the man in front of her. When the fireworks stop flying because of their kiss, Cori stepped from the line of groomsmen and walked in front of the newlyweds and hands Kizzy the long side of the wedding broom while he holds the bristled end. Simultaneously, they both squat and lay the broom on the floor in front of Audumn and Secori who has turned around towards the audience ready to jump when Aubrie or Nick say to.

"Will the crowd please stand for the woman who will always be our family princess and a man who's become like a brother to me, Audumn and Secorion Woodson!" Robert passes the microphone to Nickolas after riling up the guest for the welcoming of two families coming together.

"Are you ready, big sis?"

"Yes Nick, I'm ready."

"Are you ready, brother in law?" Aubrie pulled Nick's arm with the microphone in his hands to his mouth to ask Secori with the mic.

"Yeah Brie, I'm ready."

"Okay crowd, look at me!" Nick held his fist high above his head. "When I open my hand, I want everyone here to yell jump." Nick smiled at his mother on the front row who's standing in glee for being able to witness one of her children getting married before God calls her home. "Y'all ready?!"

"Yes!" was replied back to him from every seat on the floor in unison.

"Here we go guys!" Brie shouted to the crowd as his brother Nick pumped his fist two times above his head as if he's silently counting to open his hand on three.

And that's exactly what he did before shouting, "Jump!" with everyone else after gaining everyone's expectation.

Secorion had Audumn's hand gripped in his when they took their four-inch leap of fate into their happily ever after. When they landed, Audumn blew a kiss to her father who is very proud of the addition his daughter has brought home to be a part of his family. Secorion's dad and his Uncle Andre, couldn't help themselves and gave their son and nephew a high five to show their excitement towards their family member jumping the broom.

"You did well, my son. She's beautiful."

"Thanks pops, but please can you and unc go sit down because it's time for me to walk out with my bride." Secori grins to his dad and uncle's jolliness. "And get mom some tissues," he whispered. "She hasn't stopped crying since I said, 'I do.'"

"She just loves you son and you know how her side of the family feels about jumping the broom."

"I know, dad. I love the both of you, too." Secorion whispers.

The music came on and the singer and songwriter, Babyface's voice showered the completion of their wedding ceremony with the gifts god blessed his vocal cords with. The song chosen is the song Secorion wanted to be on the playlist for when he exits with the woman he can't shake from his mind whether his eyes are opened or closed. As the people remained standing, the song, 'Every Time I Close My Eyes,' captured the essence of what's inside his heart for Audumn while the two of them walked down the aisle and out the door in which everyone entered. Following them is Secorion's niece and nephew, Phil and Lil, Kizzy and Cori, Diana and Brian, Robert and Gayriale, Dexter and Khamil, Nickolas and Shanay, Kendra and Aubrie, and then their parents.

Pastor Colbert waited for Secorion's mother and father to step foot into the hall with the rest of the wedding party to give his closing remarks Kizzy asked him to do when all of the wedding party have exited. "This concludes the wedding ceremony of two beautiful God-fearing people. If you will please be so kind and exit in an orderly fashion to the parking lot for Mr. and Mrs. Woodson's autumn balloon release and for refreshments in the lobby. In doing this, we will allow the wedding crew to set up this room for the wedding reception that will be taking place in approximately thirty minutes. Thank you, and by the way, Ms. Diana Ross said that if you were in the wedding or a family member of the bride and groom then you better not leave until after we take pictures during the reception." Pastor Colbert raised his hand to the body language response from the guest because of his bidding. "Just kidding. Well, I hope she was just kidding." He smiled. "But I must say that I was thinking about cutting out of here early, but after she told me that, I'm staying until after we take pictures by Courtney Thibodeaux with Taken Images."

CHAPTER 16

An array of balloons sit captured underneath a canopy. As everyone exited into the parking lot, ushers hand each guest a sparkler to bring life to tonight's sky when the balloons are released shortly. With their sparklers in hand, each attendee goes to the canopy and grabs an orange, red, yellow, or green balloon to represent the lady of the hour's name. Standing in the midst of the surrounding sparkles, Audumn and Secorion kiss and scream, "We are now officially Mr. & Mrs. Woodson!" and release the balloons in their hands as everyone else did likewise.

"God bless you two lovebirds and I must say, Audumn, you look ravishing in that dress and to take care of my son for me."

"Yes, Ms. Dorion. I promise you that I will be the best bride you can ever ask for when it comes to being with your son, Secori."

"I know you will, Audumn. I knew from the first time my son told me all about you." Ms. Dorion rubs the back of Secorion's head. "You did well son and your wedding was ever so beautiful."

"Thanks mom, but where's dad?"

"He's over there mingling with the guys and my brother, probably talking about how the Bears will win the Super Bowl next year." Secorion's mom points towards a small huddle of middle aged men and he waves his father over to where they're standing.

"What's up babe, son, and daughter in law? What's shaking?" Mr. Woodson asks, taking a sip of his drink.

"Well mom and dad, me and your daughter in law have something to tell you."

"Oh, and what might this something be?" his mother asked, but her son, Cori, already told her via text that Secorion's having a baby and not to tell dad.

"Yeah son, spit it out." Mr. Woodson takes another drink. "It's not like you can't take me off my high horse already. Shoot, this is the best day of my son's life and if he's happy then I'm happy." Secorion's dad puts his arms around the both of them and a little bit of his Hennessy spills onto his son's shoulder. "Hell, the only thing that's going to make me happier than today for you two lovebirds is when you two have me and your mom's grandchild."

"And that will be in March next year." Audumn hurried and interjected or Mr. Woodson would have continued to drunkenly rant.

"What's happening in March next year?" Mrs. Woodson asks, acting surprised.

"Yeah, son and daughter, what's happening next year? I mean, did I miss something? Because one minute I was talking about you two having our grandchild and the next minute Audumn is saying next year in March."

"That's right, dad!" Secorion replied, knowing that his mom knows because he's her first born and he knows when his mother is surprised and is not. "Next year in March we are having twins."

"Twins?" Mrs. Woodson said, surprised. "You mean to tell me you two are having twins?"

"Yes ma'am." Secorion replied, silently thanking his brother for leaving out the best part.

"Oh, I am so happy for you two. First my son has gotten married and now I find out that I'm about to be a grandmother to two beautiful baby boys…Hold up, is that right?"

"We don't know yet, momma and papa Woodson. I don't have my next ultrasound for a few weeks."

"Wow son, this has turned out to be a most wonderful day or shall I say night." Secori's dad turned to his wife and gives her a big kiss. "Baby, we're about to be grandparents again!" he exclaimed, gulping down his drink before giving his daughter in law a kiss on her cheek.

"So, by Christmas we should know what to get our bundles of joy for the holidays."

"Yes ma'am," Secorion replied.

"And Audumn, are you two still coming to spend Christmas with us this year?"

"Yes ma'am. Of course we are, Momma Woodson. We will not miss it for the world. And besides, you and Mr. Woodson have visited us twice already. It's only right that we come to spend time with you now."

"And we can't wait to have you, Audumn."

"And mom, Audumn has never been to Chicago before."

"Well that will soon change, son. And when she comes, make sure to bring her to the Navy Pier."

Back inside, Taken Images is all setup to take pictures when the outside crowd came in to have a seat in the redesigned room for the wedding reception. After the wedding party sat and stood in their assigned spots, Courtney had her assistant/sister, Tiffany, adjust the lighting while she adjusted the lens on her camera. Audumn is sitting in the middle and Secorion is to the right of her with their hands overlapping each other's on top of their knees. Down below are Phil and Lil sitting on the floor in their bride and groom lookalike attire, waiting on the photographer to tell them to smile and show their missing teeth. Standing on side of the newlyweds are their parents, smiling ear to ear looking down on the blessing God blessed them with when their son and daughter were born.

Behind them are the maids of honor, the best men, then the bridesmaids and groomsmen standing according to their height and the way they walked in during the ceremony. Courtney said on three say, "Love," and when they did, she snapped a picture of a jointly happy family. No one knew it, but the picture that was captured is the last picture that will have Audumn's parents standing side by side cheerfully, making it the last picture her mom will cherish with all of her children in it until the day God calls her home.

Picture time is over and the volume of the music turning up by Beaumont's #1 D.J., Flava Dave, means that it's time to jam out and party. Secorion is taking pow wow's from the family and friends he invited, while Audumn is surrounded by family and friends congratulating her on such a glorious day. The huddle surrounding the bride dispersed back to their seats when they saw the caterers placing full course plates on the 6' round tables while asking everyone what would they like to drink with their meal. Audumn is walking back to the table of honor for the bride and groom on her dad's arm when a black woman in her late forties approaches the bride to give her felicitations.

"Hi, my name is Jenny, which is short for Jennifer, and I want to say congratulations on getting married and the bundles of joy that will soon be added to your family."

Audumn wonders who this woman is and how she knows about her babies when the only people who know are her immediate family and the people who are close to her.

"Thanks Jenny." Audumn smiles, but the smile is fake and it's only on her face not to be rude. "Are you a friend of the groom or did you come today with one of my guests?"

Jenny looks confused and wonders why Audumn has never heard of her. "No, I'm here with your…"

"Audumn, this is my friend, Jennifer, and my guest for the day." Audumn's dad, Geary, intercedes to help lighten the approach of his girlfriend.

"Your guest? What do you mean your guest? What, do you two work together or something because please don't tell me what I think you're about to tell me?" Audumn bites her lip and her face turns almost the color of her dress as she looks up at her dad. "And if you are, then why in the hell is she at my wedding when we discussed this and clearly had an agreement?"

"I know baby, but she really wanted to come see my baby girl get married. So please, can you make an exception for your old man this one time?" Geary tries to kiss his daughter on the forehead, but she leans back before he can.

"An exception!" Audumn yells over the music that turns off as soon as her voice reached its peak. "Did you give my mom an exception when you were creeping around on her with this bitch when she had cancer a few years back? Or when you left the day before Christmas last year saying you were on your way to work? Or better yet, did you give me and my brothers an exception when we stood up for you when mom had a suspicion that you were cheating on her?" Audumn turns towards Jennifer and thinks about how bad she's been wanting to see the homewrecker that has aided in taking her dad away from her mother. "Here, I guess these are for you!" Audumn takes her bouquet of flowers and throws it in Jenny's face and slides her feet out of her heels. Her dad notices that his daughter has gotten shorter and knows what's about to go down when Audumn pulls her snap on earrings off and tosses them onto the table. "I hope you two live up to your expectations when you two decide to get married. But before y'all do, I have an exceptional ass whooping for you from my mom sitting over there to your left and a congratulations ass whooping from me on you two becoming one at my mom's heart's expense."

Secorion comes over to see what has turned his wife's smile into a frown. "Audumn, are you okay and why are your shoes off?"

Audumn continues to look at her dad while answering Secorion's question. "They're off because I'm about to make an exception and accept this hoe bitch snake whore and homewrecker's congratulations on my wedding day."

"Huh?" Secorion asks, praying that Audumn isn't about to do what he thinks she's about to do.

"Audumn no!" her mother screams as her daughter lashes out to grab a handful of Jenny's hair and swings her around throwing her to floor.

"Bitch, the nerve of you coming to my wedding to ruin my day and my mom's day." The reception hall is on their feet because the commotion from the bride and this mysterious woman has now gone to the next level. "Wedding or no wedding, I'm about to do what my mom is too much of a lady to do. And that's beat your ass and throw your ugly bad built ass up out of here afterwards."

Audumn rushes her while she's down and tries to kick, but Secorion yanks her back in midair before she can land a blow. "Baby no! Please don't do this on our wedding day with all our family here visiting us."

"Put me down. This ho ain't my family!"

"No, my love. Not until you calm down."

"Yeah sis, she's not worth it. And dad, you should be ashamed of yourself bringing her here, knowing how Audumn just let you back into her life." Dexter tries to help calm the situation down before round two starts.

"What?" Jenny gets up and tries to straighten her hair that's all over her head. "I am so sorry, Audumn. I knew a few months back that you and your dad had your differences, but last month he told me that you two made up and that he told you all about me." Jenny pauses and thinks about how foolish she was in coming here. "I promise you Audumn that I wouldn't have come here today, but your dad invited me, so here I stand." Jenny realized that she perhaps ruined Audumn's wedding day by attending. "I'm sorry for coming, Audumn, but please know that this isn't my doing. Out of respect for me not being wanted here, I'll leave."

Secorion lets Audumn go when her brothers make a wall between her and the lady. "Are you okay, honey?" he asked. "Please just let her leave in peace so that we can get back to entertaining our guests."

"Hell no, I'm not okay! I'll be okay when I see the doors close behind that heifer and my dad when they get the hell up out of here."

"But baby."

"Don't but baby me, daddy! I told you what I wanted from you and you didn't comply, so now you can get up out of here too." Audumn begins to cry. "And as far as I'm concerned, I don't want to see or hear from you ever again. I hate you daddy and please go be with your whore because from this day on you're not welcome in my life or my kid's life that I'm carrying."

"But Audumn." Her dad tries to plea again.

"Just go!" Audumn points towards the exit and picks up one of her shoes that's nearby and runs out the opposite exit, crying and ashamed that everyone present has seen her get out of character on her wedding day.

"Audumn!" her mother yells when seeing her daughter dash out of the hall, but Audumn didn't stop because she's angry and she knows her mom and Ms. Boswell are disappointed in her.

Diana and Kizzy run behind her when Audumn makes her exit. Both of them are appalled at what their eyes and ears have witnessed from the time the D.J. turned off the music to Audumn's high pitched voice. They didn't say anything because Audumn was fighting with her dad and his mistress; therefore, family business is family business. And two, Audumn needed to get off her chest what she felt towards her dad over her mom being cut to the bone from his longtime cheating scandal. Sad that it had to happen today of all days, Kizzy and Diana disregarded their judgements and comments because pressure that's released is better than pressure that has been stored up any day.

"Audumn, it's me Kizzy, open up." Kizzy speaks to the latched door of the lavatory stall. "Come on sugar, we know you're in there and you're messing up that pretty dress your mom and your play momma bought for you."

"Yeah Audumn, open up. Your mom paid too much money for that dress to have her daughter sitting on a toilet in it getting it damaged by this dirty floor." Diana chimes in to help sway their friend in unlatching the door. "Please best friend, don't let that old bag mess up your day. You said what you had to say, and they're both gone. I know it hurts to see your dad with that woman, but please know that this day is not just about you."

Audumn remains silent, so Kizzy tries to make her see the bigger picture. "Diana's right, Audumn, about today. Yes, this is your day of happiness, but this is also your husband's day of happiness too, yeah. Not only him, but your mom, Ms. Boswell, your brothers, Secorion's parents, and family who flew down here, and me and Diana's day as well." Kizzy tries to pull the handle, but the door is still locked. "Audumn, we all love you and we've all waited for this day to come for you. I mean, I don't see me getting married no time soon and Diana is Diana. I guess what I'm trying to say is that when you walked down that aisle today, we all walked down that aisle with you."

"What do you mean, Diana is Diana?" Audumn giggles in the stall to Diana's question to Kizzy. "I know I'm a big bitch, thick and tall that is, but I would like to think that I can catch me a man someday."

"Oh lord." Audumn said lowly.

"And what are you oh lording about? What you need to be oh lording about is how you got me in this bathroom in this $186.00 dollar dress that I squeezed my fat ass into for your wedding day."

Kizzy hears the door latch slide after Diana made her statement. "That's a girl, Audumn," she said, pulling the stall door open so that they can talk face to face. "Please sugar, don't let this woman come between you, your husband, and those beautiful babies you have in your stomach. I understand how you feel because my mom left my dad for another man when I was fourteen, but that still didn't stop me from becoming the woman you see standing before you now."

"I feel you Kizzy, but your mom ain't disrespect you like my dad did me today by bringing that wench to my wedding."

Secorion knocks on the door and sticks his head inside. "Is everything okay, may I come in?"

"Umm sir, this is the lady's restroom."

"It's all right, Diana. It's not like he hasn't seen me on the toilet before." Audumn wipes her eyes so that Secorion won't see how much she's been crying.

"Yeah Diana, maybe he can talk some sense into Audumn and get her back to her party."

"Thanks Kizzy." Secori comes all the way inside the restroom and the door closes on the bridesmaids trying to listen or see what's going on with Audumn. "How is she?"

"She's fine now I guess, but she still needs you to talk to her." Diana steps to the side to let him pass and Kizzy does the same. "It's on you now, husband. Me and Kizzy did our part in getting her to laugh instead of cry."

"Thanks, Diana." Secorion looks at his wife staring at him with puffy eyes. "Do you mind if I have a word with my wife?"

Audumn hears nobody move when her husband asked them for some privacy. "It's okay, Chicas, I'll be alright. If you don't mind, could you please tell the guests I'll be out shortly and that I apologize for the disturbance."

Secorion waits for the girls to leave and squats to be eye level with Audumn. "I got something for you."

"What, some tissues because this roll is about out?"

"No, my love." Secorion pulls her heel she left behind from the inside of his tux. "I have your glass slipper you left at the ball when the clock struck twelve and you ran out on me." Secorion smiles big and searches under the poofy skirt until he finds her foot. "Now the question is, does it fit?"

"What do you mean does it fit? Did it fit Cinderella or her stepsisters? Because last time I checked, I'm the only Cinderella in your fairytale."

"Yes, my love, you are the only Cinderella in my fairytale." Secori slides her foot into her shoe. "Always have been and will always be. I love you, Audumn Woodson."

"I love you too, my prince, and thanks for making me your wife."

"Come on baby. Let's get back to our wedding reception because I can't wait for us to dance our first dance together as a married couple."

Cori is the lookout for his brother to tell D.J. Flava Dave when Audumn and Secorion are coming. Before his brother left to check on his wife, he told the D.J. to introduce them when they come through the door and play, "Heaven Sent," by Keyshia Cole right afterwards for their first dance together. Audumn doesn't know this because they chose another song for this special occasion. This is because Secori has kept this song a secret and always told himself that whomever he marries, "Heaven Sent," will be the song he's going to dance with the woman of his dreams too.

"Shh!" Cori gives the D.J. the thumbs up that the man and woman of the hour is coming. "They're almost here in five, four, three, two…"

"Ladies and Gentlemen, boys and girls!" Flava Dave begins his greeting. "Tonight, we have witnessed two beautiful people becoming one. And after the pouring of the sand, jumping of the broom, and the release of autumn balloons, I now introduce to you, Mr. and Mrs. Audumn and Secorion Woodson." A standing ovation is given to them when they're walking through the double doors. "By the way, my name is D.J. Flava Dave and the Woodsons want to thank everyone for coming to share this priceless moment in time with them. If you will be so kind, please step off the dance floor for Audumn and Secorion's first dance as a married couple." Flava Dave turns on the soothing, but heavenly music the groom requested. "The floor is yours, Secorion. Now show her how you get down and let the words of the great Keyshia Cole tell your woman what's in your heart."

The words coming from the speakers Secorion knows by heart because he really loves the words to this song. Doing his best ballroom dance, he looks Audumn in her beautiful hazel eyes and serenades her like he said he was going to do on his wedding day when it comes. His eyes are dreamy because Audumn is his dream girl. Caressing her sexy figure, he spins her around during the chorus and places his hand on the small of her back to dip her. When Audumn comes up, she comes up to a kiss. Not just any kiss, but an electrifying kiss. One that sent chills down her spine and made the hairs on the back of his neck stand at attention.

"You're so beautiful, Audumn," he says as the song comes to end. "And from this day forward, I will never doubt my God in heaven because you and those twins you're carrying are heaven sent just like the title of this song I believe Keyshia Cole made specifically for me and you."

"Amen to that. And I feel the same way about you, my love." Audumn kisses him again and they both turn around for a quick bow on behalf of their loving performance.

"Are you ready to party people?!" the DJ shouts into the microphone. "Because that's exactly what we're about to do. Like I said before, my name is DJ Flava Dave and I'm Beaumont's #1 DJ. What that means is that if you're not trying to cut a rug or break a leg, then you can get up off my dance floor because all you're doing is taking up space." Flava Dave turns on the, "Wobble Baby," song to get everyone onto the dance floor, young and old, so that energy and life can set the tone for tonight.

"Chicas, let's show'em how we got down in New Orleans on Bourbon Street." Kendra said, taking off her heels so that she can be the first to lead the crowd in the renown steps made to dance to the song.

"You heard her, Chicas!" Kizzy shouts, pulling Gayriale's arm to get up. "Let's get this party started. And remember girls, Chicas never let their fellow Chica get up and step by herself without all of the Chicas present doing the same. We're one girls, and that means we got each other's backs no matter what."

"Yeah, and I can definitely dig that!" Khamil kicks her heels off and runs onto the dancefloor next to Kendra.

"Um, I think that's are cue to get our asses out there and get to backing it up like Khamil and Kendra are doing with everybody else." Diana stands and looks down at Shanay who is still sitting, but she catches the hint and gets up with the rest of the girls. "That's a girl, Shanay." Diana said, walking off singing the chorus, "Get in there! Yeah, yeah! Get in there! Yeah, yeah!"

"That's what I'm talking about people. Let's have some fun to break the ice from earlier." Flava Dave said that because the crowd was a little tense after Audumn placed her hands on her dad's side piece and voiced her opinion. "Afterwards, we will have the daddy and daughter dance." Everyone looked at him when he said that. "Oh, I'm sorry. What I meant was the mother and son dance."

"No, you said it right." Robert spoke up over the music. "Only change it to sister and big brother dance. I refuse to let my sister's day be out of sort because of my dad's decisions."

"Will do, Robby! Correction, big brother and little sister dance. And then mother and son dance."

Brian goes to the DJ booth when the DJ cranks the music back up. "Hey bro, good job on the ones and two's."

"Thanks Chi-Town. Do you have any request you want played?"

"No, I don't want a song played, but I do have a request to give my big cuz a toast before they cut the cake."

"Bet that, I got you. As soon as Secorion and his mother finish their dance, the mic and floor is all yours."

The night went on as if nothing ever happened. Brian made his toast to his cousin's new future and Aubrie made his toast to his sister's new future. Both of them accepted their toast whole heartedly and afterwards, they smeared wedding cake on each other's face. Friendships were also made on this unforgettable night and the alcohol loosened everyone up a bit to dance. Audumn smiled and Secorion smiled too as they embarked on the love they have for one another while Courtney snapped her camera throughout the night making sure she didn't miss a Taken Image moment.

However, Mrs. Humphrey and Ms. Boswell stayed seated because anguish has set in the mind of Audumn's mother and tomorrow she will let her family know what's been eating her up inside. And when she does, she wanted her friend Janice next to her to help her be strong and help her children cope with the unfortunate news.

CHAPTER 17

A udumn awakes to Secorion's arm around the backside of her neck and his hand cuffing her bare breast. Yesterday was full of mixed emotions, but the night capped off with a sweet sensation of two people releasing their bodily fluids on and in one another. The wedding was everything they both imagined, despite her disarray from who she thought she saw standing in the entrance door window and her dad bringing his unwanted guest. It took a while for her to get back on track, but when she did, drinking, congregating, laughing, and dancing helped set the tone of the beginning of their happily ever after.

11:00 sounded with a loud beep from the hotel's alarm clock sitting on the nightstand next to her ear. The night before, Secorion set it so that they can have an hour's time to take a shower and finish getting their stuff together for checkout. Audumn shut it off as soon as it went off and continued to lie underneath the covers snuggled in the arms of the man who accepted all her flaws and said, I do. With her lips, she kisses his nipples and with her finger she outlined a heart shape on his stomach, making his belly jump up and down from the feeling of being tickled.

Kissing the side of his neck, she tells him to wake up, but he doesn't move because last night she showed him with her mouth and her riding abilities that he chose the right one to ask to marry him. It isn't until she strokes his rising penis that his eyes open, ready for round four, but Audumn tells him that he will have to wait for when they take a shower. But, she did promise that he will not be disappointed and that if he gets up right now, he can hit it from the back after she sees how much of him can fit in her mouth.

Time is not on their side, so their wet and wild shower scene was cut drastically. Therefore, Secorion had to settle for a quickie, on behalf of the fact that someone knocked on the door and yelled, "Checkout is at noon!" Moving at an upbeat pace, Audumn got their bags together, while Secori went down stairs to get a luggage buggy. When he got back, his wife is sitting on the bed staring into thin air with her cellphone in her hands.

"You ready, baby?" He asks with a smile while waving his hand in front of her face. "Hey babe, you're not blacking out on me again, huh?"

"No, my love, I was just thinking about the text I just got from my mom."

"What's wrong with getting a text from your mother the day after you got married?"

"Nothing's wrong with getting a text from your mother the day after you get married. But something must be wrong if it says, we have a family meeting today in room 409, the one where we got married."

"Why in the same room we got married in, and not at her house?" Secorion looks confused. "Hold up, didn't she go home last night before our reception got lit and we took the party up to the next level?"

"Yes she did, but now she's back and that's what has got me worried because something's got to be wrong if she's calling a family meeting the day after we got married."

Secorion grabs the bags she's packed off the bed and puts them on the cart. "Or maybe she just wants to stand in the room her daughter got married in one last time with her family before everyone goes about their everyday lives." Secorion helps her to her feet. "I said that to say this. Don't be negative, my love, because it could be anything your mother wants to see or talk to you about."

"Yeah, but I know my mother."

"And yeah, let's keep our minds on a positive note as we both go see what the family meeting is all about."

"I guess you're right bae, and thanks for always having the right words to say when I'm in doubt or feeling down." Audumn only agreed because she didn't want to knock her husband off the high horse he's on from being married, but inwardly she remembered that the last time her mom called a family meeting it was because she had cancer.

The phone rang at 11:55. "Do you want me to get that?" Secori asked, thinking it may be one of her brothers.

"No, it's just the front desk giving us a courtesy call to get out this room asap."

"Courtesy call, huh?" Secorion laughed. "Come on bae, let's go see what's going on so that we can get back to being honeymooners these last two weeks before I go back to work on the 1st." Secorion opens the door for Audumn to walk into the hallway. "Shit…Just thinking about how I'm fixing to be wrapped up in your arms until I go to work makes me feel like I can't wait until February when we go on our honeymoon valentine's day cruise. I wish we could've done something now, but like we agreed on, we got to keep some money saved for the babies."

"It's all good, bae." Audumn said, thanking God that they made that decision because she has a bad feeling inside. "We'll make it up to each other when that day comes."

"Okay love, now let's go downstairs and tell everyone thank you for being there for us for our wedding."

Back on the first floor, Secori tells Audumn that he's about to put the bags in the car and tell his mom and pops that he will meet them in Houston after they go and do some sight seeing with his Uncle Andre. Their plane doesn't leave until seven out of Bush Continental, but Mrs. Woodson loved seafood and wanted to see what a certain restaurant, The Aquarium, is all about. From the looks of their website, it's one of Houston's main attraction because of its gigantic fish tank and tall Ferris wheel that stands next to and above I-45. His brother and cousin, on the other hand, checked out at eight because their plane departed at one and they wanted to make sure their rental car was returned and that their bags were checked in so that they won't miss their flight. Yes, they enjoyed their time in Texas, but at the end of the day, there's no place like home.

Audumn walked into the room she got married in, curious on what's about to be said by her mother. However, that curiosity diminished when she saw Ms. Boswell standing next to her mother waiting for her to come through the doors. The room is almost empty except for a table and a few chairs that her mother told her four brothers to sit in to hear what she has to say. Audumn took her seat next to Robby, knowing this isn't about to be good because he was supposed to be gone already, but he pushed his flight back to a later time for the family meeting.

"Where's Secorion?" Robert whispered when she scooted her seat up to the table.

"He went to tell his parents we'll catch back up with them in Houston."

"Good afternoon, my children," their mother said with a laden look on her face. "I know you're all wondering why I waited until today of all days to call a family meeting, but please know that I have my reasons and what I've got to say can't wait any longer because time is not on my side."

"What do you mean, time is not on your side, momma?"

"Dexter please let your mother finish saying what she has to say." Mrs. Boswell replied. "It's already hard enough for her to have to tell you what's going on with her."

"Yes ma'am."

"Thanks Janice." Ms. Boswell takes a deep breath and says, "It's back."

"What's back?" Nickolas asks, but he already knows the answer.

"The cancer is back son, and it's not looking too good."

"What do you mean it's back, momma?" Brie begins to cry. "It's been over five years already."

"I know it has Aubrie, but the severe case of cancer I have is never really gone, but only goes into remission. Some people's cancer never comes back, but I guess that wasn't the case for me."

"Momma, please tell me that you're joking. Momma, please tell me that this is all a dream and me and Secorion are still in the room sleeping waiting to get up." Audumn puts her head down and pounds the table. "Momma, please."

"Okay kids, your mother is going to need you to be strong because it's very hard for her to be telling you this. You're all she's got and right now you need to be her strength because she is very weak from putting on a front for you these past few months." Mrs. Boswell tries to stop the tears from falling from her friend's children eyes, but they won't stop crying.

"Past few months!" Robby stands because he feels, being the oldest, he should've been known. "You mean to tell me that you've known this for some time now and haven't said nothing mom?"

"Sit down Robby and let your mother finish. Like I said before, this is hard enough on her already." Ms. Boswell said sternly.

Robert sits and his mother continues. "For the past three months, I haven't been feeling like myself. It started after Audumn's graduation when I couldn't keep anything down when we ate at the Golden Coral your father took us too. I thought it was nothing, but then at the end of June, me not being able to keep anything down started happening periodically and I began getting worried, but tried to deny what my body was telling me; that something was wrong with me. In July, that's when the abdominal pain started hurting and exhaustion started to drain all my strength. It was at that time my doctor told me to come in for a checkup so that they could run some tests."

"Is that why you weren't at the wedding rehearsal in July? Because I remembered you texted me that you went to the doctor that day and you were too tired to talk about what happened."

"Yes Audumn, and that's also why your Aunt Glynda and my niece Monica isn't here today. By them coming for your graduation, they couldn't come to the wedding and then turn around and come right back if I needed them. After my visit, I called my sister and told her that my test results came back showing that my white blood cells were high and that I would have to make a decision soon to start chemotherapy."

"Chemotherapy!" Dexter exclaims, remembering how those treatments broke his mother down to almost nothing. "But momma, it was hard enough on you back then when you had to do it the first go around."

"I know, son. But that's the other reason why I called this meeting."

"And that's?" Nicks tries to rush his mother into getting out the rest of what she's trying to say.

"I don't know what to do, kids." Mrs. Humphrey begins to sob and Ms. Boswell puts her arms around her. "For the first time in my life, I really don't know what to do."

"Aww momma, don't cry." Brie gets up and goes and hugs his mother. "I'm sorry for crying, momma. I'm here for you and we're going to fight this cancer together."

Mrs. Humphrey begins to cry louder, so Ms. Boswell speaks for her. "That's just it, you guys. She doesn't know if she can go through that pain again from being hooked up to those machines and the burning after affects from the treatments."

"But..."

"It's no buts, Audumn." Ms. Boswell rubs the back of her friend's head as she shed tears on her shoulder. "This meeting is to tell you that the cancer is back and that her doctor's appointment is Wednesday on the 16th and she wants all of you to be there to hear what the doctor has to say on moving forward. Like I said before, she doesn't know if she can handle the chemotherapy or wants to do it again, but out of respect for her kids, she will make a decision with all of you present. Her reasons for waiting until today was not because she was trying to keep you in the dark, but because she wanted her daughter to be happy walking down that aisle and not thinking about her and her sickness. She promised me that as soon as the wedding was over, she would let you know because, like she said earlier, time is not on her side."

"So, you're giving up, Momma?"

Her mother dries the few tears she can with a piece of tissue. "No Nick, I'm scared and I'm tired. And I don't know if my body can take that torching feeling again."

Secorion walks in and puts his hands on Audumn's shoulders, who has her head in her arms crying. "It's going to be all right, my love. I heard everything. I'm sorry for not coming in sooner, but I didn't want to interrupt your mother from saying what she had to say to you guys."

Audumn hears Secorion, but acts like she doesn't and speaks her mind. "But momma, I don't won't you to go through that again." Audumn manages to say through the tears dripping from her face onto the table. "I remember how much pain you had to endure mentally to keep fighting to get your body back to the way it was. I remember momma because I was there with you every step of the way."

"I know you were sweetheart, but your mother doesn't need all of this crying from you guys." Ms. Boswell continues to hold Mrs. Humphrey who can't look her children in the eyes because she doesn't know what her children will do without her if something tragic was to happen to her. "Kids, God has blessed your mother with five beautiful healthy kids and right now, she needs you to be strong for her as she gets ready to make the decision of her life. So please, if not for me, but for your mother, could you please turn the faucets off because where we're at in this uphill battle, crying is something that isn't going to help any one of us, especially your mother."

Mrs. Humphrey looks up and wipes her tears away. "Thank you Aubrie, but go sit down with your brothers and sister." Aubrie goes and sits down like his mother asked him to. "Janice is right kids when she says I really need you more than ever. My doctor's appointment is at one on Wednesday and I expect all of you to be there with me to hear what the doctor has to say about my health." Mrs. Yolanda walks to the table and stands over her kids who have their heads down wallowing in their tears. "Look at me. Audumn and Dex, please lift your heads up and look at me. This is so painful for me to be telling you this and I don't need to be worrying about my children because I need to be focused on me and me only right now. Now, can I count on all of you to stand by me and to see me through this cancer, no matter what I decide to do or how far my health holds up?"

"You know I got you, mom. We're going to get through this together."

"Thank you Robby, and that's what I need to hear from all of you right now. This is no time to have a pity party over me. Yes, I'm going to break down sometimes, but I need you guys to help me get back up. If I don't have that, then I don't want to go through this." Mrs. Yolanda's eyes begin to water again. "You guys don't know how it feels when that chemo gets into my body!"

"Momma, don't cry." Dexter says from his broken heart. "I don't want you to cry. I don't want you to have cancer. Momma, I don't know what I will do without you. Momma..." Dexter walks off, shaking his head and Aubrie goes to see if he's okay.

"See." Their mother points at Dexter who has his back to her. "It hurts me more when you cry because it makes me question God on why me above all people has to go through this when my kids still need me."

"Yolanda, don't talk like that. God is good and he's a healer, but you mustn't allow your faith to waver because he knows what's best for all us."

Audumn finally gets up and goes to her mother. "Momma, we did it once before and we're going to do again. I'll be your strength, but like Ms. Boswell said, we must trust God and not give up. I'm not giving up and I know you're not going to let me fight this cancer by myself for you."

Mrs. Humphrey puts her forehead to her daughter's. "No I won't, Audumn. And thanks for being such a fighter for me the first time we did this. And you're right." Her mother puts her hand on her daughter's tummy. "I'm not going nowhere because I'm about to be a grandma soon."

"Yeah, momma. You're about to be a grandma soon." Nick gets up and stands by his mother's side. "We got this, momma. And giving up isn't an option."

"Thank you, son."

"Come here you guys and give your mother a big hug because she needs all the love she can get from all of you." Aubrie gets Dexter to come stand with his brothers and sister like Ms. Boswell wanted. "Great, and I'm glad to see the five of you getting on one accord because your mother is going to need it. And don't forget, Wednesday the 16th at one o'clock is her appointment and I want all of you there."

"Yes, Ms. Boswell." The boys said while Audumn shook her head yes.

"Well it's settled, Yolanda. They all've agreed to go to your doctor's appointment, so therefore. I think that makes this meeting adjourned."

Secorion and Audumn left as soon as Ms. Boswell prayed over Mrs. Humphrey's health and her kid's stability to help their mother get over the mountain that she's about to climb. Riding home, Audumn's thoughts were succumbed by her mother's last encounter with cancer and until this day, she still wouldn't wish that mental and physical pain on her worst enemy. It was the enigma of not knowing what her mother's picture looked like when finished that made the ride from Beaumont fast forward to Houston. Audumn felt as if she left the Holiday Inn's exit to then entering her apartment in a matter of minutes. Secorion did drive a little over the speed limit, but not fast enough for his wife not to remember 80 miles of terrain between the two cities.

"Baby, we're home." Secori said with some sorrow in his voice. "Come on, bae. I know you're not up to it, but my mom and pops is about to pull up to visit us before I follow them to the airport." Secori hurries around the car to open Audumn's door because her eyes are open, but her body is as still as board. "Baby, we're home. Let's get you inside. My parents should be coming through the gate any minute now, so if you want to go in the room while their visiting, I totally understand. And by the way, I haven't told them about your momma's illness coming back because I'll leave that up to you if you want them to know or not."

Audumn didn't say a word to her husband. In actuality, to her it feels like she's really not there, but back home taking care of her mother like she did before. Sitting on the bed, Secori lays her down and hears a knock on the door. He knows who it is, but before he goes to answer, he asks Audumn if she needs anything.

"No, I don't love, thanks, but go and get the door for your mother and father, I'll be out shortly. Just give me a minute to get myself together. I know I probably look a mess from all that crying."

"You look fine baby, and it doesn't matter how you look because you've received some bad news that you're still processing on how to handle the situation we now have at hand."

"You're so sweet, Secori." Audumn kisses him on the lips and pushes him towards the bedroom door. "Now go and get the door for your parents."

Secorion scurried out of the room to get the door while Audumn sat up to take a deep breath and think on all she's heard the day after her wedding. Sitting there, her phone chirps from a text message from her childhood friend, Tamera.

Hey friend. Congratulation on getting married and due to my job, I'm sorry I couldn't make it. That's why I didn't commit to being a bridesmaid. However, I will be down there for Xmas and I hope we can catch up on old times. Please know that I'm happy for you and you should be getting your wedding gift in the mail any day now. I love you friend and keep being who you are. See you soon…

Tamera's text made her remember the school she got accepted into to be the veterinarian she's put in over 4 years of hard work for. Veterinarian Institute of Technology (VIT) classes start on the 28th, but from the looks of it she won't be starting school anytime soon. Knowing what she needs to do for her mother to beat this sickness again, her mind is made up with quickness. Her mother's doctor's appointment is on the 16th and when she enters Beaumont, from that day forward it will be all about her mom, her twins, and her husband. She just hoped Secorion would understand that she only has one mother and, whether he likes it or not, she's not going to leave her side until God says something different.

"We got this momma, and I promise you that you will not fight this cancer by yourself," she said, standing to her feet to go entertain her mother and father in law before they get on their plane back to Chicago.

CHAPTER 18

The days Audumn and her family thought were behind them are present again, but this time a black cloud is hovering over their family and Audumn can feel the sprinkles of turmoil starting to fall upon her. Two days have passed since she got the dreadful news and up until she woke up this morning, she was going to be the kryptonite to her mother's cancer. Now, she feels terrible and the knots in her stomach aren't unloosening as she sits holding her husband's hand with a fake smile on her face so that she doesn't worry her mother or brothers.

Today there are the same number of people present from when they had to speak with the doctor for Yolanda's first go around with cancer. Except for this time, Secorrion is here and not her father. Celeste Ball is back in the picture as well, which is her mother's big sister in Christ and is also the woman who led their mother to Christ before her sickness started. All of the family is happy that she's here because her voice is soothing and her presence seems to take anxiousness, worry, and grief from Mrs. Humphrey. Also, the siblings know from their last scare with cancer that their mother will need all the support she can get to be triumphant when this is all over with in the near future.

"How you holding up, Yolanda?"

"Oh, I'm fine I guess, Celeste." Ms. Humphrey responds, fidgeting her fingers together to calm her anxiety. "Other than the fact that I have to pee all the time and my legs feel like they're too weak to support me."

Celeste stands next to her friend who's sitting, and rubs the back of her shoulders for comfort. "I'm here, Yolanda." Mrs. Humphrey looks up at her friend who's always assured her that Jesus has the last word in anything that concerns those who love him. "We're all here friend, and I promise you that you will not go through this alone."

"Thanks, Celeste. I don't know where would I be without you, the kids, and my friend Ms. Boswell."

"Speaking of Ms. Boswell, why didn't she come today?" Aubrie asks aloud.

"Her son James is flying in from the Navy today, so she had to pick him up from the airport." Audumn answers. "But she said that she will be down here to help wherever she's needed when mom starts her chemotherapy."

Nobody noticed how Mrs. Humphrey cringed when hearing the word chemotherapy concerning her. At heart, she really doesn't want to take those painful chemo sessions, however, she must be strong to show herself and God that she's willing to do anything to be with her kids. Even it's just for one minute longer than she had before taking the chemo treatment.

"Good afternoon Mrs. Humphrey and family. My name is Nurse Porter and Dr. Von will be out shortly." Nurse Porter acknowledges everyone present with a dimpled smile and a nod of the head. "My reason for coming out ahead of Dr. Von is because the doctor wants to know who all you want present when she's giving you the prognosis of what's to come when it comes to your upcoming treatments."

"Everyone in this room is my family and if my family can't hear what's about to be said on behalf of my sickness, then I don't need to be here either because they're the reason I'm here."

"I completely understand, Mrs. Humphrey. I'm only following hospital procedures." Nurse Porter helps Yolanda to her feet when seeing that she's trying to get up. "Is everything okay, Mrs. Humphrey?"

"Yeah mom, is everything okay?" Robby puts his arm under his mom's armpit to help support his mother's weight while she's standing.

"I'm okay Nurse Porter, and thanks Robby. But my bladder is killing me and I have to go to the restroom, like now."

"I totally understand. And by the time you get back, Dr. Von should be here to speak with you and your beautiful family."

Robert and Nickolas are talking to Dr. Von when Audumn and Ms. Celeste returned with their mother. Both brother's hands are folded across their chest and their ears are pointed up as they listened, giving their full attention to the doctor who can perhaps cure their mother. Continuing to be hospitable to her current audience, Dr. Von waits for her patient to have a seat in the matching chairs along the wall so that she can be comfortable when hearing what she has to say. Aubrie and Secorrion sit along the wall perpendicular to their loved ones and as everyone got settled, Nurse Porter introduced Dr. Von to Audumn since Audumn weren't there when she came into the conference area.

"How are you feeling today, Mrs. Humphrey?"

"I'm fine, Dr. Von. I've just been feeling tired a lot lately and it feels like I'm getting fat."

"So, is everyone here that you wanted me to speak to?"

"Yes doctor." Yolanda says, looking around with cheery eyes at her intermediate family.

"Great, so I guess I'll proceed." Nurse Porter hands Dr. Von a clipboard with Yolanda Humphrey typed across the top of some papers. "Well, today Mrs. Humphrey has asked me to talk to you because on September 30th I have your mother scheduled to start her first chemotherapy session of two cycles every two weeks for six weeks and a twelve month maintenance chemo once a month when that's completed."

"So, if she's scheduled already then why are we here?" Dexter said, standing to his feet from a chair in the corner.

"Yeah Doc." Nick says dubiously. "Why are we here if mom is going to take the treatment already?"

"Your reason for being here is that Mrs. Humphrey hasn't signed off on taking the treatments. And, she also stated that the only way she will sign the form is for all of you to hear what I've got to say and agree as a family that this is what's best for your mother."

"Of course we will listen, Dr. Von." Robby steps forward and says. "We will do anything for our mother."

"Now that's what I need to hear because today these consent papers need to be signed or she can lose her seat on the 30th and I will have to find a later date, and time we do not have on our side."

"And why is that?" Audumn asks, rubbing the back of her mother's hands.

"Because I've been delaying the treatment since the day I find out I needed it." Mrs. Humphrey looks at Audumn and then at her sons and then back to Audumn. "Kids, I've been pushing this back because as a mother, there's some things you will have to sacrifice everything for out of respect for your kids and the joy that's going to be coming with it. For me, it was my precious Audumn's wedding and the twins she's carrying. I say that to say this, I don't know how long I've got left here on earth, but what I do know is that I watched my baby girl get married to a handsome man and now I want to do everything possible to see my first grandkids be born."

"Momma, you're going to be here forever." Dexter comes over and hugs his mother. "Momma, I love you and we're going to get through this just like last time."

Mrs. Humphrey can smell that her son has been drinking, but doesn't say anything and instead pats his arm around her neck. "I love you too Dex, but please I need you to hang in there for me and don't fall off the wagon."

Dexter rose up quickly when hearing his mother call him out so that only he can know what she was saying to him. *How do she know?* he thought. *I haven't drank since late last night.*

Dr. Von regained the floor when Dexter stepped away abruptly. "Now back to what I was saying, since I see that all of you are willing to sign off on your mother's chemotherapy treatments, I must further educate you on her illness and what we found in your mother's genetics." Dr. Von allows everyone to come in a little closer. "Last month, your mother and friend came into my office for some tests to clear up any worries she's been having when it comes to her battle with cancer. From the first time I saw her, I knew before the testing where my diagnosis was going to be. I knew because of the stricken look on her face, the way she walked, and when she sat in my office chair, I could see a fatty pad in her abdomen hindering her posture when sitting. I didn't say anything on behalf of the fact that I didn't want to worry her and as a doctor, I must see facts first if I'm going to give a patient that type of news concerning their health."

Dexter, Aubrie, and Nickolas look on in grief because they felt they should have seen that as well. Especially with them being around their mother on an everyday basis when they go to the house they grew up in to check on her.

Dr. Von continues. "After getting Mrs. Humphrey's consent, I scheduled her for some genetic testing. But in the meantime, I had her try to find out all she could about her family history by the day of the testing. On the day of testing, Mrs. Humphrey let me know that her great great grandmother and great aunt died of cancer, and that her aunt is in remission for cervical cancer. With this new information on your mother's medical history, we found out that there is a pattern within the women and cancer when it comes to your mother's side of the family."

Audumn swallows hard to hearing the truth in what the doctor is telling her. "So, you're saying there's a possibility that I can get cancer too?"

"Yes Audumn. When we did the genetic testing on your mother, we found that she has the Brca 1 gene."

"What's the Brca 1 gene and are you saying that I can't get cancer because I'm a boy and not a girl?" Aubrie asked.

"It means that there's a 35%-60% lifetime risk that the girls in your family may get cancer. And no is the answer to your second question. Cancer runs in your family, so that means you are at risk, but it's more likely to be a threat to the women in your families."

"Even our daughters?" Secorion looks down at his wife's stomach, not knowing if one of the buns in Audumn's oven is a girl, and if so, will she have cancer too.

"Yes sir," Dr. Von says. "Your daughters too."

"So, what should we do?" Secorion asked.

"Make sure you stay on top of your health, eating patterns, and getting your male and female checkups regularly. This is why your mother wants you here today. She wanted me to tell you from a doctor's standpoint on how grave this is and that she wants you to be aware of what's running through the DNA on her side of the family."

"So where do we sign our consent at so that my mom can be back to her normal self again?"

"Yeah doc, where do we sign at so that my mom can get back to being mom and not in all these hospitals and stuff all the time?" Nick exclaimed, backing his brother's Aubrie's question.

"You don't have to sign anywhere. It's all up to your mother from here on what she wants to do moving forward."

"Thanks Nurse Porter for the input. And to all of you, Nurse Porter is correct when saying that it's up to your mother from here and what she wants to do with these consent forms in my hands." Dr. Von taps the papers with a pen she's been holding during the meeting. "Nurse Porter and I have done what your mother has asked us to do and now we ask her, 'Do you consent to chemotherapy treatment starting September 30th at the Kelsey-Sebold Cancer Center in Houston Texas?'"

"Yes, I do, Dr. Von." Mrs. Humphrey reaches for the clipboard and pen. "And thank both of you for speaking with my family about my family history." Mrs. Humphrey hands Dr. Von the clipboard back with her signature on it. "Now kids…"

"Yes mom," they all said at once.

Mrs. Humphrey smiled big when hearing her kids respond to her mother's call. "Let's go kick this cancer's butt."

Celeste left after she helped her friend get into her son Robert's rental car. At the visit, she remained silent because she already knew what was going to be said because she's the one who's been bringing Yolanda to her appointments. As she watched her friend ride away, she raised her hand up facing the rear of the car and said a silent prayer on Yolanda's behalf:

Dear Lord, today is the beginning of my sister, Yolanda Humphrey's, fight of her life. As I am commissioned by you to stand by her side throughout these unwelcomed times, I ask that her kids stand steadfast as well. Dear Lord, I beg you to give her strength to overcome what's up ahead and a peace of mind that will give her assurance that the light at the end of her tunnel will soon overcome all the darkness in her present life. Jesus, my friend and sister needs you more than ever right now, so I pray that when she's in pain from her treatments or can't sleep because of anxiety, that it is you she leans on and draws all her strength from. I love you Father, and I thank your son Jesus that his blood allows me to pray this prayer before your throne of grace today. It is in Jesus' name, I stand in the gap for Yolanda Humphrey. And it is in Jesus name I pray as I say amen.

After getting their mother settled into her home and bed, the boys decided to go have a drink. Robby's flight departs tonight at 11:00 and he wanted to go over a few things with his brothers that he expects out of them while he's gone until Christmas. Audumn and Secorrion didn't go and instead went back home to Houston so that she can fully process the information about her mother being a Brca 1 carrier and how that may affect her and her children. At the end of the day, she concluded that she must go to her well woman checkups regularly or she could end up like her mother, fighting for her own life in her foreseeable future.

Days begin to seem longer than usual since Audumn was given the news from her mother on Monday. It's Saturday and Audumn can't seem to find her rhythm in life again. This past week she was supposed to be under the sheets with her newlywed husband, but instead she's been under the sheets by herself. Or running to the bathroom throwing up nothing because of the babies. Normally, she would be crying, but her tears dried up Friday morning and now she just has red puffy eyes. One minute she was this season's Audumn princess and the next minute, she feels she has been stripped of her crown. Not only her crown, but also her heart, mind, and her stomach.

Secorion came in from getting some things from Academy and Walmart. His time off for his wedding and so-called honeymoon will soon come to an end when he is to be on the job at the new plant in Corpus Christi, Texas on the 1st. He's saddened for his wife's unfortunate news and for his mother in law. As a man, he wants to stick his chest out and be the brave one out of the two of them, but he doesn't know how he would react if that was his mother instead of hers. Standing there with his head down, he puts the bags on the counter and looks at the darkness under the closed door to his bedroom where Audumn is laying. *This has to stop,* he thought. *This can't be healthy for Audumn or the babies.*

Light from the front room pushes its way into the bedroom when Secorion pushes the door wide opened. "Baby, wake up," he says, sliding the curtains back so that the afternoon's sunshine can liven up the room a bit. Kneeling on the side of the bed, he lifts the covers and puts his head underneath the sheets. Audumn opens her red eyes to the sunlight hitting the outside of her covers and to Secorion's perfect white smile. "I love you, Audumn. Please get up. I need you. The twins need you. And your mother needs you to get it together because you're all she's got. All I've got and all those babies you're carrying have got." Audumn strokes the back of Secorion's head while staring into his brown eyes. "Come on my love," Secorion pulls the cover from over her head and kisses her on the forehead. "I promise you that you'll feel better when you get up."

Audumn's husband sits her on the couch and turns the television on. As he's running off towards the kitchen, the leg of the coffee table trips him and causes him to stumble. Audumn smirks and then giggles and then starts laughing uncontrollably. Secorion starts laughing too, but in reality, his shin is hurting like crazy. In the kitchen, he splits a grilled pork chop, eggs, grits, and toast plate in half from Hanz Diner because the meal comes with two pork chops and not one. Gazing over the counter, he sees Audumn reach for the remote and at that very moment he knew, everything is going to be all right.

Secorion takes a seat and puts both plates on the table. "So baby," he said, grabbing both of Audumn's hands in his. "I was thinking that it might be best for you to move back in with your mother while I'm off working in Corpus Christi. You are your mother's only daughter and right now, she needs your girl skills more than ever because there's some things boys can't do when it comes to helping their mommas. Don't be mad, but I spoke with the manager of our apartments and told them our unfortunate situation. She agreed to us breaking our lease if you decide to move back to Beaumont to help with your mother full time. As for all of our stuff, I will get my Uncle Andre to put it into storage the day before I leave on the 1st. Please know that none of this is set in stone and that I'm asking you if this is something that you want to do. I'm saying what I think is best for our small family and your mother, who needs her only daughter right now." Secorion looks into Audumn eyes and a tiny tear rolls out of his eye. "I love you, Audumn. And don't shut me out like you did this week ever again. You are my wife and whatever we go through from this day on, we will go through it together."

Audumn wipes his tear. "I'm sorry love for being in my own world lately. You are my husband and I'm lucky and blessed to have a man like you. You have been nothing but good to me and as the man of this house, I stand by what you propose for what's best for all of us, including my mother. For the past week, I've been contemplating on moving back with my mother, my job, and my scholarship at VIT, but hearing and seeing you take charge has helped me make the decision that it's time for me to put everything on hold and move back home."

"That's right, my love. Remember, you have only one mother."

"You can say that again, love." Audumn grabs Secorion ears and pulls him in for a kiss. "I love you, Secorion Woodson and you're the best husband and father a woman can ever have or ask for."

Diana and Kizzy knocked on the door shortly after the two of them were going in and out of each other for an hour of makeup sex. When they got there, Secorion decided to leave and visit his uncle to tell him that he will be needing him to help move his furniture into storage on the 30th. Audumn waved him off, but she knew he was only leaving because she needed to talk to her friends and needed a woman's touch to help clear her mind completely.

"So, how you holding up, Beaumont?" Diana asks.

"I'm a lot better now since my husband gave me a reality check."

"From the looks of your hair, it looks like he gave you more than a reality check."

"Now there you go with your big self, always saying the wrong thing at the wrong time."

Audumn quickly raises her hand and says, "Stop it right there you two," because she knows Kizzy is about to go off on Diana and Diana is going to give her the fight she's looking for. "Diana's right, Kizzy. Secorion did give me a little something something extra after he gave me my reality check."

"Boo yah!" Diana points her finger in Kizzy's face and Kizzy slaps it down. "I know I smelled what I smelled when I came up in here. Not that I'm trying to be all up in your business, Audumn."

"Girl, you always trying to be all up in my business so stop fronting with that lie, Diana."

"Yeah Diana. There's a time for jokes and a time to be serious."

"All right, all right, Kizzy." Diana turns to Audumn. "I'm sorry Audumn for always cracking jokes and I'm sorry for what's going on with your mother." Diana gives Audumn a hug.

"Girl, you're okay. On the cool, I needed a good laugh because starting today I'm coming out of my shell."

"That's good Audumn because girl, we were worried about you, yeah. We haven't heard from you since you called us and told us what was going on with your mother."

"I'm sorry friends, and you guys are right. We've been through everything together and I now know that I won't be able to go through this without you."

"Yeah Audumn." Diana stands next to Kizzy. "You know we got you girl, no matter what."

Audumn group hugs her best friends and says, "I'm moving back to Beaumont," after taking a deep breath to her new truth and reality. "Secorion and I agreed that I must drop everything and move back to Beaumont to help my mother. He said that everything, including my job and school, should wait until we get on the downside of the hill when it comes to my mother's ovarian cancer treatments."

"So, you're moving, Beaumont?"

"Yes Diana, but just because I'll be living in Beaumont again doesn't mean that I won't need the both of you to help me get through this for my mother."

"Anything you need Audumn, we got you."

"Yeah Audumn, like Kizzy said, we got you."

"Thanks Kizzy and Diana for your friendship and for reminding me that I have people like you in my corner."

"Aww Audumn, you know the two of us will never leave your side. And remember, you only have one mother."

Kizzy's words and New Orleans accent ran through her brain along with Secorion's voice telling her the same thing earlier. "Yep Kizzy, you're so right." Audumn squeezes her friends a little tighter. "You only have one mother."

CHAPTER 19

September 30th is here and Audumn is through dotting her I's and crossing her T's in Houston, Texas. Everything that they needed to be packed got packed over the course of time that they had to get everything packed in. And Secorion's Uncle Andre has freed up his calendar to move their furniture into storage today. Also, he said that Secorion could stay at his house tonight, but Secorion declined because he's going to stay in Beaumont with Audumn and leave out for Corpus Christi from there in the morning.

Audumn's job was sad that she was leaving because the store isn't going to be the same without her. But her employees were even more sad for her mother because Audumn opened up to them on occasion and told them how her mom overcame the calamitous disease before. Closing the night before, she said her final goodbyes, thinking about how she had to say her final goodbyes to her last job, Magic City, six years ago for the same reasons. *I can't wait for all this to be over,* she thought without having any regrets because her mother comes first in her life right now.

Throughout the week, her and the hubby have been moving things to her mom's house and setting up her old bedroom to be just for her. To do that, they had to put her and Aubrie's twin size beds inside the garage and set up their queen size bed from their apartment. Her bedroom at her mother's house is practically an exact replica of the apartment's bedroom after she puts her nightstands in place. Except for the old wallpaper and the window being on a different wall, Audumn is at home sweet home.

"You ready, momma?" Audumn asks from her mom's bedroom doorway while her mother is sitting on the bed.

"Now I am." Mrs. Yolanda slides her feet into her comfortable Sketcher walking shoes. "Now come and help me up so that we can go get this over with."

Audumn helps her mom down her mother's steep steps. Growing up, those steps was fun to run up and down on with her friends and also, she found her dog Lady underneath them. But seeing how much weaker her mother has gotten since last week, she wishes they weren't there anymore. All buckled in, Audumn pulls off silently, praying that her mother gets through the day with the least amount of pain possible. She prayed that prayer because she can feel the shivering of her mother's body with each step she took down the stairs. Before, her mother was upbeat when fighting her cancer six years ago, but it seems that now Mrs. Humphrey just wants to get this over with and whatever happens, happens.

Driving back to Houston for her mother's chemotherapy treatments, Audumn feels alone in what she feels that her gut is telling her about this new battle she's facing with her mother. Alone because once again her brothers bailed out on her after lying about all that they're going to help and do. And just like last time, Aubrie and

Nickolas preferred not to see their mother down and feeble like this, and Dexter is nowhere to be found. *Forget them momma, we got this even if it's just gon' be me and you like last time.* Audumn looks over at her mother who's looking out the window at the passing pastures. *We don't need them, momma. We don't need anybody.*

Traffic is okay today on FM 1960 and Audumn has caught all the green lights on this beautiful day. Kelsey-Sebold is about three lights down, so she decides to stop at the Chick-fil-A approaching quickly to get her mother a snack. It's not good to take the chemo treatment on an empty stomach and they both haven't eaten anything since breakfast and that was almost four hours ago.

"Can I have four ranch chicken wraps, a coke, and a pink lemonade?"

"That'll be $7.86. Thank you and please drive-thru."

"I see you remembered."

"How can I forget?" Audumn jokes and they both laugh at how her mother had her running every five minutes to get ranch chicken wraps every time she had a craving. "Momma, you know I got you girl."

"I know you do sweetheart." Mrs. Yolanda pats her daughter's thigh. "I know you do."

Mrs. Humphrey made it on time to her 1:30 appointment. Her strength is back and Audumn can see the color of her mother's skin is back to normal. As the elevator doors separated onto the fifth floor, Audumn grabbed her mother's hand and they both took the first step off the elevator together.

"Good afternoon, Mrs. Humphrey," the lady clerk said behind the registration desk. "Dr. Whoroha will be with you shortly. Please have a seat in the chairs behind you."

"Right this way, Mrs. Yolanda." Dr. Whoroha said before they could sit down. "Follow me."

Audumn and her mother followed the woman in the white coat to an office down the hall and to the left. She thought she was going straight to the room her mother is getting her treatment in, but evidently that isn't the case. Taking a seat at the doctor's request, Audumn looks at her mom because she can't take any more bad news than what she's already accepted and currently moving on from.

"Is there a problem Doctor?"

"No Ms…"

"Audumn, Audumn Humphrey. I mean, Woodson. Audumn Woodson." Audumn stammers. "Sorry doctor. I just got married two weeks ago." Audumn shakes Dr. Whoroha's hand. "I'm her daughter if you want to know the relation."

"Thank you, Mrs. Woodson, for being here with your mother today and congratulations on your wedding."

"Thank you doctor." Audumn replied, taking a seat next to her mother who's already sitting down.

"How are you doing this afternoon, Dr. Whoroha?"

"I'm okay. Sorry I couldn't speak with you long last week when you came in with your friend, Ms. Boswell. It's just that lately we've been so busy with new patients around here, but it's always like that towards the end of the month." Dr. Whoroha takes a seat. "By the way Mrs. Woodson, I am your mother's Oncologist who will be overseeing your mother's chemotherapy."

Audumn smiles. "Nice to meet you again, Dr. Whoroha."

Dr. Whoroha smiles back and continues. "This informative meeting is to inform my patient on what we do here, what chemotherapy is, how it effects you, and to introduce you to me and your care team who you will meet when we finish talking. I see from your files that you've done this before in 2007, but a lot has changed in the last few years when it comes to chemotherapy. That's why I must have this meeting with all my patients, so that they can be introduced or reintroduced to the studies that we've proven to work in today's time." The doctor pauses to allow her patient and guest to digest the information. "Chemotherapy is a medication that selectively kills the cells in the body that are rapidly dividing. Your prescription is prescribed on the basis of the type of cancer that the patient has and to whether there's a strong chance that the cancer has spread throughout the body. As a doctor, our profession understands that cancer spreads through the bloodstream and it is for that reason we administer chemotherapy through the blood. Some type of chemos know to only kill the bad rapidly growing cells and some don't have the ability to discern the difference between good rapidly growing cells or bad rapidly growing cells. When this happens, good rapidly growing cells die. Such as blood cells, digestive tract, bone marrow, and hair cells."

"Is that why my momma's hair fell out last time?"

"Yes Mrs. Woodson, and it will most likely fall out this time as well."

"Dang!" Audumn exclaimed, remembering how her mom hated having to cut her hair last time and knowing that she will hate cutting her hair now since she finally got it to grow out.

"Not to mention the side effects that comes with each treatment." The doctor sees Audumn grimace at the sound of that statement. "I can see from the look on your faces that you two know all about that from your last altercation, so I won't go into detail on that subject too much. All I'm going to say is to eat nutritious foods, rest, and take prescribed side effect drugs if prescribed."

"Yes ma'am." Audumn replied, taking mental notes to help her mother in the best and most nonpainful way as possible.

"There's two ways to receive chemotherapy. One is intravenously and the other is orally. Intravenously, is through a PORT or an IV. The PORT is typically used for patients that will be undergoing treatment for a long period of time. And the I.V. is used when patients are undergoing chemotherapy for a short period of time. Orally is through medication prescribed by me that best gets rid of your cancer." Dr. Whoroha looks at Audumn's mom. "You, Mrs. Humphrey, I believe, received a PORT last week when I spoke with you on the floor."

"That's correct."

"I see here Dr. Von has you scheduled for six cycles. Which would be two cycles every two weeks for six weeks and a twelve month maintenance chemotherapy once a month. After looking over your files and checking your blood work from last week, I agreed and signed off on your paperwork for you to start your treatments today after your preparatory work comes back from your care team."

"What's preparatory work?"

"I'm glad you ask that, Mrs. Woodson."

"Please call me Audumn."

"Will do, Audumn. But to answer your question, preparatory work includes: blood drawn and vitals taken to make sure that your mother's white blood cells count, platelet count, and hemoglobin are high enough for treatment. Preparatory work also includes observing the kidney and liver to make sure they will be able to function correctly during the treatment as well. Don't worry, our care team

will be here to help you and answer questions every step of the way."
Dr. Whoroha asked if they have any questions and both mother and
daughter shook their heads no. "If there's not anything else, please
have a seat back in the waiting area and Nurse Javier, who is head of
our care team, will come and get you to start your preparatory work."

Audumn thought, *At St. Elizabeth in Beaumont, I had a friend
named Javier who used to sit with my mom last time when I had to run
some errands.*

"God bless you Mrs. Humphrey, and thank you Audumn for
listening to what I had to say and for coming with your mother. If
you have any questions for me throughout your chemo treatments,
please get with any member of your care team and they will bring
them to my attention. Or, if I'm not too busy, you can stop me in the
hall and ask me your question if it's something I can answer quickly.
Good day."

"Good day." Mrs. Humphrey replied, thinking about how nice
Dr. Whoroha is and feeling like she's in great hands.

"Mrs. Humphrey, is that you?"

Mrs. Humphrey and Audumn turn around at the same time,
but her mother beats Audumn in responding. "Javier!" she exclaimed,
pushing herself up using the arms of the chair. "Oh, how I'm so so
happy to see you!"

"Girl, I thought that was your name when Dr. Whoroha gave
me your chart." Javier looks at Audumn, who is all teeth because
she can't stop smiling at the sight of her hospital friend. "I was just
on my way to come get you. And Audumn girl, I see you're still
hanging in there with your mother." Javier gives Audumn and her
mother a slight hug. "Come on you two. Follow me so that we can

get this blood work over with so that we can get you to a chair and a machine."

While waiting on her blood work, Javier introduced Mrs. Humphrey to her care team of three, including him, that will be helping her throughout her chemotherapy process. Nurse Dana is also one of Mrs. Humphrey's care team workers and worked at St. Elizabeth with Javier when he was back at the hospital in Beaumont. Javier loved her work ethic and decided to tell his supervisor that he wanted to bring one of his coworkers with him if he took the job as head floor nurse. The higherups agreed and she's been assisting him ever since. All Audumn could say is, "Small world," when she shook her hand after Javier called her name to introduce herself.

The third nurse of her care team of three name is Neiko Roberson. She just graduated this year, but Javier assured Audumn and her mother that she's one of the best nurses on the floor and has gotten high accolades from the patients that she's been assigned too. "Nice to meet you, Mrs. Humphrey and Mrs. Woodson." She said, shaking her patient's and daughter's hand. "I assure you that I will do whatever is needed to help both of you get through the chemotherapy procedures."

Mrs. Humphrey's blood work came back high enough for treatment that day. Therefore, Nurse Javier escorted them to their chair and slid the curtain halfway along its track when leaving. Dana comes in as soon as he leaves and explains to her patient that the pharmacy is mixing her chemo treatment for the day. She also told Mrs. Humphrey that it generally takes about thirty minutes to begin treatment after her blood work comes back, giving the okay to administer chemotherapy. Before leaving, she hands Audumn the remote and says, "It's nice to see you again."

Audumn gets up and puts a pillow behind her mother's neck and drapes a pink blanket over her legs. "How's that, momma?" she asked, pulling her mother's Bible from her bag and then placing it on the table next to her mother.

"I'm good and could you text Janice and let her know that we made it?"

"Yes ma'am." Audumn texts Ms. Boswell what her mother asked her to and also said thank you for bringing her mother to get her PORT last week. *I don't know what I would do without Ms. Boswell,* she thought as she flipped through the channels to find something to watch.

The curtain in their section slid wide open a little after about forty minutes. Routinely, Neiko comes in and attaches the special IV to the PORT'S access point under the skin in Mrs. Humphrey's chest. After stepping away, she allows Dana and Javier to come in.

"How are you feeling, Mrs. Humphrey?" Nurse Javier asked.

"I'm fine. Just ready to go home."

"I see here that you are receiving a 60 milligram bag of Carboplatin for one hour and 400 milligrams of Doxorubicin for four hours. If there's nothing else, I'll leave you two be so that we can get you home as soon as possible."

Nurse Dana punches a few buttons on the machine and the IV line going into the PORT starts to become purple from the Carboplatin. "You're all set Mrs. Humphrey, and if you have any questions, please let your daughter know so that she can tell us." Dana leaves, but not before saying that she will see them in an hour."

Mrs. Yolanda begins to read her NIV Daily Bible that she's been reading daily to complete the Bible in a year. Her last passage to read for the day is Psalms 23. As she is reading the last words of the scriptures, a revelation appeared in her spirit on what God is trying to tell her through her studies.

Psalms 23 reads: The Lord is my shepherd; I shall not want. He makes me lie down in green pastures. He leads me beside the still waters. He restores my soul. He leads me in paths of righteousness for his name's sake. Even though I walk through the valley of the shadow of death, I will fear no evil, for you are with me; your rod and your staff, they comfort me. You prepare a table before me in the presence of my enemies; you anoint my head with oil until my cup runneth over. Surly goodness and mercy shall follow me all the days of my life. And I will dwell in the house of the Lord forever.

Caught up in the spirit, Mrs. Humphrey eyes opened up to the scriptures and she realizes what she's going through is temporary because the Lord is her shepherd right now while she's in the valley of the shadow of death. And if she's in the valley of the shadow of death, that means Jesus' rod and staff will comfort her and he will anoint her head with oil until the blessings he has for her runneth over. Not only that, but God's goodness and mercy shall follow her all the days of her life until she dwells in the house of the Lord forever.

Dwelling in the house of the Lord forever is what she liked most about Psalms 23. Mrs. Yolanda liked it most because no matter what befalls her in the valley of death that she's currently in, the end result will be her dwelling in her Father's loving arms forever.

"Momma, you're done with your first bag."

"I am?" her mother replies, looking over at the drawn down bag that held the purple solution.

Nurse Neiko comes in and changes the bag when hearing it beep. "Great job Mrs. Humphrey, only one more bag to go," she said, hanging up the orange bag of Doxorubicin onto the intravenous poles to be administered into her patient's bloodstream. "Do you need anything?"

"No, not that I know of. Well, I would like a bottle of water to go with my sliced apples I brought to snack on."

"Coming right up and what about you, Audumn?"

"Water's fine for me too, thanks."

"Will do and I'll be right back. By the way, Dana will be in shortly to turn on your machine."

The day went by smoothly for their first visit together at the doctor for chemotherapy. Mrs. Yolanda explained her revelation to her daughter on Psalms 23 and told her not to fret because the Lord is her shepherd and she shall not want while she's in the valley of the shadow of death. Audumn listened and is intrigued that she learned so much more about the scriptures from her mother in ten minutes than what she knew about the Psalm since she was a child and had to recite it at church in Ms. Boswell's class. After their Bible study, Mrs. Humphrey began to sing, "Oh how I love Jesus," in a soft tone and Audumn joined in with a big smile because that's what her momma used to sing at her chemo visits a long time ago.

Her treatment was over in no time because they both got caught up in each other's company and in the word of God. Nurse Neiko came in as if she had a stopwatch when the machine started beeping that the Doxorubicin bag was finished. Dana brought in a wheelchair while Audumn is helping her mother to her feet. Settling into the wheelchair, Mrs. Yolanda thanked her care team for making this day not as fearful as she thought it would be. Before getting on the elevator, Audumn ran back to thank Javier for being here. And to tell him that she feels that a lot of tension has been lifted off her mother's shoulders because he's there.

It was a quarter till 8:00 when they finally got onto I-45 to drive back to Beaumont, Texas. Approaching the ship channel on I-10 East, Audumn hears a low snore coming from her mother who has already fallen asleep. She wished she had time to stop and see Ms. Boswell and her friends, but she could see in her mother's face that she was tired from the long day of driving and chemotherapy. Hearing her mom snore, she's glad she made the right decision to keep straight when the exit that goes to Ms. Boswell's house came up while on the highway.

With her foot on the gas along the open interstate, Baytown Texas passed, then Anahuac Texas, then Winnie Texas, and before you knew it, Audumn is pulling into her mother's driveway at 9:55 pm. For some reason, the street light at the corner is off tonight, but then she remembers growing up that it was always a flickering light and some days it came on and some days it didn't. Allowing her mother to sleep for a few extra minutes, Audumn runs up the stairs and unlocks the door and flips the switch for the porch light to come on. Before going back out, she turns on her mother's bedroom lamp and pulls the covers back on the bed so that her mother can go right to sleep when she puts her head on her pillow. *There, all done,* she thought, turning around to see an empty 40 oz. beer bottle next to Dexter sleeping on the couch.

Back outside, Audumn opens the passenger door to her car. "Come on momma, we're home."

"Already?"

"Yes momma, already." Audumn helps her mother out the car and walks her over to the steps. "You ready?"

"Ready as I ever will be." Mrs. Humphrey replied, grabbing the hand rail and taking her first step up the stairs.

Inside, Mrs. Humphrey senses become more keen because of the chemo in her body and she smells alcohol in the air. Dexter is still asleep on the couch, but Audumn threw the bottle away so her mom wouldn't see it. Mrs. Humphrey wanted to wake him up and say something to him about it because he was doing so good the past five years with his addiction until she told him that her cancer has come back. However, her stomach begins to start churning and Audumn feels her mom hunch over in pain.

"Come on, momma. Let's get you to your bed because you need to get some rest."

"I will sweetheart and do me a favor and pray for your brother, Dexter. He's taking my sickness really hard and I can't be there for him right now like I need to be."

"Yes ma'am, and I'll talk to him in the morning."

"Thank you, Audumn." Mrs. Humphrey pulls the chain on her lamp. "Now go and get you some rest."

Audumn went outside and sat on the steps by herself like she used too with her dog, Lady. Staring at the starless night sky, she hopes for the best but in her heart, she prepares for the worst. The coolness of the night makes her wish she's in Secorion's arms and hence, wraps her arms around herself as if he's there. Tightly embracing herself for warmth, her phone vibrates and it's a text from her husband saying he's about to pull up. Headlights suddenly shine across her face while she's checking her missed calls from him ten minutes ago. Parking, Secorion jumps out with some flowers and a surprised look on his face at his wife sitting on the porch waiting on him. "Lord watch over this family. We need you right now," Audumn said to herself, standing with opened arms to greet her husband's arrival.

CHAPTER 20

"Okay Audumn, this may feel a little cold when I squeeze it onto your stomach."

Dr. Belisima applied the ultrasound gel under Audumn's bellybutton and begins to carefully rub the clear substance over her patient's abdomen. Diana is standing over the doctor, who's sitting, waiting for her to use the transducer probe so that a black and white image can appear on the monitor in front of them. Kizzy has Audumn's phone in her hands and she's facetiming the man who's made all of this possible for the three of them. As far as the lady of the hour, she's just lying there, hoping all is well with the two lives inside her.

Her hope stems from her skipping her twelve weeks prenatal visit last month that she was scheduled to take the week after the wedding. That was the visit, that she was supposed to get this ultrasound on, but due to all the chaos, having to move, and her mother's chemotherapy, she forgave herself for not taking her babies lives more seriously during her tough times. Last month is in the past and looking at the man cheesing from ear to ear on her phone in Kizzy's hand, she promised to never put her children on the back burner again for nobody, not even her mother.

Secorion is on the screen sitting at his desk in his boss's office, waiting to see his babies' faces for the first time. He would've been there with his wife, but he just left three weeks ago and it's too soon to go back home unless it's an emergency. As the doctor goes left to right and up and down in rows of three over Audumn's tummy, two separate images appear on the ultrasound monitor identifying two fetuses.

"Look Audumn, there go your babies." Diana exclaimed, pointing at the crowns of the babies' heads on the screen.

"And look, I see a nose on this baby over here and an ear on the other baby over there hiding!" Kizzy blurted out in surprise when the distinct features popped up on the screen.

"Do you see them, baby? Audumn asked Secori. "They're sooo beautiful."

"Yes they are my love. Yes they are."

"What's that?" Diana reaches over the doctor's shoulder and points at something small fading in and out on the screen.

"That my friend is a boy."

"How do you know that's a boy, doctor?" Kizzy brings the phone closer to the monitor so that Secorion can see.

"Because that..."

"Because that boy is just like his daddy!" Secorion shouts, finishing off Dr. Belisima's statement with his own words. "Don't act like you don't know what that is ladies. You've seen one, you've seen them all." Secorion laughs and then rolls his seat back to holler at his foreman. "Hey Mr. Williamson! Guess what, boss? I'm having a boy!"

"A boy?" Audumn leans over in glee to get a closer look.

"Yes Audumn, you're having a boy."

"And from the looks of it, a big boy!" Diana nudges Kizzy.

"Diana, you sho is crazy, yeah. But I hate to say it Audumn, you gon' have a girl problem on your hands. Him and his brother."

"His brother?" Audumn asked ambitiously to the doctor.

Doctor Belisima chuckles. "Now, I wouldn't go that far just yet. Let's see if we can get this baby to move or roll over some so that I can give you a conclusive answer."

"Yeah love, the other baby could be a girl like my niece Lilian."

"Oh please, please, please doctor let it be a girl." Audumn thought about her four brothers. "Because Lord knows we already have enough boys in the family."

"I feel you, girl. But two boys wouldn't be so bad because you know us girls can be something else sometimes."

"No, Diana. You're something else." Kizzy shakes her head and looks back at the screen to see if the doctor can determine the other baby's sex.

Dr. Belisima finished the ultrasound without determining the other child's sex. No matter how much she tried, she couldn't get the other baby to move in the right position so that she can get a glimpse of the child's genital area. What she did confirm and point out is that both babies' heartbeats are strong and that they both are healthy. As they all marveled at the babies' tiny heartbeats, Diana had an idea and recorded the babies' lifelong drumbeats for a gift she plans to give the twins when they're born.

"All done and as of the moment, you're fifteen weeks pregnant give or take three to five days accuracy."

"Wow baby! Did you hear that honey?" Audumn sits up and grabs her phone from Kizzy. "Our babies are 3 months old already."

"Yes, they are love. And as for now at least, we know we're having a boy to help take care of his sister."

"Sister? Why do you think our other baby is girl?"

"I don't know, bae." Secorion shrugs his shoulders through the phone. "I guess you can say I have a feeling."

"I guess if you say so, then I guess we're having a girl too."

Secorion laughs. "I love you so much Audumn, but I'm ten minutes past my breaktime my foreman gave me to call you. Tell your mom and brothers I said hi. And thank you Kizzy and Diana for filling in for me while I'm at work." Secorion kisses the screen of his phone. "Bye babe and you're going to be a great mother."

"I love you t…" Audumn tried to reply, but only got a picture of them on her screensaver because he had already hung up.

Back by their cars, Audumn feels much better after hearing her babies' heartbeats and seeing them in baby form for the first time. Kizzy and Diana wanted to go have a bite to eat, but Audumn declined because her second priority comes before eating with her friends and she tells her Chicas that she will have to take a rain check.

"Aww mannn… You never got time for us anymore."

"Diana please don't do that to me right now with everything I'm going through with my mother."

"Yeah Diana," Kizzy chimes in. "Stop thinking about yourself all the time."

"I tell you what, Diana."

"What?" Diana said sadly because she knows her friend is about to head back to Beaumont.

"Next week is my mom's third treatment at Kelsey-Sebold and instead of me going with her on that day, I will ask Ms. Boswell or one of my brothers to go so I can hang out with you two all day."

"Oh, Audumn you don't have to do that for us. We understand that you have to be there for your mother." Kizzy quickly responds.

"I'm not doing this for you. I'm doing this for me and besides…I ain't gon' lie I miss H-town and most of all, I miss my Chicas."

"And we miss you too, Audumn. And I'm sorry if I be sounding like your mom ain't important."

"It's okay Diana. Moving back home is a big adjustment for me too."

Bidding her farewells, Audumn drove off with her two friends standing in her rearview mirror, waving goodbye. With her right hand on the steering wheel, she palms the circumference of her stomach and thinks about the little penis that stood out on the monitor earlier. *What shall I name him?* she thought, but nothing came to mind because she doesn't know what the other baby inside her sex is yet. Secorion's cheesing face on her phone is what shined in her mind the most driving home. The excitement of him having a son and then bragging to his boss about it was memorable to her because she did well in blessing her husband with a son. Her only wish is that the other baby is a girl, so that she can love on her and teach her what it is to be a woman.

Aubrie is playing the PS3 when his sister pushed a ray of sunshine into the house and followed behind it. Closing the door, she asked him where Nickolas is and he tells her that Nick's at work. Her mother is asleep when she poked her head inside her mom's bedroom door to check on her. As she went back to her room to sit her handbag down, she hands her brother Brie the sonogram from her doctor's visit and walks off, awaiting her brother's response.

"Twins!" he shouts. "Big sis, you're having twins!"

"Yes Brie, I'm having twins." Audumn goes back to her mother's room and closes the door. "I'm glad you're happy I'm having twins, but momma's sleeping so you're going to have to keep it down lil brother. And besides, I told you that we're having twins when I announced my pregnancy before the trip to New Orleans."

Aubrie speaks lowly. "That's right, you did say that, huh? Now I remember why I don't remember, but now I remember because you made me remember."

"Wait what, huh? Hold up, Aubrie are you high?"

"Yep and that's why I didn't remember just now when you gave me this. Well, that and the fact that your girl Kendra was giving me some play." Aubrie hands the sonogram back to his sister and starts laughing. "If you know what I mean, big sis."

"Yeah I know what you mean. Now keep it down because you know mom be up at night and sleeps during the daytime."

"All right, all right. But I'll give you a better one. How about I just leave?"

"Brie, I don't care what you do. But if you do decide to leave, then so be it." Audumn goes inside her room and closes the door, but then opens it. "Thanks brother for sitting with momma today. I love you and I got it from here."

About three hours later, Audumn awoke to running water traveling through the pipes in the walls. The sound isn't loud; it's just that the house is at its peak when it comes to silence with the boys always being gone. She knows where the water is coming from because it's only her and her mom in the house. Also, from growing up in the room next to her parents, she heard that sound all of the time when her parents would fill up their bathtub to take a bath.

"Hey momma."

"Hi sweetheart," her mother replied, taking off her bathrobe and draping it over her walker. "Did you get you some good rest? Because I sure did."

Audumn notices scab like sores all over her mother's back while her mom is trying to lift her leg over the ledge of the tub. "Here momma. Grab my arm so that you can brace yourself better."

"Okay, but I think momma may need a little help lifting this leg a little higher too."

"Yes ma'am, and make sure you grab the handrail when you get in and get ready to sit down."

Giving her mother a bath is something that Audumn has begun to cherish. As her mother sits up in the warm water, allowing Dr. Teal's Pure Epsom Salt to soothe her bones, Audumn massages her muscles. With her mother's skin becoming fragile from her first two chemo treatments, Audumn has to be as careful as possible or she could hurt her mother and perhaps give her a nasty bruise. A bruise that can take longer than usual to heal or may not fully heal at all. With her thumbs and fingers, she gives her mom the gentle kneading she needs to get up and finish the day.

"Thank you, Audumn." Mrs. Humphrey grabs her mouth because inside its full of blisters and it sometimes hurt for her to talk or swallow.

"You all right, momma? Those sores in your mouth are bothering you again?

Her mom nods her head. "Audumn, can you make me some tea?"

"Coming right up!" Audumn hands her mother her slip after helping her dry off. "Here momma, and when you're done, I have a surprise to show you."

Mrs. Humphrey is sitting in her usual spot on the couch when Audumn came back with her tea. Taking a sip, she allows the hot fluid to coat the inside of her mouth so that the pain can be less than what it is was. Everything concerning her side effects is starting to come to a head, and its only been two cycles. The sores are all over her body, including her mouth, backside, and vagina. And on top of that, her stomach feels like it's in knots all the time and she can't poop the way her body feels she needs to poop. Feeling exhausted from the walk from the bathroom, her mind tells her that she isn't going to make it to all her chemo cycles if her body don't get any stronger than what it is now.

"So, guess what we learned about your grandchildren today, momma?"

The thought of her grandkids quickens her heart and the strength she's looking for slowly livens her bones. "Now how did I forget that you were going get your ultrasound today?"

"Um, probably because you slept all day." Audumn points to the window to show her mom that daylight will soon be nightlight in a matter of minutes.

"Audumn, you know that chemo is having me up all night and sleeping all day. But enough about me. You were saying that you learned something new about my grandkids."

"Yes we did, but I can show you better than I can tell you," Audumn said, handing her mother the sonogram.

"My, my Audumn, they're beautiful. And this one over here looks like she doesn't want to be bothered until birth."

"She? I'm sorry mom, but it hasn't been confirmed that we're having a she yet."

"Well, I'm confirming it because that's just how you were on the monitor when me and your dad saw you for the first time."

"I sure hope it's a girl."

"Me too because I can clearly see that this one over here is a boy."

Audumn laughs. "Yes he is, and he's just like his daddy."

"Huh?"

"I didn't say nothing." Audumn puts her hand over her mouth and smirks because she can't believe that she said that to her mother.

"Yeah, you better get it right," her mother chuckles. "Because that's a little too much information for these old ears to hear."

"Mom, you're only fifty-one."

"Yeah, but I'll be fifty-two in December if I can make it."

"Well December is five weeks away with your young, beautiful self. And stop talking like that momma. Because you're going to make it."

Mrs. Humphrey feels her body isn't as strong as it was before when she did her treatments years ago. "I know I will, Audumn. And I will be done with my six cycles by the time them babies come."

"That's the spirit mom, and here, take this medicine before your headaches come back and we both be in a lot of trouble."

Throughout the rest of the day, they both rejoiced at the fact that they will have the pitter patter of little feet running throughout the house next year. Mrs. Humphrey gave her daughter some tips on rubbing coco butter on the stomach to reduce the stretch marks. And walking will help the babies settle into the right position when it's time for them to be delivered. Bible study is something her mom does every day, and Audumn joins in every time because she knows that's what puts a smile on her mother's face. Not to mention that she's learning a lot about the stories she read and had to perform as a child when she went to church.

"Mom, do you need anything?"

"Not that I know of. Thanks, but why do you ask?"

Audumn thinks about her mom saying how happy her dad was when he found out that his wife is having a girl after having her two big brothers, Robert and Dexter. "Because no matter how mad I am at daddy, he's still and always will love me and he will never stop being my father."

"That's a girl, Audumn," her mother replied because she knows Audumn is going to need him more than ever as her health goes down before it gets better. "And if you hurry, you probably can catch him before he goes to sleep."

Audumn goes inside her room and closes the door. It's twenty minutes after ten and the only light in the room is the streetlight parting it's way through the crack down the center of the window curtain. Her phone lights up the room further when she touches the screen to use it, but she doesn't immediately press talk when she got to her dad's contact. "Oh, to heck with it," she said to herself, looking at the time in the top right corner of her phone. "If he answers, he answers. If not, oh well." But she then shook that thought away when he didn't and promised that she'll call again in the morning. That is, until her phone rang one minute later with her dad's picture popping up on the caller i.d. "Hello daddy," she answered and then proceeded to give him the update on his two grandchildren that the stork will soon be delivering.

CHAPTER 21

Ms. Boswell enters the curtained section that Mrs. Humphrey is getting her chemotherapy in. "Hey Yolanda."

"Hi Janice. And thanks for coming to sit with me while my son goes to the flea market to get some speakers for one of his customers tomorrow."

"Girl, stop it with all that nonsense. I told you that I was coming last time, but something came up with my granddaughter, Shanay."

"Well, you're here now, and I couldn't be happier to see you, friend." Mrs. Yolanda allows Nurse Neiko to change her chemo bag to Docetaxel, which will be her last treatment for the day. "And I know Aubrie is too because he's been ready to leave so that he can run these Houston streets."

Nurse Dana came in as Aubrie is leaving and turned on the machine to allow the yellow medication to enter her patient's body. Mrs. Yolanda and Ms. Boswell immediately started fellowshipping about the Lord when Dana slid the curtain closed so that they can have some privacy. Twenty minutes into glorifying God, praising his son Jesus' name, and praying for healing, Ms. Boswell said amen and opened her eyes. When she did, Mrs. Humphrey's machine started beeping unsteadily and the electrocardiogram attached to her index finger showed only a straight line.

"Yolanda?" Ms. Boswell asked, tapping her friend's hand vigorously. "Yolanda, Yolanda open your eyes!"

———ɯ———

"Where am I?" Mrs. Yolanda is standing upright, but it's as if she's floating because it feels like she's suspended in the sky. "Janice, are you there?" She asked the air around her while standing in fog like clouds covering her feet. "Aubrie, where are you? Can anybody hear me? Is anybody there?"

Suddenly, out of nowhere, a peculiar light becomes very bright some ways up ahead and a strong voice said, "Come!"

Mrs. Yolanda just stood there, but then realized that she can't stand there forever and took a step towards the light. When she took that step, an image of her mother and father sitting on a couch next to a fire appeared directly to the left of her. Her mother's pregnant and from the looks of it, her mom is due in the very near future. Her dad has his arm around her mother and his other hand is resting over his wife's basketball stomach. To Mrs. Yolanda's knowledge, she's never been in that house before, but her mind, body, and soul are telling her that she has. *What is this place?* She thought, touching her dad's face on the projection screen wall to see if he or she can feel each other. *Am I dead and where did everybody go?*

Unexpectedly her mother spoke. "What do you think we're having, darling?"

"A girl."

"But what if it's a boy, Donald?"

"Trust me, it's a girl."

"Well if you say so, but let's not get our hopes up. And don't forget that I'm due any day now, so we need to start thinking of some names if it's either or."

"There is no either or love. I know what my heart is telling me and it's telling me that I'm having a girl."

"Okay love, I believe you." Her mother said, looking into her dad's eyes. "So, what will be our precious daughter's name since you've got it all planned out?"

"Yolanda," her dad replied without any hesitation.

His response surprised Mrs. Humphrey and made her step back only to have her back bump into something. "What is this? A hallway of some sort?" she asked aloud, touching the sky blue wall her back found without trying. *This has to be a hall and the only way out is that light at the end of this tunnel.*

"Come," the voice said again when she looked towards the brightest light she's ever seen.

Deciding to follow the voice, she utilizes her only option and takes another step forward. This time when she did, she heard a woman's voice combined with her dad's yelling, "Push!"

"Come on Edna, your baby is almost here. Just give me one good push!" The woman doctor commanded, putting her hands between her mother's legs as if she's about to say, hike.

Out of the blue, a loud cry echoed through the delivery room and her dad kissed her mom when he saw that he was right all along. "You did it, baby! Our Yolanda is finally here!"

"Come!" the faraway voice exclaimed again from the light to let her know that's she's going in the right direction and to keep walking.

Mrs. Yolanda took another step and the sky blue wall that first showed an image displays a new image. "Go on Yolanda. Go to daddy," her mother said, holding her daughter's hands trying to get her thirteen month old to walk to her father.

"Come."

"All right I'm coming, but it's not like you're making it any easier to get there." Mrs. Yolanda responded, taking a step still wondering where she's at and why the voice won't come to her.

That step made a new image appear on the opposite wall. In it, she sees herself standing at the alter with her husband. "Do you, Geary Humphrey, take Yolanda Swarn to be your wife, to have and to hold from this day forward, for better or for worse, for richer, for poorer, in sickness and in health, to love and to cherish; from this day forward until death do you part?" The pastor that conducted her wedding stated to her husband while they both stood at the altar.

"I do."

"Come." The voice said immediately following her husband's words confirming his love for her.

With a smile on her face from all the previous images, Mrs. Yolanda takes unhesitant steps along the hallway that has proven to be a timeline of her life. *I wonder what's next?* She asked herself, but the answer is abruptly before her eyes.

"Yolanda Humphrey." The magnificent light said with authority like a rush of roaring water. "I am he who is truth and the sacrificial lamb of my Father, which art in Heaven."

"Jesus!" Mrs. Yolanda shouted directly into the alluring light that is on the other side of the ledge right in front of her. "Jesus, I need you right now," she said, falling to her knees prostrate. "I know I started to follow you late, but I feel I've waited my whole life for this moment to be with you. Since I've come to know you, it's like the devil won't let me rest and continues inflicting pain and mental depression upon me. However, throughout all that, I still proclaim that you are Lord and that this pain I have in my physical body will be no more when I receive my spiritual body. Oh Lord, you are so beautiful and worthy to be praised. Please my savior, allow me to enter your rest so that I can be at peace within you all the days of the rest of my spiritual life."

"But your time has not yet come."

"It has to be now, my Lord. My body hasn't felt this good since I was a child."

"My child, the images that were displayed before you on your journey to me was just a few of the happiest times you've experienced throughout your life. In them, you were pleased at yourself and your surroundings because they made you feel good and yet in turn, they made you smile."

"I know Jesus, but that makes me want to go with you even more. Because lately I haven't been smiling and if this cancer doesn't get any better anytime soon, my family want be smiling either."

"And that's why you're here, Yolanda Humphrey. You're here because as a follower of Christ, you must learn how to smile during the bad days as well. Yes, it may hurt inside. And yes, you will feel alone at times. However, you must be strong and carry your cross. Remember my child, that the light that you see before you is also in you and that you must let it shine so that others who are lost can see me in you and get saved. You've lived a good life and I assure you that your name is written in the book of life, but until that day comes, you must continue to let your light shine before men so that they can glorify our father which art in Heaven. Be blessed Yolanda Humphrey and go!"

"Don't leave me Jesus! Please take me with you. I don't know what I'm going to do without you back there. Please take me with you. Please Jesus! Please...."

"Momma, momma wake up."

"Aubrie get out of her face like that!" Audumn retorts as she sees her mother eyes rolling around in her head trying to focus on the light and the blurry faces around her.

Mrs. Humphrey eyes zero in on Audumn face and she sits straight up and shouts, "Audumn, I saw Jesus and he was so beautiful! He said it's not my time yet and that I need to smile more during the bad times, just as I smile through the good times!"

"That's right, Yolanda." Ms. Boswell steps out of the corner and comes to her sister in Christ's bedside. "Friend, you gave me a really big scare earlier. It was like one minute you were here and the next minute they had you on your back resuscitating you with the defibrillator."

"Mom, look how pale your skin is and how your face is shining like it's glowing."

"Well I would like to think that it should be. I mean, I did just see Jesus, Aubrie."

"Come on now, momma. Jesus?"

"Yes Jesus, son. He showed me my whole life as I followed his voice through this sky blue tunnel that was something like a timeline of every happy time in my life."

"Sky blue, huh?" Aubrie looked at his sister and then to Ms. Boswell.

"Yes sky blue, son and don't look at me like I'm crazy."

"Aubrie, I believe your mother when she says she saw Jesus. A lot of people say that they do when they have similar experience such as your mother."

"For real, Ms. Boswell?"

"Yes, for real. And their stories of what they saw coincides with the way your mother described Jesus." Ms. Boswell lays down her friend's disheveled hair with the palm of her hand.

"Thank you Janice, for believing me."

"I believe you, momma." Audumn adds in before Ms. Boswell can respond.

"Yolanda, you're my sister in Christ and I have no reason not to believe you. I'm just glad he didn't decide for you to go home today because I don't know what I would've done if..." Ms. Boswell stop midsentence and recalls the feeling she had when her friend's hand felt cold as an ice cube. "Enough about that thought. Let's just be thankful that you're back and thank God that he showed his face to you and assured you that it's not your time right now. And Aubrie"

"Yes Ms. Boswell?"

"Don't ever question your mother again. She's your mother and she has no reason to lie to you. If she said she saw Jesus, then she saw Jesus and you should leave it like that if you don't believe her. She needs you right now more than ever to listen to her and not go against her."

"Yeah, brother. Why would momma lie to us?"

"You're right sis, and momma I'm sorry for sounding like I didn't believe you."

"It's okay son. It was an unbelievable experience for me too, but it happened and I'm thankful that I'm back here with my kids."

The three of them sat with Mrs. Humphrey until night time showed its face and Ms. Boswell decided to leave. Aubrie left an hour after her because he was going back home because he had a job in the morning hooking up some speakers and amps. He wanted to stay and leave in the morning, but Audumn cut that short when the hospital said that only one can stay overnight with their mother. The look on his face became laden after he kissed his mother on the cheek and told her he's about to go. His mother knows she gave her baby boy the fright of his life and puts his forehead to hers to let him know that she loves him and that she's still here. Audumn decided to step out of the room briefly to wipe tears from her eyes because her mother scared her as well.

Audumn sat in the chair watching over her mother throughout the night. Her mother is in a peaceful state, sleeping like a baby from the medication they gave her to help her rest for release in the morning. Audumn, however, can't sleep and when she did get some shut eye it's with one eye open because her nerves are still sprinting from when she wasn't there earlier when her mother went into cardiac arrest. She was at Top Golf hitting some balls with Kizzy, Diana, and Kendra when she finally got the call from her brother that their mother had flatlined and he was five minutes away from the hospital. *Thirty minutes,* she thought, pondering between sleep spasms on how long it took for her to answer her brother's missed calls. *I love my Chicas, but I love my mother a lot more and this is definitely not going to happen again over me trying to please somebody else's fancies.*

"I'm sorry momma for not being here," Audumn mumbled before dozing off good for the first time.

"Good morning, Mrs. Woodson and Mrs. Humphrey." Dr. Whoroha knocks on the door and steps inside before they can answer.

"Good morning Dr. Whoroha and sorry about yesterday."

"Sorry for what, Mrs. Humphrey? Please note that this isn't the first time, nor will it be the last time that a patient's body rejected their chemo treatment."

"It's morning already?" Audumn yawns and stretches. "But I just went to sleep right before you knocked on the door and it wasn't morning yet."

"Well, it's morning now sweetheart and it feels good to see the sun shine again upon the blessed mother earth."

"So how are you feeling Mrs. Humphrey besides seeing the sunshine again?" Dr. Whoroha checks her vitals and listens to her heart with a stethoscope.

"I feel good, I guess. I really don't remember ever feeling bad actually. It was like everything that happened was all a dream that felt so real, but then I woke up and Audumn was standing over me."

"Are you feeling well enough to sit up on the side of the bed so that I can check your reflexes?"

"I think so." Mrs. Humphrey pushes herself up and hangs her feet over the side of the hospital bed. "How's that?"

"Just fine. Now let your legs hang loosely so that I can check your reflexes."

Dr. Whoroha taps on Mrs. Yolanda's knees, elbows, and had her follow a flashlight with her eyes to make sure her health is good enough for release. When finished, the doctor explained that her body had a chemotherapy resistance and that occurs when cancers that have been responding to a therapy suddenly begins to grow. In other words, the cancer cells are resisting the effects of the chemotherapy. Her suggestion is that they may have to develop a specific chemo resistance cell line for her next few treatments, but before Kelsey-Sebold does that, they will first change the medication because the former is very expensive.

"All done Mrs. Humphrey, and I will see you next Monday instead of the Monday after next since you didn't completely finish your cycle yesterday.

Mrs. Humphrey signs some papers and says, "Thank you Dr. Whoroha for everything."

"You're welcome and one of our staff members will be bringing you a wheelchair shortly. Good day."

"Good day Dr. Whoroha and don't worry about sending someone to bring my mom a wheelchair." Audumn stands and shakes the doctor's hand to show her gratitude. "I'm pretty sure my mother is ready to get back home to her bed as quickly as possible, so I'll go get one for her myself."

"Sure thing Mrs. Woodson and you two have a great day."

CHAPTER 22

Jack Brooks Airport is an airport in Jefferson County, which is the same county that Beaumont, Texas is in. It's also the same airport that Robby flew in on for Audumn's wedding and today, it's the airport Mrs. Humphrey's sister and niece are flying in on for an extended visit.

Bad news travels fast and being that it's December, it's a known secret that Mrs. Yolanda has lost the last three, four, and five rounds in her bout against cancer. And from the looks of it, she isn't going to make it to the sixth round because her body is too weak to try and receive chemotherapy again. The cancer is spreading and until she can get her white blood cell count up and her body stronger than what it is, that means her last cycle was the one she died on.

Last month went by like a hurricane sitting on the Humphrey family, and Audumn wishes she could rip November off this year's 2013 calendar's months. Every day of November was gloomy because Audumn had to watch her mother go downhill and she couldn't do anything to help ease her mother's pain. Aubrie and Nickolas came around to check on their mom about twice a week. However, that was only for a matter of minutes because both of them couldn't stomach how quickly their mother's health has deteriorated to practically nothing. Dexter couldn't take it from the beginning in which he was told about his mother's state, and therefore, has completely succumbed to the disease he's done so well restraining from. He's homeless, but not completely homeless because he sometimes leaves for two to three days on his alcoholic binges and suddenly out of nowhere, he'll be in his room lying there passed out from his demised adventure.

With all that going on, Audumn is thankful that this past month is over and looks forward to today. Especially since Thanksgiving turned out to be a drop a plate of food off for two and go on back to your everyday lives type of day. Audumn wanted to do something and the boys agreed on it, but it was their mother who said no because Robby wasn't going to be able to make it back home until Christmas. The boys were okay with that answer, but Audumn knew it was also because her mother misses her husband and that this Thanksgiving was the first family holiday that they were apart. The only good thing that came from that month is that Audumn got to make love to her husband and lie in his arms on turkey day and the day afterwards.

Mrs. Humphrey's birthday was December 3rd and just like last month, she didn't want to do anything because of her spirit's being down. Nevertheless, she did accept a few gifts and allowed Nickolas, Aubrie, and Audumn to buy her a birthday cake and sing happy birthday to her. Hopefully, with Audumn's aunt and cousin flying in, today will be the first day she can start getting her strength back to normal so that she can finish her treatments. If not, the Humphrey's are going to lose the palm that holds the fingers together in their family.

"Monica!"

"Audumn!" Audumn's 1st cousin, Monica, opens her arms to give her cousin a gigantic hug. "Cousin, besides you graduating from college last summer, I haven't chilled in Texas since you had me helping you clean the Y.M.C.A for your community service hours for probation."

"Yeah cousin, I had a lot of fun beating you in volleyball after we finished cleaning up each day."

"Oh whatever, Audumn. You just had to rub that in, huh?"

"And you know it." Audumn holds up the number one because her little cousin never beat her.

Aunt Glynda clears her throat. "Um…if I'm not mistaken, my daughter isn't the only one standing here."

"I'm sorry, Aunt Glynda for not speaking to you. How are you and how was your flight?"

"It was great now that I'm here with my sister. By the way, where is she?"

"She's waiting for us in baggage claims. You know, she's been in a wheelchair lately and she didn't want me pushing her way over here and then back over there just in case you needed some help with your carryon bags."

"Great and I can't wait to get to the house so that I can start being there for my sister like I should've been these past three months. By the way niece, are you still having the surprise party for your mother when we get to your house?"

"Yes, and she doesn't know anything about it. Me and Secori's flight leaves Sunday on the 12th, so today is perfect and it will give me and my husband all day Saturday to pack for our trip." Audumn turns to her cousin as they're walking. "Sorry I can't stay and hang out with you cousin the whole time you're here, but I'm thankful y'all came to relieve me while I go visit my in laws in Chicago. Momma is very dependent right now and I know the boys will be very uncomfortable giving her a bath."

"That's why we're here, Audumn." Aunt Glynda gives her niece a slight hug. "My apologies sweetheart for not coming to your wedding, but please know that I'm happy for you, proud of you, and that I can't wait for my great niece and nephew to be born."

"Me neither." Audumn smiles because her last ultrasound confirmed her other baby is a girl. "Thanks Aunt Glynda for the apology, but you're here now and that what matters most to me as of the moment. Now come, let's get mother and get her home because everyone is waiting on us."

Monica sat in the front while Mrs. Yolanda and her sister sat in the back holding each other's hands and conversing amongst themselves. Audumn couldn't help but to be delighted as she looked into her rearview mirror and saw her mother's eyes gleaming from being in the company of her only sister. The airport is only fifteen minutes away from her house and even though there's a surprise party waiting on them, Audumn wishes that she could've driven her mom and Aunt around a little longer. Be that as it may, she pulled into her driveway and parked and winked at her cousin Monica.

It took them only a few minutes to get inside the house. One would think by now that the steps in the front of the house are too troublesome a climb for Yolanda, but because of her husband, Geary, he's made the steps obsolete. How, is by building a wooden ramp up to the back porch so that she can enter with the least amount of hindrance possible. Also, Audumn told him last month that it's hard getting her mom to the car by herself with everyone being at work when she has to bring her out of the house. Being that he's slowly patching his relationship up with his daughter, he was there the next day after the call with a couple of guys, nailing and hammering until it was done. Audumn thinks that was when her mother started longing for her husband again. Because when it's all said and done, every woman needs a man's touch around the house.

"Look Audumn, Miss Mary must've had a loss in the family." Audumn's mom points towards the cars lined up on side of the road starting about fifty feet from her house. "Remind me later to call her and check on her."

"Yes ma'am. Trust me, I won't forget to remind you about all the cars in the street at Miss Mary's house." Audumn and Monica look at each other and smirked.

"What's funny?"

"Sister, can we please get inside the house? I think I've got jetlag."

"Don't rush me, Glynda. Let's not forget, I'm the oldest."

"I know, big sister. I promise you that I'll never forget." Aunt Glynda pushes the door open when her sister takes her key out the keyhole.

"Happy birthday!" The full house in front of Mrs. Yolanda and the three people behind her shouted all at the same time.

"Happy birthday, momma!" Brie and Nick exclaimed as Audumn pushed their mother towards the birthday decorations in the front room of the house.

"Happy birthday, friend."

"Thanks Celeste. Thank all of you for coming, but my birthday was on the third." She replied, crying tears of love. Love for them coming to show their support for her 52nd birthday.

"I know momma, that's why I planned this for you and insisted that you ride with me to the airport." Audumn whispers into her mother's ear from behind. "I wasn't going to let you talk me out of giving you a birthday party, so I waited to do it when Aunt Glynda got here so that you would never in a million years know what was going to happen today. And besides momma, we all love you."

"Happy birthday, Yolanda."

"Janice, you're here too? You didn't have to come all this way for me."

"There you go with that nonsense again, friend. This is your day and your family wanted to show you how much everyone loves and appreciate you."

"Happy birthday, Audumn's mom." Khamil, Diana, Kendra, Kizzy, and Shanay said as she rolled passed them to her daily sitting chair.

"Oh, I see you even got your Chicas to come to my party."

"Yes momma. We all love you. And look, my friend Tamera is here too."

Tamera gives Audumn's mom a hug. "Happy 52nd birthday, play momma."

"Thanks Tamera, and Audumn has told me so much about how good you're doing in California. Keep up the good work and I'm very proud of you."

"Momma, we have another surprise for you!" Nickolas exclaimed as his little brother hooked his phone up to the tv.

Secorion helped his mother in law out of the wheelchair and into her sitting chair. "Happy birthday, mother in law. Congratulations on seeing fifty-two."

"Thanks Secori. Thanks for being here my son and thanks for taking care of my daughter and my future grandkids."

As everyone waited for the tv to come on, Audumn brought her mother a gift from off the table to kill some time. The gift was from Ms. Celeste and it was a digital picture frame with multiple images of them from the first time they met until now, changing every few seconds. The smiles on their faces from their numerous trips out of the state and country truly uplifts Mrs. Humphrey and makes her tears of love turn into a big smile of joy. Ms. Boswell handed her friend her gift next and Mrs. Yolanda tears open the soft package like a kid wondering what present is underneath the wrapper. What she found was a purple handknitted blanket with a gold cross in the center of it.

"You shouldn't have, Janice." Mrs. Humphrey said, overlapping the blanket over her legs. "How long did this take you to make?"

"Don't worry about it. Just know that it was made out of love and God wanted you to have it."

"Attention, attention!" Aubrie shouted. "My phone is connected to the tv and my big brother has a surprise for you, momma."

Mrs. Humphrey thought, *I wonder what Nickolas is about to show me on this tv?*

The 50" screen lit up and Robby's cheerful face in his office at work reflected off the pupils of his mother's blue eyes. "Happy birthday, momma. I just wanted to let you know that you're the best mom a man can ever have. I remember us living off the government. I remember going to people's houses and getting the clothes and shoes that they didn't want anymore. I remember dad losing his job at the Coca Cola plant when it was shut down and you had to work at the daycare to put food on the table until he got back to work. I remember, momma, how you told me you wanted me to graduate high school so that I can be the first one out of my siblings to do so. I remember you taking out a loan for me to get a new car because I wrecked my car that you and pops gave me for graduation my first year living in Florida." Robby gets emotional and looks away, because as the first born, he knows the struggles his mom had to endure with a newborn baby to take care of us. "Momma, the list goes on and on and on, but I said all this to let you know that I remember, momma. And being that I remember, I will never forget. I love you mom. We all do, and just as you've never given up on us, we will never give up on you. Happy 52nd birthday, my queen, and enjoy your day."

"Here momma." Nickolas hands his mother a box. "Happy birthday mom from your four boys."

"Oh, thank you Nickolas and thank you too son if you can hear me."

"I can hear you, mom. I love you and I'll give you a call later when I get off. Happy birthday."

Their mother opened the box and found a pair of gold dove earrings and a gold necklace with a gold olive branch pendant. The three charms were a pair and it represented hope because the Bible says that Noah sent out a dove from the ark in search for land and the bird came back with an olive branch in its beak. All of her boys are not into going to church like Audumn and their mother, but they do know that their mother believes whole heartedly in what the Bible teaches. Being so, they knew that the gift that they're giving their mother is the perfect gift. Predominantly because they know that hope is all that everyone's hanging onto right now as each day is an uncertainty as to what tomorrow may bring, concerning their mother, that is.

Aubrie and Nickolas made a video with a collage of their mother's friends from Beaumont, their friends, friends from the hospital, and friends from her church, Cathedral of Faith. All of whom said, "Happy birthday, Yolanda Humphrey!" Some even expressed their love for her and what she means to them as a person and as a friend. Pastor Delbert Mack ended the video with him expressing how much he's appreciated Mrs. Yolanda as a baby in Christ growing into an adult in the Lord under his ministry. He knows from one of his members that Sister Yolanda is very ill and that's why she hasn't been to church service on Sundays. Consequently, he pleads the blood of Jesus over her and when he's finished, his church choir sang happy birthday until the tv screen went black from being turned off by Aubrie.

"We love you momma and we hope this video shows you how much we all love you." Aubrie says as he and Nick make way to give their mother a kiss and a hug.

Mrs. Humphrey is balling in tears when her sons gave her that hug. Holding them tightly, she thinks about what would she do without out them. Or worst, what will they do without her? Her mind has no answer for that question that's been popping up daily as she goes another week without chemotherapy. Her mind wants to keep pushing for her health to be back to what it used to be, yet her body is saying that she can't take the excruciating feeling that the chemo brings when it goes inside her body. This is what has her up at night and this is why she's in tears from the fear of having to leave her kids. Yes, her mind wants to do this and wants to do that, but until her body follows, she feels like fifty-two will be the last number called on her timeline.

"I love you sons, and that video was breathtaking. Thank you both. Thank all of you for this wonderful day." Audumn hands her mom some tissues. "Thanks Audumn, and thank you for throwing me this surprise party."

"Momma, you deserve it. We all know how you're less mobile these days, so we decided to bring the party to you when we knew for sure that you were going to be out of the house."

"Were you in on this too, sis? And what about you, niece?"

"Yes Auntie. That's why Audumn waited for Friday to have the party and to leave on Sunday for her trip. She wanted to wait until we get here because she knew that it will be more special if we were here when they screamed happy birthday to you."

Mrs. Humphrey laughs. "Y'all got me good, niece and sis. I didn't have a clue. And to think, I was about to send Miss Mary my condolences when that's all of your cars parked down the street."

"And look momma, my friend Diana made you your favorite dish."

"What, homemade lasagna and garlic bread?"

"Yep, and it's one of my specialties that my mom taught me growing up." Diana hands Mrs. Yolanda a plate and a fork. "Texas Toast made the garlic bread, but please know I can make a good homemade garlic bread too."

"Yeah momma, you know big girls always know how to cook."

"Whatever Audumn. And I'm not big, I'm thickalicious."

"Please don't start her up, Audumn."

"I'm with Kizzy."

"And I'm with the both of them." Khamil chimed in right after Kendra.

"All right." Audumn agreed, knowing that her Chicas are right about Diana. "Here momma, here's some lemonade."

"Thank you, sweetheart. And Diana, this lasagna is de-lic-ious."

"I told you that it's my specialty and that you were going to like it."

"Yes you did, Diana. And thanks again for this scrumptious birthday dinner."

"You're welcome, Mrs. Humphrey. You're my bff's mother and it's the least I can do for you blessing me with such a beautiful friend, inside and out."

Everyone enjoyed the latter end of the day, hanging out and having a really good time with Mrs. Yolanda. All of the gifts were opened and each gift the birthday girl held up to be seen she expressed a cheerful emotion. Gospel music was played throughout the day, but towards the end, Brie put on one of his mixtapes and started to do the Harlem shuffle with all of the girls in his sister's wedding. Secorion and Audumn joined in too and before you knew it, Ms. Celeste and Ms. Boswell got in the front of all of them right on que to show what they can do. Mrs. Humphrey just sat on the edge of her seat and moved her hands and feet to the beat as if she's doing the shuffle with them. That is, until the doorbell rang and Nickolas turned the music down to see who was at the door.

"Happy birthday, Yolanda," her husband said, holding a card and some flowers in a vase while standing in the door. "Sorry, I'm late, but look who I found."

Dexter steps from behind his dad and goes to give his mother a hug. "Happy birthday, momma. I love you."

"I love you too, son," she replied, smelling the alcohol on his breath. "Are you hungry? If so, go and get you something to eat."

"Yes ma'am."

"And Geary, those flowers are beautiful. Nick, if you don't mind, could you please take them and put them in my room on my dresser?"

"Coming right up." Nickolas said, retrieving the flowers from his dad. "Anything for the birthday girl."

Perfect! Everything turned out perfect, Audumn thought from the kitchen as she looked into the living room at how much joy her mother has on her face. It's sad to say, but Audumn hasn't seen that look on mother's face in a long time and hopes that today will be the beginning of joy being present in her life again. Daily, she talks to her mom and uplifts her on what she has to be thankful for and today, her mother is able to see what Audumn's been telling her for the past two months.

"So babe, are you ready for our trip to the windy city because it's cold as hell up there?"

Audumn smiles at her husband's dumb analogy as he puts his arms around her and cuffs her belly. "Yes, my love. Ready as I'll ever be," she replied, hoping that her mother will be okay the three weeks that she will be gone.

CHAPTER 23

"Baby, wake up." Audumn is lying next to Secori with a big cheesy smile. Her hair is unkempt from the night before and her breasts are standing at attention.

Secori wakes up to the grey morning light that will soon be daylight. "Baby, you can't be waking me up with your stuff all in my face. I almost did something to you."

"What were you going to do to me? Audumn replies teasingly and then they both burst into a snickering laughter. "Aww baby, I can't believe you remembered…"

Secori kisses his wife's nose. "What do you mean you can't believe that I remembered the first day I woke up next to you and your boobs was all in my face?" Secorion looks at his wife's lips. "And you had that big cheesy smile on your face like the one you have on your face now."

"Like this?" Audumn smiles her biggest smile ever, showing her pretty white teeth.

"Yes, my love. Just like that."

"Also, my love, that was the first day you called me baby." Audumn kisses his neck, his chest, and then drags her tongue down to the base of her husband's penis. "And look at us now, laid up in your momma's house doing the nasty."

"But baby, my parents should be getting up any minute now."

"I don't care about that right now. But please be quiet so that I can make some seven in the morning love to my husband." Audumn licks up the shaft of his penis and then kisses the head of her favorite part of Secorion's body.

"Okay baby, but we got to be quiet." Secorion whispers. "And you got to promise me that we're going to get out of the house today."

Audumn takes his pole out of her mouth. "I promise," and goes to sucking on his sack, while twisting and stroking his penis.

"Oh baby, don't stop." Secori grips the sheets and bites his bottom lip.

Standing, Audumn tells her husband to hang his feet over the side of the bed so that she can have a seat on his rocking chair. Secorion quickly complies to his wife's wishes, disregarding the weird feeling about how he's about to make a real live porno in his parents' house. With his slippery penis in her hand, she turns around and puts her husband inside the slit that changed into a rhombus when his head divided her opening. Audumn's back is to him, so he holds on tight to her hips while she works the helm of the S.S. Lady. Well, at least, that's what his imagination is thinking as Secorion reads, Lady tatted across the top of her back moving up and down as if they are on the water. *God damn, my wife is giving me the business early this morning,* he thought as the daylight highlighted the cream from Audumn's upside down V building onto his pelvic area.

Secorion sits up and squeezes her colostrum breast, while pushing down on her shoulder with his other hand. As he's holding her there, she puts his fingers in her mouth and moans while he pulsates his penis inside her vagina. "You like this pussy, huh?" she whispers. "That's why you married me." Secorion stands while he's still inside her so that he can hit it from the back. Audumn complies to her husband's wishes and toots her ass up while laying across the bed. "Oh, how I love being married," Secorion exclaimed as he slams inches of himself inside his beloved until the best feeling in the world starts to tingle inside his testicles.

Secorion climaxed every drip of him inside Audumn as she grinded and pushed back as hard as she could to make sure nothing got lost. After pulling out, Audumn dropped to her knees and started slurping the side of his shaft as it went down from the thirty minute workout it had to endure. Secorion thought, *I ain't never leaving no fire head like this.* Audumn thought, *His ass ain't going nowhere after seeing how good I'm getting at sucking his dick.* When they finished, Audumn felt her babies move from all the disruption, but then chuckles at the fact that her kids just caught their parents having sex.

"All right now bae, it's time to get dressed. We've been in this house five days now and I'm ready to show you my city."

"But baby, it's cold out there." Audumn comes out the shower teeth chattering. "See!"

"Don't give me that. And besides, you promised, so get dressed and meet me in the kitchen for a quick breakfast. And oh, by the way, if I were you, I would bundle up and put on that jacket I bought you at the airport."

"Why?"

"Because my little brother is about to be here in like twenty minutes to drop off my niece and nephew, so we can hitch a ride to the Dan Ryan on 95th Street on his way to work."

"But I'm a Texas girl, we don't do the cold and we especially don't do the snow." Audumn finished her sentence, but Secori closed the door to his room right after she said, "But."

The temperature is fair today for the 17th day of December. Yes, it may be twenty degrees outside, but it's a different type of cold and Audumn's Texas bones realized that they can handle it. Holding Secorion's hand, they cross the busy street and snake their way through the CTA buses until they step foot onto the Dan Ryan grand platform. Secorion pays for their tickets using his dad's Ventra Card, which is Chicago's way of payment to ride the city's transportation. Two one day tickets pop out the bottom of the ticket machine with rainbow colors on them that represented the different colors of the trains the passengers choose to ride.

"What? That's to ride the bus?" Audumn asks, going down some stairs wondering why they're not going back towards the buses.

"No, the train."

"The train!" Audumn goes through a turnstile when her husband scans her ticket.

"Yes my love, and it's time for you to see my city and what better way to do than by riding the L downtown to Monroe?"

People start coming through the turnstile in a rush when hearing the sound of the train clacking loudly on the tracks getting closer. "Is that what people in Chicago call the train out here?"

"Yes ma'am, and I grew up riding the L with my friends when we wanted to get away from our hood, Calumet Park." The train comes to a screeching halt and the doors separate for the mass number of people to get on. "Now come my love, let me show you the city by riding the Red Line."

The ding donging of the bell and the computer voice startled Audumn when she got onto the train. "Doors closing. 87th is next. Doors will open on the left on 87th."

"You good, bae? You act like you've never been on a train before."

"I haven't. My parents always drove or we caught the Grey Hound when we traveled."

"Well, let's find you a window seat so that you can get a good look at the Chi at its best."

Audumn found her a window seat and immediately became a fan of riding through the city, seeing the stages of Chicago from the lower, middle, and upper class of people. Traveling the Red Line today turned into traveling the Green line the next day. After the Green Line, Audumn convinced Secorion that every day she wanted to travel a different color train on the L because she wanted to know everything about the city her husband grew up in.

Secorion just laughed because it was eight different rails and they were long to ride, even if it was just for sightseeing. Instead, he took her every day to see something different so that she can fulfill whatever it is she's looking for about him in his hometown. Thus far, within a seven day span of touring the city, Audumn feels she's accomplished seeing everything possible she wanted to see or what her husband wanted her to see.

Back on the Red Line today, Audumn wants to take a Christmas Eve walk downtown so that she can soak up the jolly atmosphere with her husband and the twins inside her. Cori just met a girl a few weeks ago and they've been hitting it off, hence, he thought this would be the perfect opportunity to introduce her to his big brother and his sister in law. Audumn is all for it because she wants to hang out with a girl from the Chi just so she can feel her vibe. Secorion didn't tell her that after their walk, he's going to take her to the Winter Fest at the Navy Pier. It's a surprise and that's also the reason he's taken her to see all the other main attractions but the Navy Pier.

Such as the famous Michael Jordan statue, the White Sox stadium, and the Kris Kringle Market where you can get into the Christmas spirit downtown while eating some delicious Chicago entrees. Audumn's favorite was the Chicago style pizza, but she did say the Chicago dog was the best hotdog she's ever eaten in her life. In fact, she can't wait for the Red Line to stop on Monroe so she can get her a slice of pizza on their walk-through of Millennium Park and by the frozen Lake Michigan.

Her babies are craving pizza and it's one of the main reasons she wanted to come back to the first place Secorion took her while riding the Red Line. However, Audumn thought she could kill two birds with one stone because she wanted to see the steel Cloud Gate Bean again. She just thought it was so cool how humongous the bean is and how unique in design it is at the same time. Not to mention, when one is standing directly under the twelve-foot arch that curves underneath the bean, that it looks like a Kaleidoscope when you're looking up at your reflection.

Audumn and Cori's girlfriend, Nicole, became cool real fast. Partly because they both loved each other's accents and they both were hungry. Also, she was very laid back after smoking weed throughout the day with Cori when they could. After getting their hunger fix situated, the four of them took funny pictures in front of the shiny bean while savoring the embellishment of the huge Christmas ornament balls throughout the park. The walk to Navy Pier from Millennium

Park is thirty minutes, so they begin their Christmas hike through downtown admiring the skyscrapers, architectural buildings, hotels, condos, and the lake. As they got closer, the secret came out of the bag as music and lifelike holiday figures started to line the sidewalk along with tourists taking pictures on their way to Navy Pier.

"Finally, we made it," Secorion said, rubbing his hands together for warmth.

Audumn looks at Secorion and his brother. "Let me guess, we were coming here all along."

"Yep!" Nicole laughs. "It was hard not telling you too because you're real and it feels like I've known you all my life."

"Oh baby, this place is beautiful. Please, please, please say that we're going in." Audumn pokes out her bottom lip and give him her pouting eyes.

"No need for all that bae. Of course we're going in."

"Yes sir, and you better believe it." Cori grabs Nicole's hand. "Because we for damn sho didn't walk all this way for nothing."

When they first got there, they walked inside of a big glass room full of exotic trees, Christmas fountains, and an array of flowers. The room is warmer than outside because of the small forest, so everyone skedaddled in when it was agreed that they were going inside. Shaking off the cold, Audumn whips out her camera and begins making memories with her new friend, husband, and brother in law. As she twirls around about the fountain, she stops when her eyes fell upon a tall Ferris wheel on the other side of the glass turning ever so gradually.

"Ouu baby, can we ride it?"

"Just hold up bae, we'll get to that after we go to the Winter Fest." Secorion points to a sign that says, 'Winter Fest,' with an arrow pointing to the right next to it.

"Oh, alright."

"Come on now sister in law, you can't be serious about going back into the cold to ride the Ferris Wheel?"

"Yeah Audumn, it is cold out there and we still need to warm up from that long walk from the park. But shit, you know you my girl, so after I get something hot in my system, I'm down."

"And bae, they've got rides in the Winter Fest if I'm not mistaken. Well, at least they did when mom and pops used to bring me and Cori back in the day."

The first thing Audumn noticed when she enters the Winter Fest is a yellow Minion Christmas tree and she thought it was cool. That is, until she approached it and saw right behind the yellow tree was a divergent number of Santa's from all cultures around the world. Seeing the diversities in their attire to match their homeland was intriguing and they all agreed that it is a sight to see how each culture dressed for this particular holiday. It was the Polar Express horn that grabbed their ears and then their eyes from the magnificent sculptures. As they're waiting in line, Secorion buys Audumn a Polar Express teddy bear as a souvenir before getting on the train.

"All aboard!" the conductors bellows.

Audumn squeezes her polar bear and pumps her fist two times. "Toot! Toot!"

Side by side, the four of them sit in two rows on the small indoor train. As they toured the massive event center, Christmas carols and kids' voices singing along sounded from the speakers throughout the building. Nicole was the first to see the indoor Ferris wheel hiding behind the inflatable slide and pointed it out to Audumn. Audumn eyes widened as soon as she saw it because she hasn't rode one since she was a teenager at the South East Texas State Fair. When they exited the train, they hurried and got in the line with the inflatable slide first because it wasn't that long and the Ferris wheel had nobody in line because they had so many seats to fill.

"Whew!" Audumn exclaims when Cori and Nicole helped her to her feet from her slide. "That was a rush for me and the twins." Audumn rubbed the lower part of her protruding stomach. "Ain't that right you two in there?"

"Watch out!" Secorion comes sliding down at full speed and bounces off the slide onto the cement right as Cori grabs Audumn from his path.

"Damn bro, you all right?" Cori and the girls laughed.

"Come on, baby. I got you."

"Thanks bae, but I ain't getting on that no more."

"Shit, I wouldn't either if my ass feels like yours does right now."

"Oh shut up, Cori. That shit hurt for real."

Audumn don't want them to fight, so she interjects. "Come on now guys, can we ride the Ferris wheel already? I think it's time we all take a chill pill and then get back to having fun."

"I'm down with taking a chill pill or whatever Audumn said."

"You said it right, Nicole." Audumn tugs Secorion's sleeve. "Baby, you can rest on the ride. And Cori, stop picking on your brother."

"Okay sister in law, but you know I'm full of them green trees and that shit was funny as hell."

On the Ferris wheel, Audumn rested her head on Secorion's shoulder. While up high, they're able to get a full view of the arena and soak in the holiday scenery. Cori and Nicole are behind them in another cart making out, so Audumn puts her hand down her husband's pants to give him a quick hand job.

"You're so crazy baby these past few days."

"What?" Audumn squeezes his testicles and smiles. "You don't like it?"

"Now I wouldn't say all that. I actually do like it."

"Baby, I just feel so free out here with you and your family. And not to mention my pregnancy hormones have been going through the roof since you've been around me every day and not at work."

"I know it feels good for you to take a break sometimes bae, and for what it's worth, I'm proud to see how you're hanging in there with your mother."

Audumn takes her hand out of his pants when the ride rotates for the next riders to get off down below. "But baby, I love you and I don't want you to feel like I don't have time for you."

"Audumn, we're a team in this, so never feel like you've got to please me or be out of your character to make up for something we're doing as a team."

"So, my situation after our wedding doesn't make you feel some type of way? Because I know it's not what you expected."

"Baby, anything that happened after we said, 'I do,' is what I expected when it comes to us. That includes my job, your job, your school, our babies, and your mother."

"Please exit to your right and thanks for riding the Mrs. Clause Ferris wheel." The operator's assistant unlatched the latch that held them inside the cart. "Thanks again and Merry Christmas."

"Merry Christmas to you too." Audumn replied and then finished her conversation with her husband while waiting for Cori and Nicole. "Thanks for today, bae. As a matter fact, thanks for the past two weeks. If you haven't noticed, I'm telling you now that I'm worried about my mother, but having my Aunt Glynda at home with her has given me a sense of peace."

"I know, sweetheart. And I also know that you most likely wouldn't have come to Chicago in the state she's in, but because of your love for me, you came."

Audumn kisses Secorion as his brother and girlfriend are walking up. "I love you, Secorion Woodson."

"There you two go again with all that lovey-dovey stuff."

"Go on with all that lil bro, don't act like you weren't getting your freak on when we were up there in the air standing still."

"Yeah, I was." Cori smacks Nicole on the ass. "That's just what we were doing up there."

"What?" Audumn asks, looking a little confused.

"Getting our freak on!" Nicole answered and they all started laughing.

"So, you ready for me to beat you on the ice skates, bro?"

"I don't think you got it in you no more, Cori."

"Shoot, you're crazy! I always got it in me if I'm going to race your old ass or my big cuz B.G."

"Fool, we're two years apart and you know you ain't never beat Brian in an ice skating race!"

"But that was then, and I bet B.G. can't beat me now."

"Hold up, hold up. I just realized you two are talking about ice skating. I'm sorry Secori, but I ain't getting on no ice. There comes a time in every woman's life where she must draw a line in the sand and this is one of those times."

"I'm with Audumn and she shouldn't be getting on no skates pregnant, anyway. Also, I don't feel like skating today either, so you two can go have some macho fun while me and my girl watch y'all kill yourself."

"Sounds like a plan to me. Unless Secorion is scared I'm going to embarrass him in front of his wife."

"I ain't never scared when it comes to beating my little brother." Secorion playfully pushes his brother. "Baby, I'll be right back. Give me a sec, this won't take long."

"No, please hubby, take all the time you want. Just as long as you don't try to get me to put on some ice skates."

It was the time that brought the enchanting day to an end. Secorion and his brother knew that their mom liked to bake cookies and look at old family pictures on Christmas Eve; therefore, they made sure that they made it back to the Red Line by 6:30 so that they can be home by 8:00. Cori's car is parked at a chicken restaurant across the street from the Dan Ryan transit station. When they get there, he presses the alarm for them to get in and goes inside and pays the girl behind the counter for allowing them to park their car there. Not only did he pay her, but he also did it in a flirtatious way and Nicole noticed them through the restaurant's window. Knowing that this is not the time or place for addressing it, she decides to let this one go because she had so much fun with his family today.

Mrs. Dorion is putting the first batch of cookies in the oven when Jack Frost rushed inside her home when the front door opened. The cool breeze is felt by her granddaughter and grandson, which in turn, made them drop their spatulas in the cookie dough and run to meet their daddy and uncle. Audumn looks at how cute they are and can't wait for them to play with their 1st cousins. What really makes her smile is that both of her kids will never feel left out because they each will have someone to play with.

"Secori, our babies just kicked." Audumn hurries and puts her husband's hand on her stomach. "Feel right here," she said with a big grin on her face that her kids moved around when hearing their big cousins.

"Yes bae, I feel it. Wow, and it's way stronger than the last time they were playing around in there."

"They must've heard Phil and Lil."

"No, they must've smelled them cookies and them pies I made from scratch." Secori's mom walks in and gives Audumn a hug. "Audumn, when was the last time you ate because my grandchildren are probably hungry for some of Grandma's cookies?"

"I guess you're right, Mrs. Woodson, now that I think about it."

"Great, because I make a sweet potato pie to die for. How about you Nicole, do you want a slice until the cookies come out of the oven?"

"Yes ma'am, and thanks."

"Mom, where's dad?" Cori manages to say as he watches his mother make haste to the kitchen.

"Dad's out getting a fifth of Hennessy."

"Sounds like a plan to me." Cori fist bumps his brother because they're about to get wasted with their pops like old times sake.

Mr. Woodson got home shortly after his wife took out the old pictures. With Christmas music playing throughout the house, she explained each picture to Audumn and Nicole. She showed pictures of her deceased dad and how much her big brother, Andre in Texas, looks just like him. Her mother, Serena, who died giving birth to her, was a breath of fresh air in the pictures she showed of her. After each viewing of the photos of her mom, she kissed each picture as she put it back into the photo album. Audumn liked going over her kid's family tree, but what she really liked the most was the picture of Secorion, Brian, and Cori playing with the water hose.

"Aww, how cute." Audumn says gullibly.

"Yeah right Audumn, you know we looking all jacked up with no shoes on, but at least it ain't that picture on your momma's refrigerator of all of y'all."

Audumn eyes got big when she realized what picture he's talking about. "Okay, okay. I'm calling a truce."

"I would too if….Nah, I ain't gon' do you like that if you're throwing up the white flag, bae."

"By the way, where's Brian?"

"Oh, B.G. texted me earlier saying he's gon' come thru in the morning because he had a big fish on the line." Cori replies.

"What's that?"

"Trust me, you don't want to know." Nicole and Secori said at the same time in response to Audumn's questions.

Christmas Eve came to an end at two something in the morning. Audumn and Nicole didn't know how competitive Cori and Secorion were in everything, but tonight they found out during the games of gin, dominoes, and spades. They wanted to quit when Phil and Lil went to bed at eleven, but both of their guys are hell bent on who would beat who in partners with their girlfriends. Finally, Cori wins the tie breaker and rubs it his brother's face as Secori walks off without responding. Audumn, in turn, tells Nicole and Cori goodnight when noticing that her husband is turning in for the night.

"You're staying here tonight, brother in law?"

"No, but my kids are. Me and Nicole about to go get high and have some victory sex for beating you."

"Oh, stop that Cori," Nicole jokes. "They played all right."

301

"Nicole, not you too?" Audumn is taken aback. "Alright, tomorrow is round two then and you better bring your A game because I'm not going back to Texas losers to you two."

Secorion is asleep when she finally got a chance to lay next to him. As she is snuggling to find comfort, she thinks about how her mother's been doing since she's been gone. Every day when she calls to check on her, her mother assures her that everything's okay and that she's feeling fine. To Audumn's ears, it sounds great, but when it comes to getting a true diagnosis from her mother on her health, Mrs. Humphrey will always say she's fine. Settling under the arms of her husband, she thinks about the day her mother rung the cancer bell the first time and falls asleep in her happy place, wishing that this day will come again. *You did it, momma!* she dreamt as her mom rung the bell. *No, we did it Audumn and I will always be with you,* her mother replied as they stood there in the hospital.

"Knock! Knock! Knock!" A hard knock comes from the other side of the bedroom door.

"Go away Cori, we just fell asleep!"

The door pushes open and his niece and nephew climbs on top of their Uncle. "Uncle! Uncle! Get up, it's Christmas!"

"Yes, it is my precious babies and Uncle's sorry for yelling at you." Secorion slides his arm from underneath Audumn's head. "Come on, kids. Let's go see if Santa ate the cookies you and Granny left out for him. And afterwards, we're going to open a few of the presents he brought you."

"Come on, come on Uncle." Phil said when seeing his uncle is moving sluggishly. "We're ready to open our presents."

CHAPTER 24

The phone call Audumn's dreaded the most came on a Saturday, one day before the 2014 New Year's Day. Secorion isn't around when her phone rings with back to back phone calls from every family member in her intermediate family. Audumn wished he had been when she finally got to her phone because what she heard through the receiver isn't what she wanted to hear while being 1,099.6 miles away.

Her next door neighbor and friend, Khamil, is the first person she talked too because that's who dialed her phone first when she's going through her missed calls. "Audumn, call your mom. I don't know what's going on down there by your house, but one minute all of your family cars were there and the next minute, they were gone." Audumn immediately hung up her phone and called her mother, only for it to go to the voicemail without ringing. Next, she called her Aunt Glynda, but she didn't pick up either after it rang and rang and the voicemail came on to leave a message. *What's wrong with my mom and Aunt's phone?* she thought as she dialed her cousin Monica's number for the second time.

"Audumn!" Monica exclaimed, racing over to Robert. "Robby and Brie, I got Audumn on the phone."

"Hey sis, Brie just got off the phone with Secorion because we couldn't reach you. Sorry to ruin your vacation with your in laws, but mom fell down this morning really bad and now she's in the hospital."

"What?" Audumn is shocked by what she's hearing and she can't do anything but hold the phone and cry. "Is she going to be all right, Robby? What did they say?"

"Stop crying sis; everything's going to be fine until you get back home on Tuesday."

"Tuesday!" Secorion tries to call, but Audumn doesn't answer. "I'm coming home today!"

Mrs. Woodson sits on the couch next to Audumn and asks, "Is everything okay?" in a whisper.

Audumn shakes her head no, and finishes talking to her oldest brother. "Where's mom Robby? I want to talk to her."

"She's sleeping right now from the morphine because she bruised her hip really bad." A silent pause came between the phone lines. "Audumn, are you there?"

"Why brother? Why does this always have to happen when I'm not around? I wasn't around when she first got this shit a long time ago. I wasn't around when she died back in November. And now I'm not around when she took her fall."

"Now sister, it's no need for all that. Mom is very ill and we both know that she would never ask any of us to stop our everyday lives on behalf of her sickness. And as far as you coming back early sis, please don't, because I think that would hurt momma even more if you do. Audumn, momma really loves Secorion and all she's been talking about is how she feels at peace knowing that you're married to him and are getting to know his family like a wife is supposed to. I promise you, little sis, that mom isn't going anywhere by Tuesday when your flight comes in at Jack Brooks Airport."

"But Robby...!"

"There's no buts, Audumn. Please do that for me and momma." Aunt Glynda and Nick come out from visiting Mrs. Humphrey. "Say sis, it's me and Brie's turn to go to the back and visit momma. I'm going to have to let you go and give little cousin back her phone. Call me back later and I assure you that I will let you talk to mom, even if I have to wake her up. I love you and will talk to you later."

Mrs. Woodson puts her arm around her daughter in law and lays Audumn's head on her chest. She doesn't know the fullness of the conversation Audumn just had with her brother and cousin, but she does know that whatever it is that was said, it wasn't the news Audumn wanted to hear. Both of them was enjoying the day in each other's company in the kitchen as she showed Audumn how to make Secorion's favorite fried green tomatoes and homemade ice cream. This is the reason why she missed her phone call, but inwardly, Mrs. Woodson is kind of glad she did so that she can share some time with Audumn before she went back home. It isn't because she feels no sympathy for Audumn's situation, but because the sad news she just received wasn't going to change if she had answered then or now.

New Year's came and New Year's went. In actual fact, to Audumn, it felt like the same year instead of a new year, but then she realizes that this year started off with her mom in the hospital and last year didn't. Audumn tried to enjoy the joy of starting her first year together with her husband, but that didn't work out well and she's been in the bed crying since nine o'clock on New Year's Eve. Mrs. Dorion sat with her and motherly assuaged her for the three days she lied in bed, waiting for her plane to leave to go back home to her mother. Secorion did as well, but Audumn gave him the clearance to hang out with his brother and cousin because she knew that's what he wanted to do. He didn't imply it, but Audumn knows how much he was looking forward to this trip to his hometown and she didn't want to drag his spirits down with hers on behalf of her mother once again. At least, that's what she thought, but then he assured her until the day they flew out that she's not in this alone and that whatever she needs for him to do, then he will do it to make her feel better in any kind of way possible.

Their plane flew into Jack Brooks Airport at one in the afternoon and Audumn and Secorion were at the hospital by two-thirty. Nick is the one who picked them up because he was out and about looking for his brother, Dexter, who is nowhere to be found and his mother keeps asking for him to know his safety. Nickolas begins to fill the two of them in as soon as they close the doors to his car. He let them know that their mother doesn't look the same from the time they left for Chicago back in December. Aunt Glynda and Monica flew home yesterday. Dexter can't be found, but is okay because he sees that his bed has been slept in from time to time. And that today, Dr. Von gets the results back from their mom's Pet-Ct scan that will tell the severity of the stage of cancer in which their mother is in. Everyone from her intermediate family, besides Dexter, is waiting on them in Mrs. Humphrey's room so that they can give the doctor the okay to come and give the news of her findings.

"Good afternoon everyone, and I'm glad to see you've made it back home safe, Mr. and Mrs. Woodson." Dr. Von walks in holding an iPad and goes to the side of her patient's hospital bed. "How are you feeling today, Mrs. Humphrey?"

"I'm fine." Mrs. Humphrey said in a raspy voice. "If that's what you call it; I'm still here?"

"Great. And are you in any pain as of the moment or need anything to make you feel more comfortable?"

"Everything's okay now that my daughter has made it back home. Other than that, I'm just really weak and feel like I can't do anything for myself."

"That's understandable, Mrs. Humphrey, considering your condition." Dr. Von checks her pulse and then checks her heart with her stethoscope. "Mrs. Humphrey, I know you're missing one of your sons here today, but is it okay if I proceed in showing your Pet-Ct scan with your husband and the children you have present?"

Mrs. Humphrey replied, "Yes," in sorrow because her son Dexter isn't here with the rest of her family.

Dr. Von takes her iPad off the table she sat it on and turns to face her patient's family. "As everyone in the room knows, your loved one was admitted to St. Elizabeth Hospital on December 31st of last year and on that day, we did a Pet-Ct scan to see where we're at in our fight against her ovarian cancer. Today, those results have come back and unfortunately, your mother is in stage IV in her battle. Which means the metastatic cancer has spread to other parts of the body. We know for a fact that the cancer is in her lymph nodes on behalf of the painless swelling in her neck and armpits, persistent fatigue, unexplained weight loss, and the occasion shortness of breath. Lymph nodes are small structures in the body that work as filters for harmful substances. They contain immune cells that can help fight infection by attacking and destroying germs that are carried in through the lymph fluid."

"What does all this mean, doctor?" Mr. Humphrey asked in denial of what he's hearing about his wife's health.

"It means that after discovering that the cancer is in her lymph nodes, then it most likely will be in her bones as well." Dr. Von shows the family the 3D picture of Mrs. Humphrey's body, showing where all the cancer has spread highlighted in green. She also swiped screens to her patient's bone X-rays to point out what she knows is terminal for her patient. "Please come in a little closer so that I can point out what I need to show you on her X-rays." Secorion steps back so that they all can get as close as possible to see the iPad's screen. "You see right here where it looks ragged and not solid on the bone?"

"Yes." Robert said quickly when seeing the differences in the bone structure of a healthy bone and not a rugged one.

"Well, that's not a good sign with everything else I've stated previously and with that said, I recommend hospice for Mrs. Humphrey because at this stage, there's nothing we can do to treat the cancer that has now spread to her bones."

"Hospice?" Tears fall from Mrs. Humphrey's eyes when she heard what no patient wants to hear from their physician.

"Yes Mrs. Humphrey, I recommend the Beaumont Hospice Center to further assist you in being as comfortable as possible as you transition to the next stages of life concerning this disease."

"Momma, are you okay?" Brie divides his siblings and makes his way to his mother's bedside. "Momma, can you hear me?

"Yolanda, can you hear our son talking to you?"

Dr, Von shines a light in her patient's eyes, which are staring into space and causes her to blink and snap out of it. "Mrs. Humphrey, I know hospice sounds frightening, but in fact, hospice is a part of medicine that we utilize when somebody has a terminal illness that can't be cured. Hospice also focuses on the spiritual needs of patients, pain, emotional destress, and keeping patients comfortable as they live out the rest of their lives as freely as possible."

"Yeah momma, that doesn't sound as bad as I thought hospice is all about."

"Your daughter is right in saying that, because people don't know the fullness of what hospice does for medicine, such as helping you not be a burden on your family and having a 24-hour medical staff to help take care of you for as long as you have left."

Nick walks on the other side of the bed and grabs his mother's hand. "Momma, we're going to be right here no matter if you're at home, in this hospital, or on hospice."

"But what about Dexter?"

"Momma, please don't stress about Dex." Nickolas replied. "He has a whole lifetime to get it right and I assure you that I am my brother's keeper and won't let you down when it comes to his wellbeing."

"Me too, momma." Brie responded, followed by Audumn, then Robert.

"And I will be there for him too, Yolanda. Not only as his father, but also as a shoulder for him to lean on."

Mrs. Humphrey sees all the love she has around her and recalls how hospice helps take some of the burden off of her family during this time of crisis. "I'll go, Dr. Von." Mrs. Humphrey grabs her son Nick and Aubrie's hands tight. "With healthy young men as these and a daughter whose got my back to the end, I have no choice but to finish this fight in faith and running to the finish line until my father in Heaven calls me home."

"Now that's the spirit, Yolanda. And I know we haven't been on the best of terms this past year, but don't think I don't love you or worse, that you don't have me in your corner also."

"Thank you, Geary, for those kind words and thank you for being here for me and my kids, despite what we're going through."

"If there's not any further question concerning what we've just discussed, then I guess I'll be leaving. Oh, and here's the number and address to the Beaumont Hospice Center. They will be expecting your call, so give them a call in the morning. Thanks Mrs. Humphrey and family, and I wish you the best of luck on your journey and fight against cancer. Have a blessed day."

The Beaumont Hospice Center is a one floor facility on a side street off of a side street and everything from the road to the front door spelled death. The front lawn is bare and if it wasn't for the freshly painted black bench and the staff's cars parked around back, one would think that the building is vacant from the street. On the way, Mrs. Yolanda kept her spirits up because last night she prayed for healing and the hospice center is only one step closer to her miraculous recovery.

Audumn and Robert are the only two who brought their mother in to the Beaumont Hospice Center. Their reasoning being because they all agreed that it would be best if just them two go so that all of them won't crowd their mother as she's getting settled into her room. And from the looks of the outside of the building, they both are glad they are the ones who came because their two baby brothers would've started complaining as soon as they figured out where the GPS was taking them.

"Good afternoon, my name is Yolanda Humphrey and I'm here to see Dr. Burk and to be admitted to a room."

The clerk looks over her appointment book and sees her name. "Yes, here we go Mrs. Humphrey. Right this way."

Robby pushed his mother down the poorly lit halls and faded tiles that used to be white when the center first opened. From the outside, you would think that the building isn't as big as it is because the length of the building goes towards the back and not towards the sides. As they went down the long hall, Audumn glanced in some of the rooms to see how the other residents/patients are living. And yes, to no surprise, all of them looked like they were just lying there in sorrow, waiting on their day to check out and check into the after-life. Suddenly, the lady in scrubs cut in front of their mother and they came to a halt at room 2D. Robby quickly avoided her, but her sudden stop almost got her legs broken from the footrest of the wheelchair.

"Here we are, Mrs. Humphrey."

"What, no excuse me?" Robert asked in frustration.

"Oh, excuse me, and Dr. Burk will be with you shortly."

Robby shook his head as she is walking back to her desk. "Audumn, I'm starting to really not like this place."

"Son, God brought me here for a reason. I've come too far to give up now."

"I know that's the truth, momma." Audumn looks at Robert with a blank expression. "Come on Robby, let's get mom into her bed."

It took both of them to get their mother into that high hospital bed. Even with the bed being as low as it goes, both of them knew that their mother will never to be able to get out of the bed by herself if she tried too. Especially with her legs being weak and her arms not being strong enough to support her to get down from that height. Audumn adjusted the mechanical bed to what her mother asked and then started brushing her hair so that she can be presentable for the doctor. While she did that, Robert put his mother's clothes inside the drawers, pictures on her nightstand, and handed his mother the Bible so that she can read it like she does every day and at night before she goes to bed. Mrs. Humphrey just sat back and smiled at the fact of how much her kids love her and will always be by her side.

Dr. Burk walks in, looking at his clipboard, but then looks up when he stops in front of their mother. "Good morning Miss… umm…"

"Her name is Yolanda." Robert feels a little irritated that he doesn't know his mother's name.

"Yes, Mrs. Yolanda Humphrey."

"Good morning to you too, Dr. Burk, and I'm ready to start my next steps to getting back to taking my chemo treatments."

"Chemo treatments!" Dr. Burk exclaimed. "You do know this is a hospice center?"

"Yes doctor, but I also know that God is not finished with me yet."

"Well I hate to tell you this Mrs. Yolanda, but you have stage IV cancer and this is a place where people like you come to die."

"What did you just to tell my mom, you son of a bitch?"

"Whoa there, young man, I'm just stating the facts."

"But you didn't have to say it like that, doctor." Audumn said angrily. "It's a shame that you've seen death so much that you don't give a damn to learn your patient's name before you come to their room to greet them."

"Momma, what's wrong?" Robert shoves the doctor out the way and goes to his mother's bedside. "Momma, don't cry, say something."

"I'm going to die, Robert. What do you want me to say, son?"

"Momma, don't mind this idiot. We ain't staying here anyway." Audumn lowers the bed back down. "Robert, get momma's things! I'll take care of her my damn self before I let her stay in this hell hole with Dr. Giggles over there."

"And Dr. Jerk or whatever the hell your name is, that lady over there is my momma and I love her with all my heart. I guess what I'm trying to say is that she raised me to treat women with respect and therefore, I will never treat a woman or a mother like you did her today from the time you came into this room." Robert looks Dr. Burk square in the eyes. "Now honestly doctor, would you want somebody to talk to your mother like that in the state my mother is in?"

"I...I guess not."

"Well, don't talk like that to my momma then or better yet, the next patient you have that's a woman, treat her like you would want your mother to be treated." Robert goes over to the side of his mother's bed to help her get inside her wheelchair. "Goodbye doctor. We're not letting my momma stay in this gloomy ass place and we will see ourselves out from here."

Days after the cataclysmic conversation with the wonderful Dr. Jerk, Audumn and her siblings got their mother's bedroom together to fit her dire needs. Robby and Brie put the electrical hospital bed together while Nick added more handrails in the master bathroom and around the tub. When they finished, they all helped move the furniture so that their mom can get to all the essential rooms in the house when she wants too. Mrs. Humphrey just sat there in a daze, staring at what her house has become due to her sickness. *What happened to my home?* she thought, remembering all the good times she's had at home with her husband and her kids.

"Momma, that's it for me." Robert said, squatting to be eye level with his mother. "I talked to Dexter last night and he said he's going to do better. He says he's sorry for not coming around much, but he can't see you sick like this. He also said not to worry about him and to get better. I love you momma, and Nick and Brie are about to drive me to the airport. I'm sorry I can't stay longer, but I already overstayed my stay and I have to get back to the office to start my new year. However, I promise you that I will come back at the drop of dime if you need me too." Robert kisses his mother's hand and starts to cry because in his heart he feels like this is the last time he will see his momma alive. "I love you, momma. I love you so much and hate that I've got to go."

"I love you too, son. I'll be all right."

"Robby, we got to go. Your flight is leaving in an hour."

"Audumn, why don't you and Aubrie get Robby's bags to the car and me and big bro will be out right behind you?"

Audumn listened to Nickolas and helped Aubrie get their big brother's things to the car. And just like Nick said, the two of them came walking down the steps shortly after. Nickolas had his arm around his brother as he wept within his hands. Brie jumped out of the driver's seat and went and opened the back door while his sister went to help Robert get himself together. When he flopped down onto the backseat, he closed the door and rolled the window down. "Take good care of her, Audumn. Call me if you need anything. I love you and I'm counting on you."

Robert's genuine tears of love for his mother and his, "I'm counting on you," statement is all she needed to see and hear for the path she's been placed on to take care of her mother. With Nick and Brie gone, she entered the house, hoping they'll stick around to help this time, but if they didn't, then so be it. Secorion left for work yesterday, so her total focus will be on her mother to help keep her as comfortable and pain free as possible. Some women would run from what she's about to endure, but Audumn looked forward to it because her mother would do the same for her.

"Momma, are you okay? What's wrong?"

Mrs. Humphrey is back in her stupor in her newly arranged bedroom. "Why Audumn? Why me of all people to get cancer? I don't smoke or drink and I go to all my well woman checkups, only to still end up right here in this empty room awaiting my day to die."

"Please momma, don't say that."

"But it's true. And Dr. Burk said it to confirm it."

"Momma that guy didn't know what he was talking about, so forget him."

"Yeah, but that guy is the only person who told me the truth about all this, when from the beginning, everybody else gave me false hope."

"But momma, you're wrong in thinking about your sickness that way when you believe in Jesus." Audumn helps her mother to her bed and gives her some tissues to wipe her eyes. "I know this may sound crazy momma, but your sickness has brought me closer to God than I've ever been. Not only your sickness, but to you too momma. I mean, I never saw a woman be this strong in battling something that I know for a fact that I couldn't do myself. I say that to say, the Bible says that the devil had to ask permission to attack Job because of his faithfulness to the Lord almighty. Just think momma, if the devil went to God to ask permission to attack this family with cancer, which one of us would step up to say, give it to me and not my kids."

Audumn tucks her mother into bed and lowers it a little with the remote. "I believe momma that God chose you for this journey for a reason because he knew that you couldn't take it if it was one of us the devil decided to give this disease to."

Mrs. Humphrey wipes her tears and looks her daughter in her hazel eyes and smiles. "You know what sweetheart, I think you're right in saying that God chose me for a reason."

"Momma, you got to realize that up until this time, nobody in our intermediate family has had to go through anything like this. And we must be real with ourselves because tragedies strike all families someday or another."

"You know, I never thought of this that way."

"I didn't either, but I've been reading Job lately because what you're going through is something similar to what he went through."

"Wow, my baby has been reading her Bible on her own."

"Yes ma'am, and you taught me that when I saw how much you've changed from reading it."

"Thank you, sweetheart. I really needed to hear that. And I'm sorry for that rant a few minutes ago. Our God is an awesome God."

"Yes he is momma, and he and his son Jesus will have the last word when all this is over."

"Get thee behind me, Satan! The devil has no place in my house!"

"Amen momma. Amen."

That positive thinking lasted Audumn's mom exactly four days. In actuality, it was the third day that the little color in Mrs. Humphrey's skin started to fade. It was also the day her smile started to turned into a frown. Audumn thought the distant look in her eyes was just for a brief moment because on the fourth day, the sparkle of life was present again in the two windows to her soul. Today however, it's different. Lately, her mother's words have been few since Dr. Burk told her the harsh news, but today, she has said nothing but two, maybe three words, and they were mumbles. Audumn asked her mother what she said, but she just stared right through her as if she wasn't there.

Ruth got there the following week after the paperwork and insurance got worked out from Mrs. Humphrey walking out of the hospice center. It can only be God, as her eyes are enlightened to see Audumn and her sister in Christ lying in bed. Audumn is also overjoyed to see her mother's friend from her first chemo treatments. With her being here, Audumn feels a little pressure released from within because Ruth loves her mother and also loves God.

This go around, Mrs. Boswell sat, read, and prayed with her mother during her chemotherapies in Houston. But the last time, it was Nurse Ruth who took her time and love with Mrs. Humphrey and in doing so, they became good friends. This is why it can only be God. First, Mrs. Humphrey had Dana and Javier from her first time taking chemotherapy. And now, God has blessed her with Ruth, her praying partner. What's ironic, is that this is Ruth's first hospice job because last week she asked to be transferred from the hospital because her friend died on hospice and no one was there to pray over her before she passed.

"Good morning Audumn, and what a joy it is to see you and your mother again."

"I wouldn't say joy, Ms. Ruth, due to what's all going on, but I am happy to see you too. I can sure use some joy, though, if you have some to pass around. My brothers were coming around, but ever since my momma stopped talking, I haven't seen them as much."

"Oh, she's not speaking?" Ruth puts her bag down and goes to observe her friend and patient.

"Yes ma'am, and she just stares into space looking at nothing all the time."

"That's from decreased blood flow to the brain due to the cancer spreading all over her body." Ruth tilts her over to see her back. "When was the last time you moved her?"

"Yesterday when my dad came over to help me get her in and out of the bathtub."

"Great job. Do you know how to move her by yourself because you don't need to be straining with that pregnant belly of yours?"

"No, not really."

Ruth grabs two pillows from off the sitting chair. "Audumn, this is important because in the state your mother is in, she can get bed sores really easy if she's not moved twice a day. Normally, you would move a patient every two hours, but with her tissue tolerance I doubt that will be suitable for your mother."

Audumn's first day with her hospice nurse was the little help she needed to clear her head. She learned how to move her mom using two pillows and a sheet. Ruth prayed and read the Bible over her mother like she used to. And she got a chance to go walking like her husband and obstetrician told her too. When she got back from her walk, Ruth left when Audumn relieved her. Her eight hour shift ended at two, but Audumn told her that she could leave early since it's a quarter till. From there until the next nurse gets there at 6:00 pm, she's on her own again and it's at that time her mother spoke some rational and heartbreaking words.

"Au...Audumn..." Mrs. Humphrey stammers as her eyes focus on her daughter sitting in the chair across from her. "Audumn, sweetheart."

"Momma, I'm here." Audumn said excitedly, looking into her mother's blue eyes looking back at her.

"Audumn, I love you."

"I love you too momma. And I'm right here, okay?"

"I know, sweetheart." Mrs. Humphrey gently pats her daughter's hand that is clasped inside hers. "Audumn, do you remember the last time when I had cancer I made you my power of attorney over my life and Robert power of attorney over my finances?"

"Yes ma'am." Audumn starts to cry as she sees her mother eyes tearing up.

"I want you to know that I never changed it and that you have the last say so over my life on whether I live or die."

"But momma you're not..."

"Listen, Audumn, to my wishes, my love." Mrs. Humphrey lips are really dry and Audumn gives her a sip of water. "Please Audumn, honor me and don't let me go on no breathing machine. If it comes down to that, then I want you to give me one week. If I'm not better by than then, pull the plug."

The next two words were the hardest two words Audumn ever had to say to her mother concerning something she wanted her to do, but that she didn't want to do. "Yes ma'am."

"Thanks, my love, for those words on Job last week. I love you and God couldn't have blessed me with a better daughter than you."

As soon as she made her peace and said what she needed to say, Audumn's mom turned her head away from her daughter and slowly faded back into her inertness. *Kids say goodbye to your grandma. The best grandma that you will never know, but you will always have.*

CHAPTER 25

"Dex, wake up! Momma's not breathing too good and Nurse Ruth wants us to come here right now!"

Robby. Dexter jumps up out of his three hour slumber and dashes to his mother's room. "What's wrong?" he asks, seeing that all his brothers are in the room and it must not be good because Robert is back home so quickly. "Is momma okay?"

Mrs. Humphrey is lying on her side with a fan blowing in her face because her chest is breathing irregularly. Her eyelids are nearly shut, but you can see the whiteness of her eyeballs rolling endlessly within her head. Audumn is in a chair holding her mother's hand because that's all her mom wanted to do before she got into this dormant state. The reason why Ruth called this family meeting is because of the terminal secretions in her patient's throat causing her not to swallow or spit. Therefore, she needs everyone to agree to put their mother on a ventilator because Mrs. Humphrey can't decide for herself.

Ruth rubs an ice popsicle she made on their mother's lips. "As you can see boys, your mother is experiencing terminal secretions in her throat from her muscles not retracting as they should. And in them not doing so, it's not allowing her to swallow or spit. Not only that, but your mother's breathing won't sustain her too much longer with the way she's breathing at the moment. This too, has a name and it's called chain stokes. Chain stokes usually happens near the end of a patient's life and it's a clear sign to let the loved ones of the patient make their peace with their loved one. It's also the time the loved one's family must decide if they're going to put their loved one on a ventilator or not, or the patient will be transitioning soon if they don't."

"I vote yes; we put her on a breathing machine. Momma ain't going nowhere and you never know, she might can get better."

"But look at her, Dex! Audumn shouts. "Stop running, big brother, and come look at her!"

"But Audumn, I vote yes too. We at least gotta fight with momma until the very end."

"I vote no; we don't put momma on a breathing machine. I think it's time we let momma go."

"Yeah, I understand what you're saying Robby, but Dex and Nickolas have a point. I don't want to see momma like this either, but I do want to say that we tried until we couldn't try no more." Aubrie replies.

"I vote no, but first let me tell you why I vote no." Audumn lets her mother's hand go and stands to confront her brothers. "I vote no because two weeks ago mom's last words to me was to not let her go on a breathing machine for no more than one week. She said that if she's not better in seven days for me to pull the plug because I'm power of attorney over her life and Robert is power of attorney over her finances."

"But we already voted Audumn and you're out numbered three to two."

"I know we voted Dexter, but if you go over there and look at your mother for once for a change, then you will see that in one week she's not going to get better."

Ruth comes over and grabs Dexter hand and brings him over to his mother. "Dexter, your mother is holding on because you and your siblings haven't told her it's alright to go on to be with the Lord. In death, hearing is the last thing to go, so please be careful on what you say in front of her."

Dexter starts sobbing over his mother. Up until today, he's only peeked into his mother's room to check on her, but never came within six feet of her. "I'm sorry, momma. I'm so sorry, momma. This is so hard for me. I never thought that you would be the one to get sick. You're my hero, momma. You've always been my Superwoman." Dexter begins to whine like a baby. "And you've always been there for me too, momma."

"It's okay, Dexter. Let it out son, your mother needs to hear your voice."

Dexter looks back at his brothers and dries up his tears. "Momma, I love you and it's no longer about me, but about what's best for you." Dexter kisses his mother between the eyes and whispers in her ear something nobody in the room can hear. "Nick and Brie, I'm with Audumn and Robby. I vote no."

"Audumn, did momma really tell you that she didn't want to be on a breathing machine long?"

"Yes she did, Aubrie."

"Well I vote no too because I'm riding with momma if that's what she wanted."

"Me too, sis. Aubrie's right. If that's what momma told you, then I vote no too."

"Great decision guys because your mother is tired and ready to leave this place, but first, she needs all of you to do what Dexter just did."

"What's that, Mrs. Ruth?" Robby asks, looking at his mother's weary body.

"You all need to tell her that you're going to be okay and that it's alright for her to go be with God. Not only tell her, but mean it when you do say what you have to say."

All five of them went one by one to their mother with sorrowful words, but stepped away with a sense of delightfulness surrounding them. For the first time, all of them are on one accord to the realization that this is it and that their mother isn't going to get well like they all hoped for. Brie cried the longest, but finally got ahold of himself and wished his mother the best on her next adventure in life. Nick didn't show too much emotion and is glad that his mother will not have to suffer anymore. Audumn, on the other hand, washed her mother's feet with her tears because she recalled a sinful lady did it to Jesus before he went on to die on the cross. While she dried her feet with a towel, Ruth anointed Mrs. Humphrey's head with olive oil just as the same sinful lady did in the Bible before washing Jesus' feet. When they were done, Robby and Dexter kissed their mother on each side of her cheeks as their mother's breathing patterns started to become rapid. Searching radically for air, their mother takes a real deep breath, holds it, and then lets it out, never to breath on this side of life again.

"Goodbye, Sister Yolanda Humphrey. May God's favor forever be upon your kids and grandkids. It was truly an honor to be here to assist you as you went on to be with the Father. Be blessed and praise God that by his son's stripes you are healed and that from this day forward, you will be pain free. In Jesus name, amen and amen."

Days of mourning traveled endlessly through the Humphrey's house throughout the week and the following week. People from her church and job came by in the mornings, evenings, and nights dropping off food, flowers, and envelopes with money in them. Audumn and the boys accepted the gifts as each of their mother's friends and people who knew her paid their respects to a woman who fought for her life down to her last breath. Celeste came by the most because she made it her business to be there for her sister in Christ's children like she promised her friend that she would do after her first cancer surgery years ago. Ms. Boswell drove from Houston twice during that week leading up to the funeral. She came by with her niece, Kendra, and her grandchild, Shanay, to clean up the house from top to bottom so that the family's guests would enter a clean house when they chose to come by. Their dad helped too, but he mostly stayed away on behalf of the guilt he has in his heart for cheating on his wife and not being there for her like he should've been while she was in her last days.

The funeral is on a Saturday, eleven days after their mother passed away on January 24th. The eleven day span gave everyone who wanted to attend Mrs. Yolanda Humphrey's homegoing services an ample amount of time to clear their schedule to attend. Such as their dad's side of the family, who would be flying in from out of town, and their Aunt Glynda and cousin Monica who would be flying in from South Carolina. Both, Glynda and Monica had just left Beaumont on the 2nd of January, and yet, here they're back again to bury their sister and their aunt after celebrating Christmas with her last year. It's like a gigantic void sitting in the center of their chests where their heart would be due to their mother, sister, aunt, friend, and wife not being there to fill the empty space. As they took their seats on the front pew of the Cathedral of Faith Baptist Church, Pastor Mack waited for the last line of people to have a seat after viewing the body displayed in front of the gathering.

"A death has occurred, and in an instant, everything has changed. We're painfully aware that life can never be the same again. That yesterday is over. That relationships, once rich, have ended. But there's another way to look upon this truth. If life now went on the same without the presence of the one who has died, we can conclude that that life we remember made no contribution, filled no space, or meant nothing. The fact that this person left behind a place that cannot be filled is a high tribute to this individual. Life can be the same after losing a trinket, but never after the loss of a treasure. Good morning, my name is Pastor Delbert Mack and I will be presiding over Mrs. Yolanda Humphrey's funeral service today." Pastor Mack pauses to gather his thoughts and proceeds. "The poem I just read to you is a direct contrast to what has brought us all together here today. And that is that life has changed as we know it because of the treasure that has now left with Sister Humphrey when God decided to call her home. We come today, church, not just to mourn the passing, but also to celebrate the life of Yolanda Humphrey. Our time today will be filled with some tears. But it's okay to cry because you're in a safe place. However, this day will also bring joy as we remember the good times shared with our beloved. The name Yolanda means violet flower. And if anyone knew her, they would concur that she was exactly that. Unlike the color purple, which is a mixture of red and blue, violet is an actual color. In actuality, if you were to look up the definition of violet, you will find that it means love, modesty, virtue, affection faithfulness, and a good luck symbol for women. All of which describes our dearly departed, lying here before us today."

Wow, I never knew that your name meant so much, momma. Audumn thought, zoning off into thoughts of her mother. *Momma, I now know why God placed me and my brothers in such a blessed womb.*

"As we can see from the time she was given her name, Sister Yolanda was predestined to shine her light upon this world from the time she took her first breath until the time she took her last. I can go on and on about Sister Humphrey as her pastor and overseer of the flock she was a member of, here at Cathedral of Faith. Hence, my words wouldn't come close in describing the fullness of life that this violet flower shined in the lives of those who truly knew her, cared for, fellowshipped with her, and loved her. With that said, the family have asked that Audumn Woodson come say a few words on behalf of their mother and on behalf of their family."

Secorion kissed his wife on the lips and said, "You got this," and "I love you."

Cathedral of Faith is a big church and even though the church isn't filled to its capacity, quite a few people from Beaumont turned out to pay their respect to Mrs. Yolanda. Standing before everyone present, Audumn stood there in awe at how many lives her mother's life has touched during her fifty-two years on earth. Her dad noticed that she's standing there without speaking and got up to check on her, but she put her hand up for him to sit down.

"I'm okay, daddy." Audumn spoke into the microphone. "I'm just standing here overjoyed at how many people came out to show their support for my mom, Mrs. Yolanda Humphrey. People, I want you to know that this is an amazing experience for me today. I say that because I came up here in sorrow, but seeing all of you here has changed that. My mom was special to me in so many ways. She was there to kiss my booboo when I fell off my bike. And she was there to put butter on my hand when I touched the iron after daddy told me not too." Audumn dries her tears with a tissue and stops herself from breaking down crying. "Last year was the best year of my entire life. I know that may sounds baffling due to us being at a funeral on the 4th day in February. Nonetheless, it was and will forever be, the climax chapter in the book of Audumn's Love until the day God decides to call me home. Last year, I graduated college and got accepted into a great veterinarian school. I also got pregnant by the man of my dreams who asked me to marry him at the end of the previous year. After that, me and the hubby went on a trip with my friends and family to New Orleans just to get away from all the pressure of being pregnant with twins and getting married soon." All of her brothers and friends looked at each other, grinning, because they know how chaotic it was being at the hands of Diana and Kizzy during wedding rehearsals. "By the way, the wedding was lovely and I want to thank everyone for making that day special for me and my husband, Secorion Woodson." Audumn closes her eyes and takes a deep breath. "And last, but not least, I got to spend some priceless mother daughter time with my mother."

"Come on, sweetheart. It's all right here." Mr. Humphrey points towards his heart as if to say, speak from your heart.

"When I came up here, I said last year was the best year of my life despite what all went on with my mom's downhill battle against cancer. How, is because I'm not here to speak on the negative or the bad things concerning my mother, but the good things that will live within my spirit and be cherished for a lifetime. Today, or any day, is not the time to be sad over someone not being in pain or suffering any more. If anything, this should be a time of rejoicing because of what I just previously stated. My mom lived a good life and raised five kids with the help of my dad. I know she only lived fifty-two years, but look at what she leaves behind. And on top of that, God has blessed us with two new additions to our family and that too stems from my mother's offspring." Audumn looks directly at her intermediate family. "Daddy and brothers, I just want you to know something I've learned from mom and from reading my Bible. What I've learned is that, we've been praying for our mother to be healed, but who's to say God didn't answer our prayer in healing her. I know he may not have healed our mom the way we thought she should be healed, but he did heal her. Reading the Bible has taught me that God's time and the things he does or so chooses to do, we can't control or wonder about because our minds can't fathom the big picture in what he's doing. I mean, who would've thought that it would be my mom's sickness that would bring me back home to my family after not talking to you for years after I graduated high school. Not only that, but it was her sickness that made me care for her during her last years of her life and because of that, I got to know my mother in ways that I couldn't have imagined if she didn't get sick. I know it's sad, brothers, and I know it hurts, but we must look at the positives and remember mom for all the love she gave us growing up and as adults." Audumn looks back towards the congregation. "Thank everyone for taking time out of your day to come to my mother's funeral and be blessed as God blesses."

Pastor Mack proceeded after Audumn kissed her mother's forehead in the casket and sat back down. "Thank you, Mrs. Woodson, for those powerful words on behalf of your mother and family. If there's not anyone else from the family who desires to speak, I ask that everyone will turn their Bibles to John chapter 14 verse 8 as I read from the scriptures in which Sister Yolanda wanted to be read and preached upon at her funeral. She also asks, that as you read or listen to the scriptures to think of her while you do." Pastor Mack pauses and thanks Sister Celeste Ball, Mrs. Humphrey's friend, for giving him the scriptures two nights ago. "In today's text, church, we have Jesus telling his disciples that he is in the Father and that the Father is in him. As previously stated, I will start at verse 8 and end at verse 12. And from there, I will go on to verse 27 and end at verse 31." Pastor Mack listens for the fluttering of pages to stop as everyone turned their Bibles to desired text for the day. "The scriptures reads; Phillip said to him, 'Lord, show us the Father, and it is enough for us.' Jesus said to him, 'Have I been with you so long, and you still do not know me, Phillip? Whoever has seen me has seen the Father. How can you say, show us the Father? Do you not believe that I am in the Father and the Father is in me? The words that I say to you I do not speak on my own authority, but the Father who dwells in me is doing his works. Believe me that I am in the Father and the Father is in me, or at least believe on the evidence of the works themselves. Very truly I say to you, whoever believes in me will also do the works that I do; and greater works than these will he do, because I am going to the Father (ESV)." Pastor Mack tells everyone to go to verse 27. "Peace I leave with you; my peace I give you. I do not give to you as the world gives. Do not let your hearts be troubled and do not be afraid. You heard me say, 'I am going away and I am coming back to you. If you loved me, you will be glad that I am going to the Father, for the Father is greater than I. I have told you now before it happens, so that when it does happen, you will believe. I will not say much more to you, for the prince of this world is coming. He has no hold over me, but he comes so that the world may learn that I love the Father and do exactly what my Father has commanded me (NIV). Amen and that concludes are scripture reading that the lady of the hour asked to be read at her homegoing ceremony."

"Amen," came from the pews in unison, but then silence filled the sanctuary as people closed their Bibles to begin listening to the word of God.

"If you don't mind Cathedral, I would like to expound on what was said in these scriptures that I feel is the reason why Sister Humphrey said, when you read them to think of her as you do." A few people in the audience nodded their heads in agreement with the Pastor saying a few words to elaborate on the text. "In the first set of verses we read from John 14:8-12, we have Jesus explaining to one of his disciples that if you know Jesus, then you know the Father as well. Not only that, but if you saw Jesus, then you've seen the Father as well. He then went on to say that his words and the works that he's done were not done by him, but through him by the Father, so that everyone can believe and do great things such as he did. That's why verse 12 says, 'Very truly I tell you, whoever believes in me will do the works I have been doing, and they will do even greater things than these (NIV).' You see church, I believe that Sister Yolanda chose these words of Jesus today to remember what she said and did for her Lord and savior Jesus Christ. I believe that she has also chosen this text on behalf of people not being saved and prepared when they die; because, this entire passage speaks about believing in Jesus and if you believe in him, then you should also believe in the Father. Meaning, that Sister Humphrey walked with the Father just as Jesus did. And spoke only Godly words concerning the Kingdom in Heaven, just as Jesus did. Therefore, you too, should believe in the Father because you all have witnessed the miraculous work the good Lord has done in her from the time she accepted Jesus' sinless sacrifice on the cross."

Robby and the boys know what the pastor is saying is true because they saw the change in their mother first hand from the time she came home saying that she was saved. Mr. Humphrey, however, is balling in tears and can't stop due to guilt and not taking his wife's walk with Christ seriously like she did when she wanted him to go to church with her. *I'm sorry Yolanda. I'm so sorry...*Audumn puts her arm around her dad and begin to console him. "Daddy it's gon' be all right. Momma's in Heaven now."

Pastor Mack went on to explain the latter end of the scriptures Mrs. Humphrey wanted to be read. "In verses 27-31, Jesus said that peace is what he's leaving with his disciples here on earth when he dies on the cross. Not just any peace, he said, but his peace. Which is not a peace of this world, but a peace that surpasses all understanding. A peace that's going to get Sister Yolanda's family through those rough times when they're missing their loved one. The peace I'm talking about can only be given from on high and to receive it, you have to be saved. Just as Sister Yolanda was saved and is now sitting with Jesus at the right hand of the Father, you too can be as well when you get called home to be with your maker. Being that this is not a church service, but a funeral, today I ask that if you're not saved and you believe that Jesus Christ died for your sins, to repeat after me." Pastor Mack waits until he has everyone's full attention. "Father, I am a sinner."

"Father, I am a sinner." The majority of the service stated.

"I believe that, by according to your word, that Jesus died for my sins and rose again on the third day."

"I believe that, by according to your word, that Jesus died for my sins and rose again on the third day," everyone repeated.

"Please Jesus, come into my life so that I can be made whole."

"Please Jesus, come into my life so that I can be made whole."

"In Jesus' name, Amen."

"In Jesus' name, Amen."

"Great job new believers and I, Pastor Mack and the Cathedral of Faith Baptist Church, welcomes you to the body of Christ. Now, before I allow the family or friends to say any last words on behalf of the deceased, Mrs. Yolanda Humphrey would like for you to keep John 14 verse 28 on your mind when you think of her or miss her." Pastor Mack picks up his Bible off the podium and reads, "If you loved me, you would be glad that I am going to the Father, for the Father is greater then I.' Amen, and the floor is now open for any last remarks before we close out this lovely funeral service. Be blessed."

Ms. Boswell is the last one to speak after following Secorion and Aunt Glynda.

She spoke about how they became friends from their kid's playing with each other. It takes a village to raise a child and even though in the beginning Sister Yolanda didn't know the Lord, she still understood that and allowed Ms. Boswell into her only daughter's life. Truly, she will be missed, but Ms. Boswell emphasized that her friend was saved, that she read the scriptures daily, gave when she could, loved her kids, loved God, and is where her soul has longed for since the day she accepted Jesus Christ into her heart. Before she sat down, Audumn walked over to her and gave her a hug. "Thank you, play momma, for those kind words on behalf of our mother," she said as she ushered Ms. Boswell back to her seat.

"This concludes our service and the family would like to thank everyone present for coming and to make sure you sign the guest book in between Sister Yolanda's high school picture and portrait on the tripods outside the doors behind you. Also, if you're attending the burial ceremony, then you can either follow in line behind the hearse or you can meet the family at the Magnolia Cemetery on Pine St. off of I-10 East." Pastor Mack turns to walk off, but then remembers something Audumn asked him to do after she finished speaking. "One more thing, church, the repast will be in the kitchen around back when we leave the cemetery and Audumn has requested that we all sing, 'Oh How I love Jesus,' when we exit the building to our cars. She also said, that this is one of her mother's favorite songs that she would always sing before, during, and after her chemo treatments. Amen and let's start singing on three for our dearly beloved and violet flower, Sister Yolanda Humphrey. One, two and three!"

"Oh, how I love Jesus!" The congregation begin to sang the famous hymn. "Oh, how I love Jesus! Because he first loved me!"

CHAPTER 26

"Hi momma. Sorry I didn't come yesterday on Valentine's Day, but life for me has changed since you're not here anymore." Audumn and Secorion stands eye to eye with her mother's mausoleum picture on the headstone. "I'm still staying in the house as of the moment, but when Secorion's job is up at the end of March and I have these babies mid-March, I'll be moving back to Houston where I'll have a better support system. I don't know if Dad told you when he came to visit you the other day, but he said that he'll be moving back into the house whenever I leave." Audumn touches the purple flowers in the flower holder. "I see Nickolas or Aubrie has recently been here because dad said that your flowers were dying when he came and that he would bring fresh one's later."

"Yeah, mother in law, they're beautiful and violet just like you and what your name means." Secorion smells them and smiles. "Sorry I didn't get to know you a lot longer, but the time I did, I can say that I'm thankful to have met you and thankful that you blessed this world with my wife, Audumn."

Audumn tears up when hearing her husband's empathy for her and her mother. "Honestly momma, I came here today because yesterday was the first holiday since you've been gone that I had to go through without you. Being 31, my Valentine's Days have been great due to my husband the past couple of years, but yesterday, it didn't feel so great, momma. Mainly because the Valentine's Days that I remembered are the ones when I was little girl and you and daddy would come inside my room first thing in the morning with a Valentine's Day basket." Audumn rubs her hand around her round stomach. "Those was the days, momma, and even though it hurt yesterday, today I feel a lot better since I'm here talking to you." Audumn winces because of pain in her lower back.

"Baby, are you okay?"

"Yes, my love. Just a few cramps I guess." Audumn feels her abdomen tightening. "Baby, I think I'm about ready to go. Could you go to the car, so that I can tell my mother goodbye?"

"Yes babe, and rest in peace Mrs. Humphrey. I love you." Secorion walks off to his wife's request, but not before he says, "I'll be in the car if you need me."

"Momma, I'm about to go now because your grandkids are kicking my butt today." Audumn laughs and puts a heart shaped box of chocolate on the stand attached to the mausoleum wall next to her picture. "But before I do, I want you to know that I will be starting school this fall so that I can finish what I started and make you proud as this family's first veterinarian. Oh, and don't worry about granddaddy Christmas' caroling collection because I'll make sure the next generation knows the history behind the old records."

Audumn manages to smile, but the pain in her back seems to not be going away. "Momma, I'm not feeling too good today, so I think that's my cue to go. I love you, and thank you for showing me how to be a good mother to my kids. Rest in Glory and thank you Father for accepting my mom into the pearl gates of your kingdom. In Jesus' name, amen. Goodbye momma and see you soon in Heaven years."

Secorion is holding the passenger door for his wife when Audumn comes wobbling to the car. Her hands are around her belly and her nose is scrunched up from the mild abdominal cramps that seem to not be going away. Falling into the seat, she struggles, trying to get her right leg inside the car, but her husband is there to help her. He can tell something's not right with his wife, but as of the moment, he just wants to get her home so that she can lie down and rest. As he backed out, he thought about how Audumn's been grieving the loss of her mother and really wishes her mom was alive to see their kids be born. *Damn,* he thought as he pounded the steering wheel in frustration because he knows that's a pain that he will never be able to fix in his wife's life.

It isn't until he made a right turn to get onto the expressway when he notices a reddish brownish stain on Audumn's crouch. "Baby, look, you're bleeding."

"Huh, what?" Audumn opens her eyes from the uneasiness in her stomach.

"Baby, you're bleeding." Secorion points between her legs.

"For real, bae?" Audumn manages to say, but then realizes what her husband is saying. "Secorion, my babies! Quick get me to hospital!"

"Baby, you think it's about to happen now?"

"Ahhhhhh! Audumn squeezes the armrest in unthinkable pain. "Yes, now!"

Secorion presses the gas pedal hard when seeing his wife is serious about the pain she's having. The babies are not due until next month, however, Dr. Belisima did say that twins have a tendency to come early. Weaving through after work traffic, Audumn tells Secorion to hurry up because she has to pee really bad and it feels like it's coming out. Secorion quickly looks down, but then does a double take because her seat is drenched and the carpet is too. He wants to stop or pull over, but that isn't going to do anything if the babies are coming right now.

"Baby, I think your water broke."

"I think so too honey because it feels like I've been peeing for over four minutes." Audumn breathes in and out real deep. "And since I told you to go to the hospital, my pains have ramped up to being six minutes apart and lasting a little under one minute."

Secorion hurried and exited Calder to go to St. Elizabeth Hospital because he recalled reading something about the 5-1-1 rule. Which is that a woman is near going into labor when her contractions are five minutes apart, last for one minute, and have been that pattern for one hour. So far, Audumn is near scratching two of those numbers off that list and if she keeps this up, she'll be completing the 5-1-1 rule by the time she reaches the hospital. In other words, Audumn's right and these babies are coming real soon.

Audumn's Cadillac comes to an abrupt halt outside of the emergency room. "Baby, stay right here while I go get a wheelchair."

"Okay, just hurry up Secori!" she exclaimed in an angry tone.

Secorion understands his wife is in a lot of pain, so he brushes off her mean remarks as he makes haste to the electric doors. "Miss, my wife is about to have twins." He tells the clerk behind the desk.

"Quick, I need a wheelchair and if possible, someone to help me get my wife to wherever she needs to be to have the babies."

"The wheelchairs are to your left and I'm calling a nurse now to assist you."

"Yes ma'am, and thanks."

Audumn is shaking in pain from the contractions running ramped through her body when Secorion opens her car door. Her body is shivering as he lifts her out the seat and puts her in the wheelchair. "It hurts bad, baby," she said, twisting and turning to find comfort. Secorion pushes a little faster when seeing that it's a strong possibility his babies are coming today. As soon as the electric doors divided, a male nurse is there to greet them with a gurney. Secorion helps stand Audumn up and then steps out of the way because another male nurse told him that he has it from there.

"Quick, Jack! After we get her on the stretcher, page Nurse Vickie and tell her to get the LDR room ready," the first guy who greeted them said. "Ma'am, everything's going to be alright, okay? We're about to get you to a room."

"Oh my gosh! Ouu…" Audumn squeezes Secorion's hand as hard as she can. "He's really low. I can feel it."

The doors to the elevator open. "5-1-1!" Secorion blurted out. "When we were in the car, we were at 6-1-1 when it came to her contractions after her water broke, so now we're most likely at 5-1-1 or lower. At least, that's what I think."

"Great to know that. Jack, when we get up to the floor get me an epidural and catheter ready. This baby is about to come right now."

"Babies!"

"What's that, ma'am?" Jack asks.

"Twins!" she screamed.

"We're having twins, sir." Secorion replied for her when the doors dinged open on the sixth floor. "And we're not due until three more weeks."

It didn't take long to administer the epidural. Audumn only felt a pinch, but twenty minutes later she became relaxed and only slightly felt the contractions, therefore the anesthesia worked. Oxygen is given to her to help her breathe for added support during the delivery. While she's getting propped up for her babies' grand entrance, Secorion puts on a cap and hospital gown over his clothes. The medicine makes Audumn laugh at him, but the babies dropping lower makes her smile turn into a frown.

A woman obstetrician comes inside the room in a haste after hearing Audumn is in the transition phase. "How are you doing, Mrs. Woodson? My name is Dr. Price and I'll be delivering your twins today. Sorry that your doctor isn't here on such a short notice, but I assure you that you're in great hands." Dr. Price takes a seat on a stool between her patient's legs. "Okay Mrs. Woodson, your cervix is now in the transition phase. I am about to do a cervical sweep to help encourage labor and to stimulate the uterus to soften the cervix." Dr. Price sticks her middle finger into the cervical opening. "Now, this may hurt a bit but the epidural may help ease the pain."

Audumn belly is out and her shirt is raised to her breasts. She wanted to hold one of Secorion's hands, but he wanted to see his first child come into the world and hence, decides to hold one of her legs instead. That, and he didn't want to get his hand crushed the way she did when they were on the first floor waiting for the elevators.

"Okay Mrs. Woodson, it's time to push."

"Yeah baby, push." Secorion said excitedly, awaiting to see the beginning stages of his son coming out of her vagina.

"I can see the head." Dr. Price exclaimed.

"Yeah, my love, you're doing great."

"Can I feel his head?" Dr. Price agrees and Audumn reaches over her crotch and touches her son's crown. "Aww, he feels so beautiful."

"Come on Mrs. Woodson, push. Your first child is almost here."

Audumn pushes again and her son pops out covered in vernix which is the waxy, cheese-like, white substance found coating the skin of newborn babies. "Look at him, he's perfect," she said joyfully, crying to sound of his cry as she held him for the first time.

"Congratulations, honey. You're now the mother of a beautiful, handsome, baby boy."

"Come on, Mrs. Woodson. Give him a big kiss and let Nurse Vickie bring him to get cleaned up so that I can get you ready for baby number two."

"Mommy loves you son." Audumn replied as the nurse took the baby to get checked for any infirmities.

"Okay, when you're ready, you can push."

"Ready." Audumn nods her head yes at Secorion.

"Push!" Secorion shouts, holding his wife's hand to help her in the best way he knows how.

"Okay Mrs. Woodson, you're doing great. Now could you give me a very small push." Dr. Price sees the crown and knows that one more push should bring the second twin into this world.

"You're doing great, babe." Secorion kisses Audumn's sweaty forehead. "I love you so much. And you look so beautiful lying there."

"Nice and slow. She's almost here."

"Can I touch her?"

"Yes, you may touch her."

Audumn reaches over her crotch again and feels the top her daughter's head. "Aww... Baby, I love her with all my heart already."

"Here she is." Dr. Price said, holding the wailing baby in the air for both of them to see.

"Yay, baby you did it!"

"No, we did it Secorion." Audumn looks her husband in the eyes as she receives her baby girl from Dr. Price.

"Hi sweetheart." Secorion smiled to his daughter's loud cry, which is louder than her big brother's. "I'm your daddy and I'm going to love you and love you and then love you some more."

Secorion goes to the room where the twins are getting a welcome to the world make over.

Audumn's eyes follow him into the room adjacent to the LDR and she feels relieved that he's going to be in there with the kids while Dr. Price finishes up with the after birth procedures. Secorion is pleased to be able to see his kids get weighed and measured for the very first time outside their mother's womb. Nonetheless, he turned away when Nurse Vickie put a gentle suction on the babies' nose and throat. He thought it look painful, but then said it couldn't have felt worse than them getting a shot of vitamin K to help their blood clot. Last, but not least, the nurse puts beanies on the babies' heads and wraps the twins in pink and blue blankets to show their sex.

"Are you ready, dad, to bring your babies to see their momma?"

"Yes ma'am, I am!" Secorion excitedly said as the nurse put a baby in each one of his arms to be carried.

Dr. Price is still working on Audumn when Secorion came inside the LDR holding their children. Even though she's still in the delivering position as they stitch her up, she doesn't feel a thing when her husband puts both of her offspring in her arms for the very first time. Words can't explain how she feels after having her kids travel through her canal with the help of her ushering them into this world to be with her forever. Secorion whips out the camera and immediately starts taking pictures of her holding the twins and Audumn can't wait to show her family, Kizzy, and Diana. "Smile, my love." Secorion said, taking a selfie of all four of them. Audumn saw the picture after he snapped it and thought about the joy her mother felt when Robby was born. *I love you momma and we now share a bond as women through your grandkids' childbirth.*

"Look bae, they're going to be yellowish brown like me. And guess what?"

"Please don't make me guess, Secori. I've been through a lot today."

"Our baby boy was born at 4:26 pm Central time. Weighed 4 lbs. 16 oz. and is 16.5 inches long. And our baby girl was born at 4:32 pm. And weighed 4 lbs. 2 oz. and is 15.75 inches long."

"Wow baby, they look so healthy to say they came early."

"That's because they have great genes."

Audumn stares at her babies' skin and relishes at raising little brown kids because her and her brothers are real light skinned and can sometimes pass for white with the glance of the eye. "Aww baby, they're so beautiful. And look she has your eyes and button nose."

"I know, right? But lil man over there has your lips and chin for sure." Secorion draws a circle in the air around his son's mouth and starts laughing at how much his son has his mother's jawline.

"What are you two going to name them?" Nurse Vickie asks, standing next to them so that she can bring the babies to the nursery. Being that the twins came prematurely, she wants to do a more thorough checkup according to hospital procedures for kids born early.

"I'm at a loss for words. Honestly nurse, I did think of some names, but my wife has lost someone very dear to her and I feel it's only right I grant her this opportunity to name the next generation to her side of our family."

"That's very sweet, son. And sorry to hear about your loss, Mrs. Woodson."

"Thank you, but this is all God because I was just leaving my mom's mausoleum today when my water broke." Audumn smiled at the last words she told her mother at the graveyard about showing her how to be a good mother.

"Wow, ain't that something? Look at God."

"Yes Lord, Nurse Vickie. You said it right. Look at God." Secorion repeated what she said and then turned back towards his kids and wife. "So, bae can you think of any names right now before the nurse take the babies to the nursery? Or do you want to wait till later?"

Dr. Price wishes them both the best and exits while Audumn is contemplating on her kids' names. With both babies in her arms, she closes her eyes and allows her mind to travel to every corner of her brain, looking for anything that sincerely means anything to her. Finally, her mind landed on a colorful open autumn field with a Jack in the bean stock tree right in the center of it. The sight of the tree and the autumn field paint an incomparable picture in the heart of her brain, causing the corner of her lips to turn upward.

"What bae? I see you're grinning from ear to ear. Did you come up with anything?"

"Yes, my love." Thinking about her love for Tree, she opens her eyes and says, "I'm going to name our son, Summer, and our daughter, Fall," while touching her

X's and O's necklace Tree gave her when they first met.

"Oh, what beautiful names for the twins, Mrs. Woodson. Great job today, you two. Now, if you don't mind, I need to get your kids to the nursery. Someone will be in here shortly to get you to a room and Summer and Fall will be in to join you a little later. Be blessed."

"Same to you, Nurse Vickie." They both said at the same time as she left with their kids.

Secorion turns to his wife. "Baby, those names are beautiful and perfect being that your name is Audumn. So, tell me, how did you come up with those names or is it because your name is Audumn?"

"Secorion, life comes in seasons and those seasons do change. I chose those names because if I can't teach my children anything else, I want them to remember that. And I'm going to let them know that that's what their names mean to me and that trees will die and grow in those seasons that they thought didn't go so well. But, in actuality, some trees did bear fruit."

"Wow that's deep love." Secorion kisses his wife. "Just think bae, we're now the parents of Summer Woodson and Fall Woodson. Hold up, what's going to be their middle names?"

"Boy, you're asking me to do too much after going through all that pain to give birth to your kids." Audumn tells him to get a pen and he finds one in a drawer behind him. "Okay daddy, your first job, besides helping me give birth, weighing, and measuring the babies is to come up with your twins' middle names." Audumn starts giggling.

"All right Mrs. Audumn Danyalle Woodson. Two middle names coming right up!"

The End